big
NATE
SAY GOOD-BYE
TO DORK CITY

More

big NATE

adventures from

LINCOLN PEIRCE

Big Nate From the Top

Big Nate Out Loud

Big Nate and Friends

Big Nate Makes the Grade

Big Nate All Work and No Play

Big Nate: Game On!

Big Nate: I Can't Take It!

Big Nate: Great Minds Think Alike

Big Nate: The Crowd Goes Wild!

Big Nate's Greatest Hits

Big Nate: Welcome to My World

Big Nate: Thunka, Thunka, Thunka

big NATE

SAY GOOD-BYE TO DORK CITY

by LINCOLN PEIRCE

Andrews McMeel
Publishing®

a division of Andrews McMeel Universal

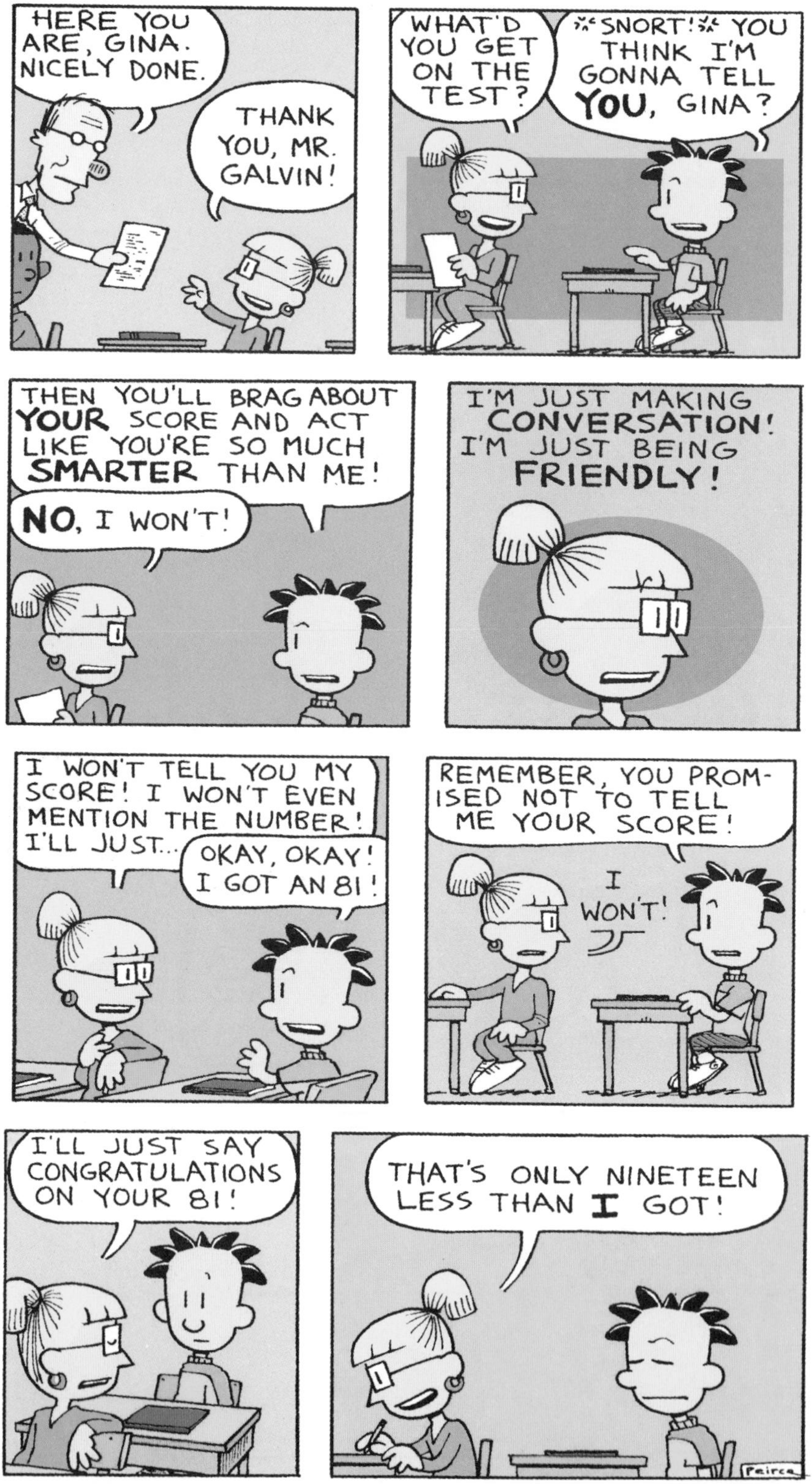
HERE YOU ARE, GINA. NICELY DONE.
THANK YOU, MR. GALVIN!
WHAT'D YOU GET ON THE TEST?
SNORT! YOU THINK I'M GONNA TELL YOU, GINA?
THEN YOU'LL BRAG ABOUT YOUR SCORE AND ACT LIKE YOU'RE SO MUCH SMARTER THAN ME!
NO, I WON'T!
I'M JUST MAKING CONVERSATION! I'M JUST BEING FRIENDLY!
I WON'T TELL YOU MY SCORE! I WON'T EVEN MENTION THE NUMBER! I'LL JUST...
OKAY, OKAY! I GOT AN 81!
REMEMBER, YOU PROMISED NOT TO TELL ME YOUR SCORE!
I WON'T!
I'LL JUST SAY CONGRATULATIONS ON YOUR 81!
THAT'S ONLY NINETEEN LESS THAN I GOT!
Peirce

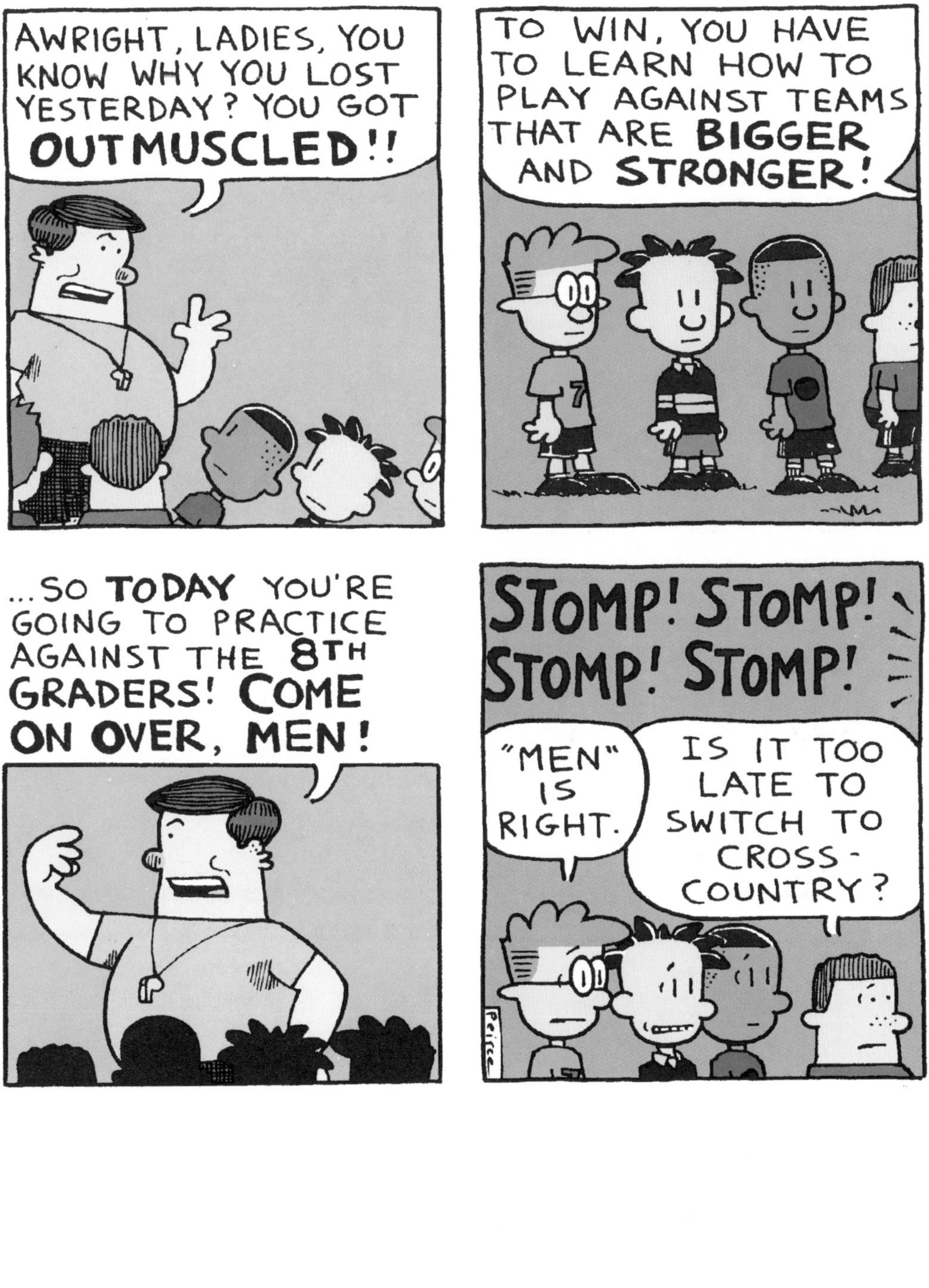
AWRIGHT, LADIES, YOU KNOW WHY YOU LOST YESTERDAY? YOU GOT **OUTMUSCLED**!!
TO WIN, YOU HAVE TO LEARN HOW TO PLAY AGAINST TEAMS THAT ARE **BIGGER** AND **STRONGER**!
...SO **TODAY** YOU'RE GOING TO PRACTICE AGAINST THE **8TH GRADERS**! **COME ON OVER, MEN**!
STOMP! STOMP! STOMP! STOMP!
"MEN" IS RIGHT.
IS IT TOO LATE TO SWITCH TO CROSS-COUNTRY?
Peirce

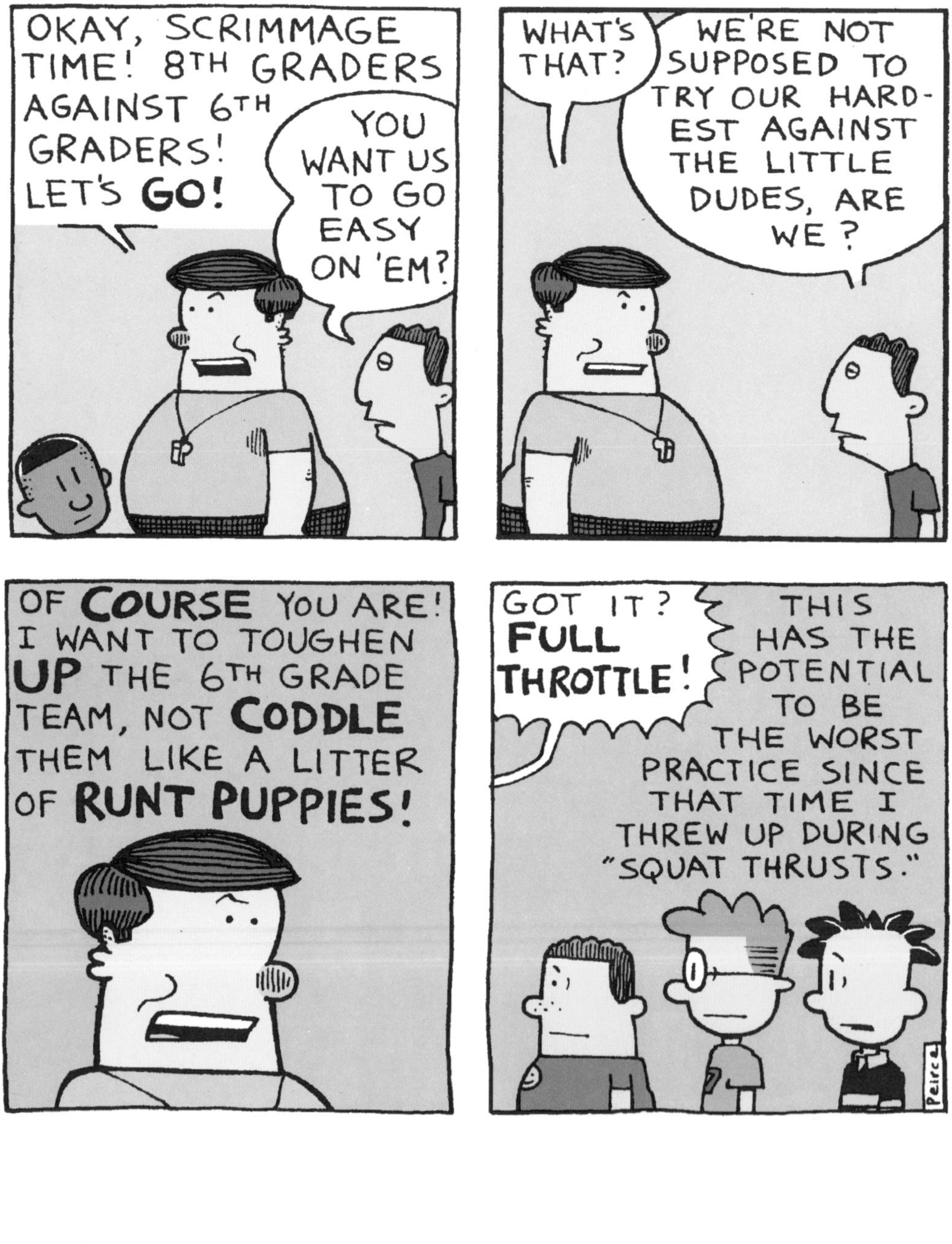
OKAY, SCRIMMAGE TIME! 8TH GRADERS AGAINST 6TH GRADERS! LET'S **GO!**
YOU WANT US TO GO EASY ON 'EM?
WHAT'S THAT?
WE'RE NOT SUPPOSED TO TRY OUR HARDEST AGAINST THE LITTLE DUDES, ARE WE?
OF **COURSE** YOU ARE! I WANT TO TOUGHEN **UP** THE 6TH GRADE TEAM, NOT **CODDLE** THEM LIKE A LITTER OF **RUNT PUPPIES!**
GOT IT? **FULL THROTTLE!**
THIS HAS THE POTENTIAL TO BE THE WORST PRACTICE SINCE THAT TIME I THREW UP DURING "SQUAT THRUSTS."
Peirce

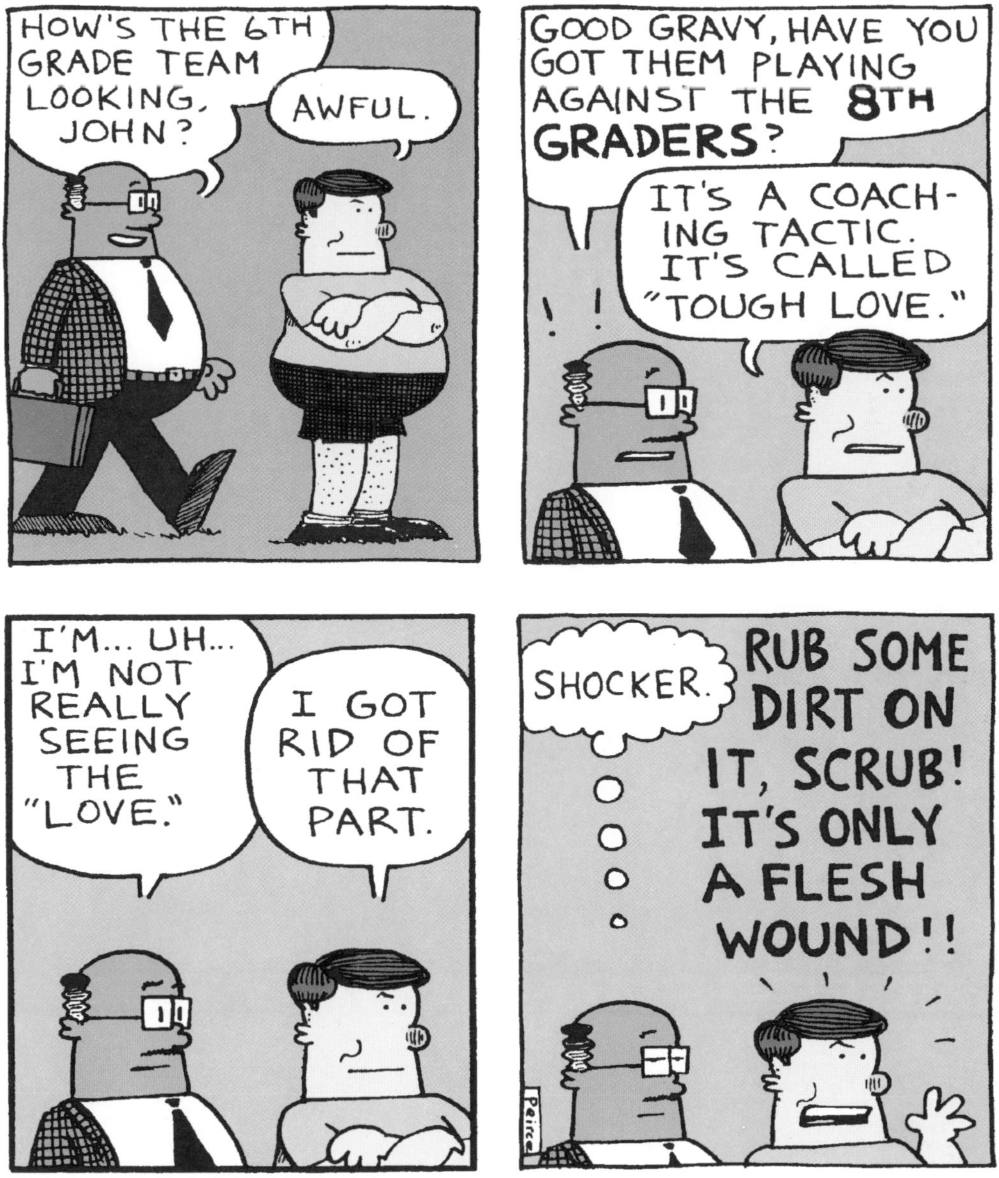
HOW'S THE 6TH GRADE TEAM LOOKING, JOHN?
AWFUL.
GOOD GRAVY, HAVE YOU GOT THEM PLAYING AGAINST THE 8TH GRADERS?
IT'S A COACHING TACTIC. IT'S CALLED "TOUGH LOVE."
I'M... UH... I'M NOT REALLY SEEING THE "LOVE."
I GOT RID OF THAT PART.
SHOCKER.
RUB SOME DIRT ON IT, SCRUB! IT'S ONLY A FLESH WOUND!!
Peirce

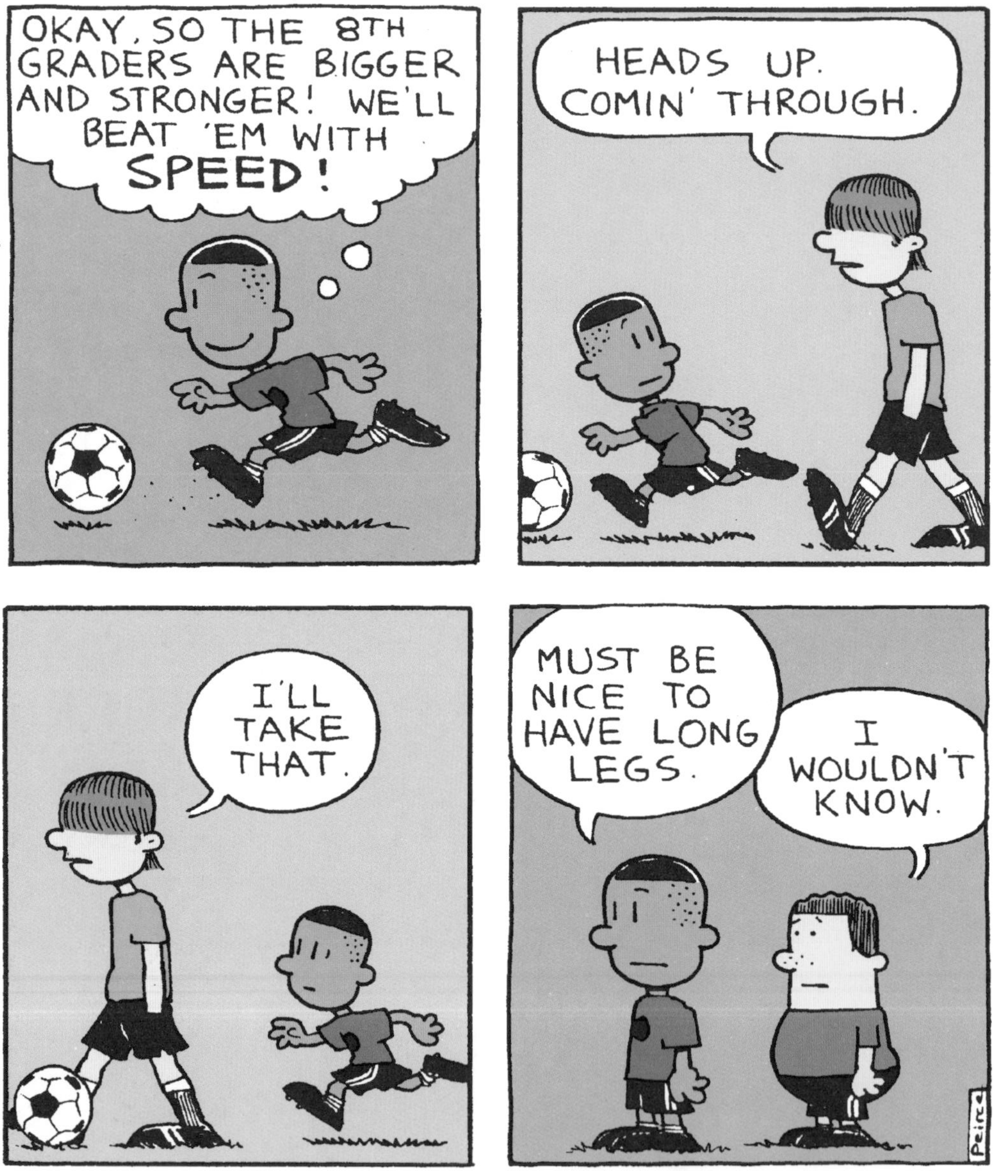
OKAY, SO THE 8TH GRADERS ARE BIGGER AND STRONGER! WE'LL BEAT 'EM WITH SPEED!
HEADS UP. COMIN' THROUGH.
I'LL TAKE THAT.
MUST BE NICE TO HAVE LONG LEGS.
I WOULDN'T KNOW.
Peirce

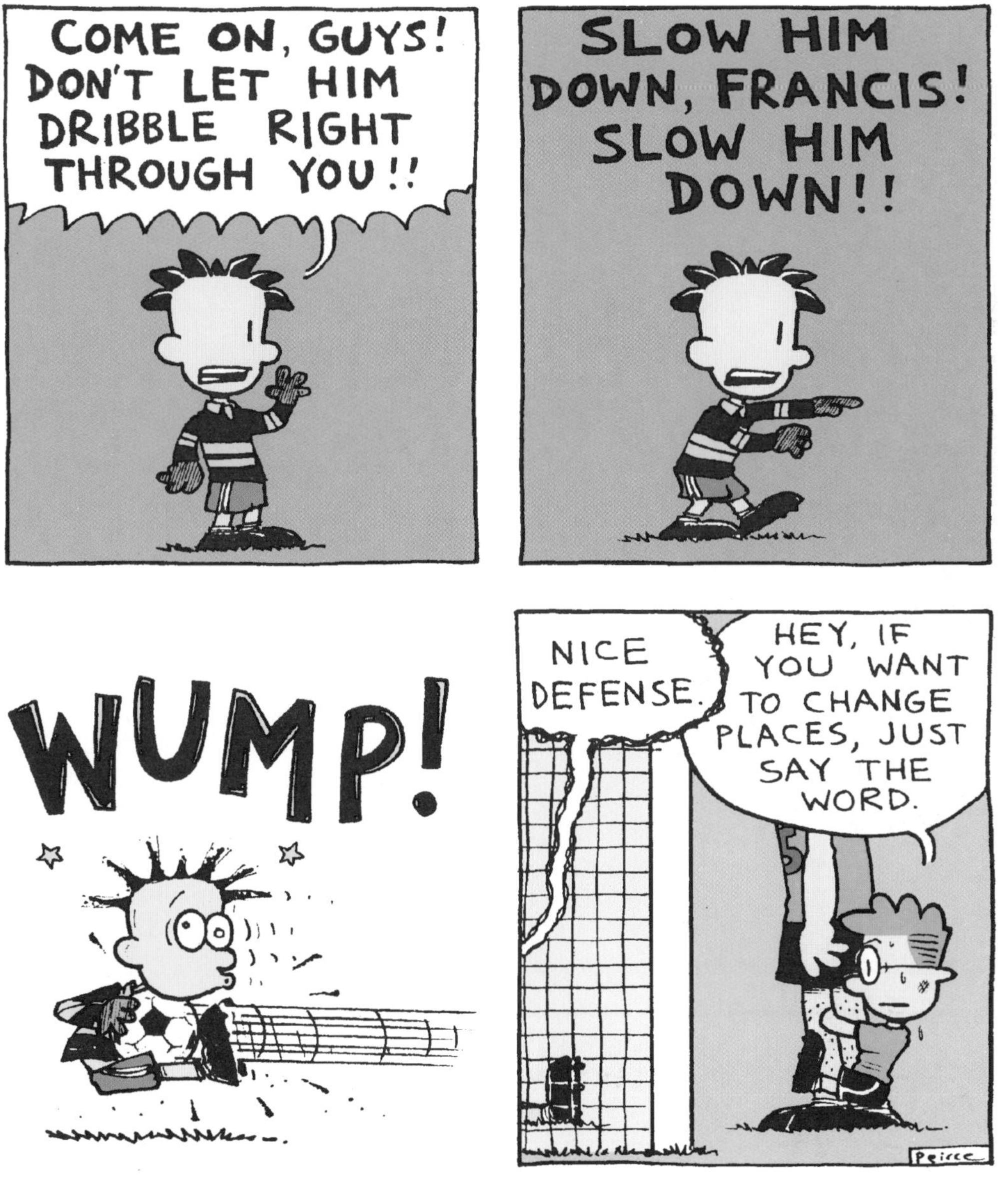
COME ON, GUYS! DON'T LET HIM DRIBBLE RIGHT THROUGH YOU!!
SLOW HIM DOWN, FRANCIS! SLOW HIM DOWN!!
WUMP!
NICE DEFENSE.
HEY, IF YOU WANT TO CHANGE PLACES, JUST SAY THE WORD.
Peirce

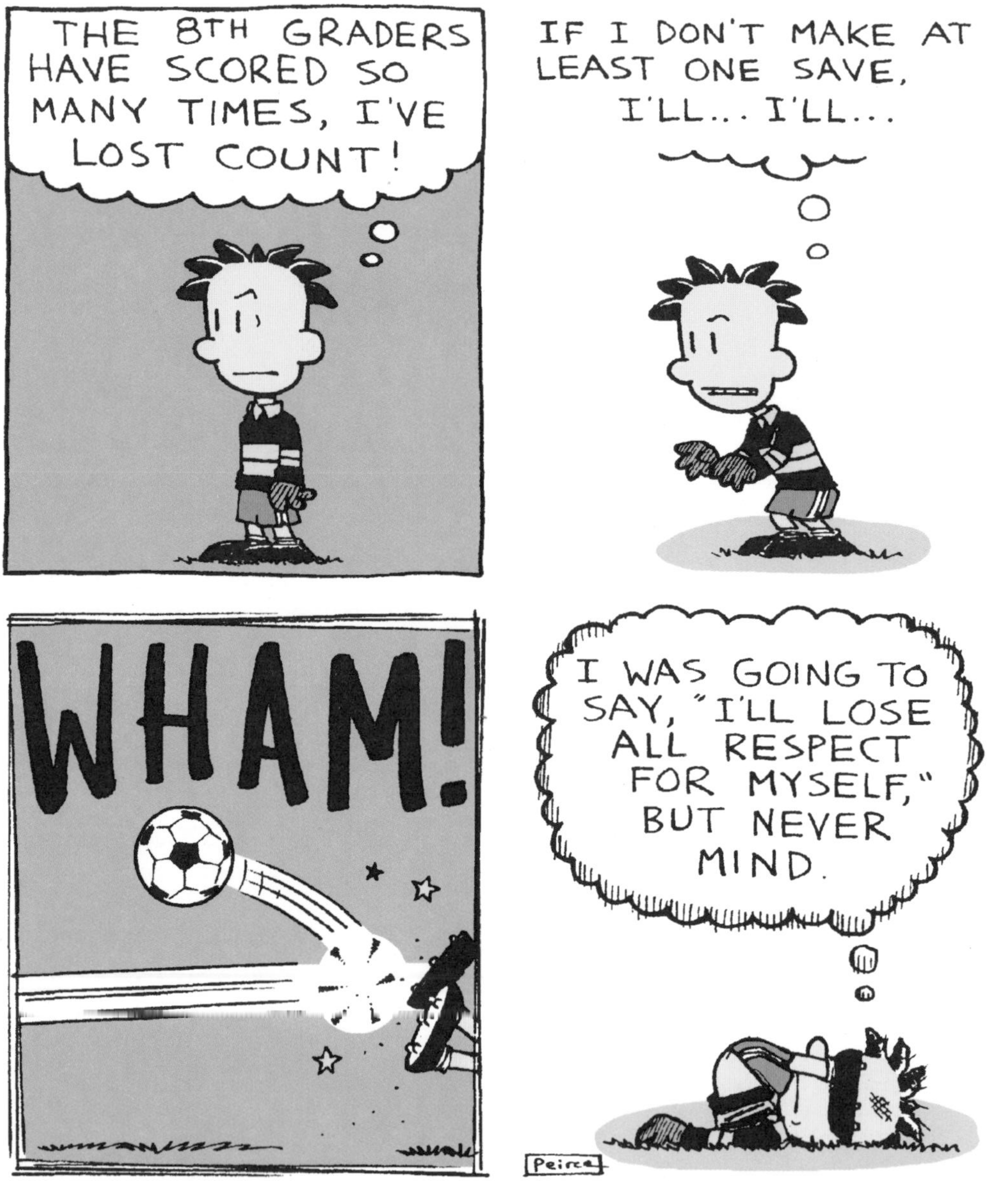
THE 8TH GRADERS HAVE SCORED SO MANY TIMES, I'VE LOST COUNT!
IF I DON'T MAKE AT LEAST ONE SAVE, I'LL... I'LL...
WHAM!
I WAS GOING TO SAY, "I'LL LOSE ALL RESPECT FOR MYSELF," BUT NEVER MIND.
Peirce

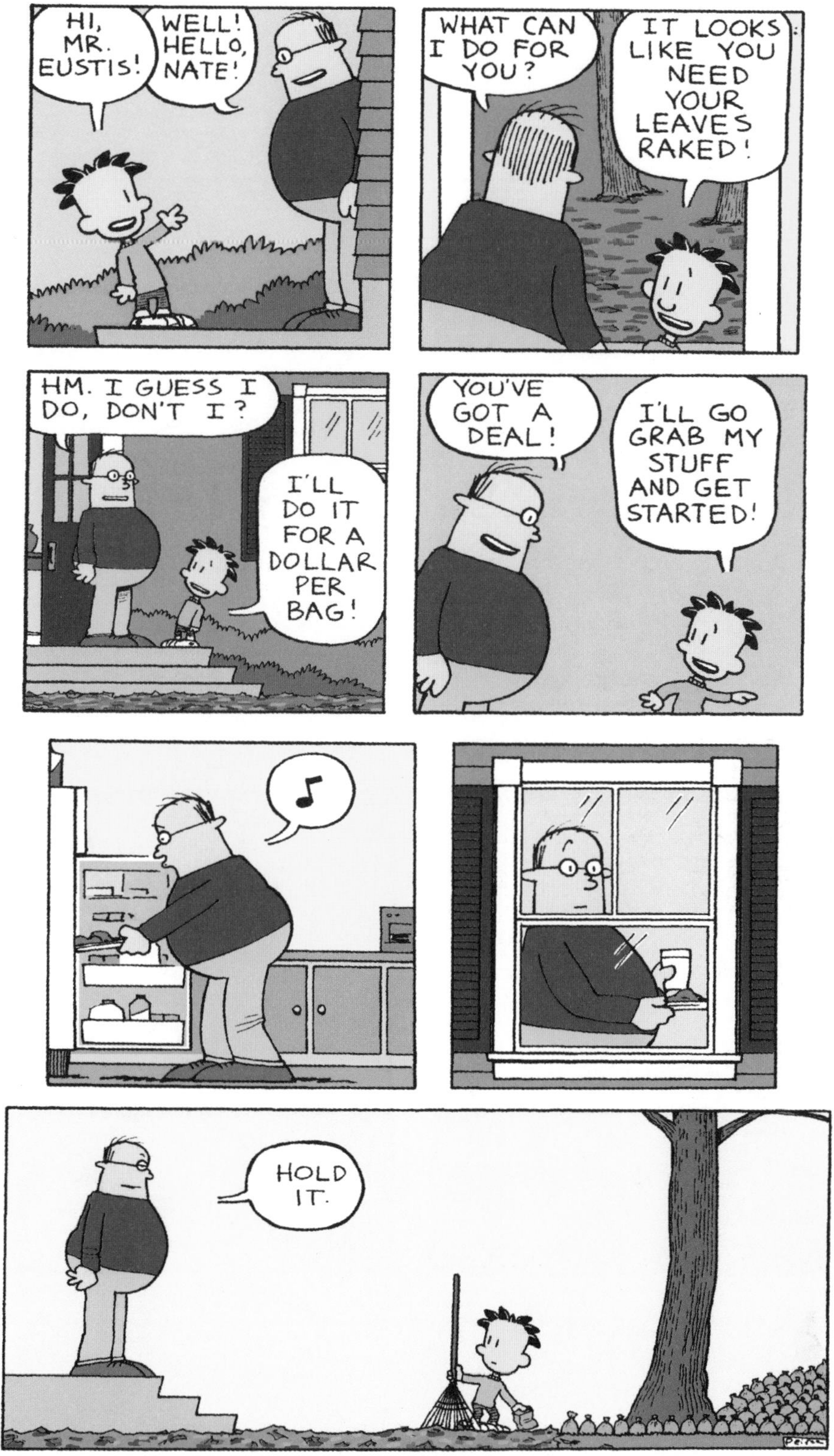
HI, MR. EUSTIS!
WELL! HELLO, NATE!
WHAT CAN I DO FOR YOU?
IT LOOKS LIKE YOU NEED YOUR LEAVES RAKED!
HM. I GUESS I DO, DON'T I?
I'LL DO IT FOR A DOLLAR PER BAG!
YOU'VE GOT A DEAL!
I'LL GO GRAB MY STUFF AND GET STARTED!
HOLD IT.

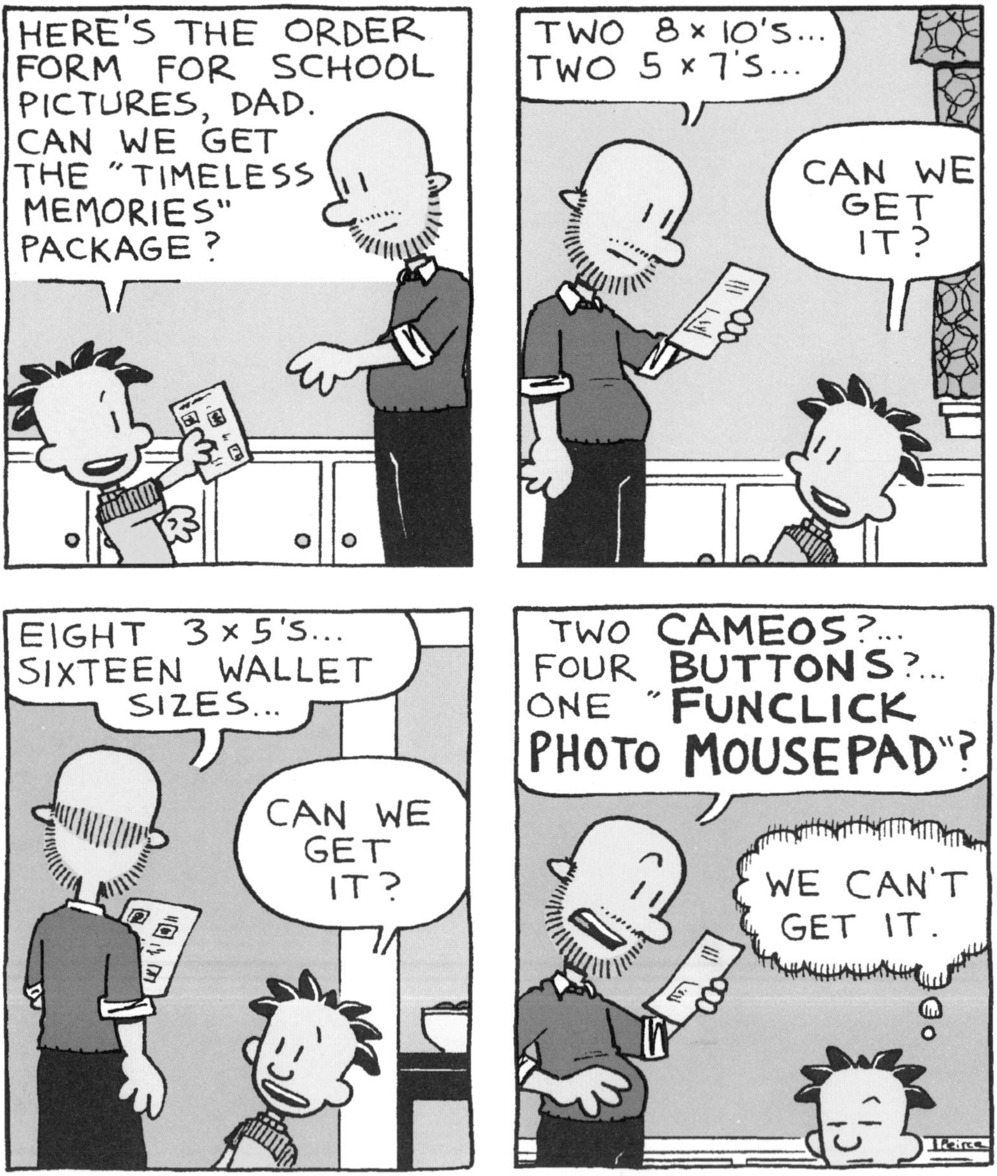
HERE'S THE ORDER FORM FOR SCHOOL PICTURES, DAD. CAN WE GET THE "TIMELESS MEMORIES" PACKAGE?
TWO 8 x 10'S... TWO 5 x 7'S...
CAN WE GET IT?
EIGHT 3 x 5'S... SIXTEEN WALLET SIZES...
CAN WE GET IT?
TWO CAMEOS?... FOUR BUTTONS?... ONE "FUNCLICK PHOTO MOUSEPAD"?
WE CAN'T GET IT.
J Peirce

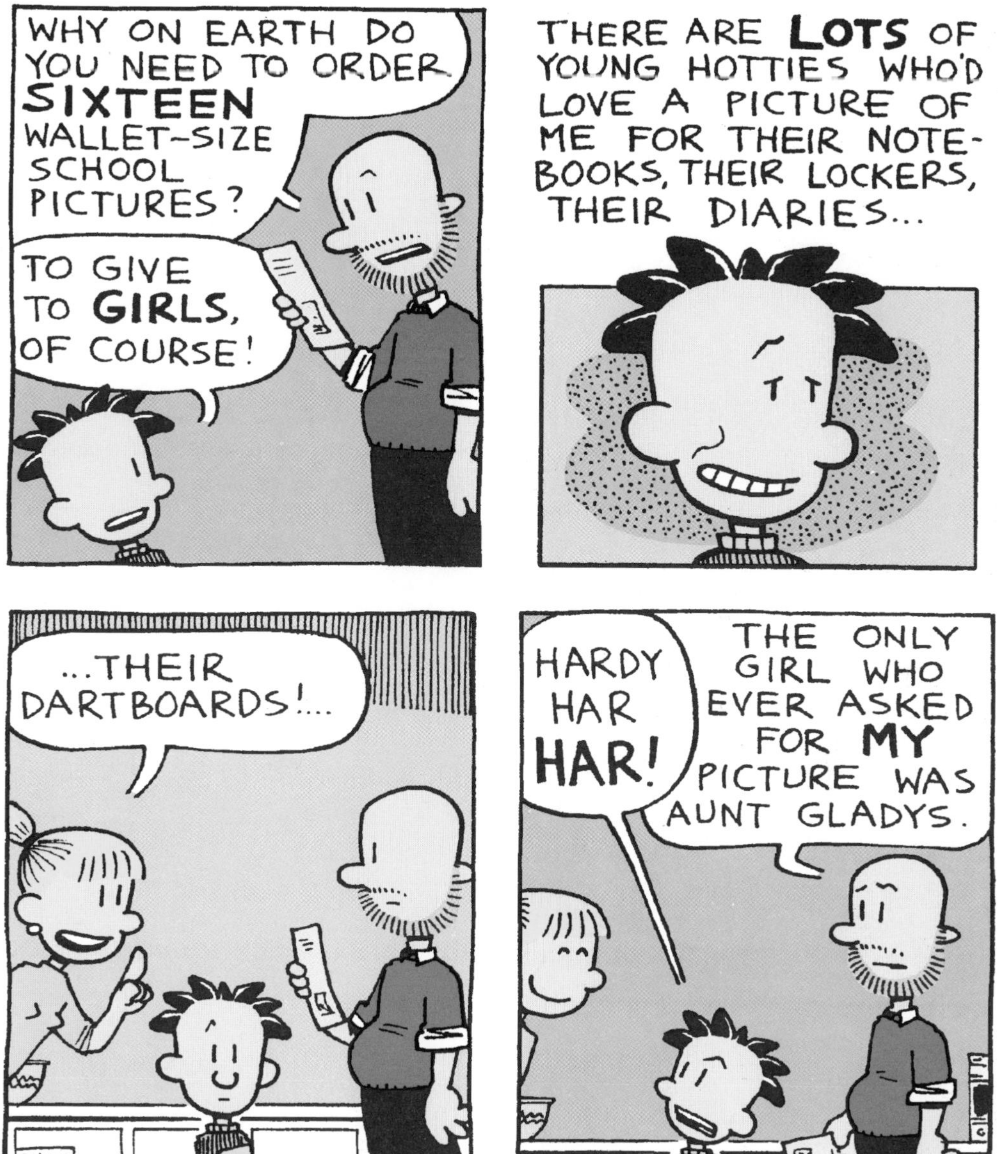
WHY ON EARTH DO YOU NEED TO ORDER **SIXTEEN** WALLET-SIZE SCHOOL PICTURES?
TO GIVE TO **GIRLS**, OF COURSE!
THERE ARE **LOTS** OF YOUNG HOTTIES WHO'D LOVE A PICTURE OF ME FOR THEIR NOTE-BOOKS, THEIR LOCKERS, THEIR DIARIES...
...THEIR DARTBOARDS!...
peirce
HARDY HAR **HAR!**
THE ONLY GIRL WHO EVER ASKED FOR **MY** PICTURE WAS AUNT GLADYS.

NATE, YOU **DON'T** NEED A SCHOOL PICTURE PACKAGE WITH SO MANY BELLS AND WHISTLES!

OKAY, OKAY. FORGET THE "TIMELESS MEMORIES" PACKAGE.

HOW ABOUT THE "TREASURE CHEST"?

NO.

THE "PRECIOUS KEEPSAKES"?

NO.

THE "DREAM WEAVER"?

NO.

THE "CLASS-ROOM COMPANION"?

NO.

THE "CHEAP DAD"?

HERE WE GO! THE "PENNY-WISE"!

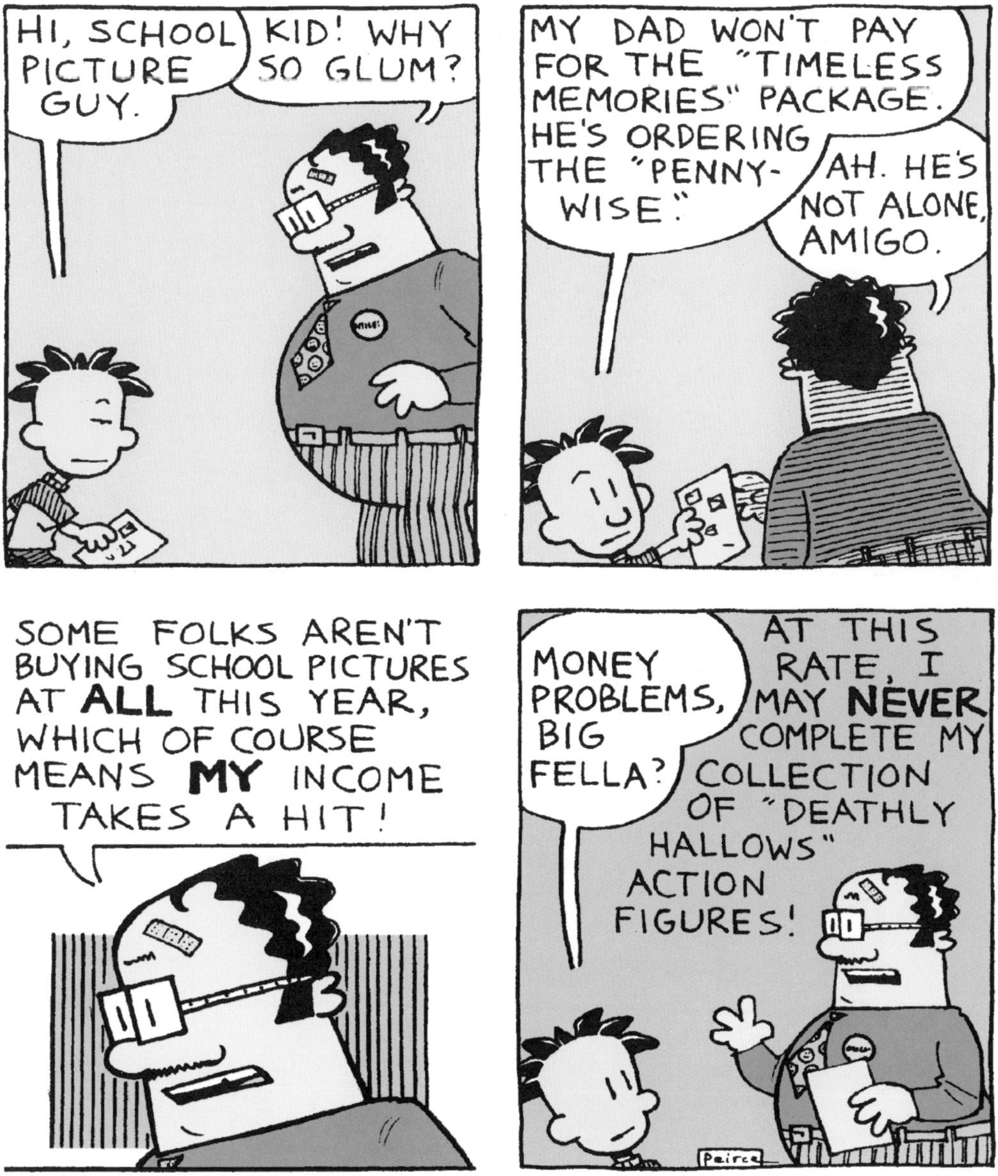
HI, SCHOOL PICTURE GUY.
KID! WHY SO GLUM?
MY DAD WON'T PAY FOR THE "TIMELESS MEMORIES" PACKAGE. HE'S ORDERING THE "PENNY-WISE."
AH. HE'S NOT ALONE, AMIGO.
SOME FOLKS AREN'T BUYING SCHOOL PICTURES AT **ALL** THIS YEAR, WHICH OF COURSE MEANS **MY** INCOME TAKES A HIT!
MONEY PROBLEMS, BIG FELLA?
AT THIS RATE, I MAY **NEVER** COMPLETE MY COLLECTION OF "DEATHLY HALLOWS" ACTION FIGURES!
Peirce

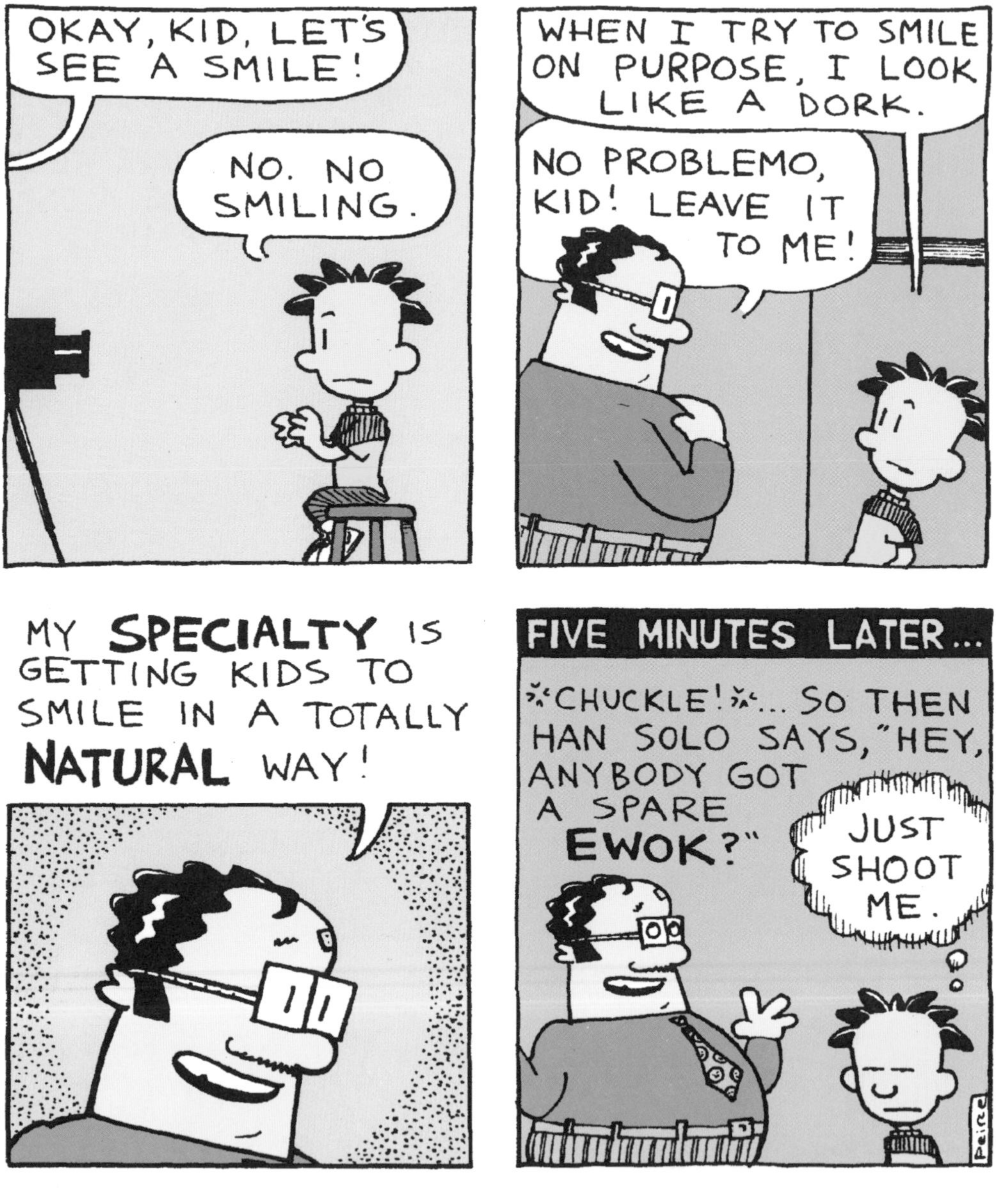
OKAY, KID, LET'S SEE A SMILE!
NO. NO SMILING.
WHEN I TRY TO SMILE ON PURPOSE, I LOOK LIKE A DORK.
NO PROBLEMO, KID! LEAVE IT TO ME!
MY SPECIALTY IS GETTING KIDS TO SMILE IN A TOTALLY NATURAL WAY!
FIVE MINUTES LATER...
CHUCKLE!... SO THEN HAN SOLO SAYS, "HEY, ANYBODY GOT A SPARE EWOK?"
JUST SHOOT ME.
Peirce

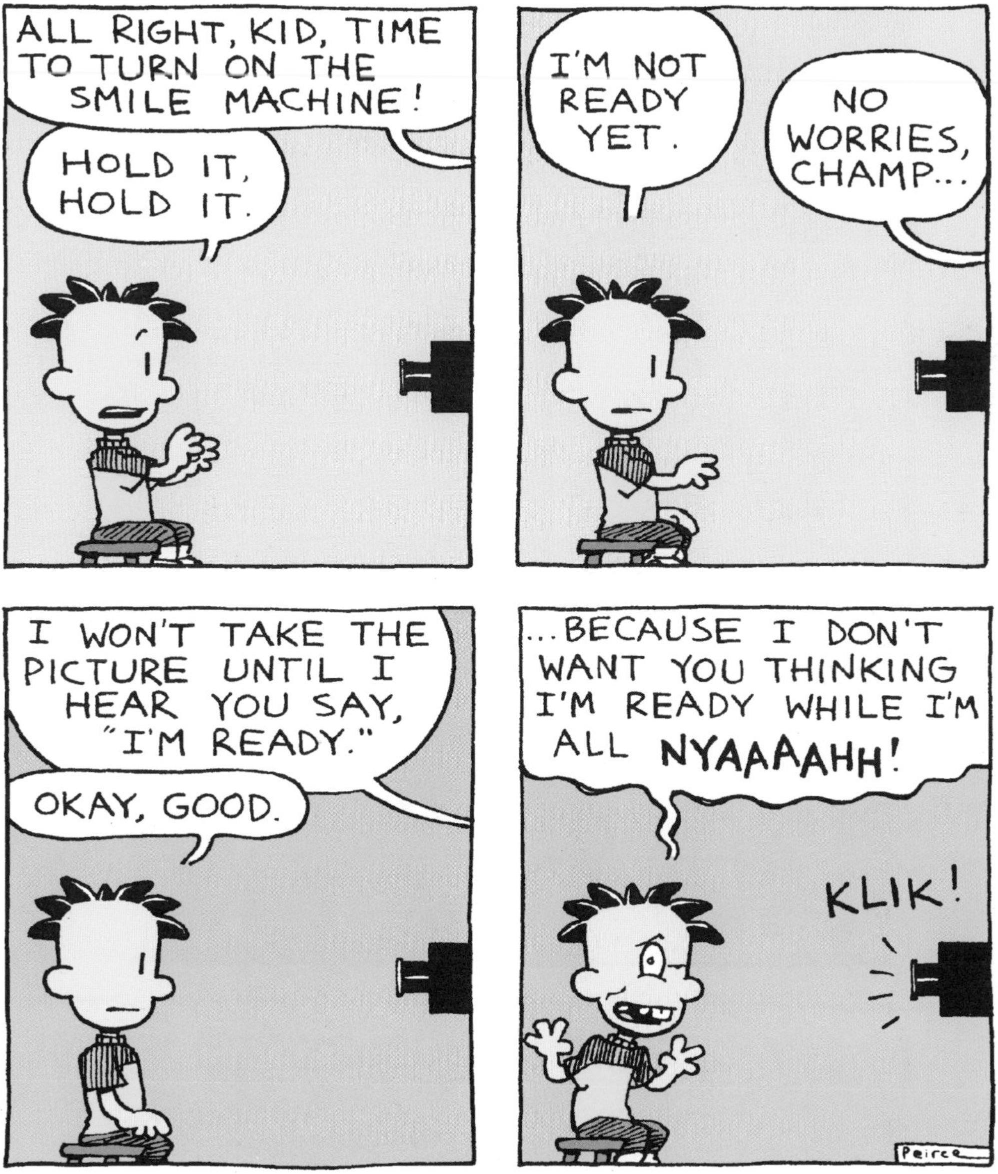
ALL RIGHT, KID, TIME TO TURN ON THE SMILE MACHINE!
HOLD IT, HOLD IT.
I'M NOT READY YET.
NO WORRIES, CHAMP...
I WON'T TAKE THE PICTURE UNTIL I HEAR YOU SAY, "I'M READY."
OKAY, GOOD.
...BECAUSE I DON'T WANT YOU THINKING I'M READY WHILE I'M ALL NYAAAAHH!
KLIK!
Peirce

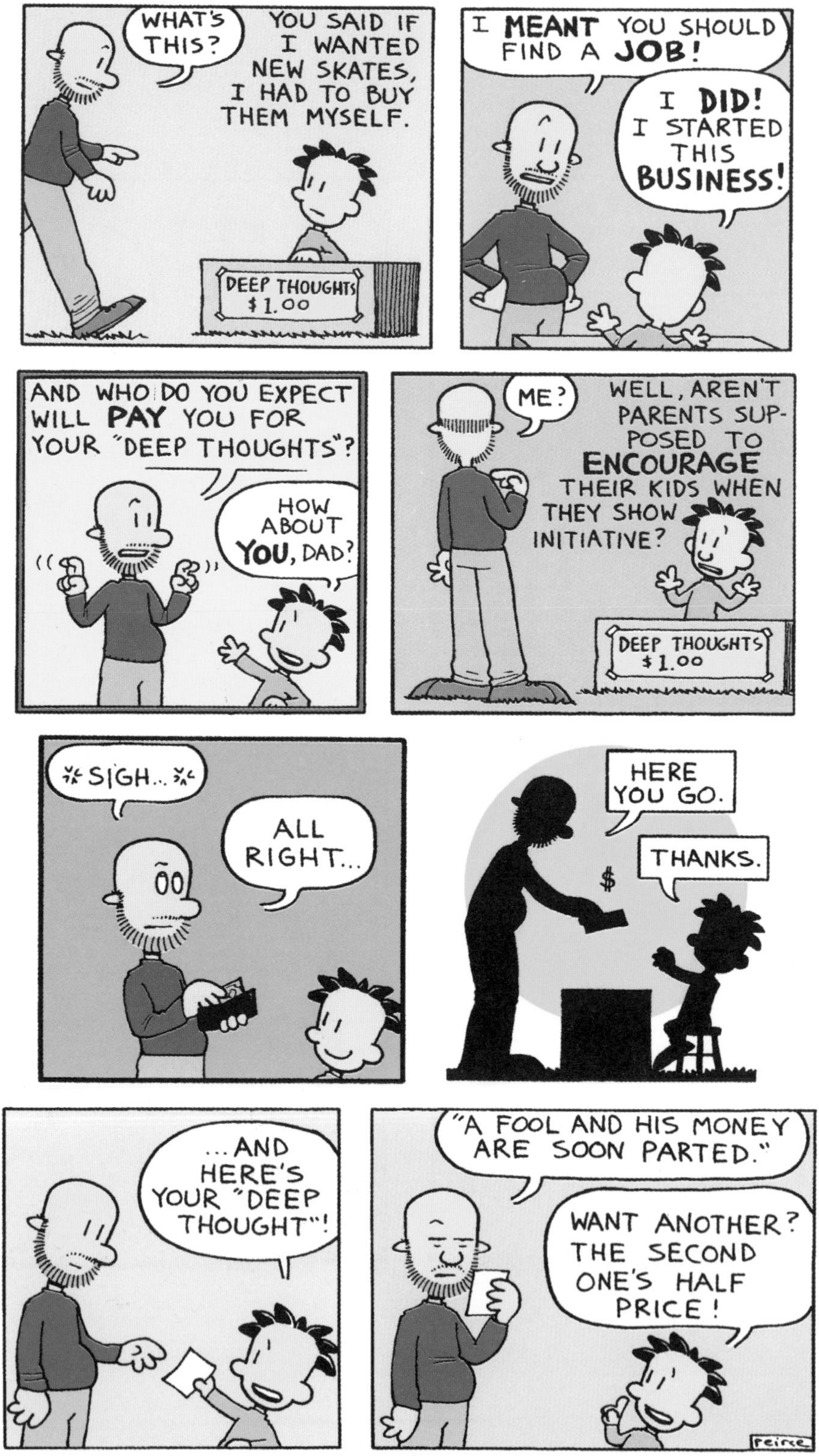
WHAT'S THIS?
YOU SAID IF I WANTED NEW SKATES, I HAD TO BUY THEM MYSELF.
DEEP THOUGHTS $1.00
I MEANT YOU SHOULD FIND A JOB!
I DID! I STARTED THIS BUSINESS!
AND WHO DO YOU EXPECT WILL PAY YOU FOR YOUR "DEEP THOUGHTS"?
HOW ABOUT YOU, DAD?
ME?
WELL, AREN'T PARENTS SUPPOSED TO ENCOURAGE THEIR KIDS WHEN THEY SHOW INITIATIVE?
DEEP THOUGHTS $1.00
SIGH...
ALL RIGHT...
HERE YOU GO.
THANKS.
$
...AND HERE'S YOUR "DEEP THOUGHT"!
"A FOOL AND HIS MONEY ARE SOON PARTED."
WANT ANOTHER? THE SECOND ONE'S HALF PRICE!
peirce

I'M BACK!
YES!
WE'RE ALL SET FOR HALLOWEEN!
AWE-SOME! WHAT'D YOU BUY? DID YOU BUY SOME GOOD CANDY?
LET'S JUST SAY I'M DOING MY PART TO HELP MAKE THIS A HEALTHY HOLIDAY!
WAIT, WHAT?
YOU SEE, I WAS READING AN ARTICLE ABOUT THE CHILD-HOOD OBESITY EPIDEMIC...
OH NO...
Peirce

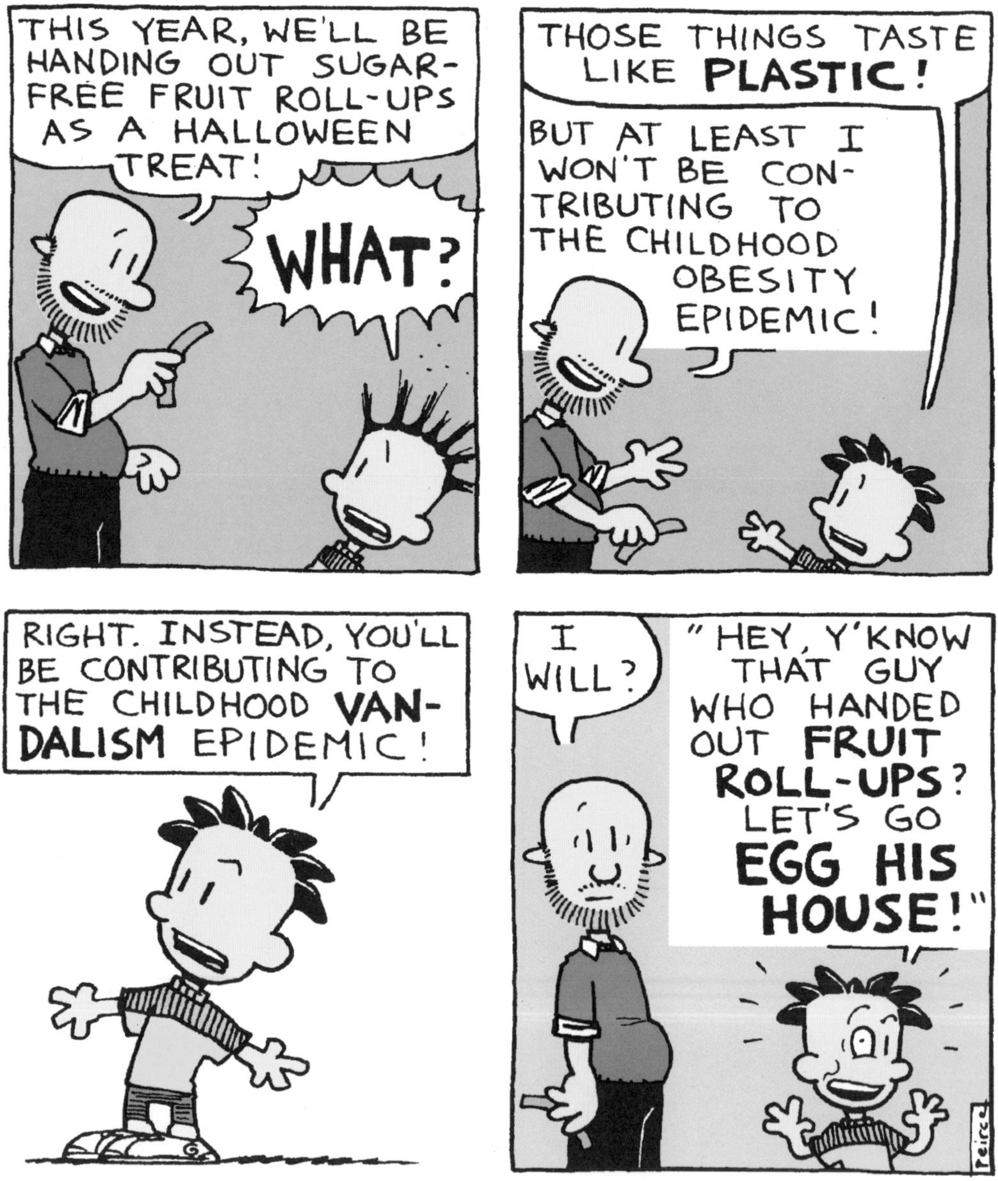
THIS YEAR, WE'LL BE HANDING OUT SUGAR-FREE FRUIT ROLL-UPS AS A HALLOWEEN TREAT!
WHAT?
THOSE THINGS TASTE LIKE PLASTIC!
BUT AT LEAST I WON'T BE CONTRIBUTING TO THE CHILDHOOD OBESITY EPIDEMIC!
RIGHT. INSTEAD, YOU'LL BE CONTRIBUTING TO THE CHILDHOOD VANDALISM EPIDEMIC!
I WILL?
"HEY, Y'KNOW THAT GUY WHO HANDED OUT FRUIT ROLL-UPS? LET'S GO EGG HIS HOUSE!"
Peirce

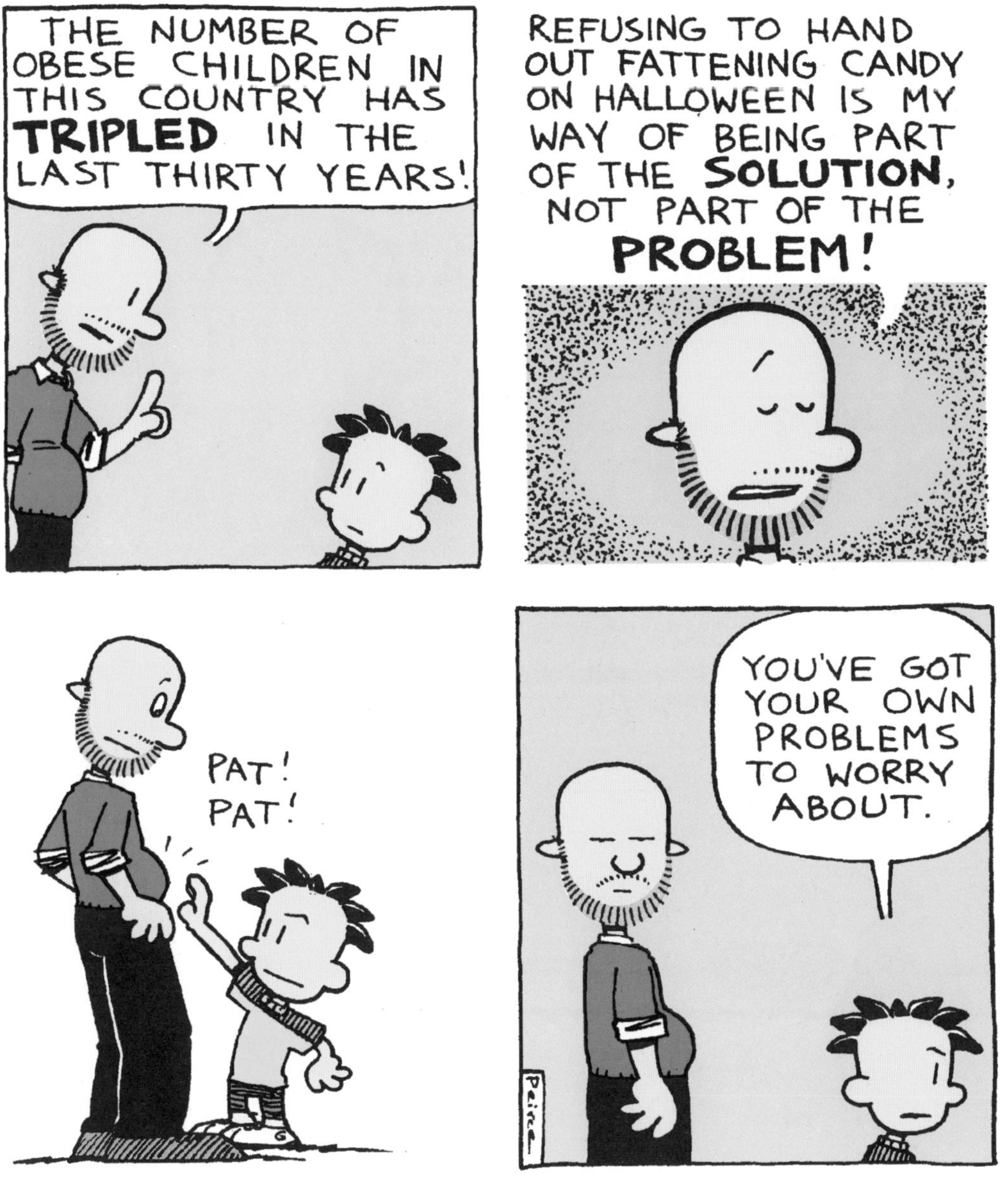
THE NUMBER OF OBESE CHILDREN IN THIS COUNTRY HAS **TRIPLED** IN THE LAST THIRTY YEARS!
REFUSING TO HAND OUT FATTENING CANDY ON HALLOWEEN IS MY WAY OF BEING PART OF THE **SOLUTION**, NOT PART OF THE **PROBLEM**!
PAT! PAT!
YOU'VE GOT YOUR OWN PROBLEMS TO WORRY ABOUT.
PEIRCE

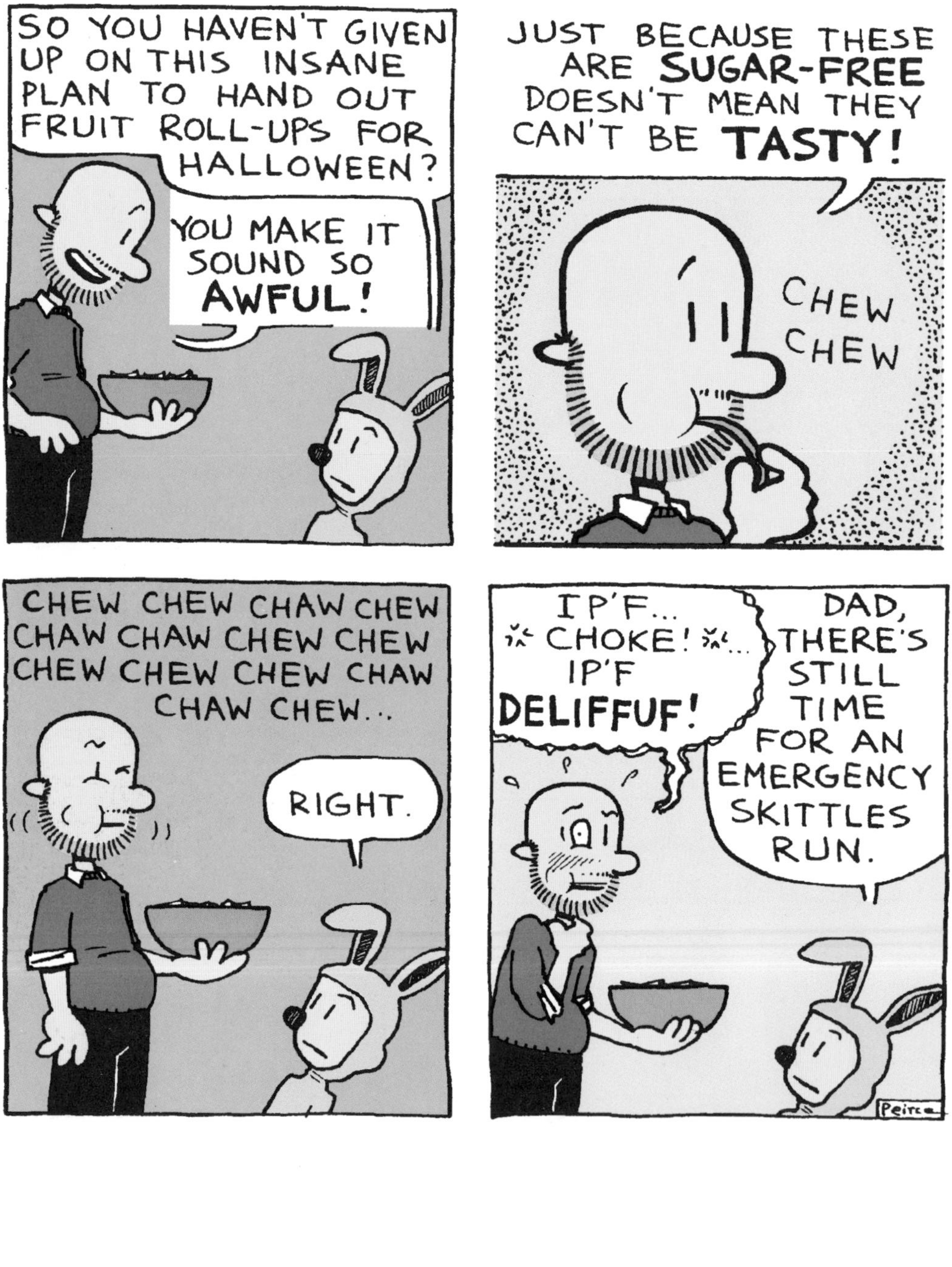
SO YOU HAVEN'T GIVEN UP ON THIS INSANE PLAN TO HAND OUT FRUIT ROLL-UPS FOR HALLOWEEN?
YOU MAKE IT SOUND SO AWFUL!
JUST BECAUSE THESE ARE SUGAR-FREE DOESN'T MEAN THEY CAN'T BE TASTY!
CHEW CHEW
CHEW CHEW CHAW CHEW CHAW CHAW CHEW CHEW CHEW CHEW CHEW CHAW CHAW CHEW...
RIGHT.
IP'F... CHOKE!... IP'F DELIFFUF!
DAD, THERE'S STILL TIME FOR AN EMERGENCY SKITTLES RUN.
Peirce

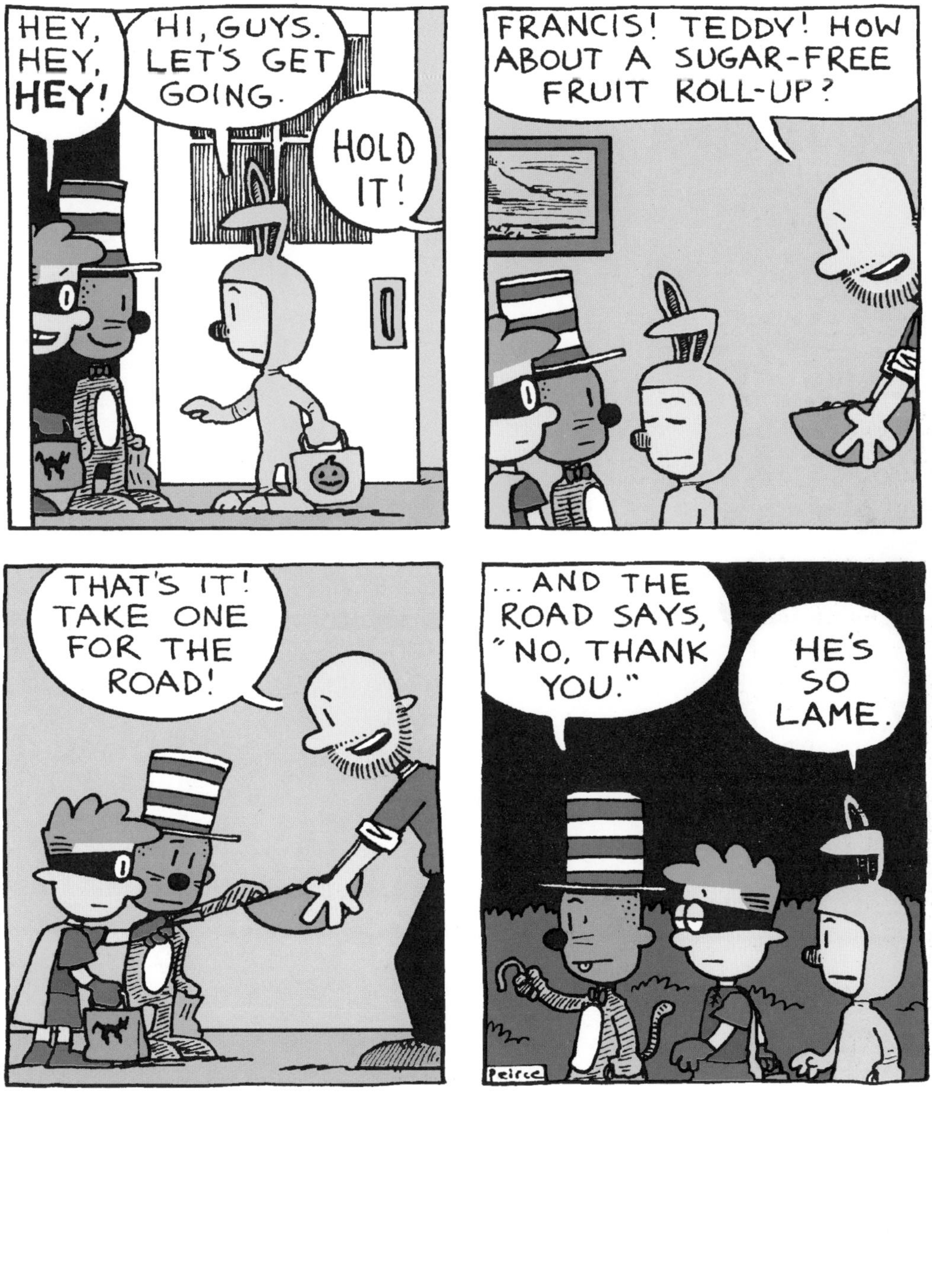
HEY, HEY, HEY!
HI, GUYS. LET'S GET GOING.
HOLD IT!
FRANCIS! TEDDY! HOW ABOUT A SUGAR-FREE FRUIT ROLL-UP?
THAT'S IT! TAKE ONE FOR THE ROAD!
...AND THE ROAD SAYS, "NO, THANK YOU."
HE'S SO LAME.
Peirce

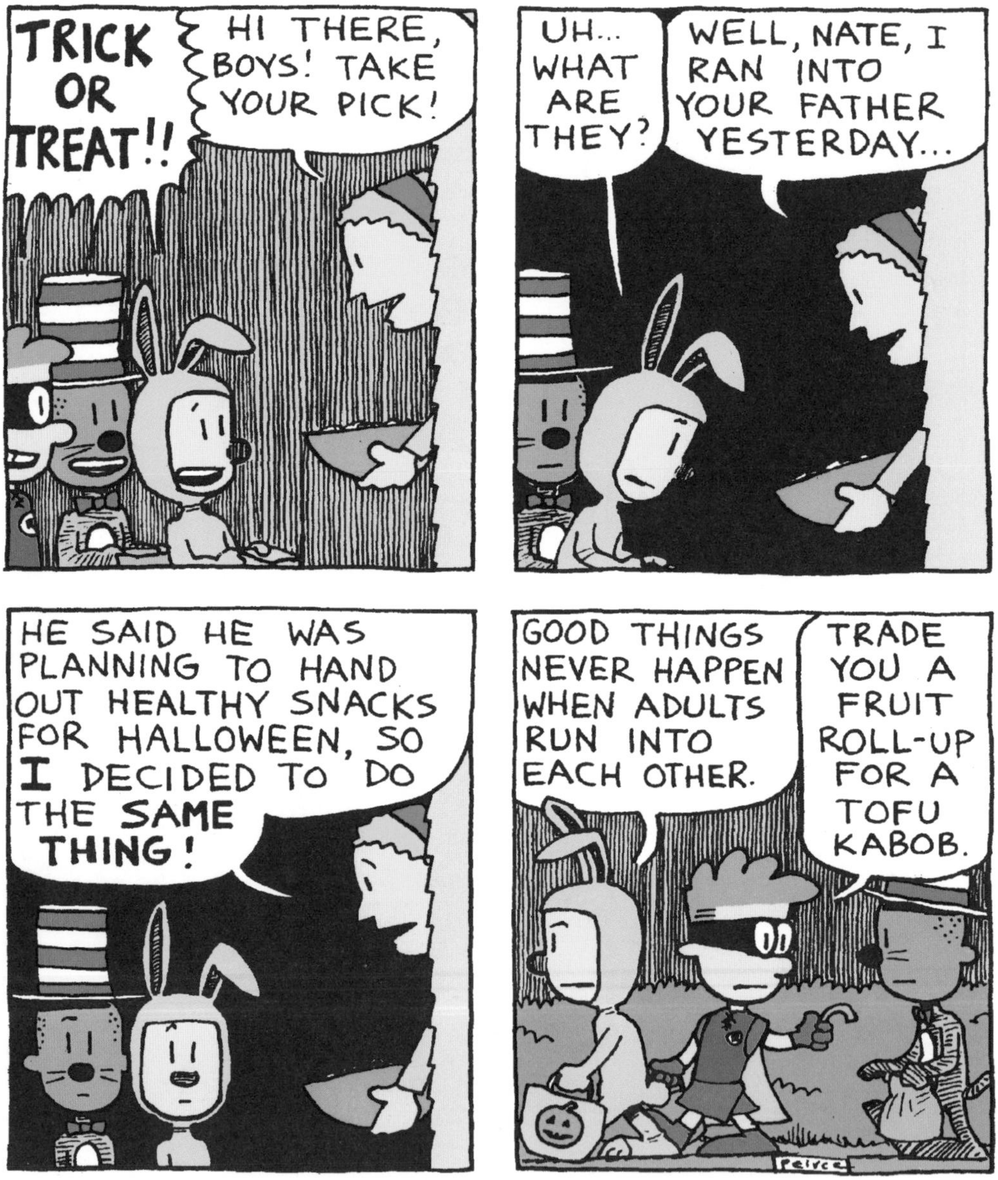
TRICK OR TREAT!!
HI THERE, BOYS! TAKE YOUR PICK!
UH... WHAT ARE THEY?
WELL, NATE, I RAN INTO YOUR FATHER YESTERDAY...
HE SAID HE WAS PLANNING TO HAND OUT HEALTHY SNACKS FOR HALLOWEEN, SO **I** DECIDED TO DO THE **SAME THING!**
GOOD THINGS NEVER HAPPEN WHEN ADULTS RUN INTO EACH OTHER.
TRADE YOU A FRUIT ROLL-UP FOR A TOFU KABOB.
peirce

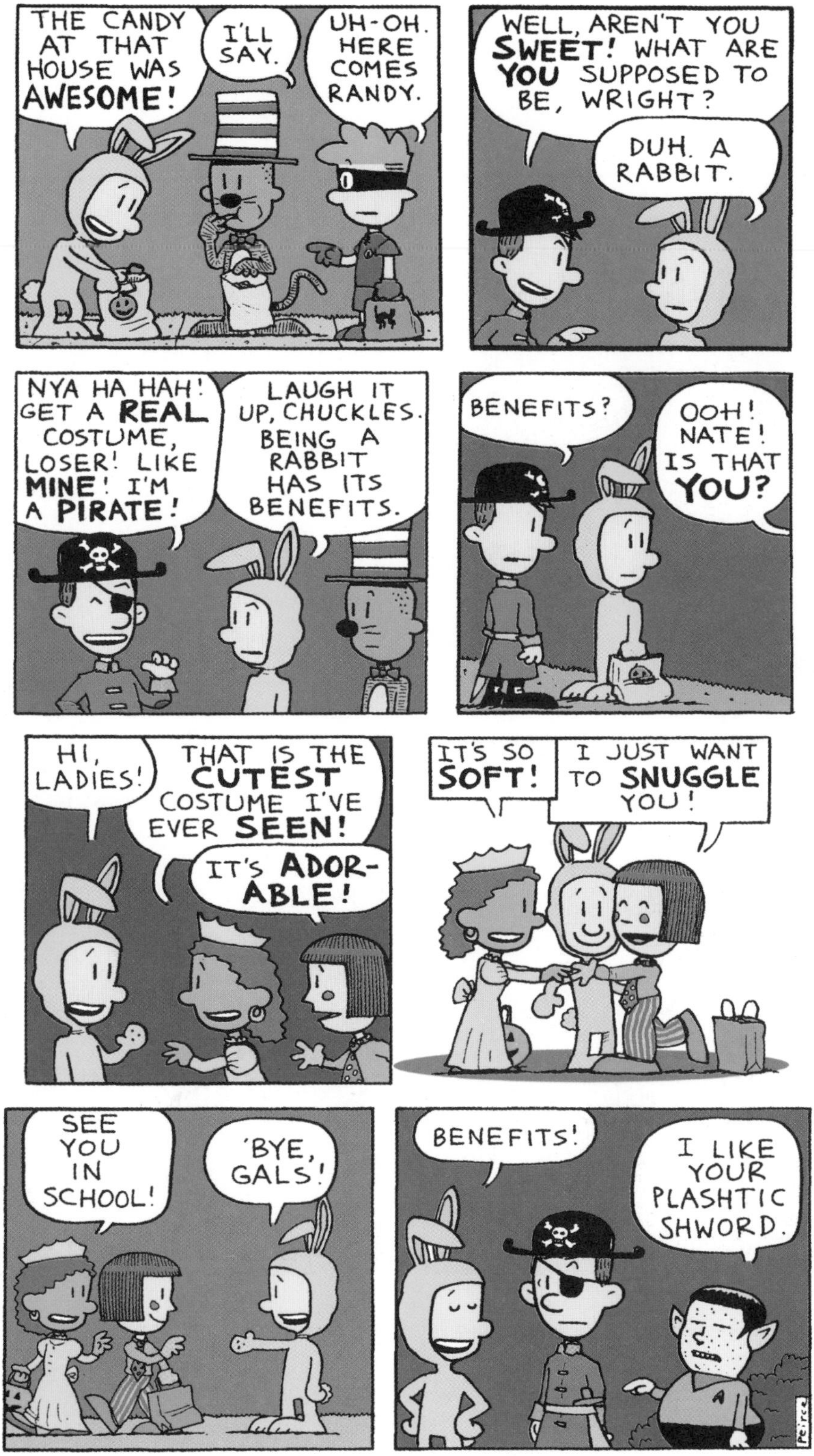
THE CANDY AT THAT HOUSE WAS AWESOME!
I'LL SAY.
UH-OH. HERE COMES RANDY.
WELL, AREN'T YOU SWEET! WHAT ARE YOU SUPPOSED TO BE, WRIGHT?
DUH. A RABBIT.
NYA HA HAH! GET A REAL COSTUME, LOSER! LIKE MINE! I'M A PIRATE!
LAUGH IT UP, CHUCKLES. BEING A RABBIT HAS ITS BENEFITS.
BENEFITS?
OOH! NATE! IS THAT YOU?
HI, LADIES!
THAT IS THE CUTEST COSTUME I'VE EVER SEEN!
IT'S ADORABLE!
IT'S SO SOFT!
I JUST WANT TO SNUGGLE YOU!
SEE YOU IN SCHOOL!
'BYE, GALS!
BENEFITS!
I LIKE YOUR PLASHTIC SHWORD.
Peirce

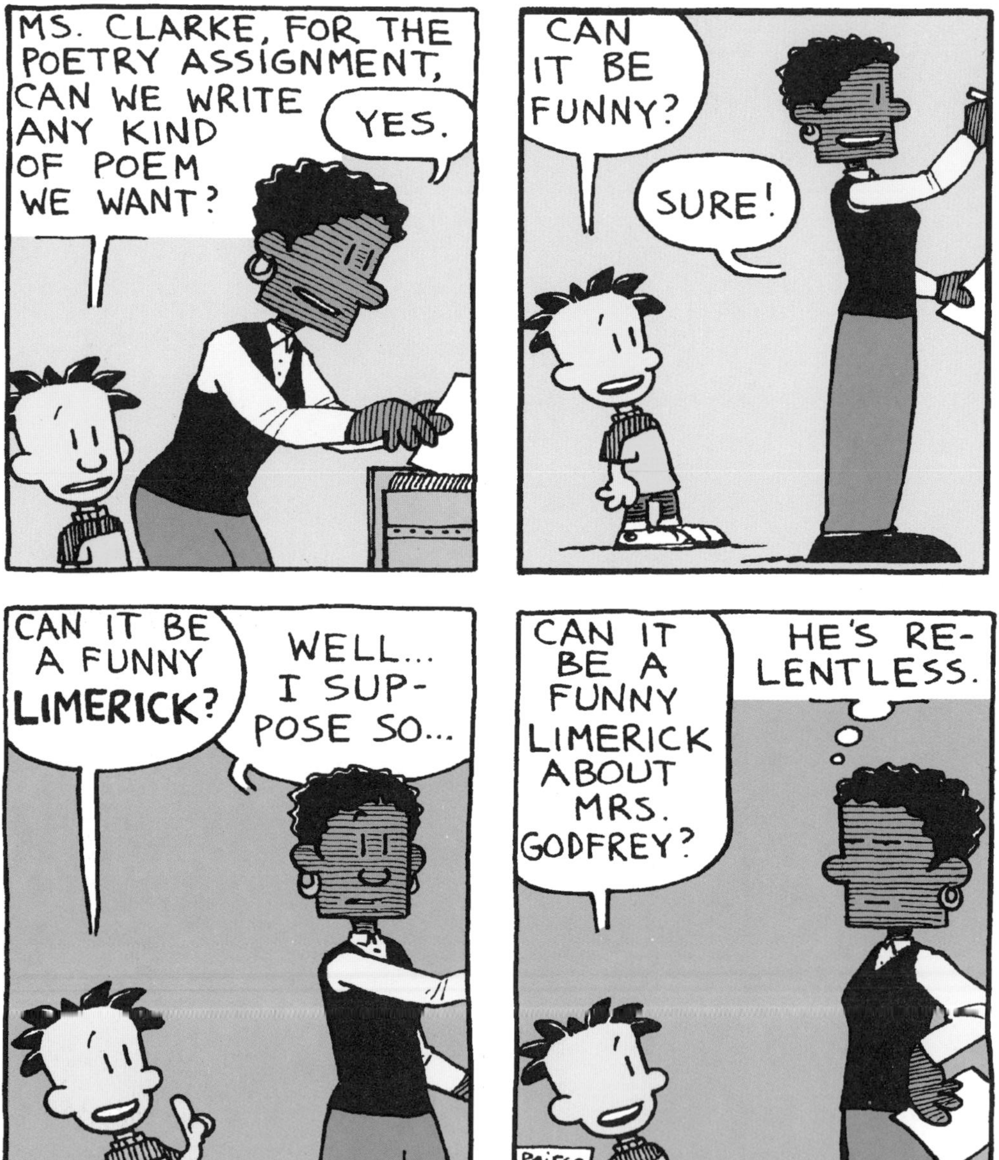
MS. CLARKE, FOR THE POETRY ASSIGNMENT, CAN WE WRITE ANY KIND OF POEM WE WANT?
YES.
CAN IT BE FUNNY?
SURE!
CAN IT BE A FUNNY **LIMERICK**?
WELL... I SUPPOSE SO...
CAN IT BE A FUNNY LIMERICK ABOUT MRS. GODFREY?
HE'S RELENTLESS.
Peirce

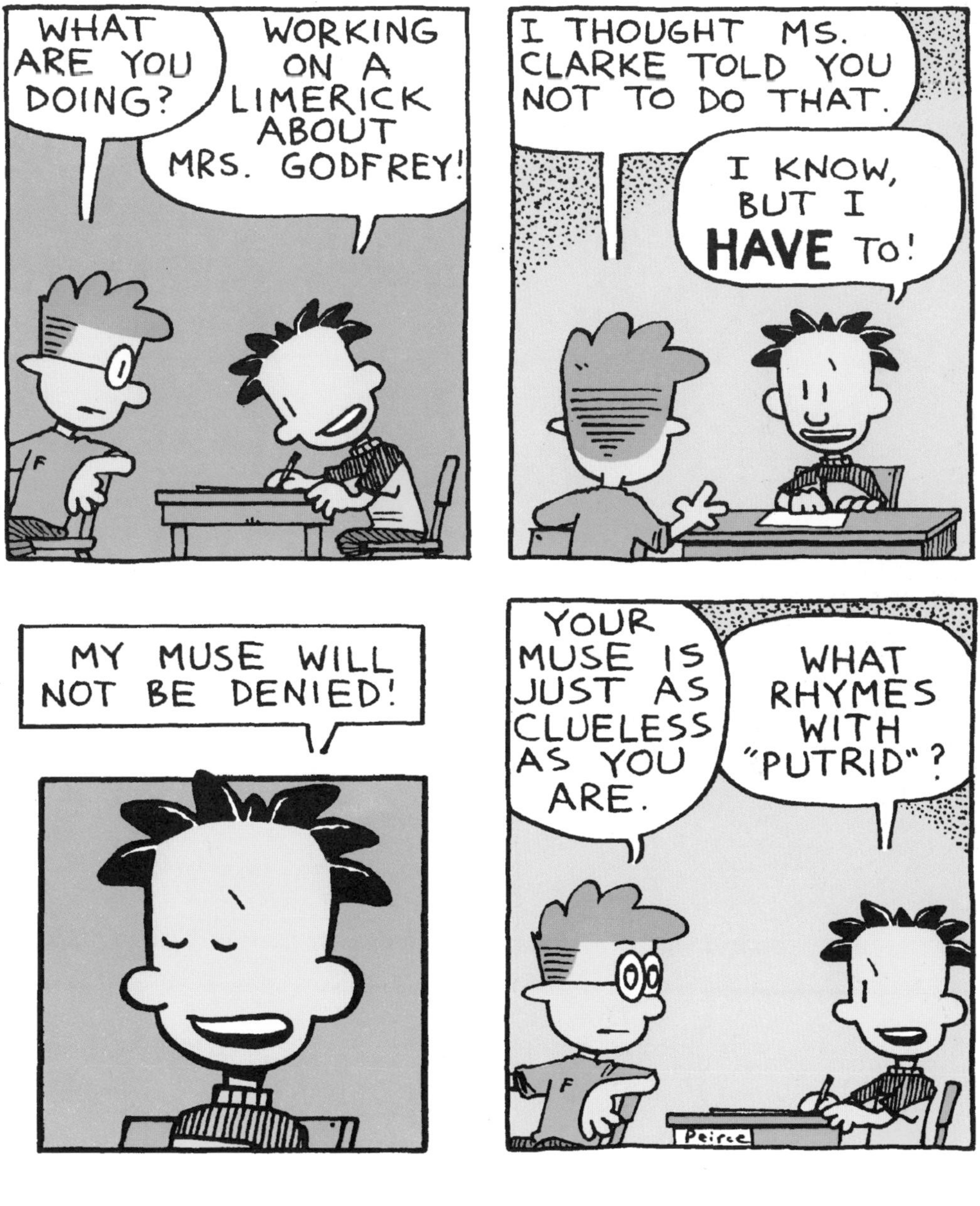
WHAT ARE YOU DOING?
WORKING ON A LIMERICK ABOUT MRS. GODFREY!
I THOUGHT MS. CLARKE TOLD YOU NOT TO DO THAT.
I KNOW, BUT I HAVE TO!
MY MUSE WILL NOT BE DENIED!
YOUR MUSE IS JUST AS CLUELESS AS YOU ARE.
WHAT RHYMES WITH "PUTRID"?
Peirce

SO DESPITE WHAT I SAID, YOU'RE WRITING A LIMERICK ABOUT MRS. GODFREY?

WHA-?... WHOOP!... I... UH... ✳ULP!✳

HM. I'VE CHANGED MY MIND, NATE. YOU MAY CONTINUE WORKING ON THIS AFTER ALL.

REALLY?

ABSOLUTELY. PROVIDED YOU SHOW IT TO MRS. GODFREY WHEN YOU'RE DONE.

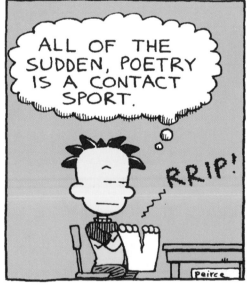

ALL OF THE SUDDEN, POETRY IS A CONTACT SPORT.

RRIP!

Peirce

MS. CLARKE, I CAN'T THINK OF WHAT TO WRITE MY POEM ABOUT.

IT COULD BE **ANY-THING**!

POETS WRITE ABOUT LOVE, ABOUT NATURE, ABOUT THINGS THEY OBSERVE, THINGS THEY IMAGINE...

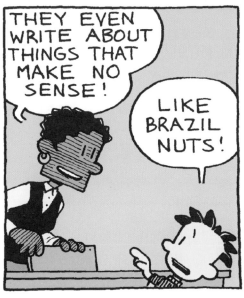

THEY EVEN WRITE ABOUT THINGS THAT MAKE NO SENSE!

LIKE BRAZIL NUTS!

UH... OKAY...

BRAZIL NUTS ARE A TOTAL MYSTERY.

Peirce

AHEM! A HAIKU. BY NATE WRIGHT.
BRAZIL NUTS IRK ME.
ALL THEY DO IS TAKE UP SPACE.
AND THEY TASTE LIKE DIRT.
YAAYY!
CLAP CLAP CLAP CLAP CLAP CLAP CLAP CLAP CLAP CLAP CLAP CLAP CLAP CLAP
I STRUCK A NERVE!
BRAZIL NUTS ARE THE DETROIT LIONS OF THE MIXED NUTS WORLD.
peirce

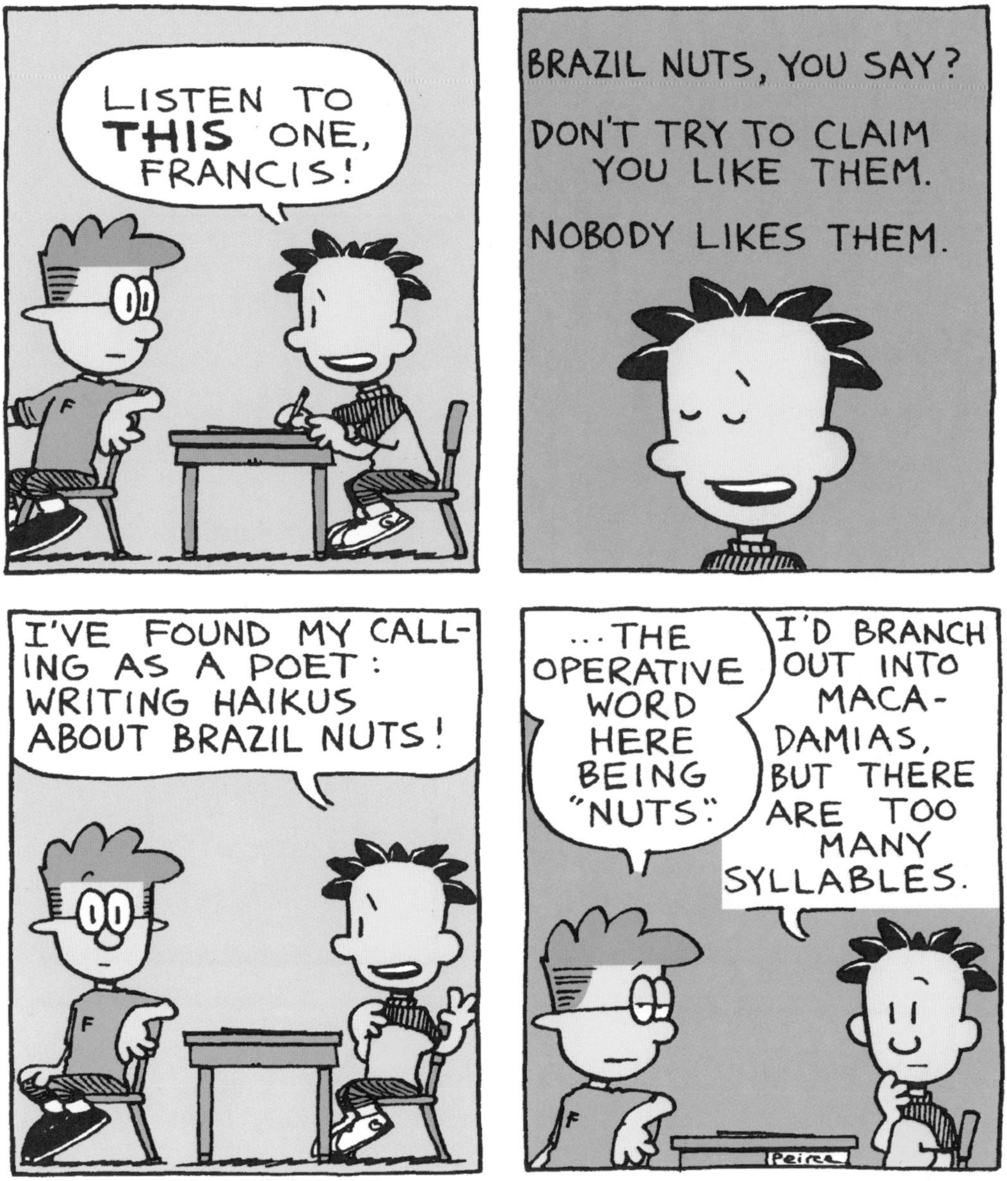

LISTEN TO **THIS** ONE, FRANCIS!
BRAZIL NUTS, YOU SAY?
DON'T TRY TO CLAIM YOU LIKE THEM.
NOBODY LIKES THEM.
I'VE FOUND MY CALLING AS A POET: WRITING HAIKUS ABOUT BRAZIL NUTS!
...THE OPERATIVE WORD HERE BEING "NUTS."
I'D BRANCH OUT INTO MACADAMIAS, BUT THERE ARE TOO MANY SYLLABLES.
PEIRCE

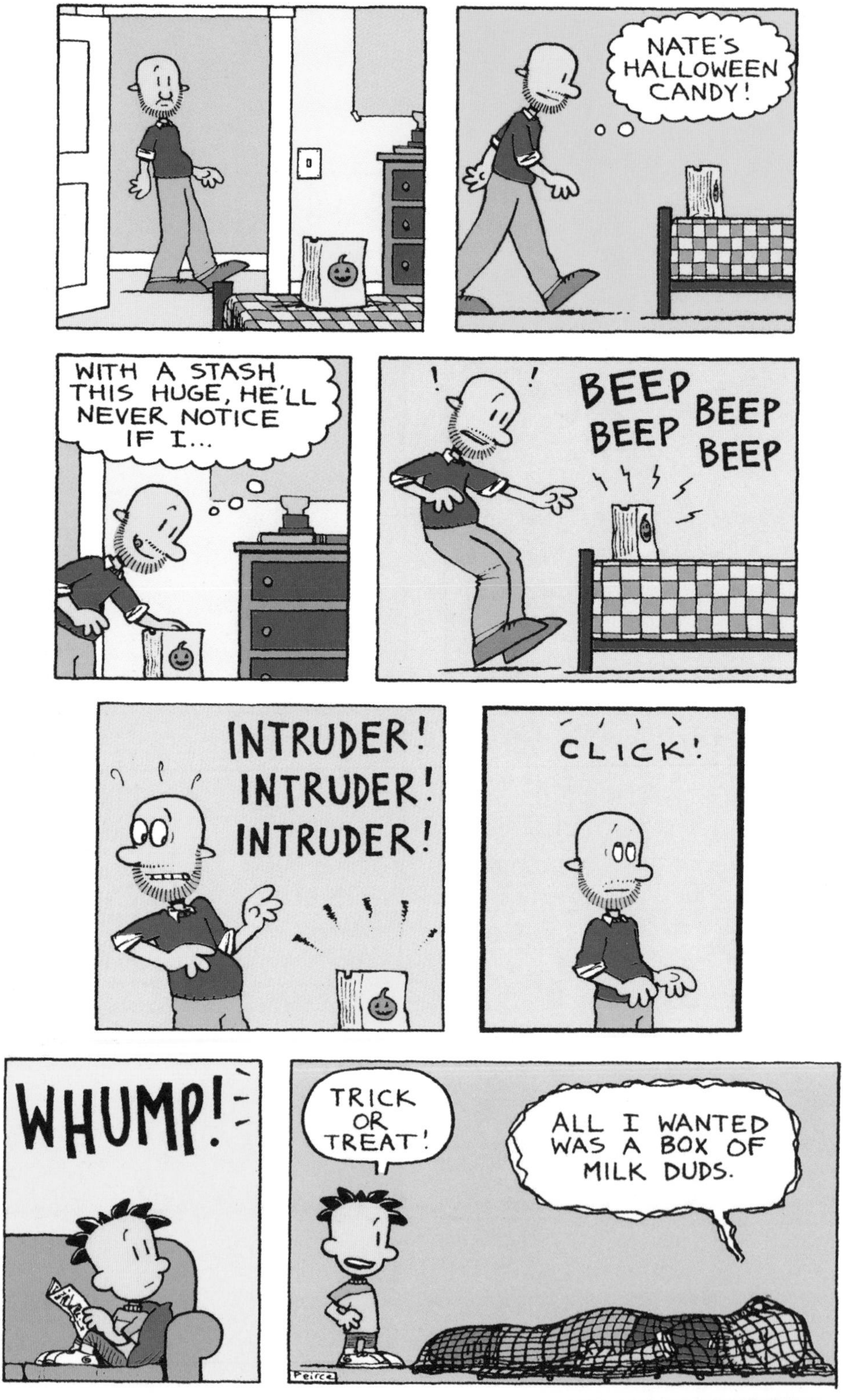
NATE'S HALLOWEEN CANDY!
WITH A STASH THIS HUGE, HE'LL NEVER NOTICE IF I...
BEEP BEEP BEEP BEEP
INTRUDER! INTRUDER! INTRUDER!
CLICK!
WHUMP!
TRICK OR TREAT!
ALL I WANTED WAS A BOX OF MILK DUDS.
Peirce

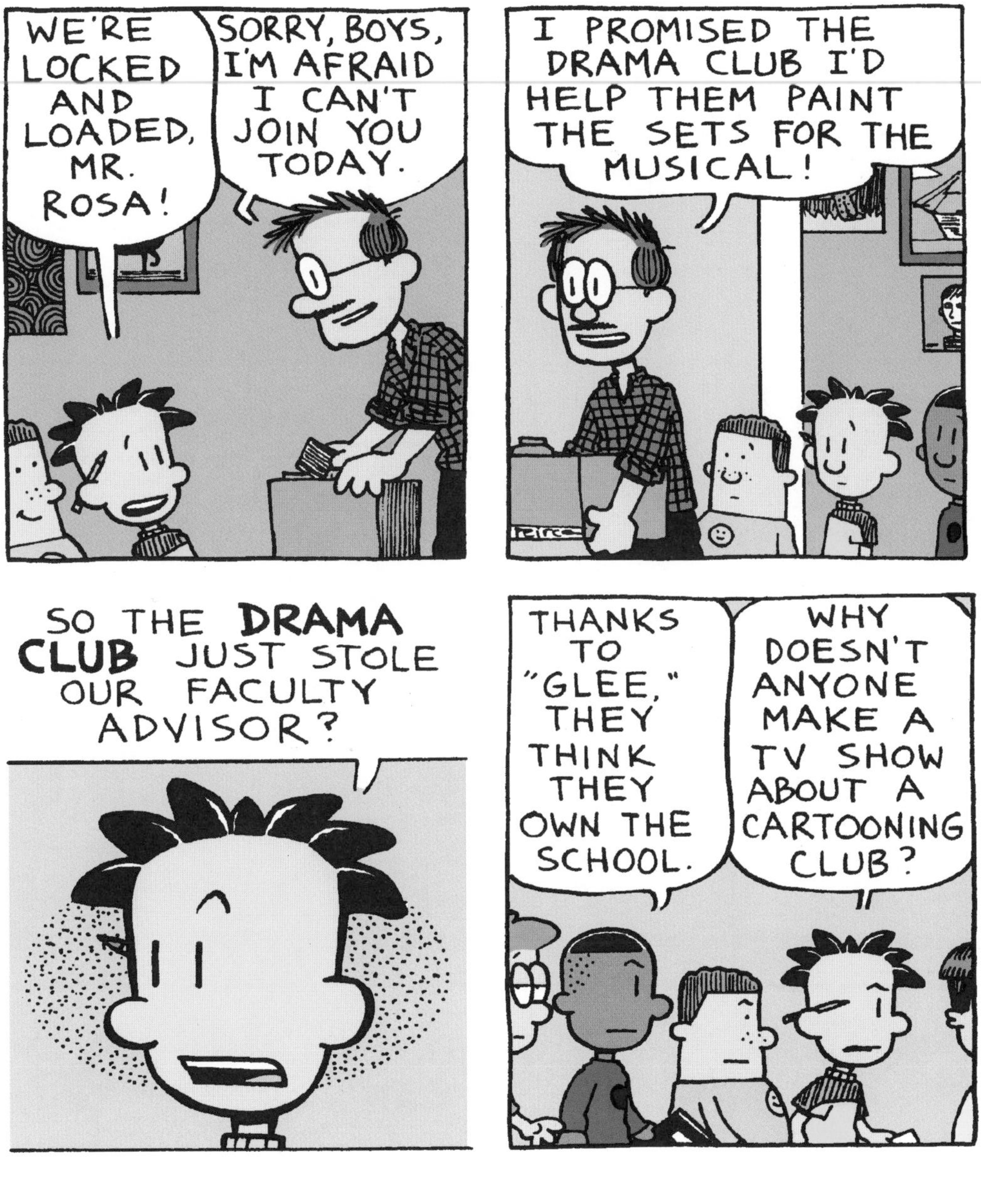
WE'RE LOCKED AND LOADED, MR. ROSA!
SORRY, BOYS, I'M AFRAID I CAN'T JOIN YOU TODAY.
I PROMISED THE DRAMA CLUB I'D HELP THEM PAINT THE SETS FOR THE MUSICAL!
SO THE **DRAMA CLUB** JUST STOLE OUR FACULTY ADVISOR?
THANKS TO "GLEE," THEY THINK THEY OWN THE SCHOOL.
WHY DOESN'T ANYONE MAKE A TV SHOW ABOUT A CARTOONING CLUB?

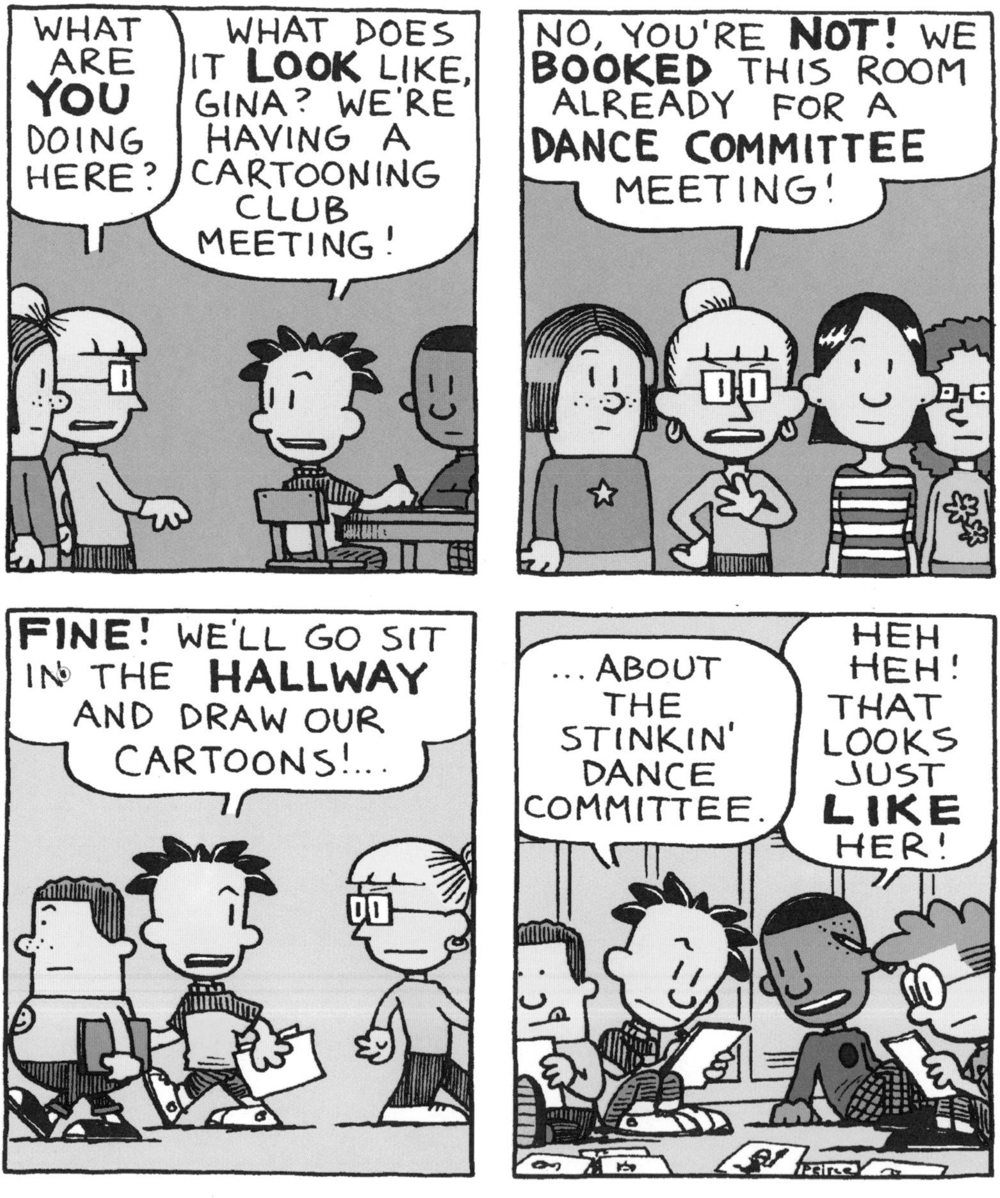
WHAT ARE YOU DOING HERE?
WHAT DOES IT LOOK LIKE, GINA? WE'RE HAVING A CARTOONING CLUB MEETING!
NO, YOU'RE NOT! WE BOOKED THIS ROOM ALREADY FOR A DANCE COMMITTEE MEETING!
FINE! WE'LL GO SIT IN THE HALLWAY AND DRAW OUR CARTOONS!...
...ABOUT THE STINKIN' DANCE COMMITTEE.
HEH HEH! THAT LOOKS JUST LIKE HER!

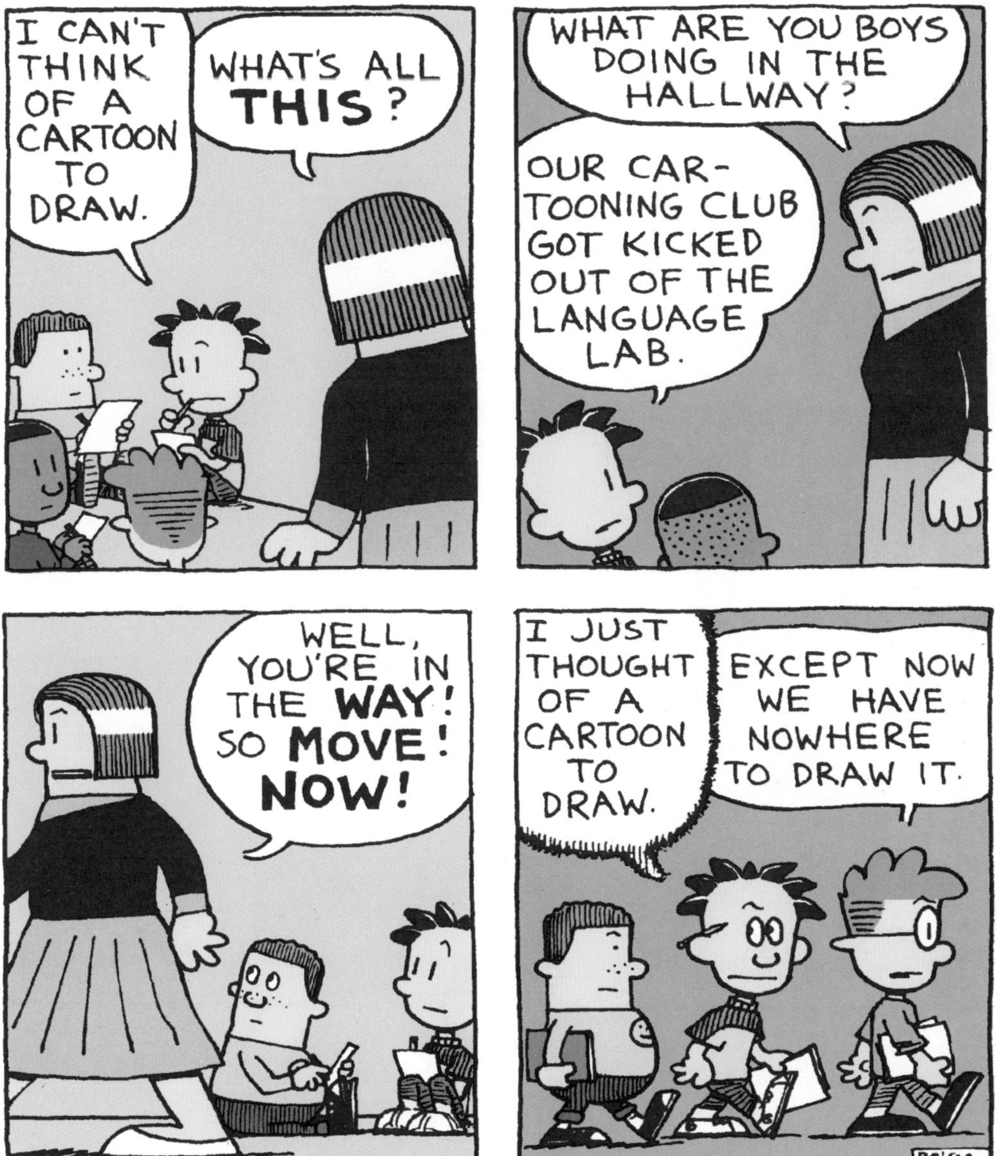
I CAN'T THINK OF A CARTOON TO DRAW.
WHAT'S ALL **THIS**?
WHAT ARE YOU BOYS DOING IN THE HALLWAY?
OUR CAR-TOONING CLUB GOT KICKED OUT OF THE LANGUAGE LAB.
WELL, YOU'RE IN THE **WAY**! SO **MOVE**! **NOW**!
I JUST THOUGHT OF A CARTOON TO DRAW.
EXCEPT NOW WE HAVE NOWHERE TO DRAW IT.
Peirce

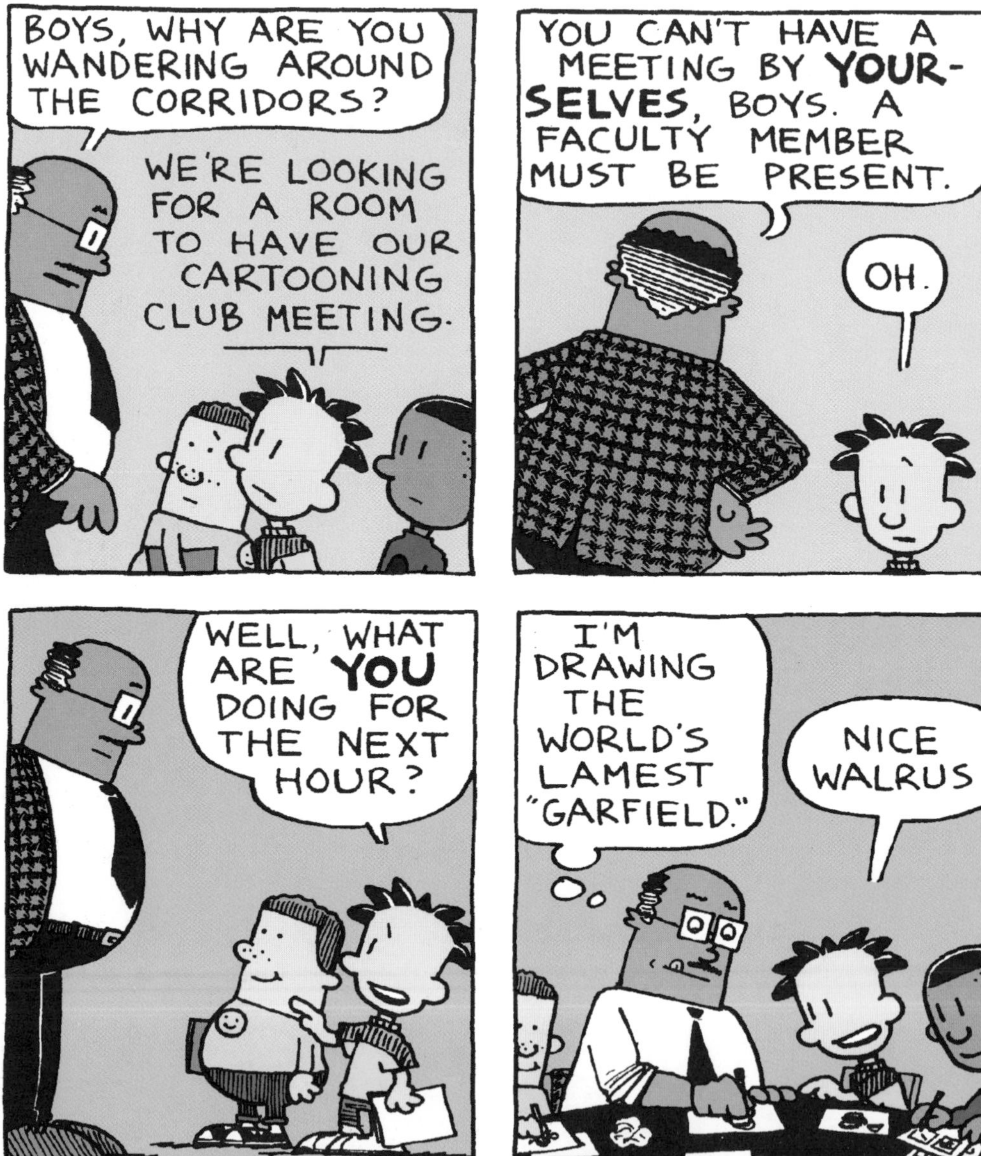
BOYS, WHY ARE YOU WANDERING AROUND THE CORRIDORS?
WE'RE LOOKING FOR A ROOM TO HAVE OUR CARTOONING CLUB MEETING.
YOU CAN'T HAVE A MEETING BY YOURSELVES, BOYS. A FACULTY MEMBER MUST BE PRESENT.
OH.
WELL, WHAT ARE YOU DOING FOR THE NEXT HOUR?
peirce
I'M DRAWING THE WORLD'S LAMEST "GARFIELD."
NICE WALRUS.

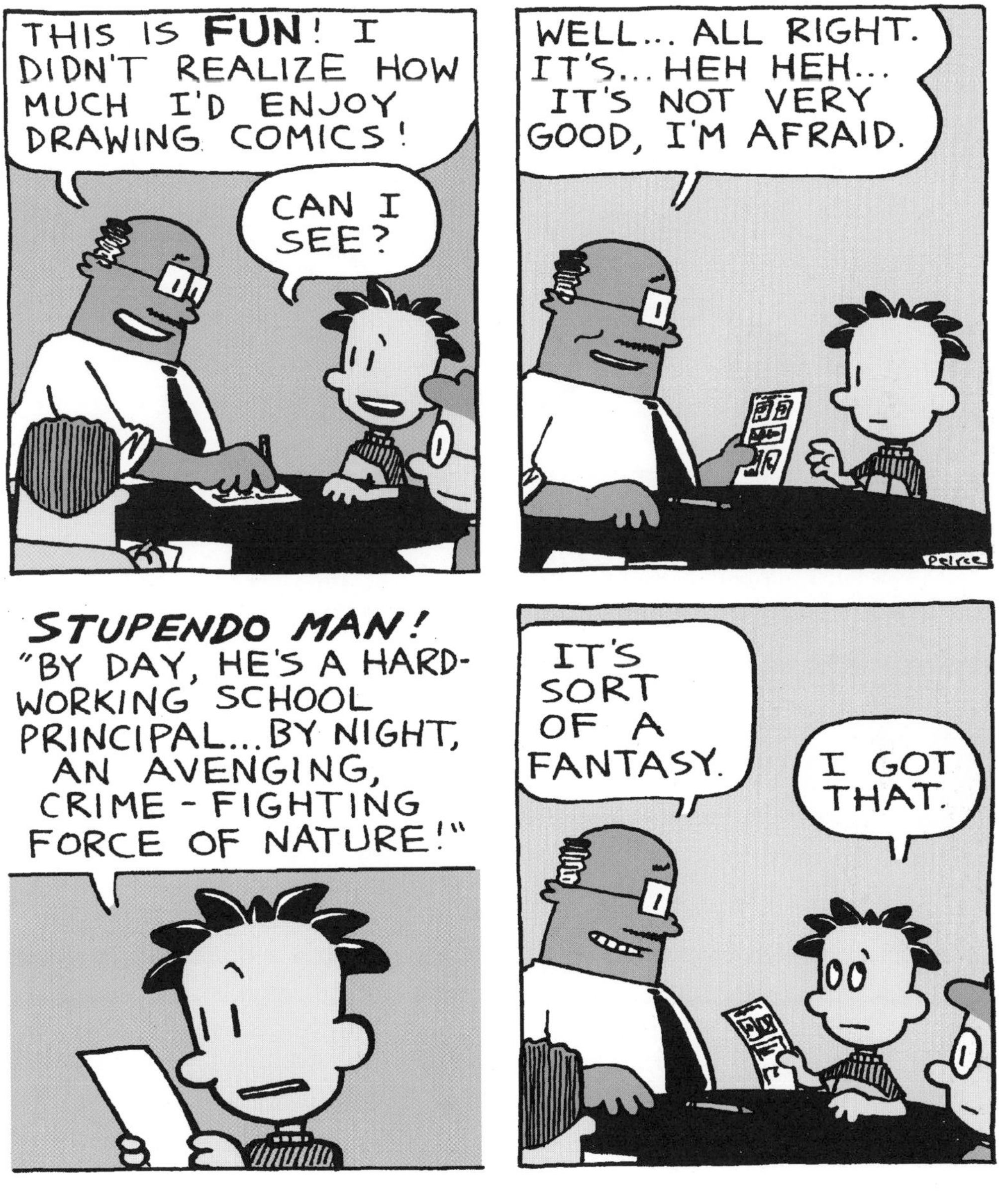
THIS IS FUN! I DIDN'T REALIZE HOW MUCH I'D ENJOY DRAWING COMICS!
CAN I SEE?
WELL... ALL RIGHT. IT'S... HEH HEH... IT'S NOT VERY GOOD, I'M AFRAID.
Peirce
STUPENDO MAN! "BY DAY, HE'S A HARD-WORKING SCHOOL PRINCIPAL... BY NIGHT, AN AVENGING, CRIME - FIGHTING FORCE OF NATURE!"
IT'S SORT OF A FANTASY.
I GOT THAT.

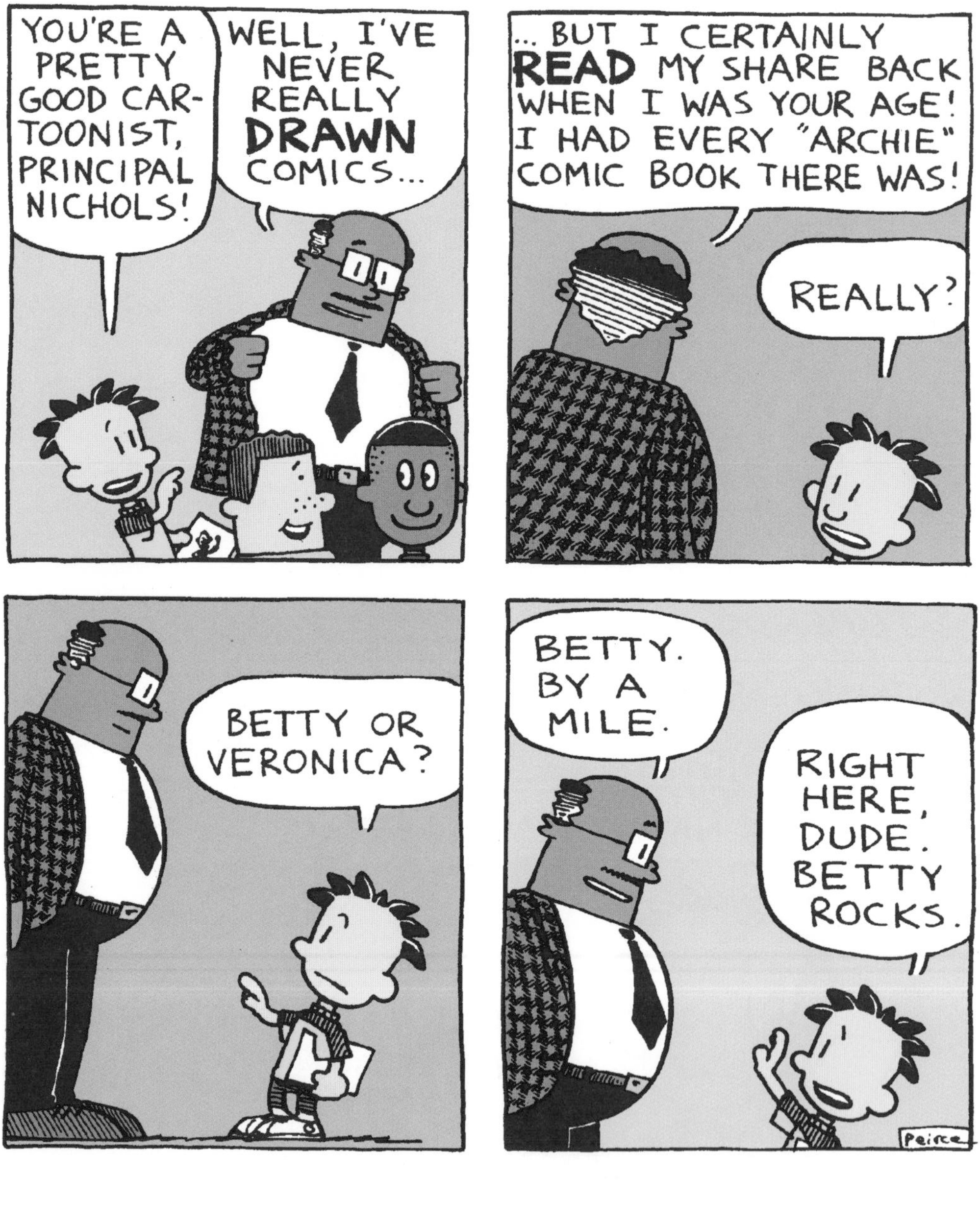
YOU'RE A PRETTY GOOD CAR-TOONIST, PRINCIPAL NICHOLS!
WELL, I'VE NEVER REALLY **DRAWN** COMICS...
... BUT I CERTAINLY **READ** MY SHARE BACK WHEN I WAS YOUR AGE! I HAD EVERY "ARCHIE" COMIC BOOK THERE WAS!
REALLY?
BETTY OR VERONICA?
BETTY. BY A MILE.
RIGHT HERE, DUDE. BETTY ROCKS.
Peirce

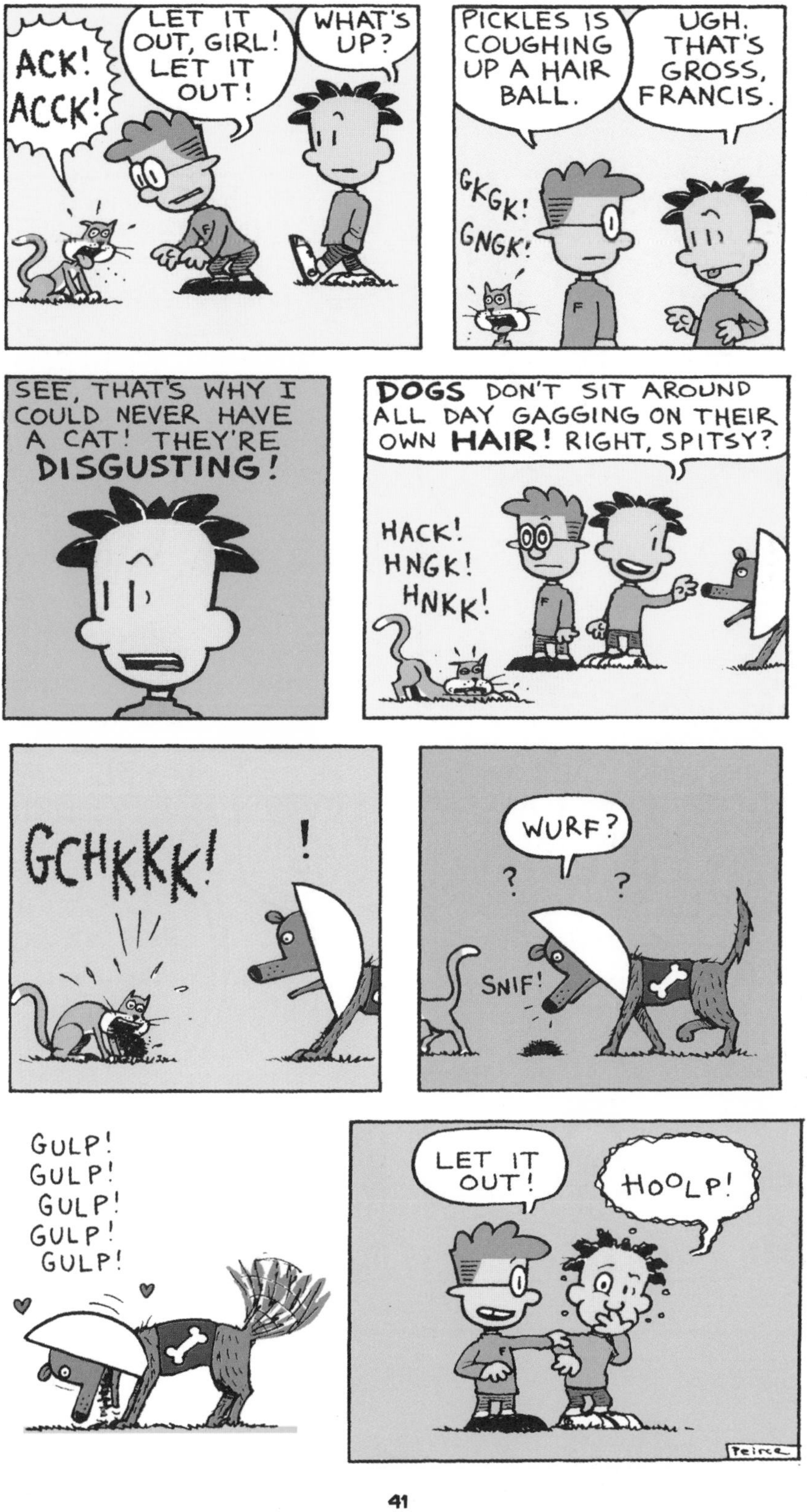
ACK! ACCK!
LET IT OUT, GIRL! LET IT OUT!
WHAT'S UP?
PICKLES IS COUGHING UP A HAIR BALL.
UGH. THAT'S GROSS, FRANCIS.
GKGK! GNGK!
SEE, THAT'S WHY I COULD NEVER HAVE A CAT! THEY'RE DISGUSTING!
DOGS DON'T SIT AROUND ALL DAY GAGGING ON THEIR OWN HAIR! RIGHT, SPITSY?
HACK! HNGK! HNKK!
GCHKKK!
!
WURF?
? ?
SNIF!
GULP! GULP! GULP! GULP! GULP!
LET IT OUT!
HOOLP!
Peirce

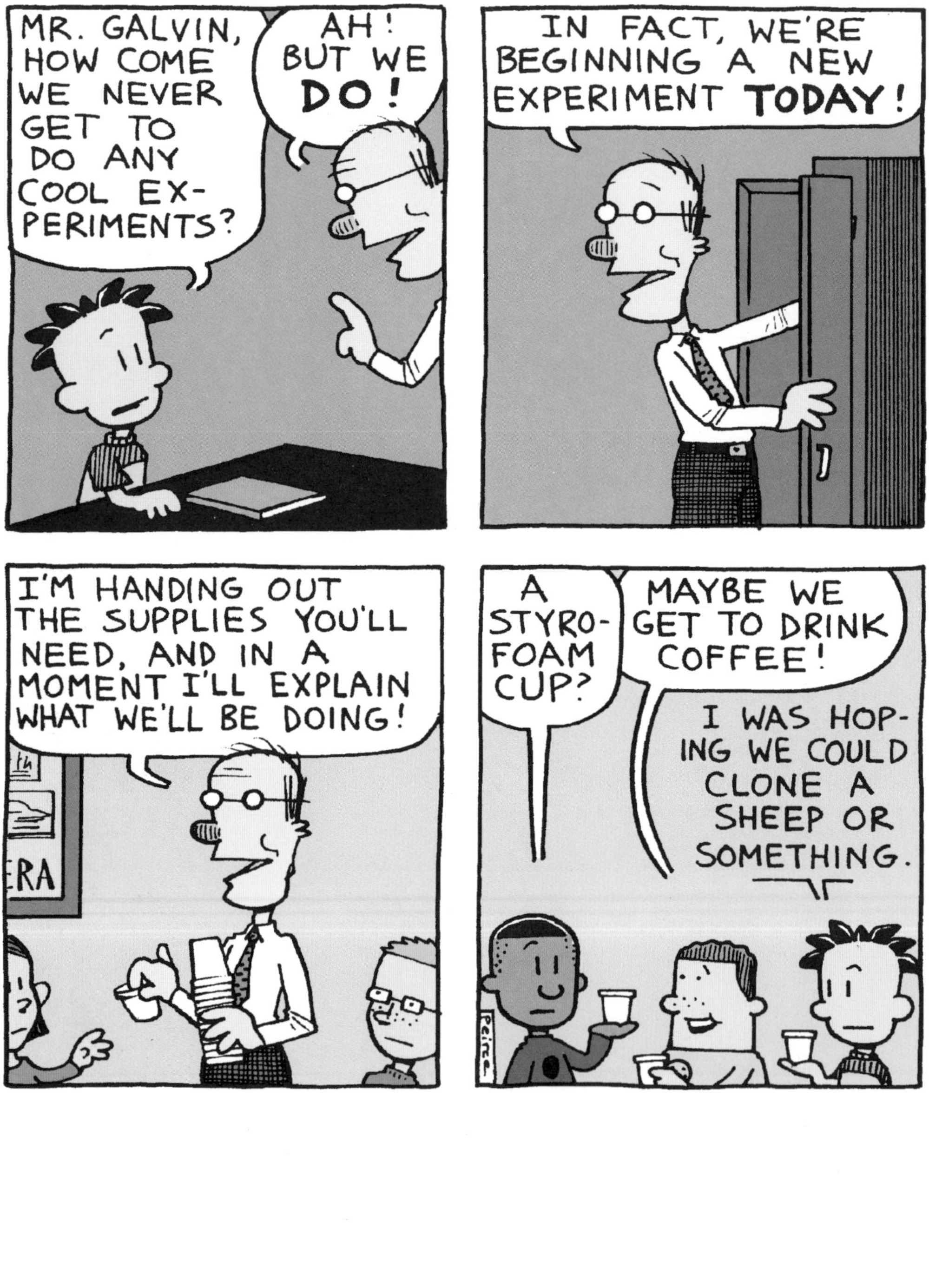
MR. GALVIN, HOW COME WE NEVER GET TO DO ANY COOL EX-PERIMENTS?
AH! BUT WE **DO**!
IN FACT, WE'RE BEGINNING A NEW EXPERIMENT **TODAY**!
I'M HANDING OUT THE SUPPLIES YOU'LL NEED, AND IN A MOMENT I'LL EXPLAIN WHAT WE'LL BE DOING!
ERA
A STYRO-FOAM CUP?
MAYBE WE GET TO DRINK COFFEE!
I WAS HOP-ING WE COULD CLONE A SHEEP OR SOMETHING.
peirce

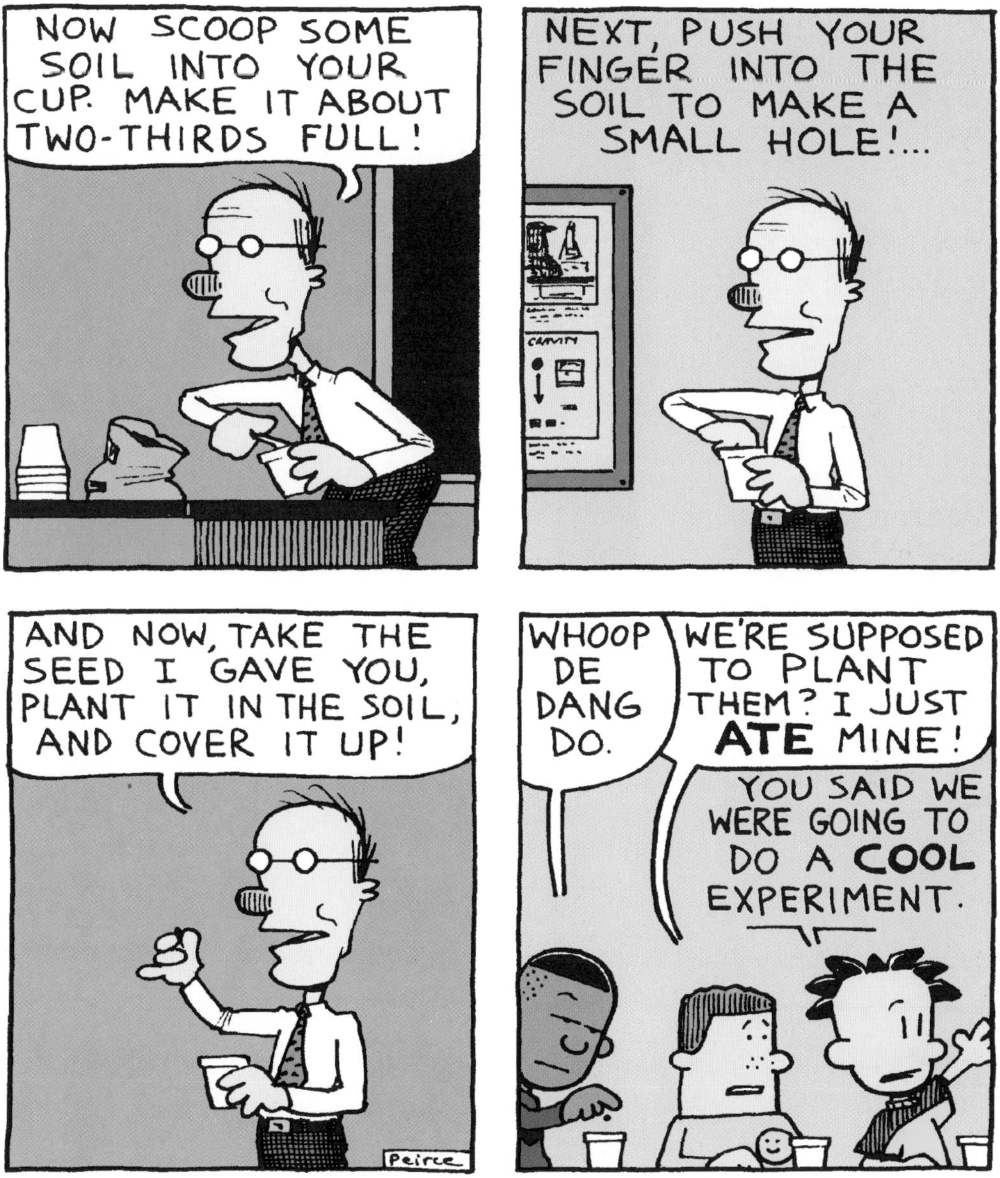
NOW SCOOP SOME SOIL INTO YOUR CUP. MAKE IT ABOUT TWO-THIRDS FULL!
NEXT, PUSH YOUR FINGER INTO THE SOIL TO MAKE A SMALL HOLE!...
AND NOW, TAKE THE SEED I GAVE YOU, PLANT IT IN THE SOIL, AND COVER IT UP!
Peirce
WHOOP DE DANG DO.
WE'RE SUPPOSED TO PLANT THEM? I JUST **ATE** MINE!
YOU SAID WE WERE GOING TO DO A **COOL** EXPERIMENT.

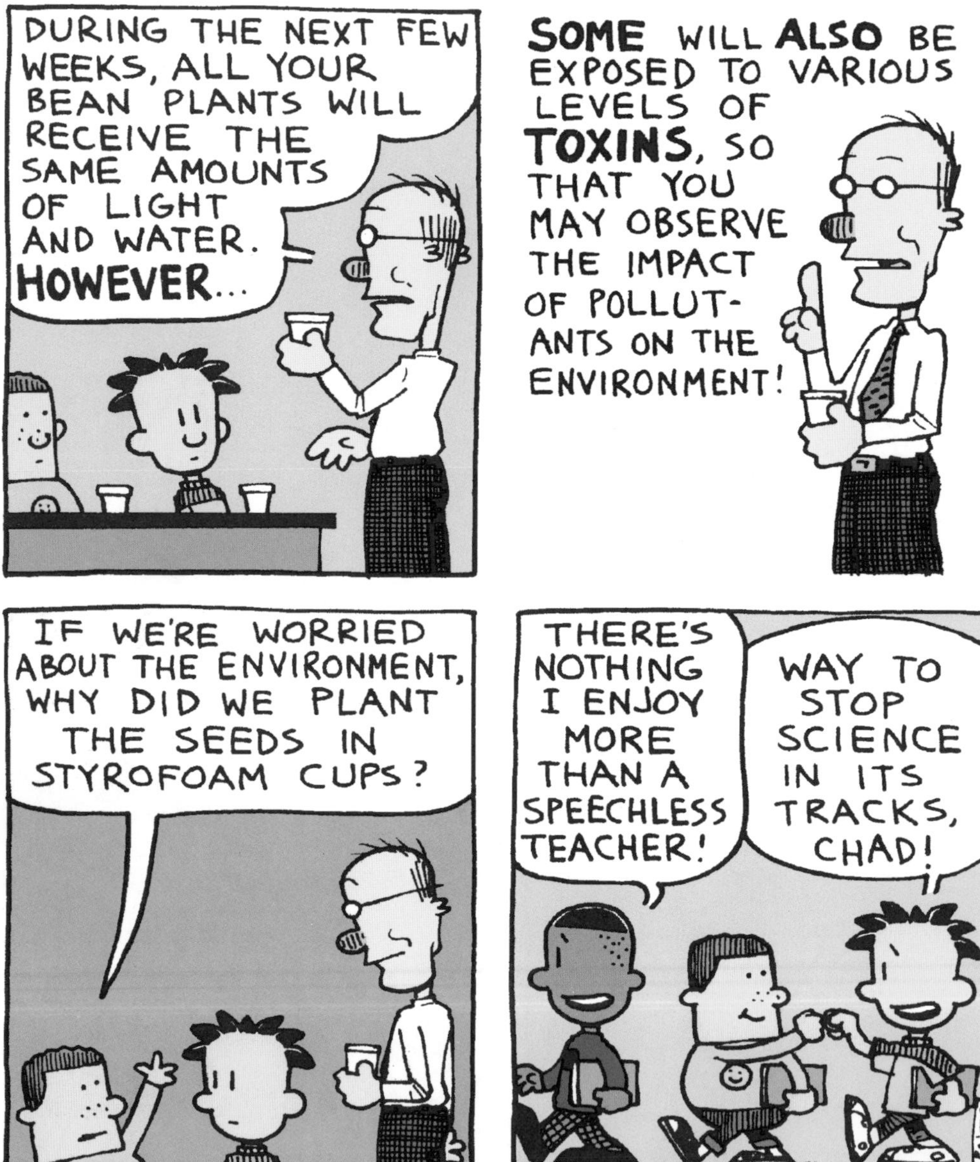
DURING THE NEXT FEW WEEKS, ALL YOUR BEAN PLANTS WILL RECEIVE THE SAME AMOUNTS OF LIGHT AND WATER. HOWEVER...
SOME WILL ALSO BE EXPOSED TO VARIOUS LEVELS OF TOXINS, SO THAT YOU MAY OBSERVE THE IMPACT OF POLLUTANTS ON THE ENVIRONMENT!
IF WE'RE WORRIED ABOUT THE ENVIRONMENT, WHY DID WE PLANT THE SEEDS IN STYROFOAM CUPS?
THERE'S NOTHING I ENJOY MORE THAN A SPEECHLESS TEACHER!
WAY TO STOP SCIENCE IN ITS TRACKS, CHAD!
PEIRCE

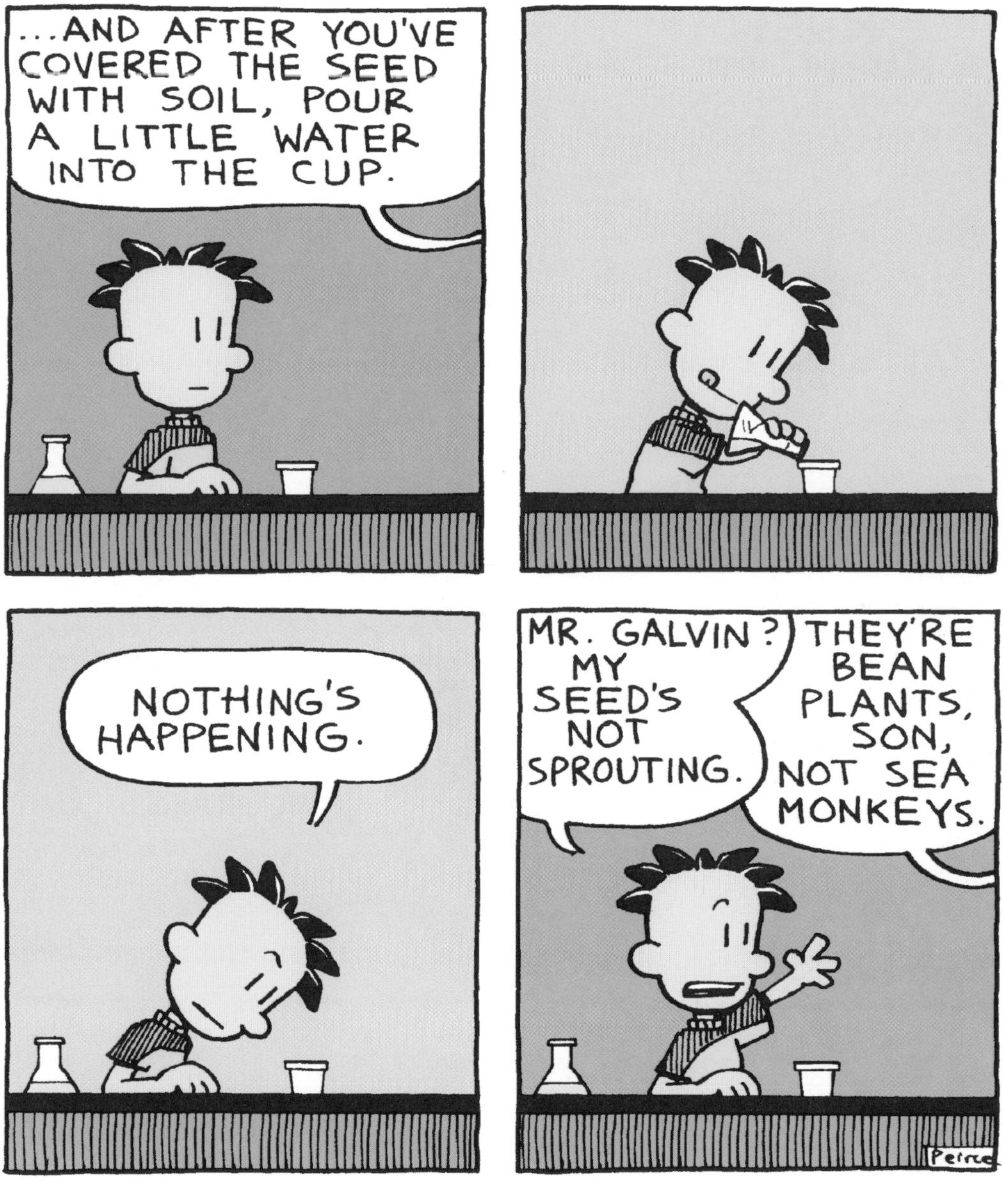
...AND AFTER YOU'VE COVERED THE SEED WITH SOIL, POUR A LITTLE WATER INTO THE CUP.
NOTHING'S HAPPENING.
MR. GALVIN? MY SEED'S NOT SPROUTING.
THEY'RE BEAN PLANTS, SON, NOT SEA MONKEYS.
Peirce

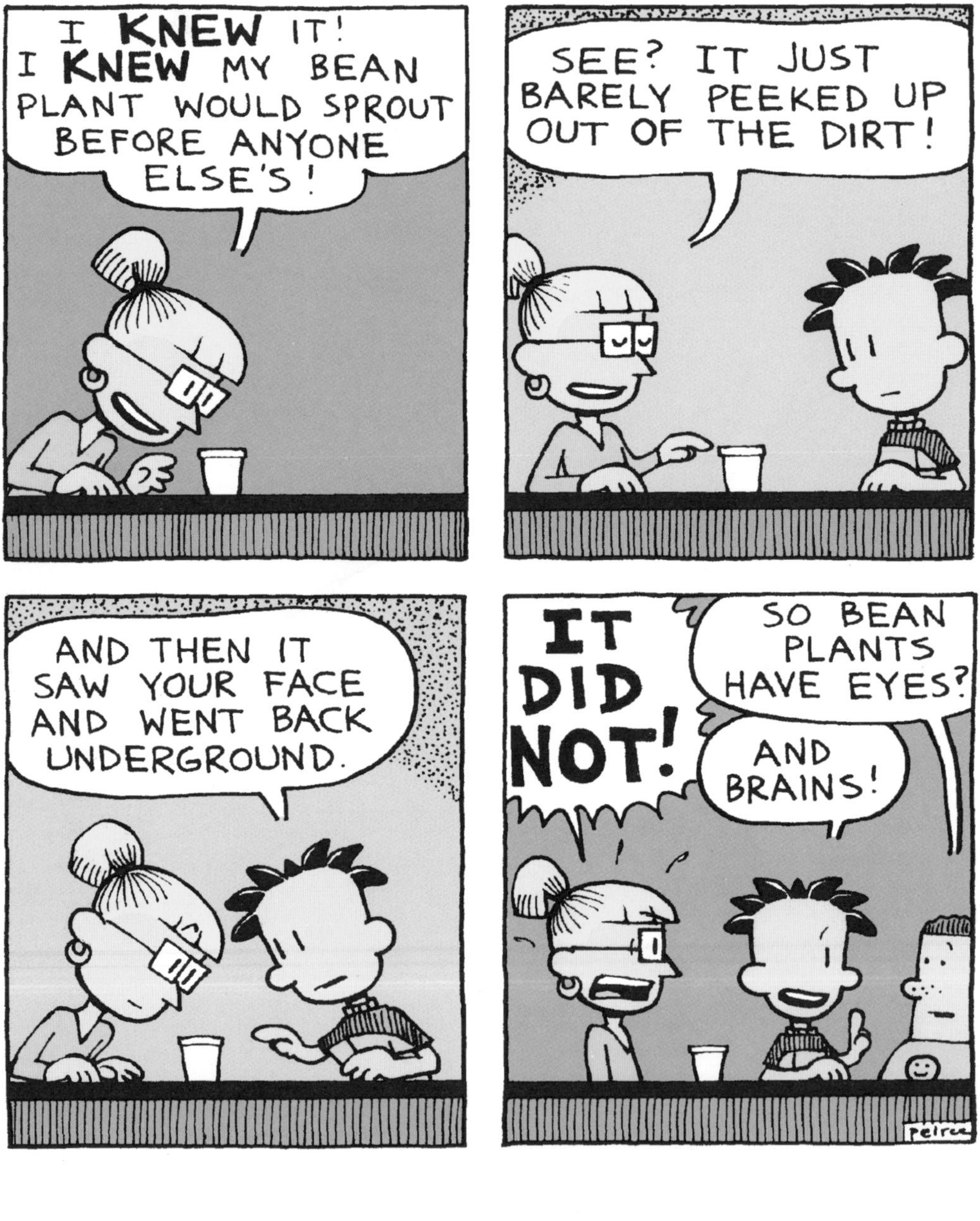
I KNEW IT! I KNEW MY BEAN PLANT WOULD SPROUT BEFORE ANYONE ELSE'S!
SEE? IT JUST BARELY PEEKED UP OUT OF THE DIRT!
AND THEN IT SAW YOUR FACE AND WENT BACK UNDERGROUND.
IT DID NOT!
SO BEAN PLANTS HAVE EYES?
AND BRAINS!
peirce

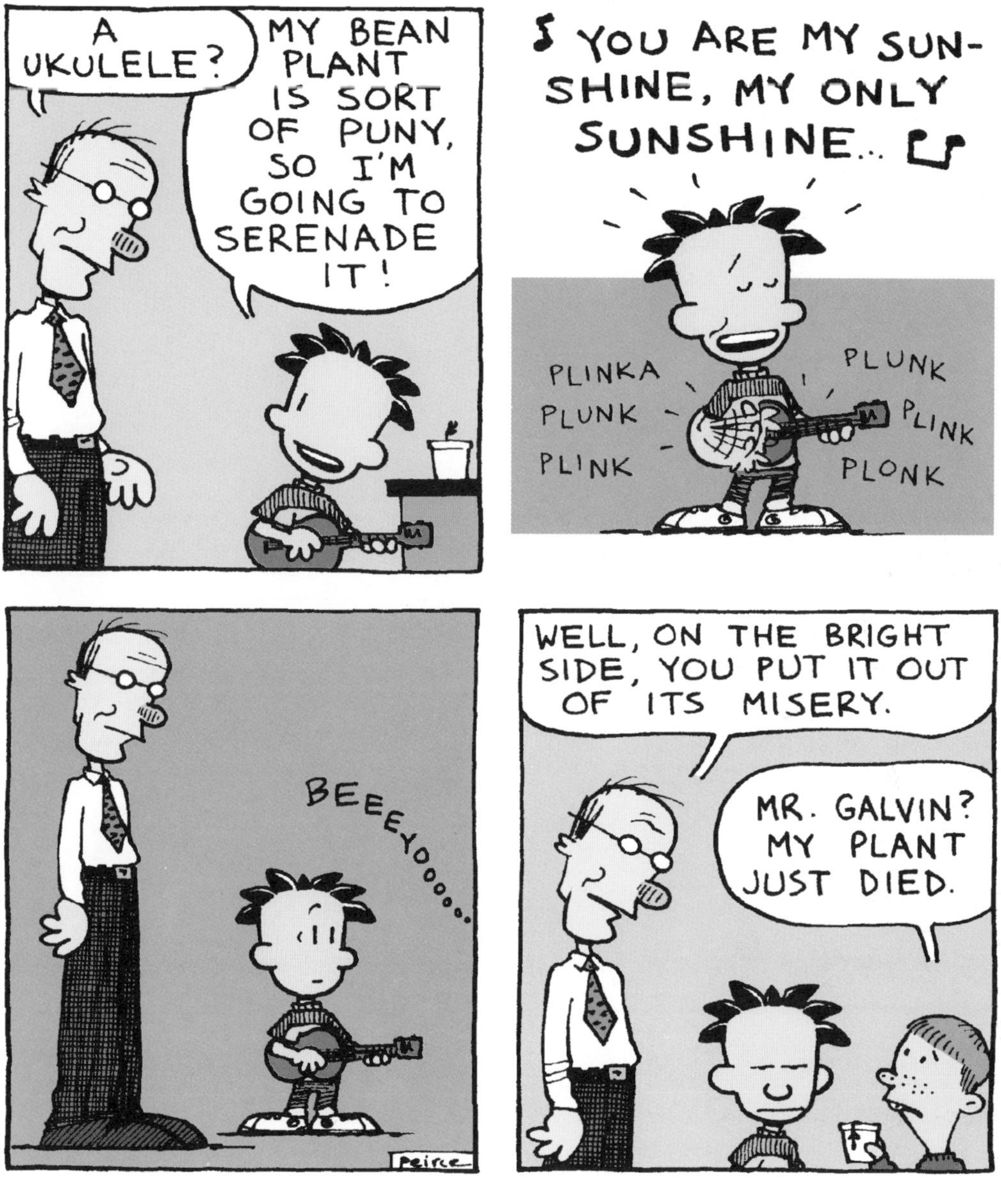
A UKULELE?
MY BEAN PLANT IS SORT OF PUNY, SO I'M GOING TO SERENADE IT!
YOU ARE MY SUN-SHINE, MY ONLY SUNSHINE...
PLINKA
PLUNK
PLINK
PLUNK
PLINK
PLONK
BEEEEYOOOOO..
WELL, ON THE BRIGHT SIDE, YOU PUT IT OUT OF ITS MISERY.
MR. GALVIN? MY PLANT JUST DIED.

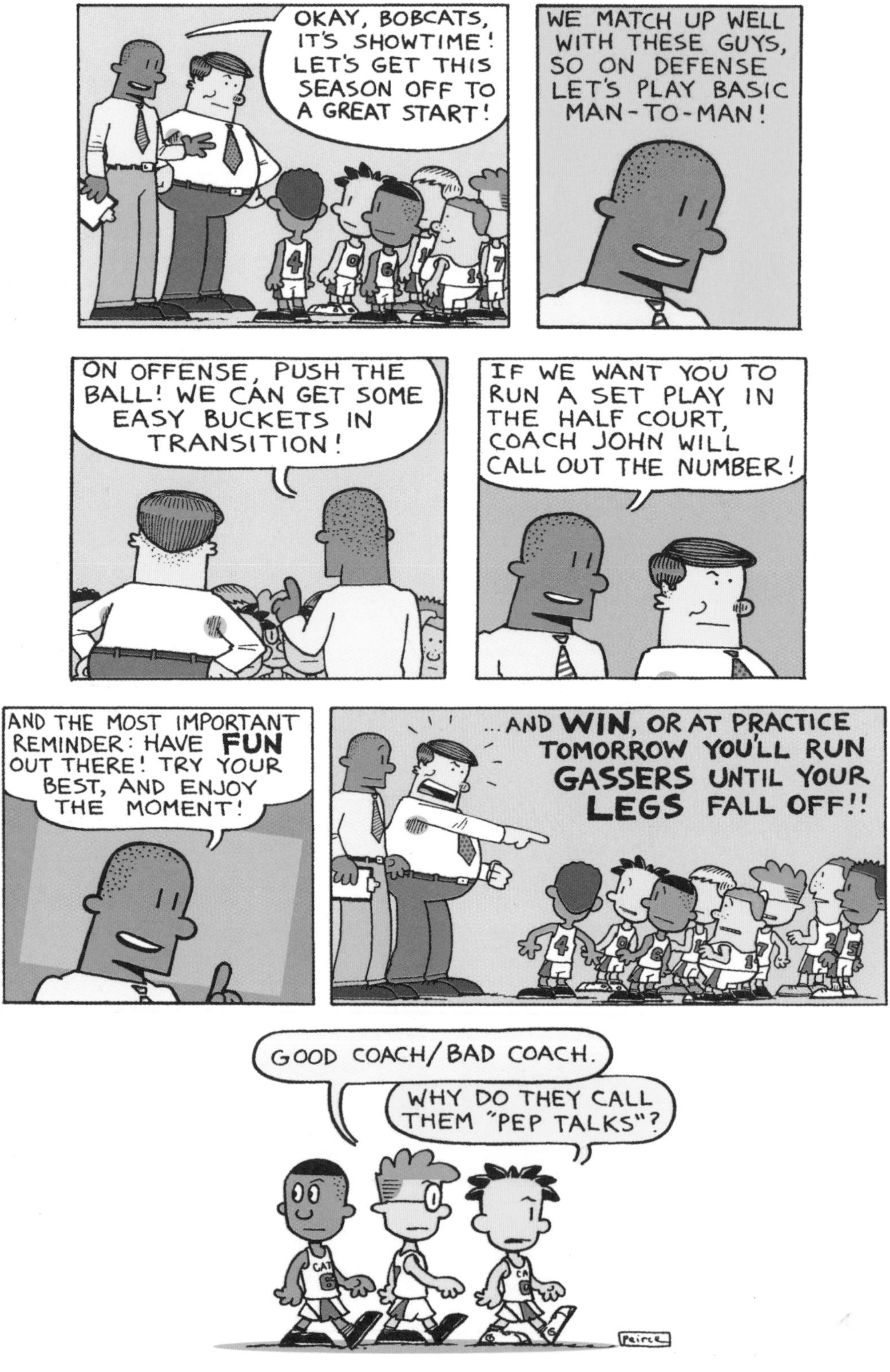

OKAY, BOBCATS, IT'S SHOWTIME! LET'S GET THIS SEASON OFF TO A GREAT START!
WE MATCH UP WELL WITH THESE GUYS, SO ON DEFENSE LET'S PLAY BASIC MAN-TO-MAN!
ON OFFENSE, PUSH THE BALL! WE CAN GET SOME EASY BUCKETS IN TRANSITION!
IF WE WANT YOU TO RUN A SET PLAY IN THE HALF COURT, COACH JOHN WILL CALL OUT THE NUMBER!
AND THE MOST IMPORTANT REMINDER: HAVE FUN OUT THERE! TRY YOUR BEST, AND ENJOY THE MOMENT!
...AND WIN, OR AT PRACTICE TOMORROW YOU'LL RUN GASSERS UNTIL YOUR LEGS FALL OFF!!
GOOD COACH/BAD COACH.
WHY DO THEY CALL THEM "PEP TALKS"?
Peirce

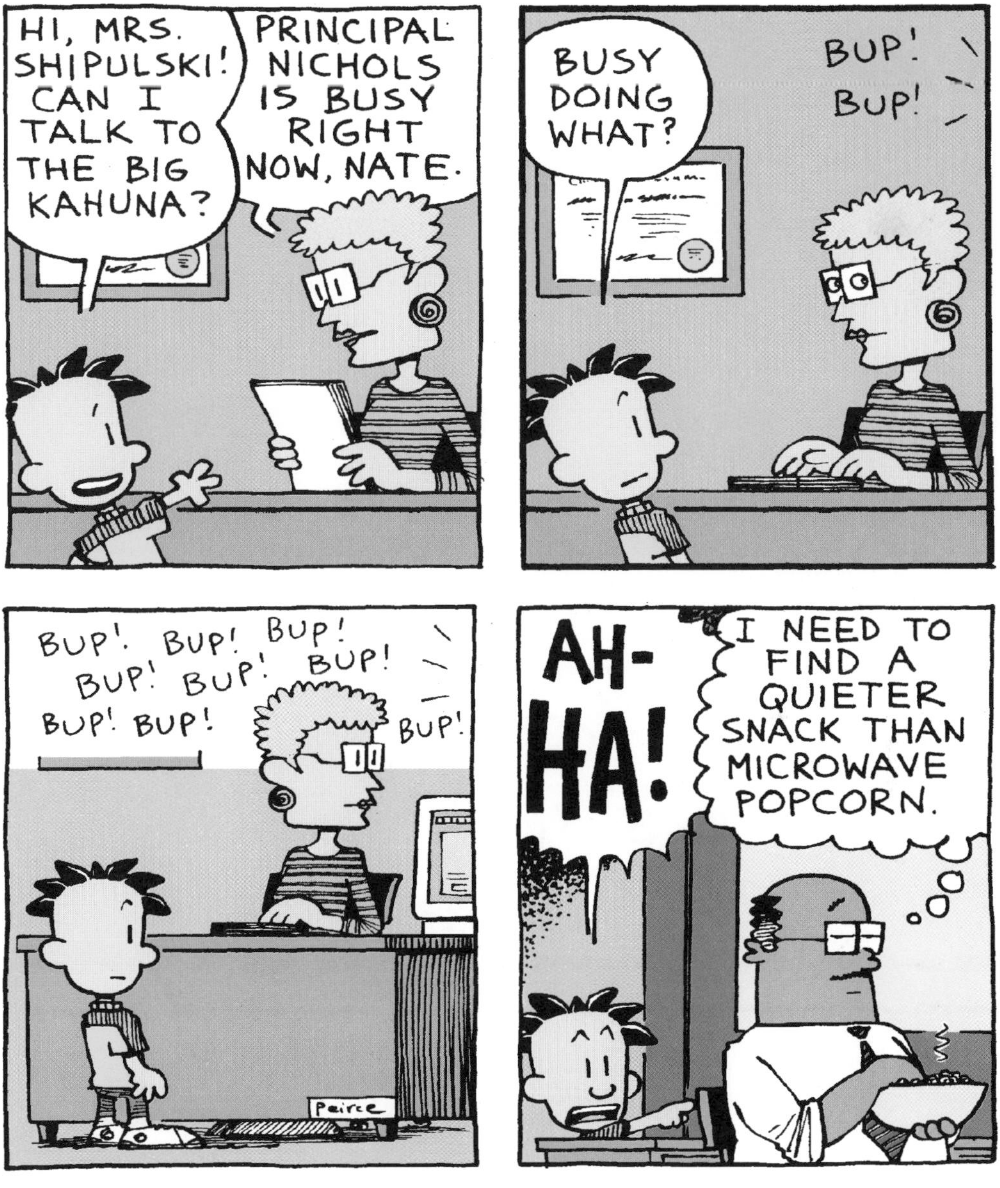
HI, MRS. SHIPULSKI! CAN I TALK TO THE BIG KAHUNA?
PRINCIPAL NICHOLS IS BUSY RIGHT NOW, NATE.
BUSY DOING WHAT?
BUP! BUP!
BUP! BUP! BUP! BUP! BUP! BUP! BUP! BUP! BUP!
Peirce
AH-HA!
I NEED TO FIND A QUIETER SNACK THAN MICROWAVE POPCORN.

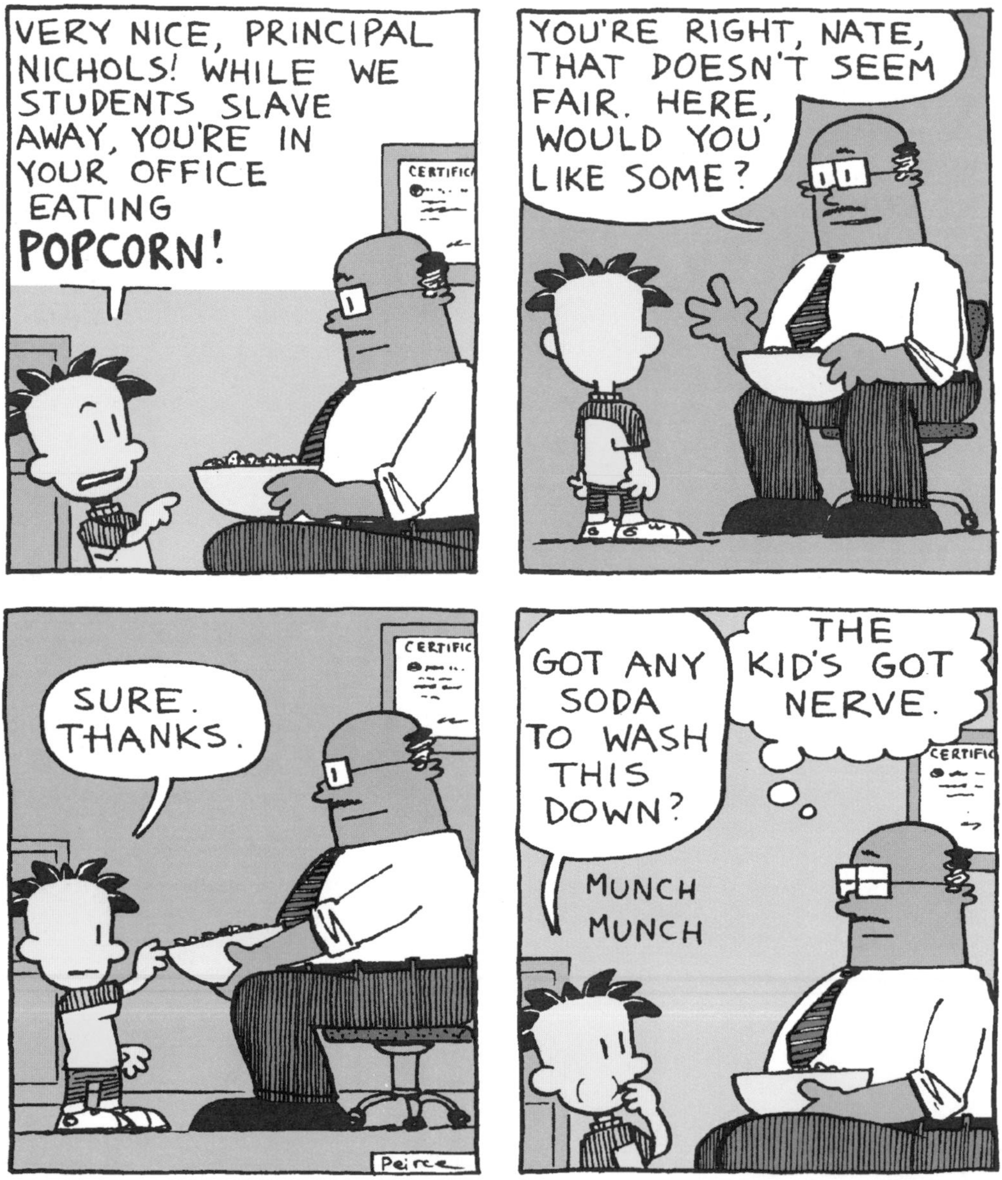

VERY NICE, PRINCIPAL NICHOLS! WHILE WE STUDENTS SLAVE AWAY, YOU'RE IN YOUR OFFICE EATING **POPCORN**!
YOU'RE RIGHT, NATE, THAT DOESN'T SEEM FAIR. HERE, WOULD YOU LIKE SOME?
SURE. THANKS.
Peirce
GOT ANY SODA TO WASH THIS DOWN?
MUNCH MUNCH
THE KID'S GOT NERVE.

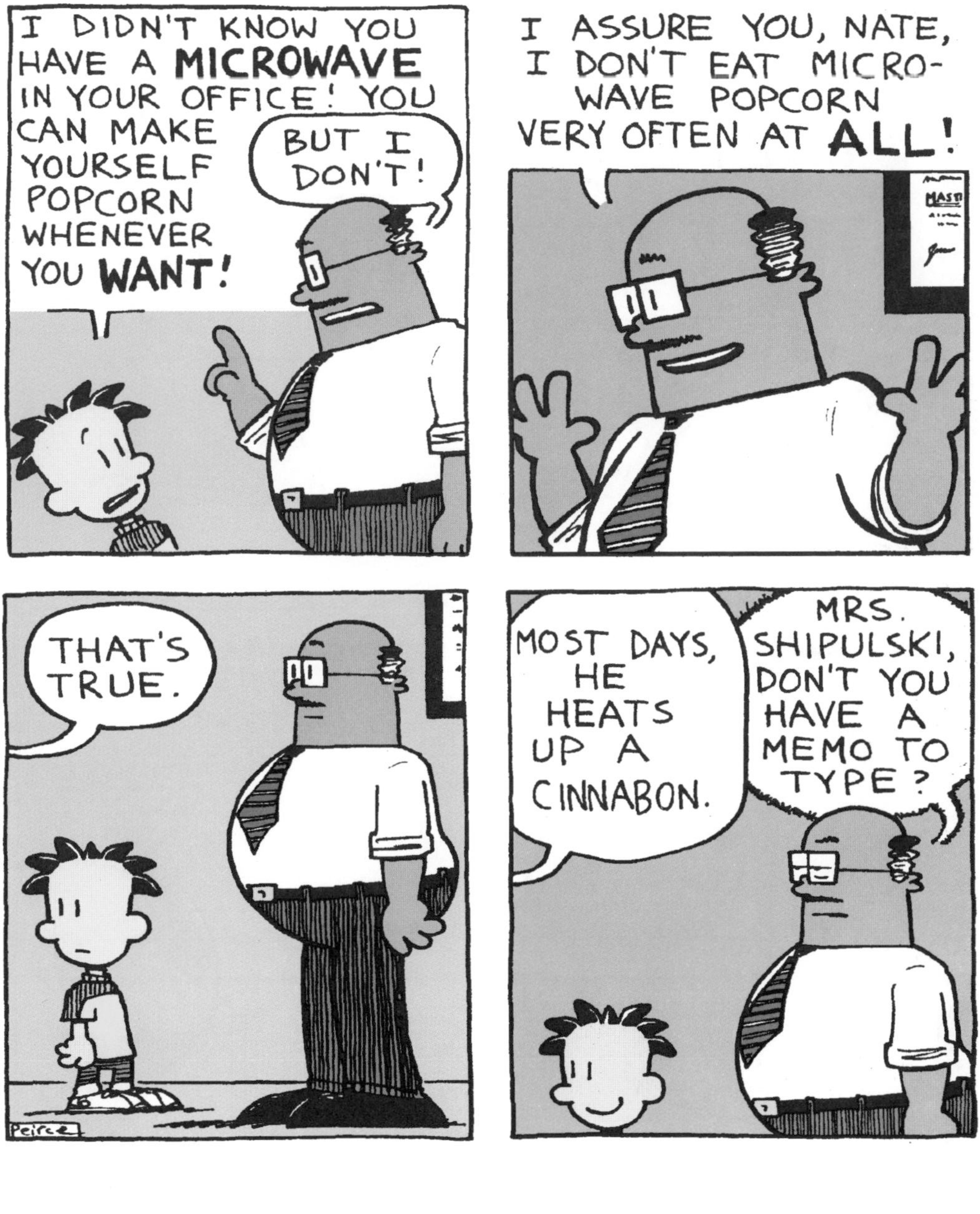

I DIDN'T KNOW YOU HAVE A MICROWAVE IN YOUR OFFICE! YOU CAN MAKE YOURSELF POPCORN WHENEVER YOU WANT!
BUT I DON'T!
I ASSURE YOU, NATE, I DON'T EAT MICRO-WAVE POPCORN VERY OFTEN AT ALL!
THAT'S TRUE.
MOST DAYS, HE HEATS UP A CINNABON.
MRS. SHIPULSKI, DON'T YOU HAVE A MEMO TO TYPE?
Peirce

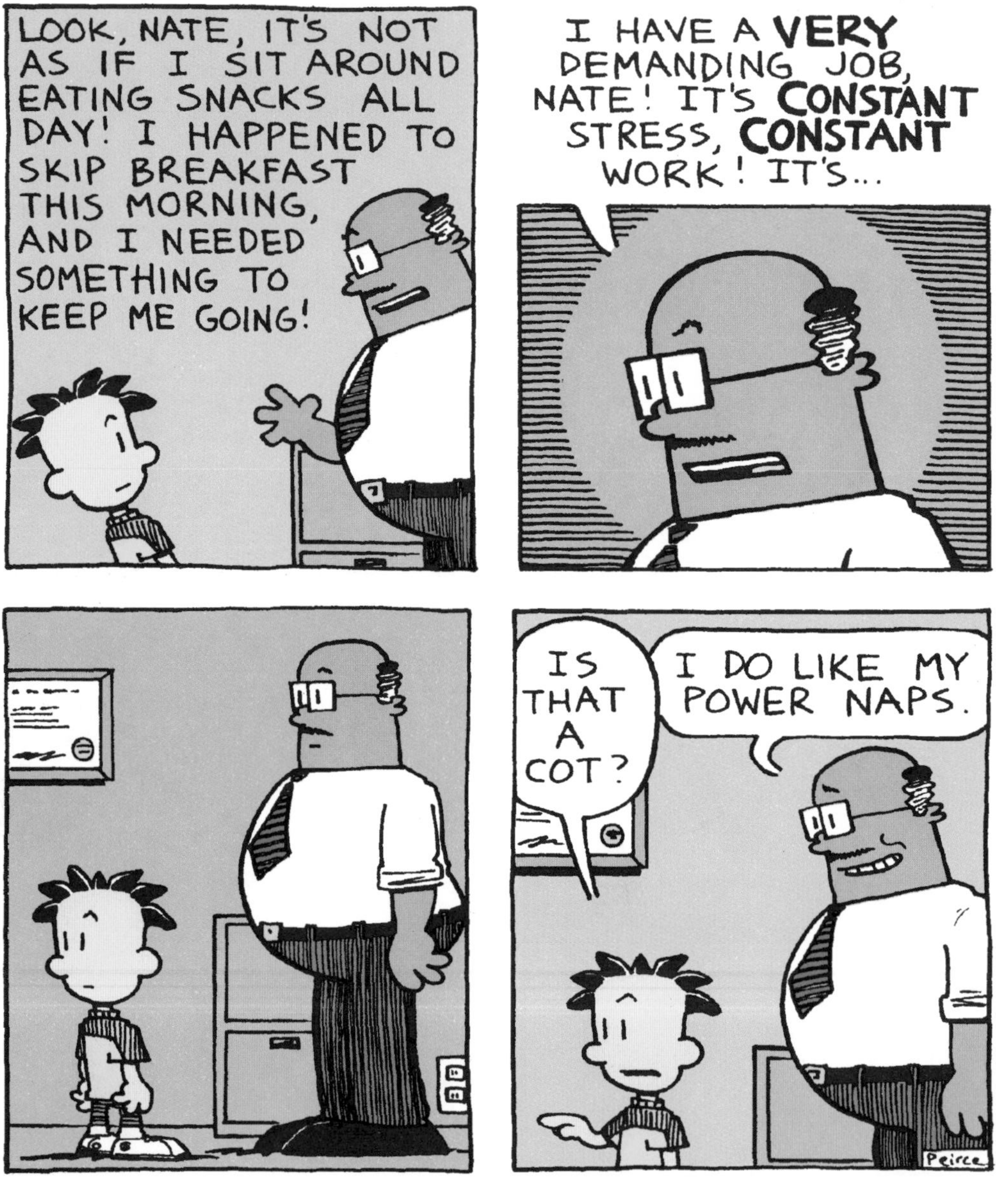
LOOK, NATE, IT'S NOT AS IF I SIT AROUND EATING SNACKS ALL DAY! I HAPPENED TO SKIP BREAKFAST THIS MORNING, AND I NEEDED SOMETHING TO KEEP ME GOING!
I HAVE A VERY DEMANDING JOB, NATE! IT'S CONSTANT STRESS, CONSTANT WORK! IT'S...
IS THAT A COT?
I DO LIKE MY POWER NAPS.
Peirce

DOESN'T IT IRK YOU, MRS. SHIPULSKI?
DOESN'T WHAT IRK ME, CHILD?
THE PRINCIPAL HAS A MICROWAVE IN HIS OFFICE TO FIX HIMSELF SNACKS ALL DAY! YOU DON'T HAVE ANYTHING!
...EXCEPT A BODY MASS INDEX OF 18.6.
I DON'T EVEN KNOW WHAT THAT MEANS.
NEITHER DOES THE PRINCIPAL.
Peirce

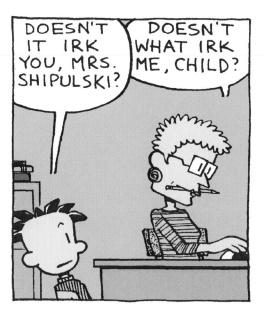

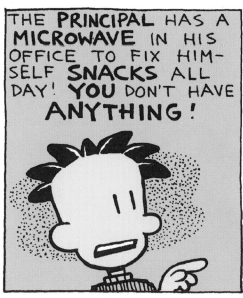

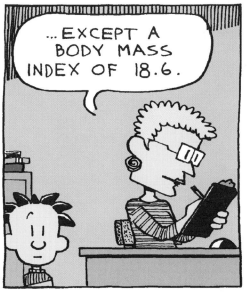

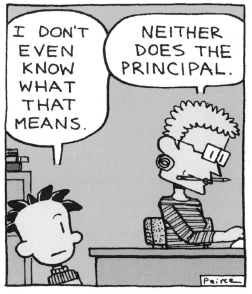

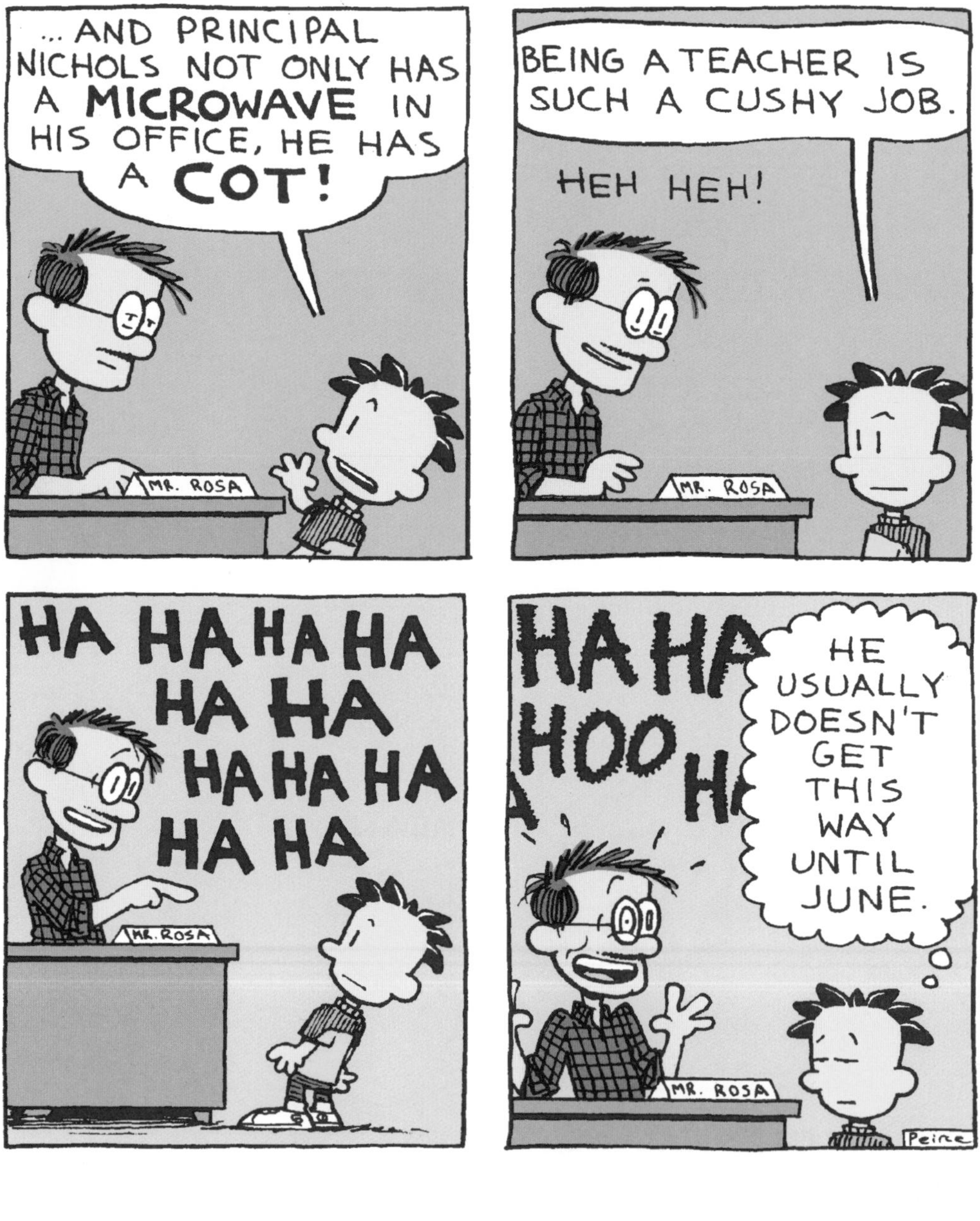

...AND PRINCIPAL NICHOLS NOT ONLY HAS A **MICROWAVE** IN HIS OFFICE, HE HAS A **COT**!
MR. ROSA
BEING A TEACHER IS SUCH A CUSHY JOB.
HEH HEH!
MR. ROSA
HA HA HA HA HA HA HA HA HA HA HA HA HA
MR. ROSA
HA HA HOO
HE USUALLY DOESN'T GET THIS WAY UNTIL JUNE.
MR. ROSA
Peirce

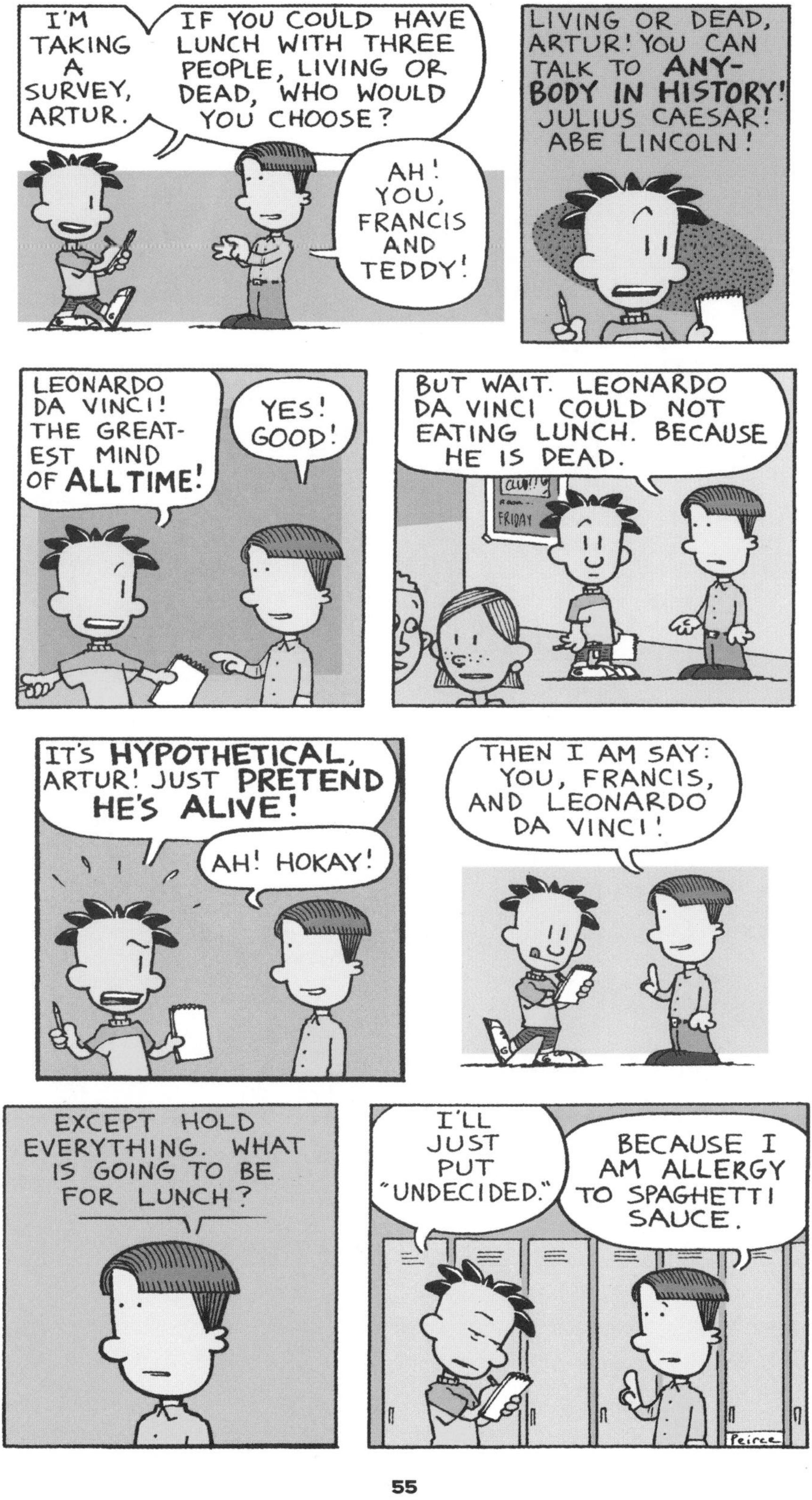
I'M TAKING A SURVEY, ARTUR.
IF YOU COULD HAVE LUNCH WITH THREE PEOPLE, LIVING OR DEAD, WHO WOULD YOU CHOOSE?
AH! YOU, FRANCIS AND TEDDY!
LIVING OR DEAD, ARTUR! YOU CAN TALK TO ANYBODY IN HISTORY! JULIUS CAESAR! ABE LINCOLN!
LEONARDO DA VINCI! THE GREATEST MIND OF ALL TIME!
YES! GOOD!
BUT WAIT. LEONARDO DA VINCI COULD NOT EATING LUNCH. BECAUSE HE IS DEAD.
FRIDAY
IT'S HYPOTHETICAL, ARTUR! JUST PRETEND HE'S ALIVE!
AH! HOKAY!
THEN I AM SAY: YOU, FRANCIS, AND LEONARDO DA VINCI!
EXCEPT HOLD EVERYTHING. WHAT IS GOING TO BE FOR LUNCH?
I'LL JUST PUT "UNDECIDED."
BECAUSE I AM ALLERGY TO SPAGHETTI SAUCE.
Peirce

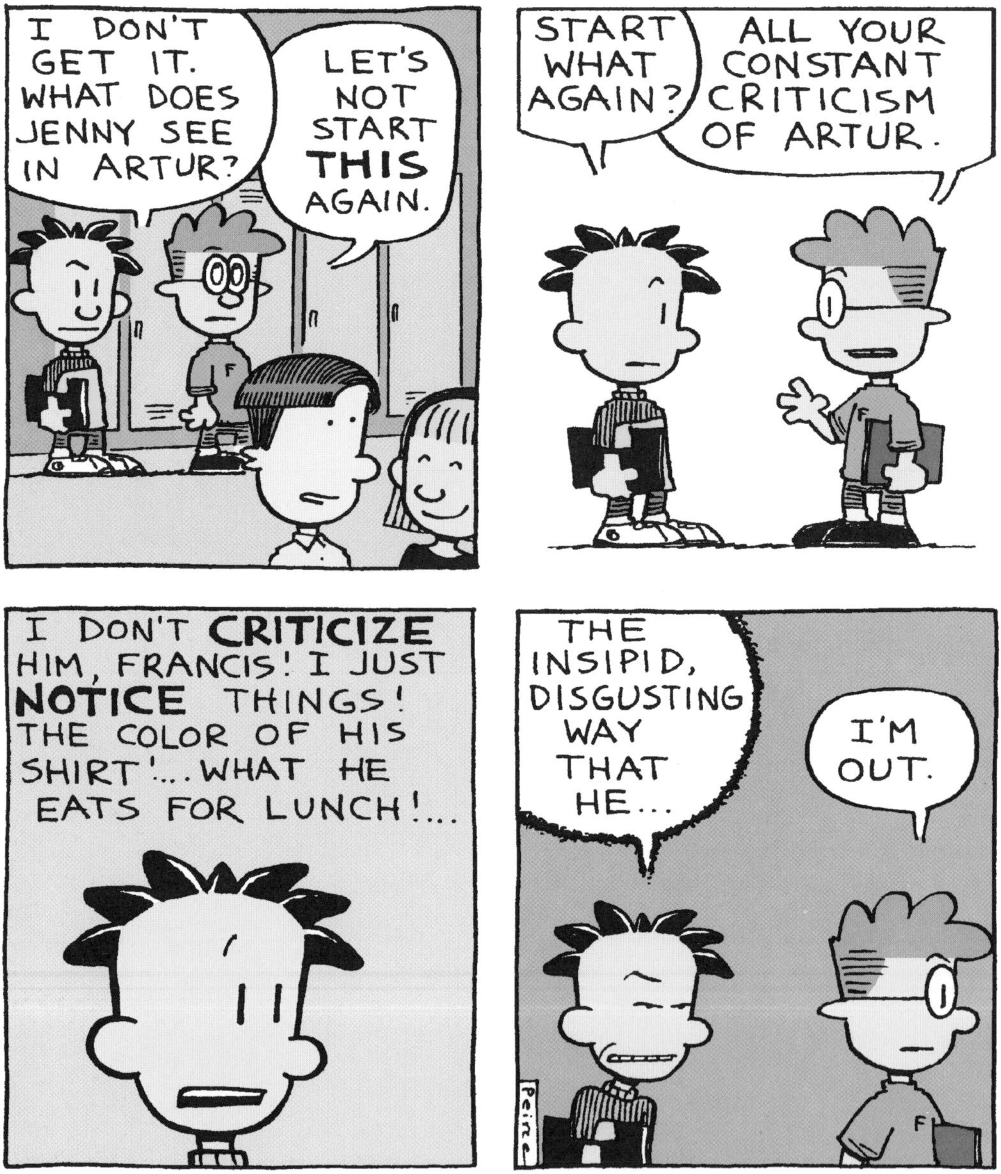
I DON'T GET IT. WHAT DOES JENNY SEE IN ARTUR?
LET'S NOT START **THIS** AGAIN.
START WHAT AGAIN?
ALL YOUR CONSTANT CRITICISM OF ARTUR.
I DON'T **CRITICIZE** HIM, FRANCIS! I JUST **NOTICE** THINGS! THE COLOR OF HIS SHIRT!... WHAT HE EATS FOR LUNCH!...
THE INSIPID, DISGUSTING WAY THAT HE...
I'M OUT.
Peirce

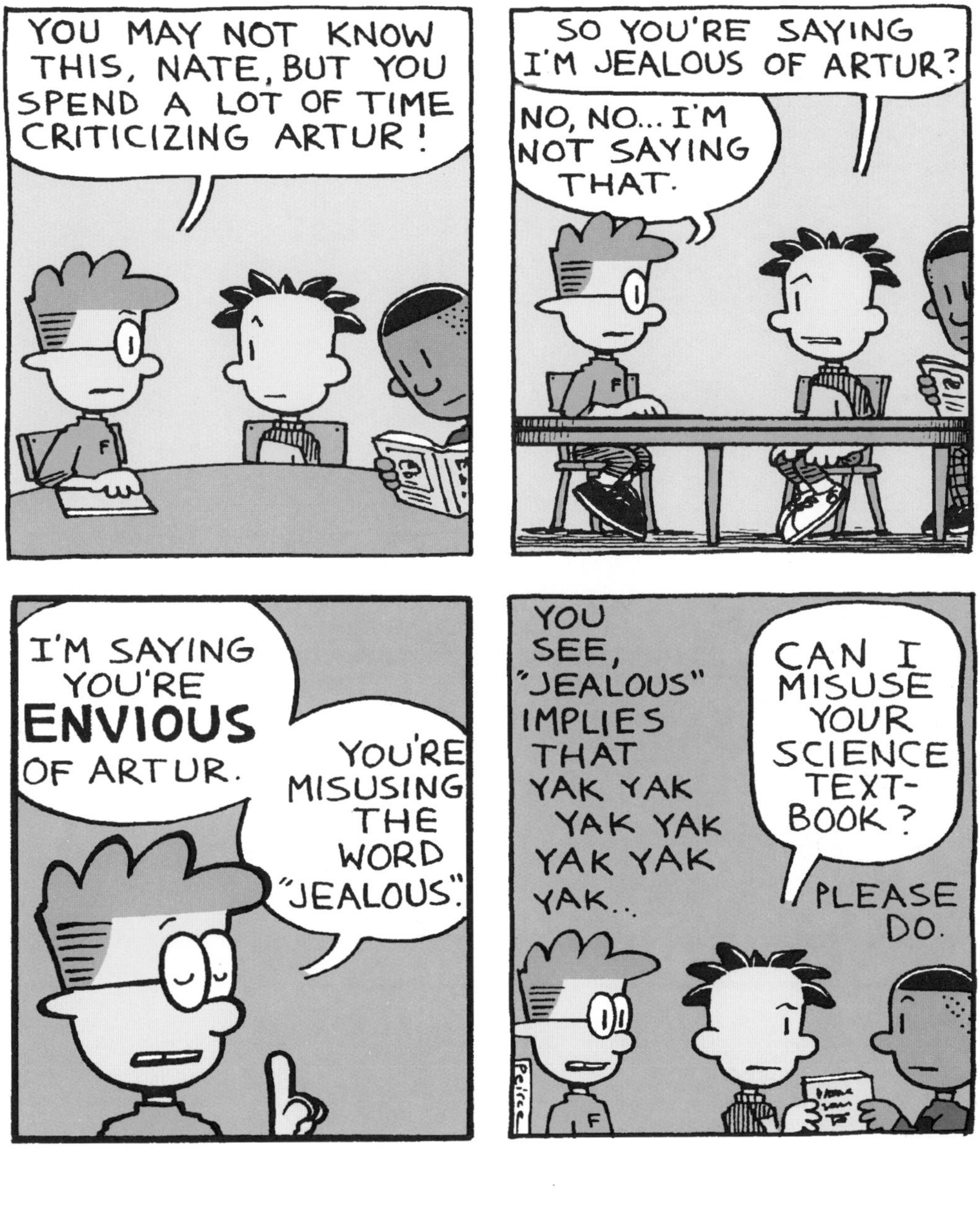
YOU MAY NOT KNOW THIS, NATE, BUT YOU SPEND A LOT OF TIME CRITICIZING ARTUR!
SO YOU'RE SAYING I'M JEALOUS OF ARTUR?
NO, NO... I'M NOT SAYING THAT.
I'M SAYING YOU'RE **ENVIOUS** OF ARTUR.
YOU'RE MISUSING THE WORD "JEALOUS".
YOU SEE, "JEALOUS" IMPLIES THAT YAK YAK YAK YAK YAK YAK YAK...
CAN I MISUSE YOUR SCIENCE TEXT-BOOK?
PLEASE DO.
PEIRCE

YOU'VE GOT IT ALL WRONG, FRANCIS! I'M **NOT** ENVIOUS OF ARTUR!

OH, REALLY?

WELL, YOU'RE ALWAYS COMPARING YOURSELF TO HIM!

WHAT? NO, I'M **NOT**!

I DON'T NEED TO COMPARE MYSELF TO **ANYBODY**! I'M VERY SECURE WITH WHO I AM!

...**WAY** MORE SECURE THAN **ARTUR** IS!

RIGHT.

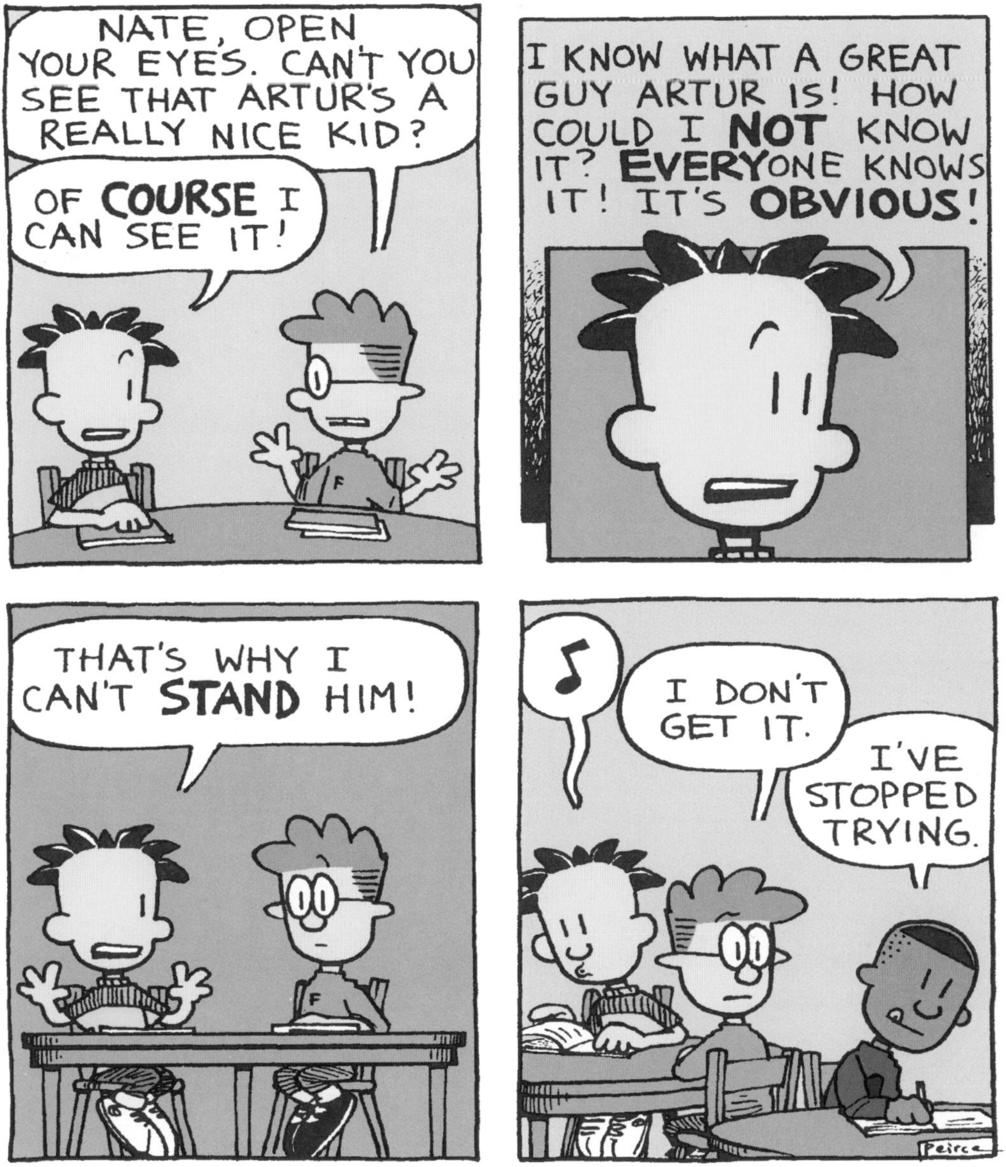
NATE, OPEN YOUR EYES. CAN'T YOU SEE THAT ARTUR'S A REALLY NICE KID?
OF COURSE I CAN SEE IT!
I KNOW WHAT A GREAT GUY ARTUR IS! HOW COULD I NOT KNOW IT? EVERYONE KNOWS IT! IT'S OBVIOUS!
THAT'S WHY I CAN'T STAND HIM!
♪
I DON'T GET IT.
I'VE STOPPED TRYING.
Peirce

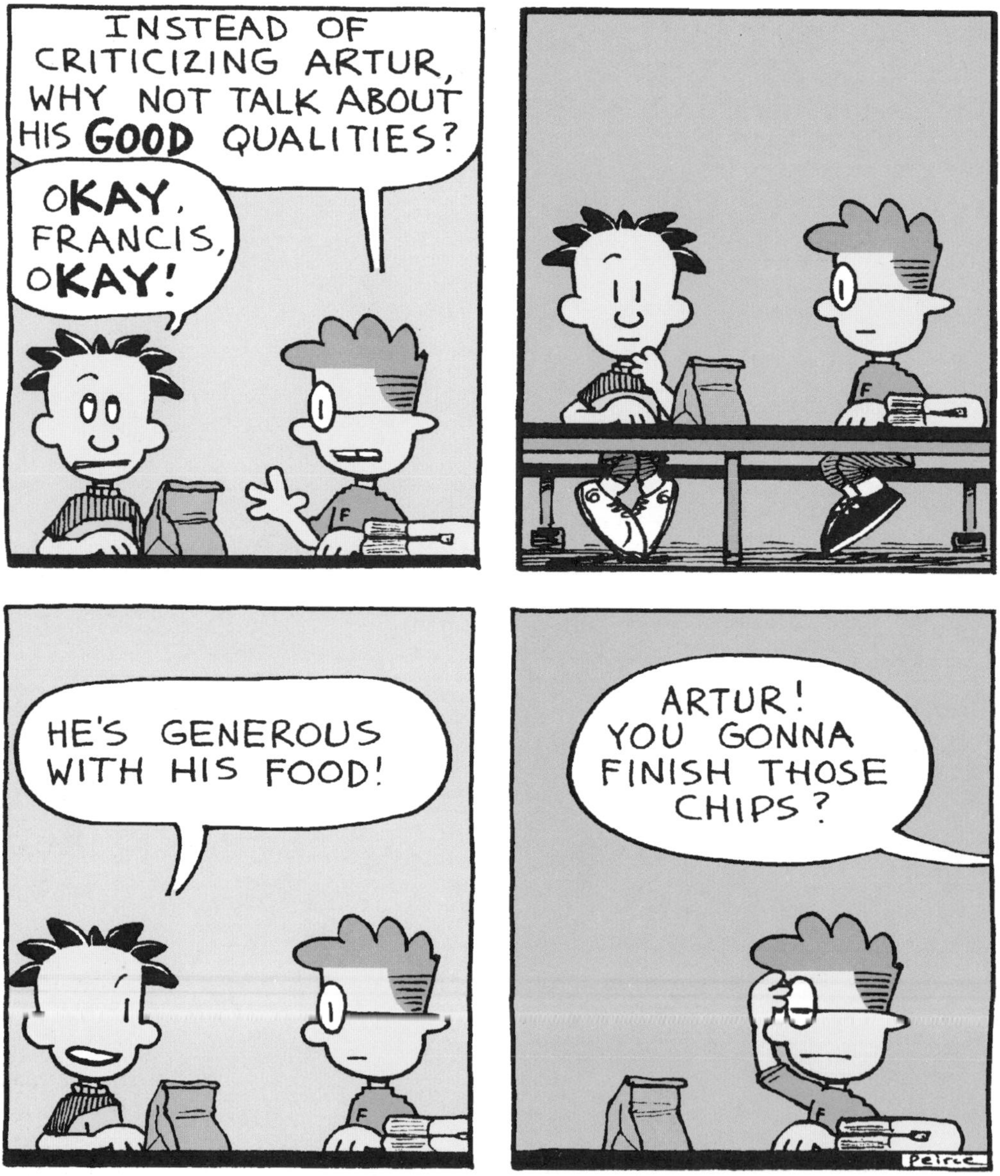
INSTEAD OF CRITICIZING ARTUR, WHY NOT TALK ABOUT HIS GOOD QUALITIES?
OKAY, FRANCIS, OKAY!
HE'S GENEROUS WITH HIS FOOD!
ARTUR! YOU GONNA FINISH THOSE CHIPS?
Peirce

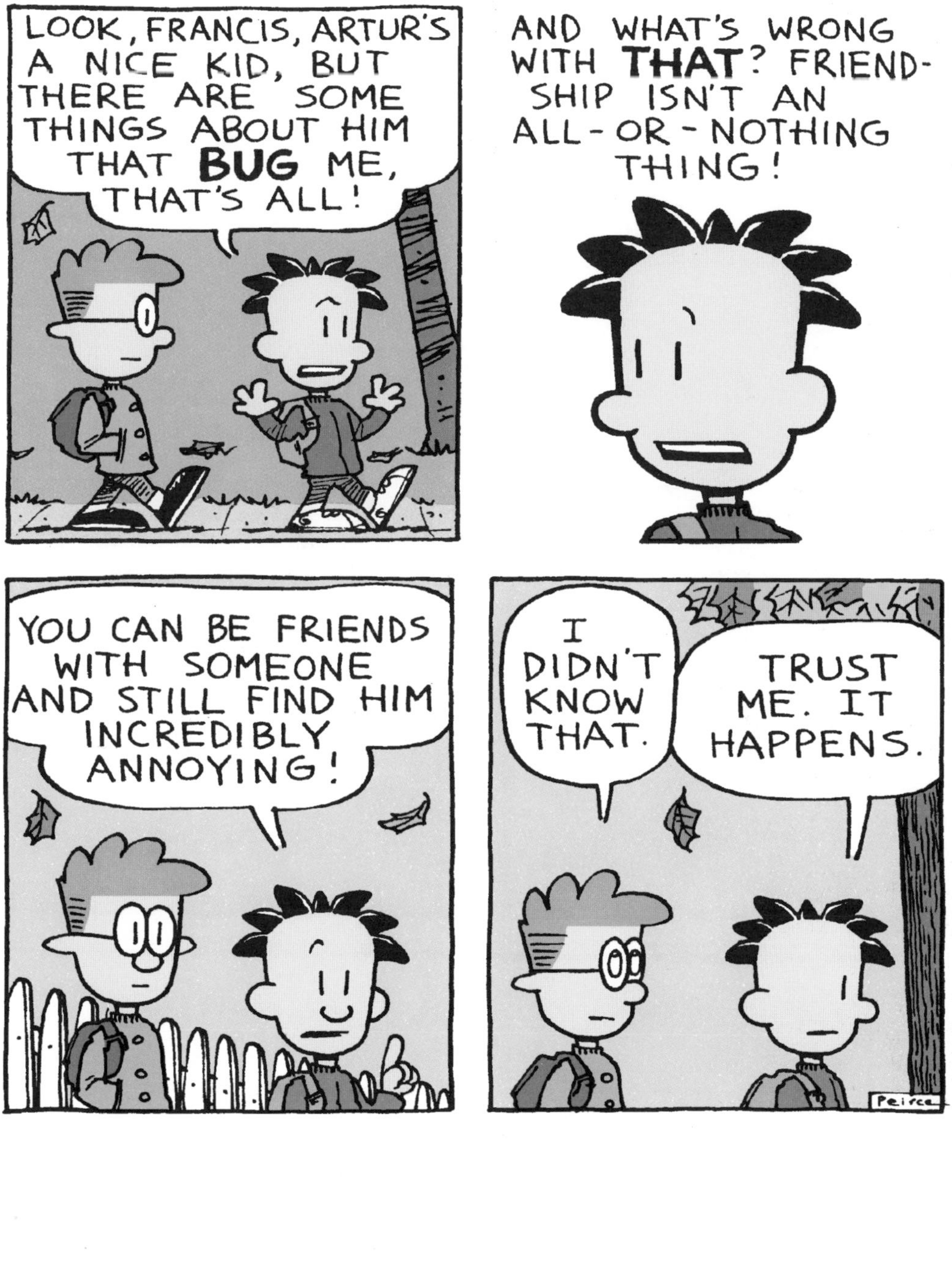

LOOK, FRANCIS, ARTUR'S A NICE KID, BUT THERE ARE SOME THINGS ABOUT HIM THAT **BUG** ME, THAT'S ALL!
AND WHAT'S WRONG WITH **THAT**? FRIENDSHIP ISN'T AN ALL-OR-NOTHING THING!
YOU CAN BE FRIENDS WITH SOMEONE AND STILL FIND HIM INCREDIBLY ANNOYING!
I DIDN'T KNOW THAT.
TRUST ME. IT HAPPENS.
Peirce

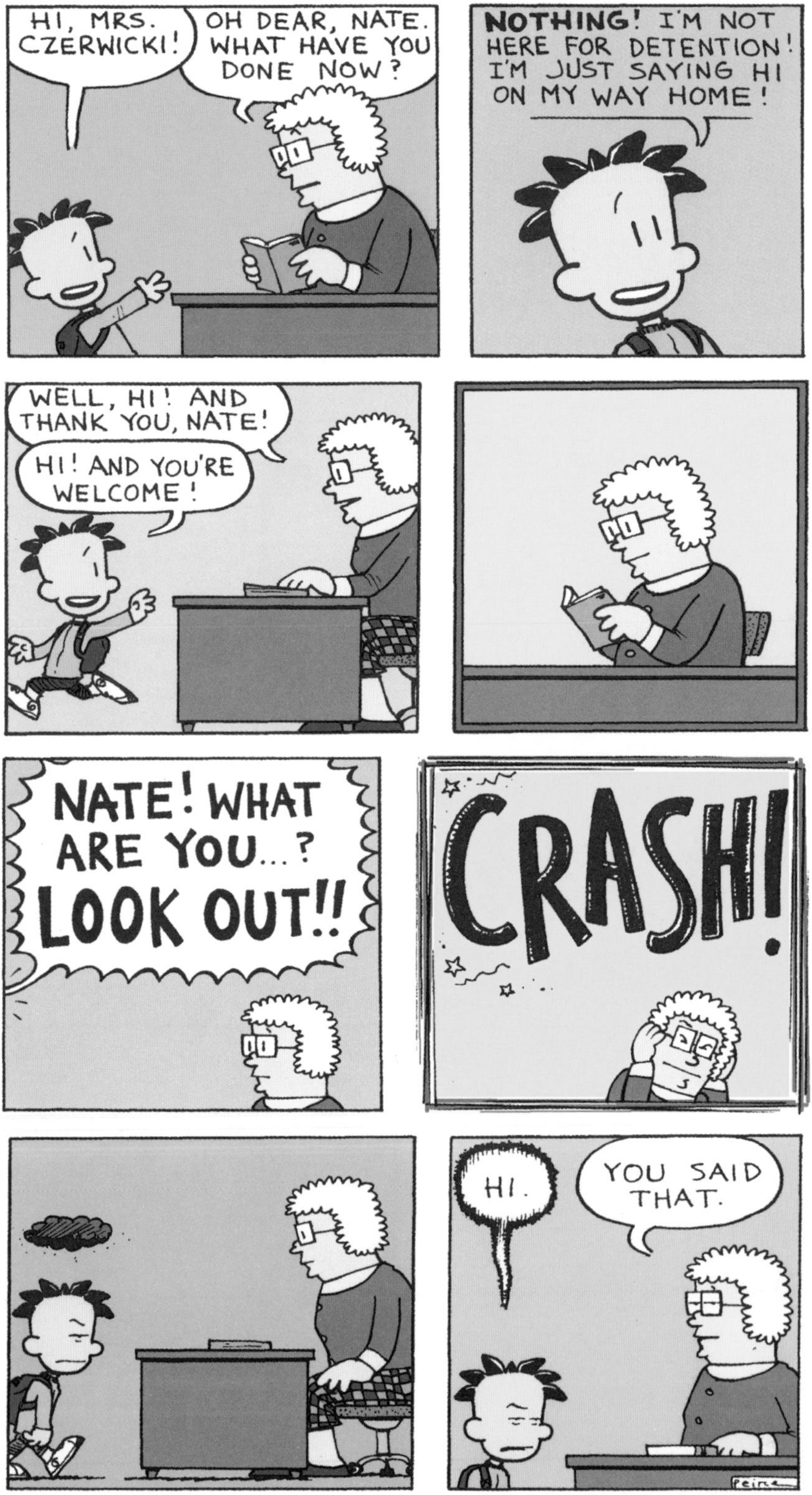
HI, MRS. CZERWICKI!
OH DEAR, NATE. WHAT HAVE YOU DONE NOW?
NOTHING! I'M NOT HERE FOR DETENTION! I'M JUST SAYING HI ON MY WAY HOME!
WELL, HI! AND THANK YOU, NATE!
HI! AND YOU'RE WELCOME!
NATE! WHAT ARE YOU...? LOOK OUT!!
CRASH!
HI.
YOU SAID THAT.
peirce

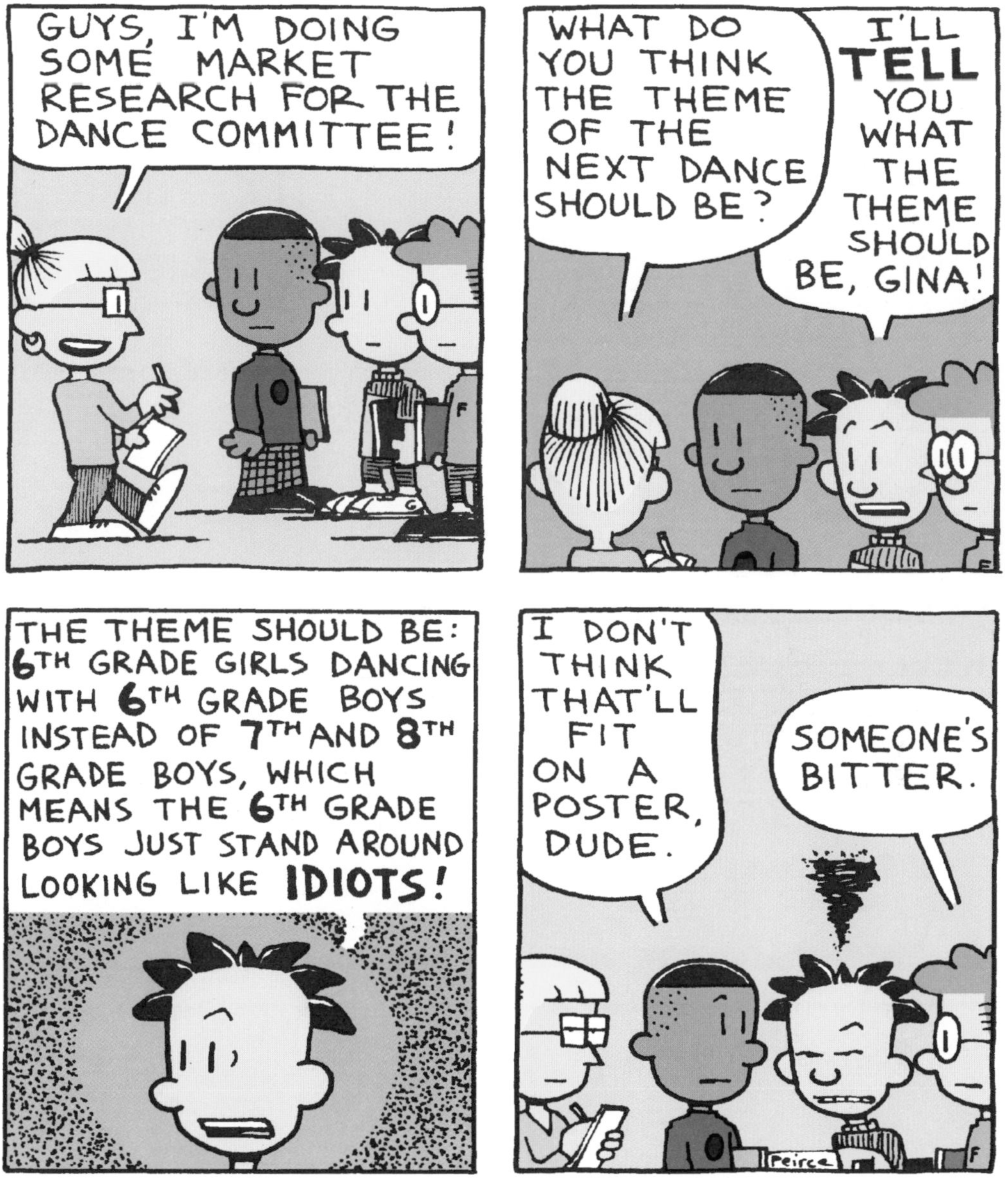
GUYS, I'M DOING SOME MARKET RESEARCH FOR THE DANCE COMMITTEE!
WHAT DO YOU THINK THE THEME OF THE NEXT DANCE SHOULD BE?
I'LL **TELL** YOU WHAT THE THEME SHOULD BE, GINA!
THE THEME SHOULD BE: 6TH GRADE GIRLS DANCING WITH 6TH GRADE BOYS INSTEAD OF 7TH AND 8TH GRADE BOYS, WHICH MEANS THE 6TH GRADE BOYS JUST STAND AROUND LOOKING LIKE **IDIOTS**!
I DON'T THINK THAT'LL FIT ON A POSTER, DUDE.
SOMEONE'S BITTER.
Peirce

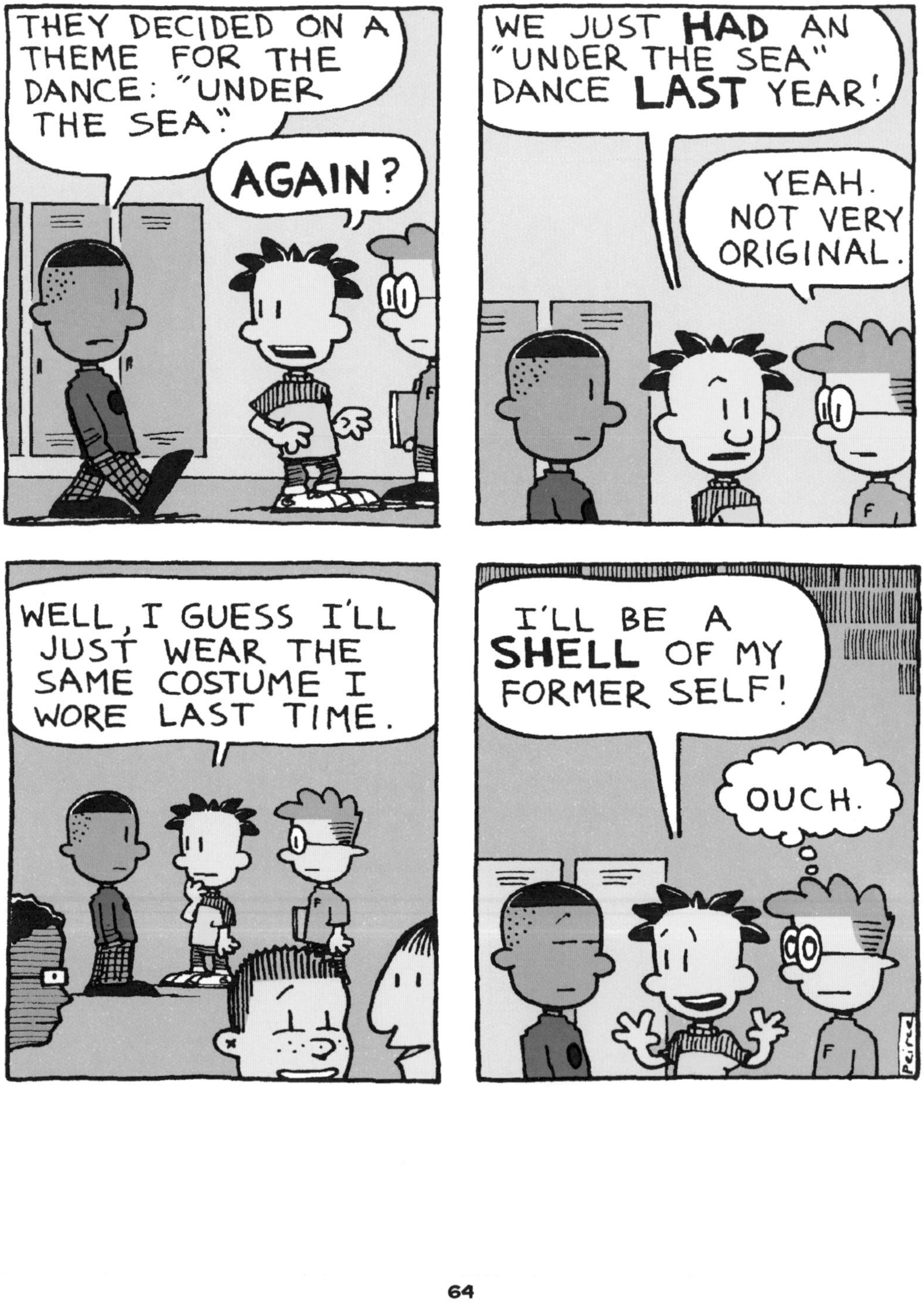
THEY DECIDED ON A THEME FOR THE DANCE: "UNDER THE SEA."
AGAIN?
WE JUST HAD AN "UNDER THE SEA" DANCE LAST YEAR!
YEAH. NOT VERY ORIGINAL.
WELL, I GUESS I'LL JUST WEAR THE SAME COSTUME I WORE LAST TIME.
I'LL BE A SHELL OF MY FORMER SELF!
OUCH.
Peirce

GUYS! I CAN'T BELIEVE WE DIDN'T THINK OF THIS **BEFORE!**

WHAT?

THE THEME OF THE DANCE IS "UNDER THE SEA," RIGHT? IT'S **OBVIOUS** WHO'D BE THE PERFECT BAND TO PERFORM!

"ENSLAVE THE MOLLUSK" WILL ROCK AGAIN!!

BUP! BUP! **BOW!** BUP! B-B-B- **BOW!**

HE'S AIR DRUMMING.

I PREFER THAT TO THE REAL THING.

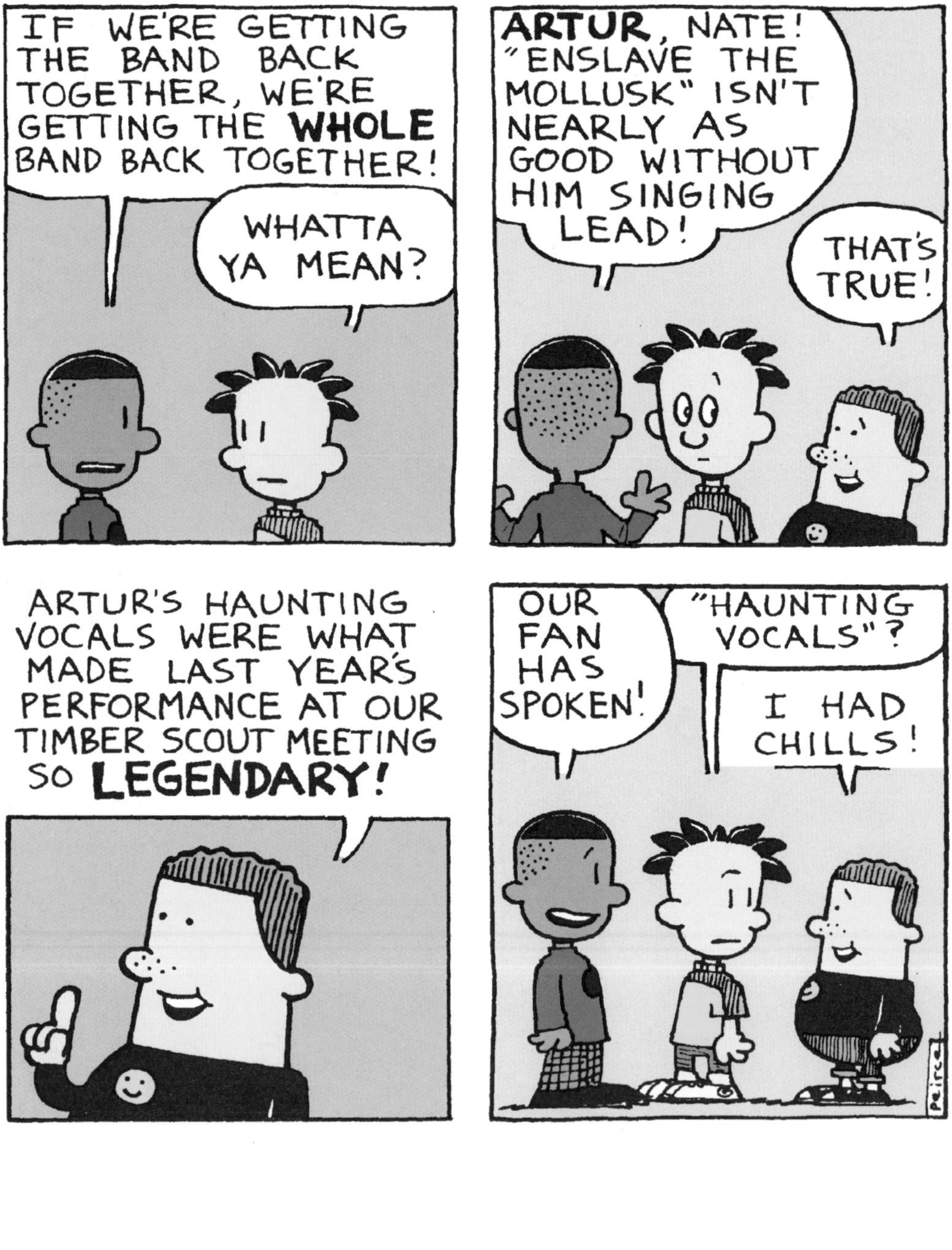
IF WE'RE GETTING THE BAND BACK TOGETHER, WE'RE GETTING THE **WHOLE** BAND BACK TOGETHER!
WHATTA YA MEAN?
ARTUR, NATE! "ENSLAVE THE MOLLUSK" ISN'T NEARLY AS GOOD WITHOUT HIM SINGING LEAD!
THAT'S TRUE!
ARTUR'S HAUNTING VOCALS WERE WHAT MADE LAST YEAR'S PERFORMANCE AT OUR TIMBER SCOUT MEETING SO **LEGENDARY!**
OUR FAN HAS SPOKEN!
"HAUNTING VOCALS"?
I HAD CHILLS!
peirce

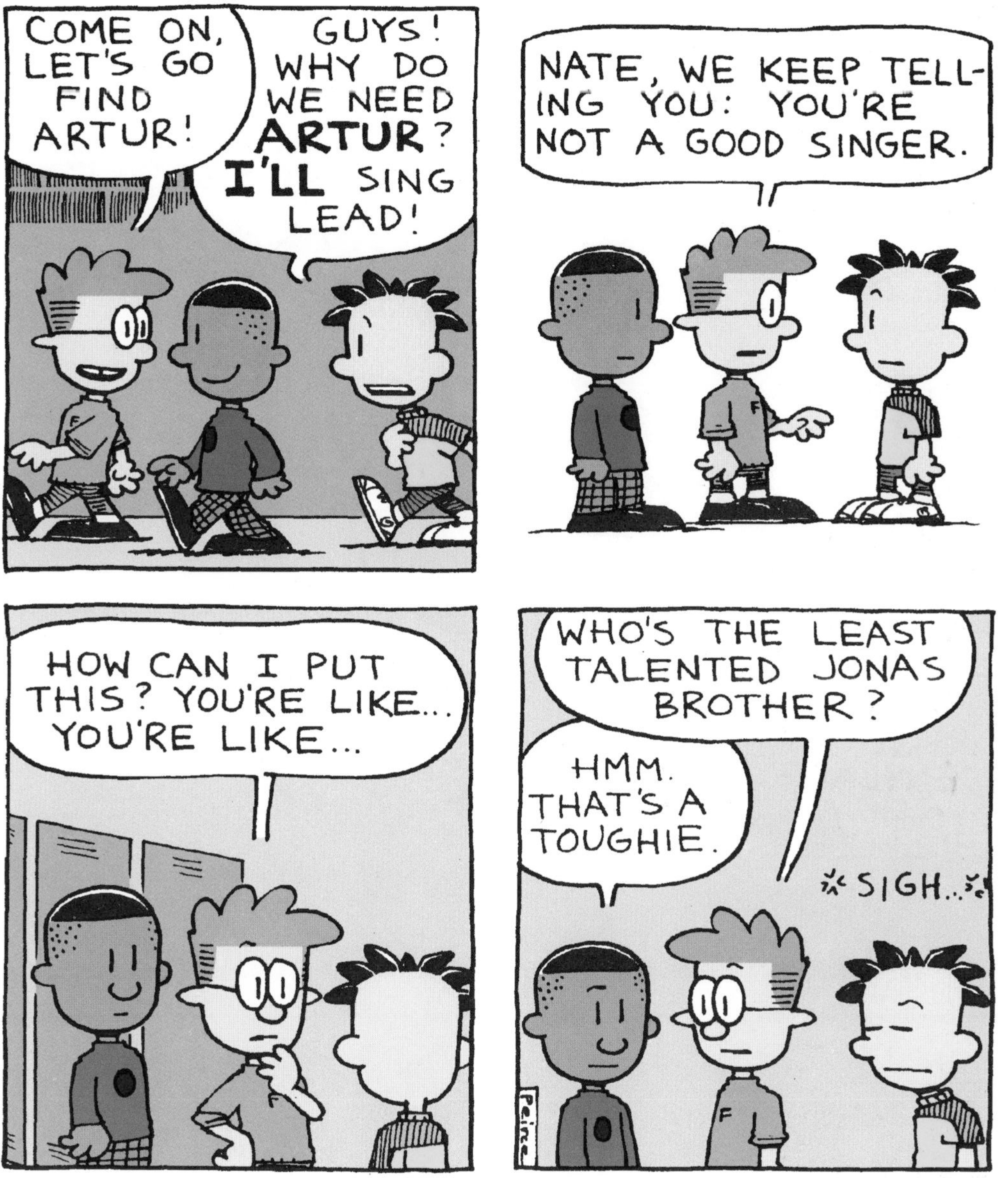
COME ON, LET'S GO FIND ARTUR!
GUYS! WHY DO WE NEED ARTUR? I'LL SING LEAD!
NATE, WE KEEP TELLING YOU: YOU'RE NOT A GOOD SINGER.
HOW CAN I PUT THIS? YOU'RE LIKE... YOU'RE LIKE...
WHO'S THE LEAST TALENTED JONAS BROTHER?
HMM. THAT'S A TOUGHIE.
SIGH...
Peirce

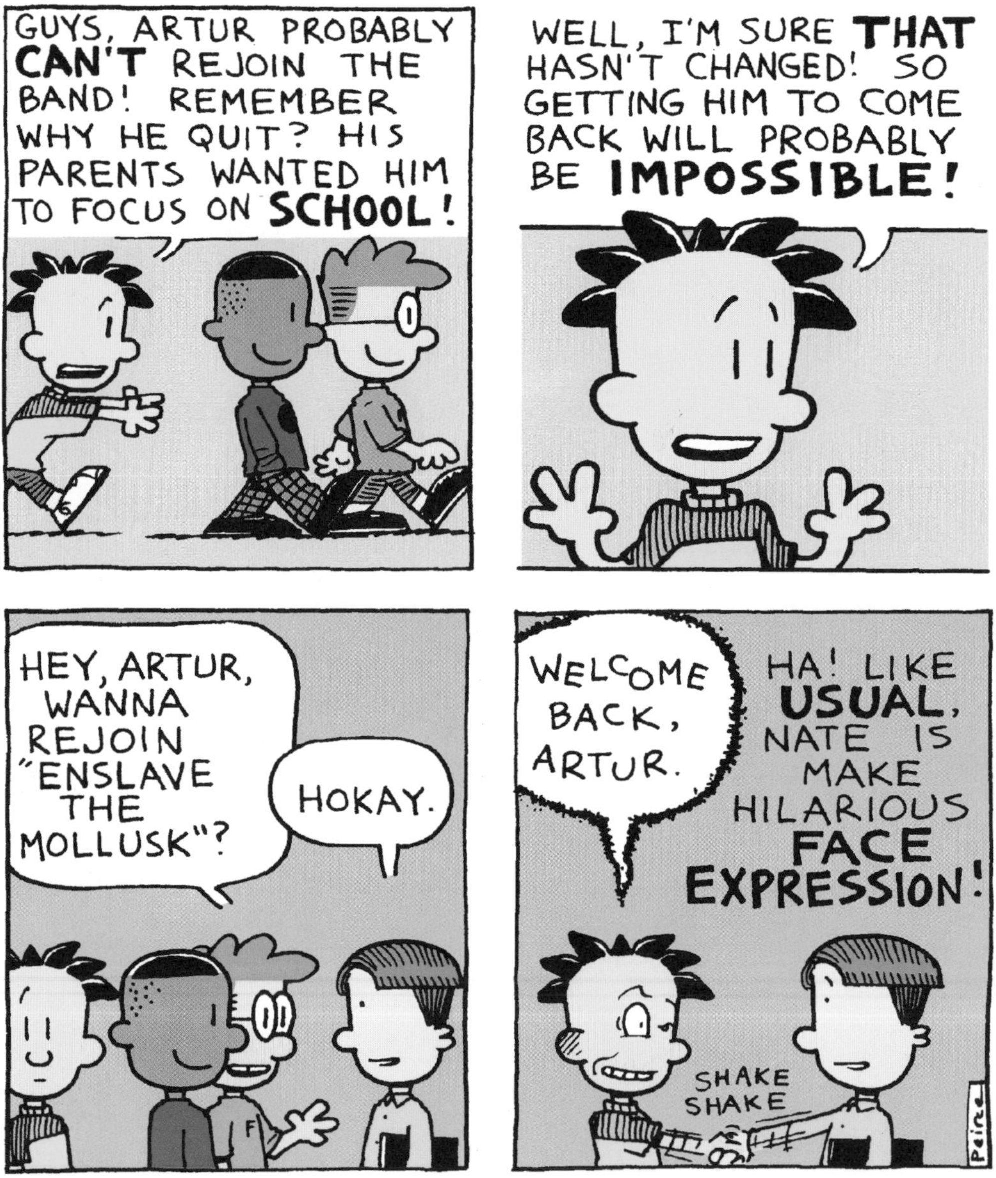
GUYS, ARTUR PROBABLY CAN'T REJOIN THE BAND! REMEMBER WHY HE QUIT? HIS PARENTS WANTED HIM TO FOCUS ON SCHOOL!
WELL, I'M SURE THAT HASN'T CHANGED! SO GETTING HIM TO COME BACK WILL PROBABLY BE IMPOSSIBLE!
HEY, ARTUR, WANNA REJOIN "ENSLAVE THE MOLLUSK"?
HOKAY.
WELCOME BACK, ARTUR.
HA! LIKE USUAL, NATE IS MAKE HILARIOUS FACE EXPRESSION!
SHAKE SHAKE
Peirce

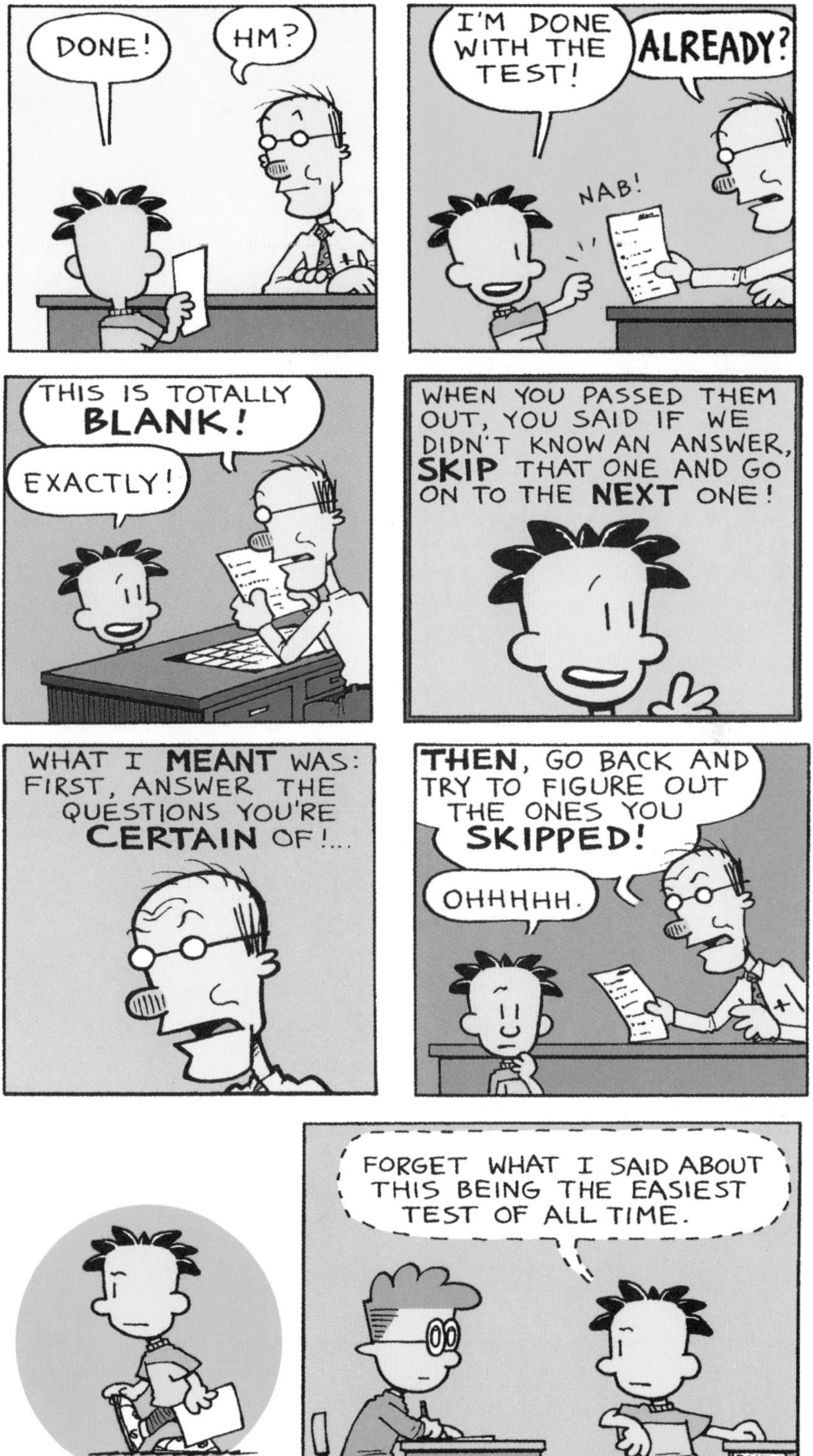
DONE!
HM?
I'M DONE WITH THE TEST!
ALREADY?
NAB!
THIS IS TOTALLY BLANK!
EXACTLY!
WHEN YOU PASSED THEM OUT, YOU SAID IF WE DIDN'T KNOW AN ANSWER, SKIP THAT ONE AND GO ON TO THE NEXT ONE!
WHAT I MEANT WAS: FIRST, ANSWER THE QUESTIONS YOU'RE CERTAIN OF!...
THEN, GO BACK AND TRY TO FIGURE OUT THE ONES YOU SKIPPED!
OHHHHH.
FORGET WHAT I SAID ABOUT THIS BEING THE EASIEST TEST OF ALL TIME.

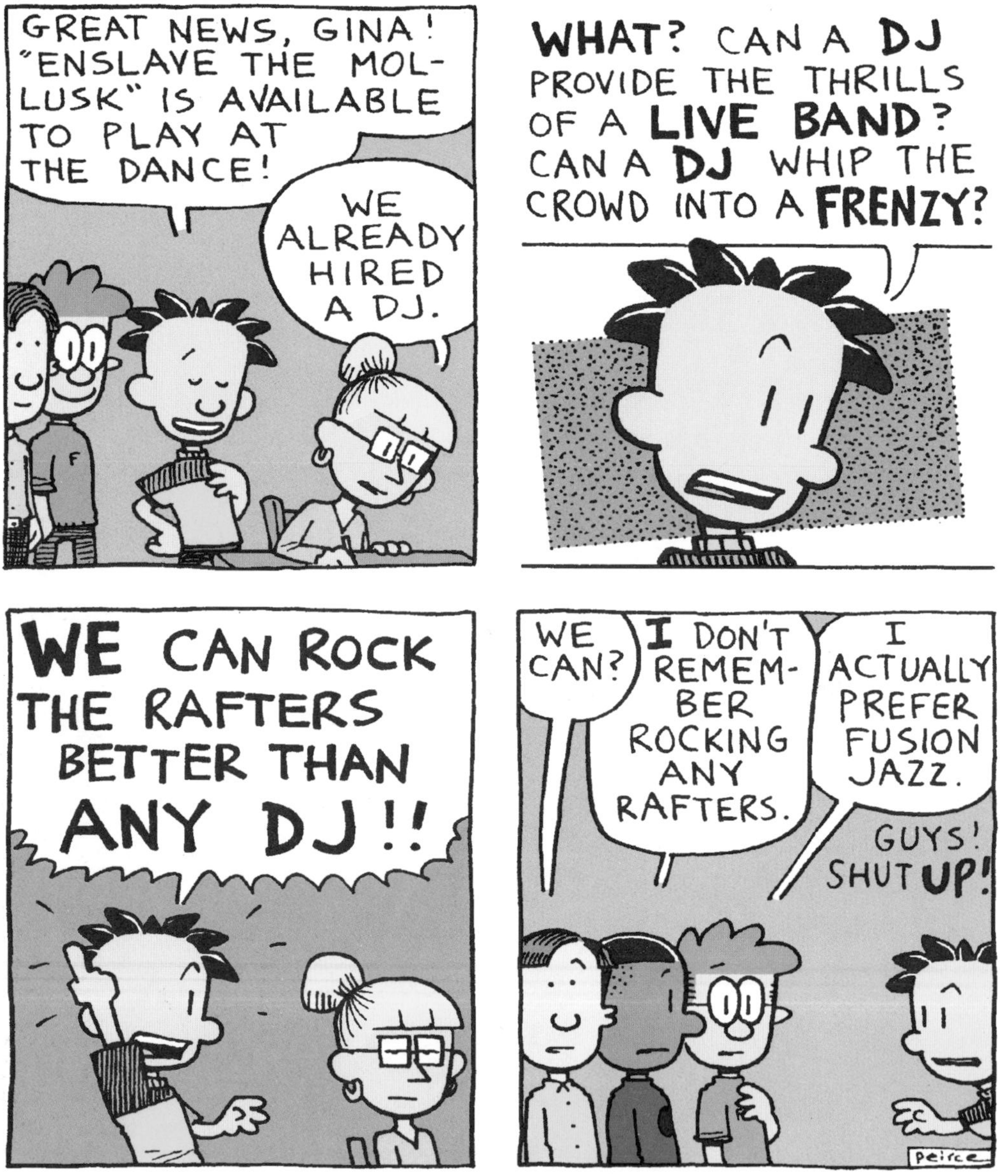
GREAT NEWS, GINA! "ENSLAVE THE MOL-LUSK" IS AVAILABLE TO PLAY AT THE DANCE!
WE ALREADY HIRED A DJ.
WHAT? CAN A DJ PROVIDE THE THRILLS OF A LIVE BAND? CAN A DJ WHIP THE CROWD INTO A FRENZY?
WE CAN ROCK THE RAFTERS BETTER THAN ANY DJ!!
WE CAN?
I DON'T REMEM-BER ROCKING ANY RAFTERS.
I ACTUALLY PREFER FUSION JAZZ.
GUYS! SHUT UP!
peirce

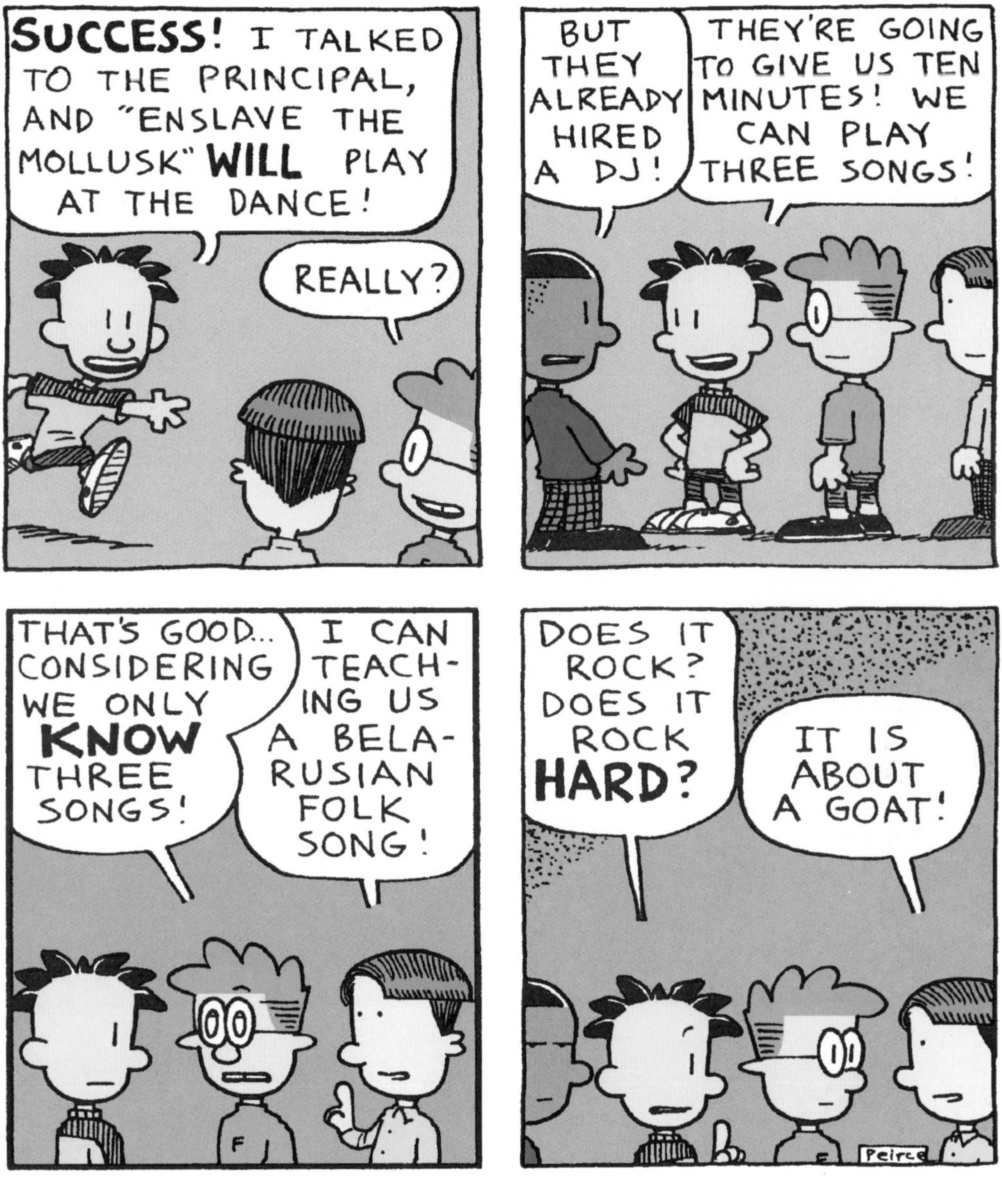
SUCCESS! I TALKED TO THE PRINCIPAL, AND "ENSLAVE THE MOLLUSK" WILL PLAY AT THE DANCE!
REALLY?
BUT THEY ALREADY HIRED A DJ!
THEY'RE GOING TO GIVE US TEN MINUTES! WE CAN PLAY THREE SONGS!
THAT'S GOOD... CONSIDERING WE ONLY KNOW THREE SONGS!
I CAN TEACH-ING US A BELA-RUSIAN FOLK SONG!
DOES IT ROCK? DOES IT ROCK HARD?
IT IS ABOUT A GOAT!
Peirce

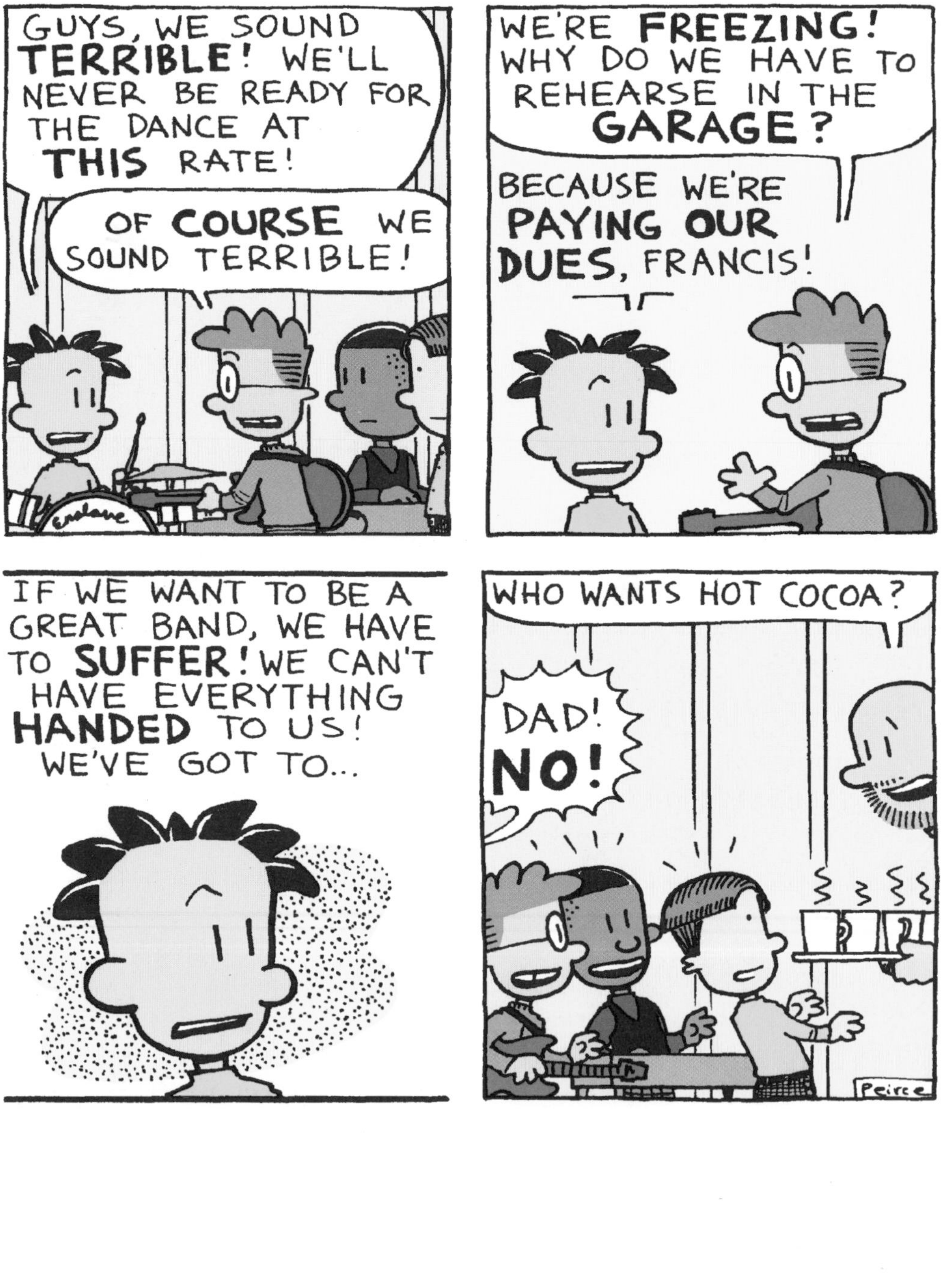
GUYS, WE SOUND **TERRIBLE**! WE'LL NEVER BE READY FOR THE DANCE AT **THIS** RATE!
OF **COURSE** WE SOUND TERRIBLE!
WE'RE **FREEZING**! WHY DO WE HAVE TO REHEARSE IN THE **GARAGE**?
BECAUSE WE'RE **PAYING OUR DUES**, FRANCIS!
IF WE WANT TO BE A GREAT BAND, WE HAVE TO **SUFFER**! WE CAN'T HAVE EVERYTHING **HANDED** TO US! WE'VE GOT TO...
WHO WANTS HOT COCOA?
DAD! **NO!**
Peirce

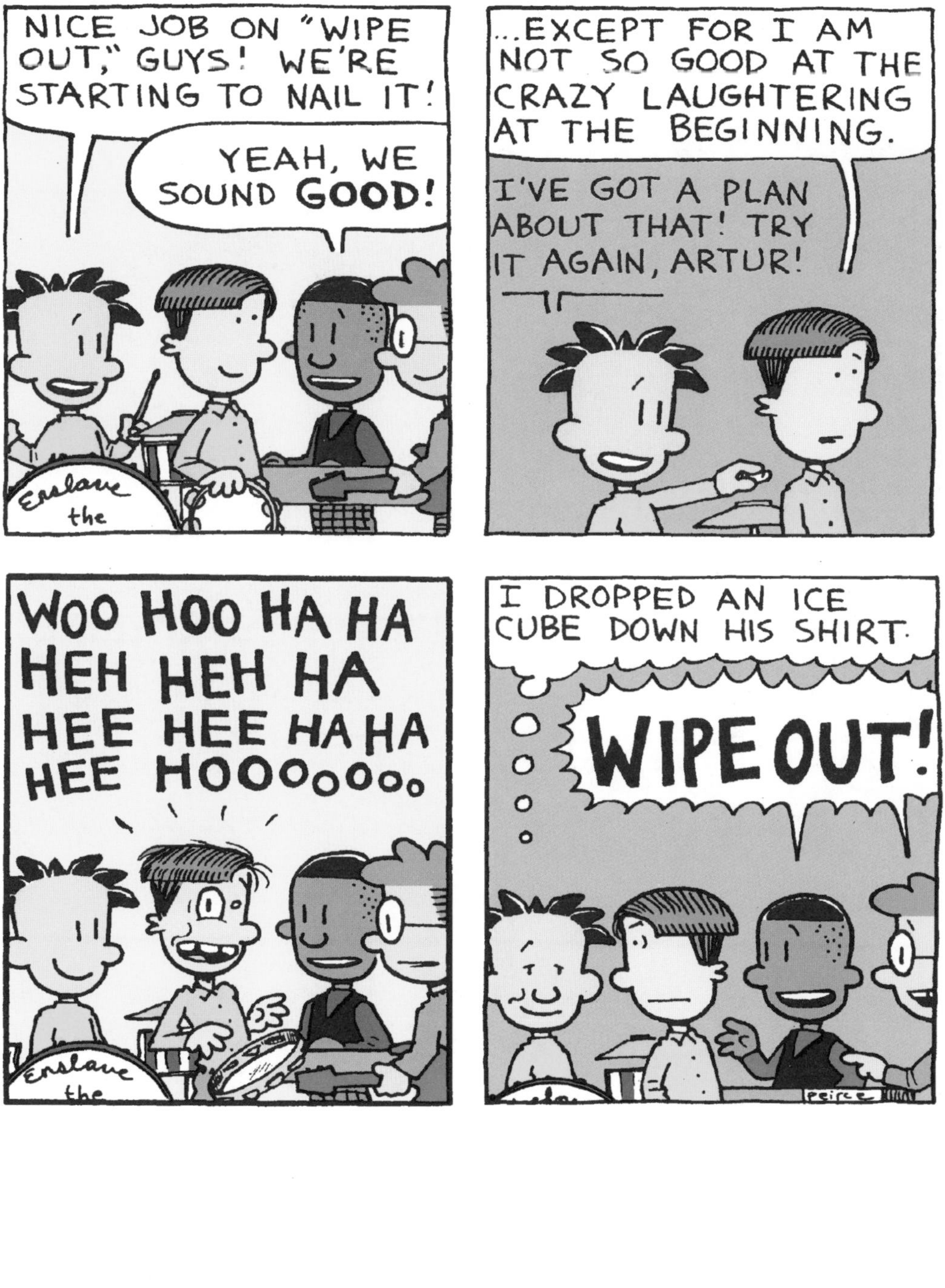
NICE JOB ON "WIPE OUT," GUYS! WE'RE STARTING TO NAIL IT!
YEAH, WE SOUND GOOD!
...EXCEPT FOR I AM NOT SO GOOD AT THE CRAZY LAUGHTERING AT THE BEGINNING.
I'VE GOT A PLAN ABOUT THAT! TRY IT AGAIN, ARTUR!
WOO HOO HA HA HEH HEH HA HEE HEE HA HA HEE HOOOoooo
I DROPPED AN ICE CUBE DOWN HIS SHIRT.
WIPE OUT!

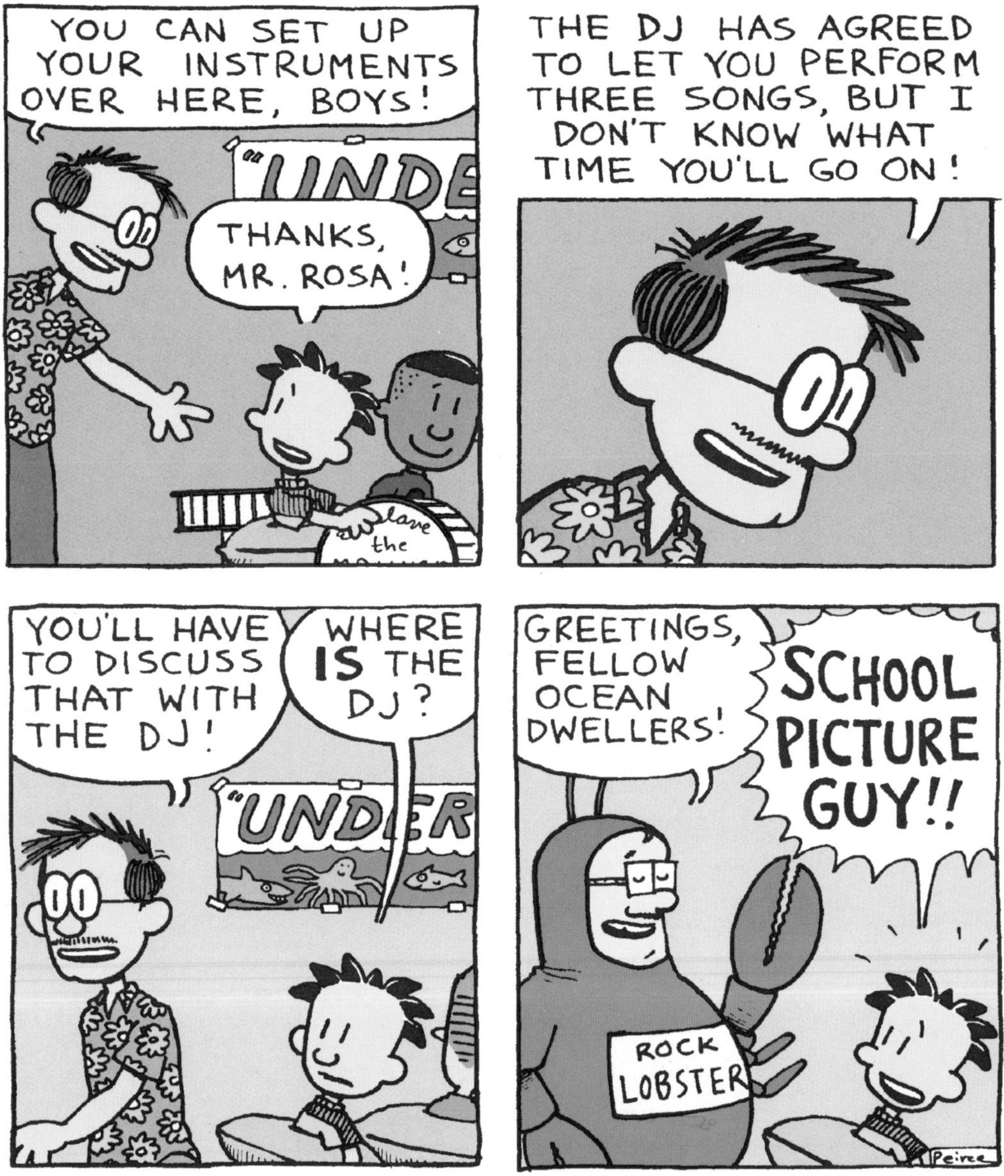
YOU CAN SET UP YOUR INSTRUMENTS OVER HERE, BOYS!
THANKS, MR. ROSA!
THE DJ HAS AGREED TO LET YOU PERFORM THREE SONGS, BUT I DON'T KNOW WHAT TIME YOU'LL GO ON!
YOU'LL HAVE TO DISCUSS THAT WITH THE DJ!
WHERE **IS** THE DJ?
GREETINGS, FELLOW OCEAN DWELLERS!
SCHOOL PICTURE GUY!!
ROCK LOBSTER
Peirce

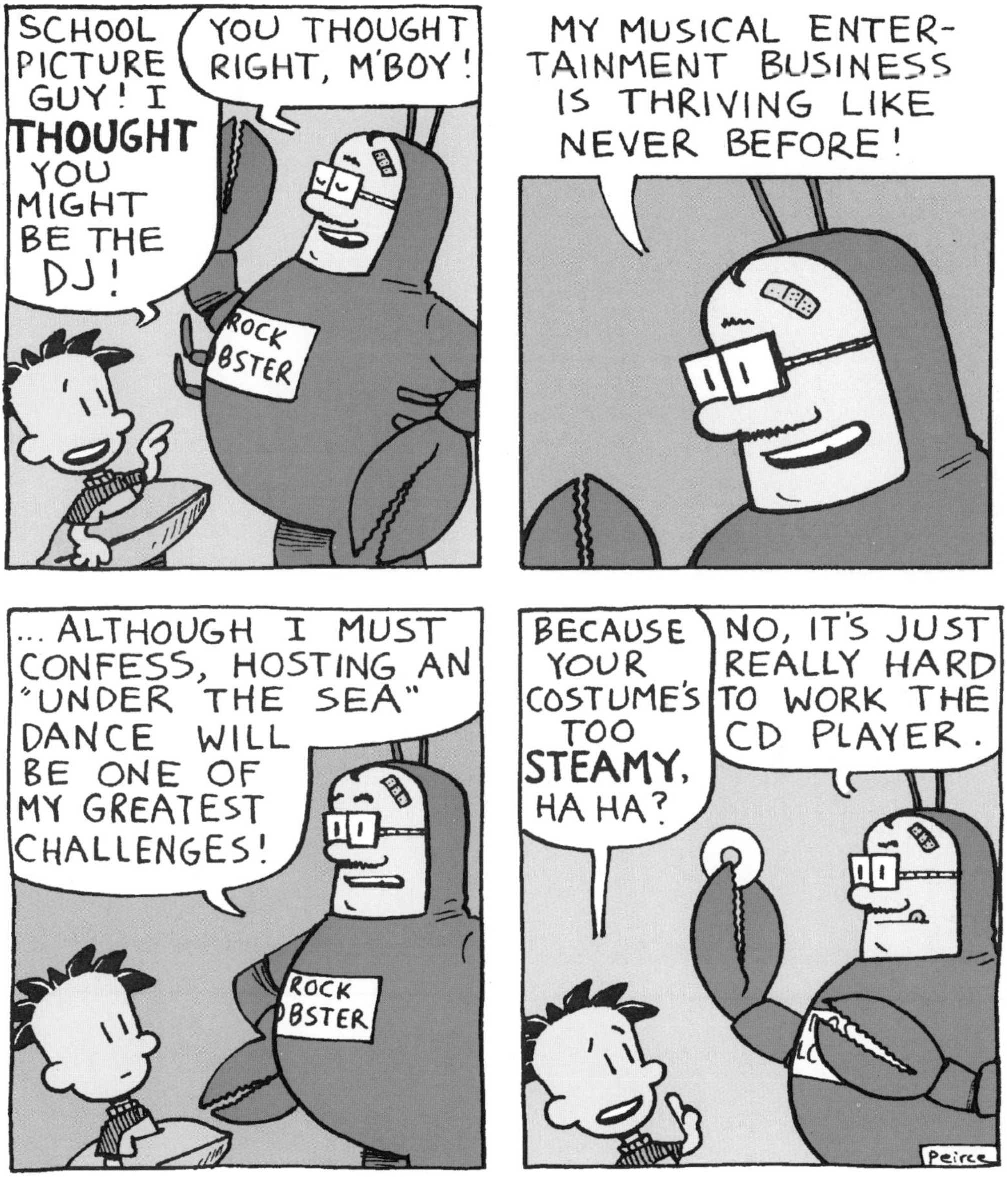
SCHOOL PICTURE GUY! I **THOUGHT** YOU MIGHT BE THE DJ!
YOU THOUGHT RIGHT, M'BOY!
ROCK BSTER
MY MUSICAL ENTERTAINMENT BUSINESS IS THRIVING LIKE NEVER BEFORE!
...ALTHOUGH I MUST CONFESS, HOSTING AN "UNDER THE SEA" DANCE WILL BE ONE OF MY GREATEST CHALLENGES!
ROCK BSTER
BECAUSE YOUR COSTUME'S TOO **STEAMY**, HA HA?
NO, IT'S JUST REALLY HARD TO WORK THE CD PLAYER.
Peirce

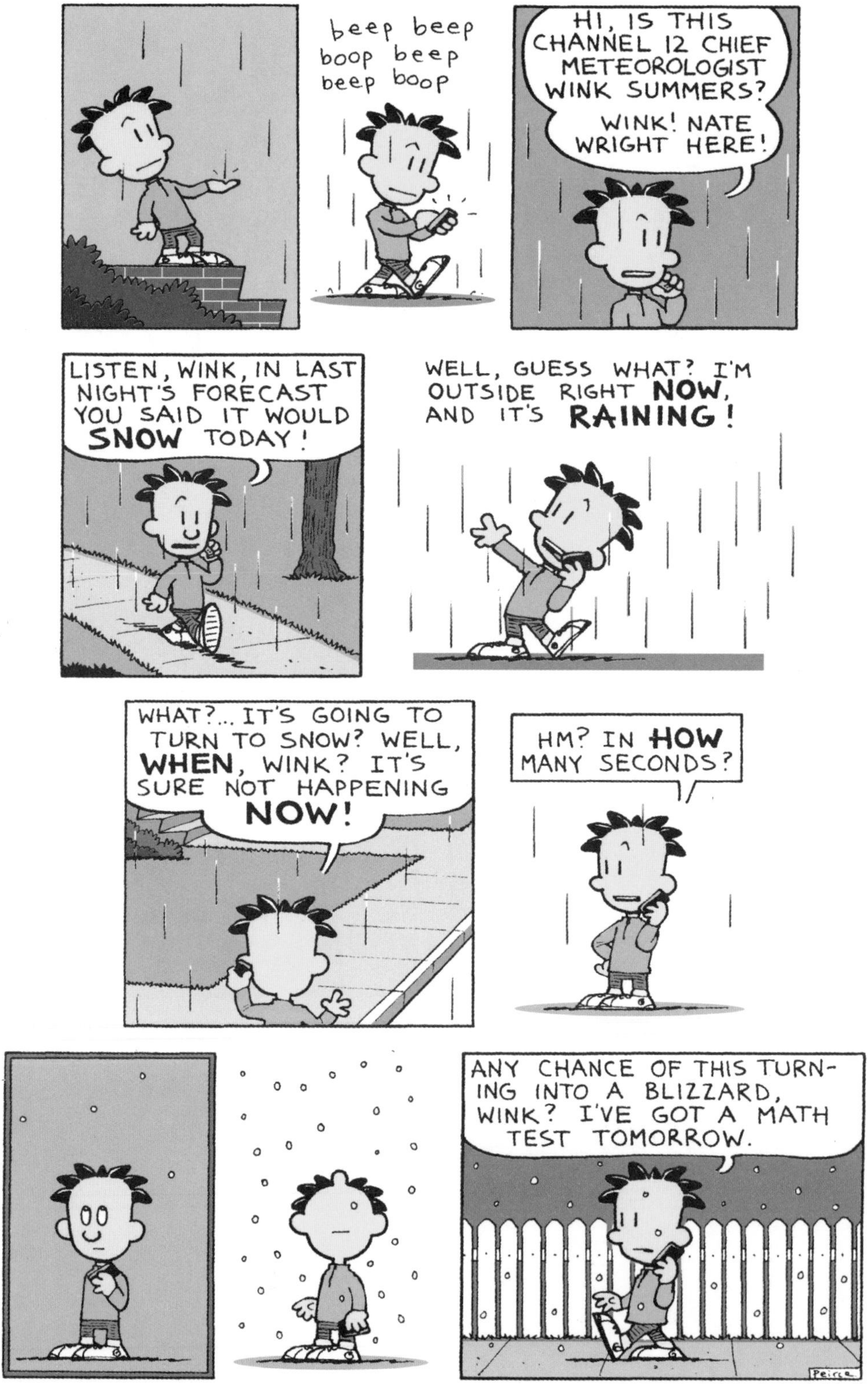
beep beep
boop beep
beep boop
HI, IS THIS CHANNEL 12 CHIEF METEOROLOGIST WINK SUMMERS?
WINK! NATE WRIGHT HERE!
LISTEN, WINK, IN LAST NIGHT'S FORECAST YOU SAID IT WOULD **SNOW** TODAY!
WELL, GUESS WHAT? I'M OUTSIDE RIGHT **NOW**, AND IT'S **RAINING**!
WHAT?... IT'S GOING TO TURN TO SNOW? WELL, **WHEN**, WINK? IT'S SURE NOT HAPPENING **NOW!**
HM? IN **HOW** MANY SECONDS?
ANY CHANCE OF THIS TURNING INTO A BLIZZARD, WINK? I'VE GOT A MATH TEST TOMORROW.
Peirce

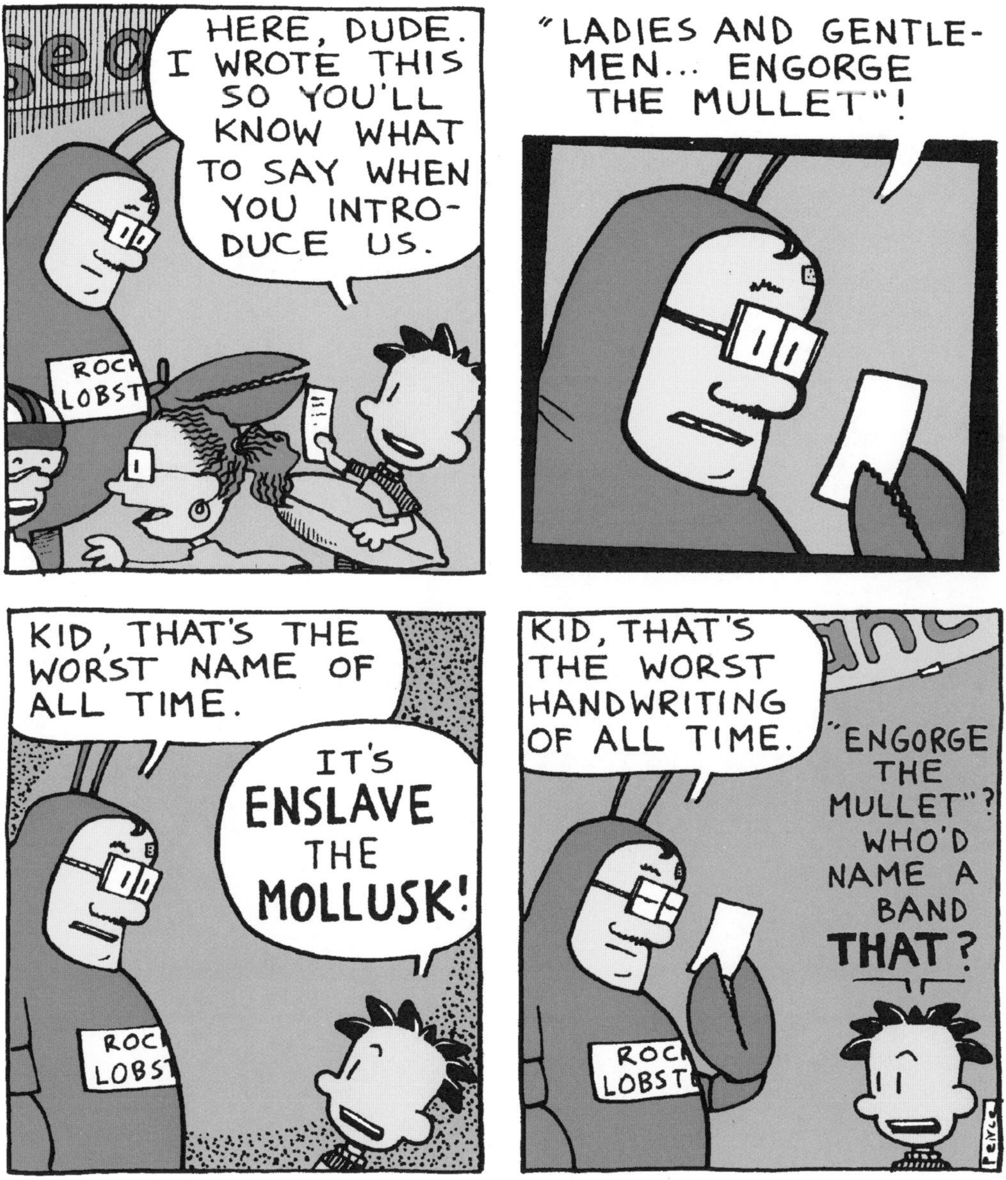
HERE, DUDE. I WROTE THIS SO YOU'LL KNOW WHAT TO SAY WHEN YOU INTRODUCE US.
ROC LOBST
"LADIES AND GENTLEMEN... ENGORGE THE MULLET"!
KID, THAT'S THE WORST NAME OF ALL TIME.
IT'S ENSLAVE THE MOLLUSK!
ROC LOBST
KID, THAT'S THE WORST HANDWRITING OF ALL TIME.
"ENGORGE THE MULLET"? WHO'D NAME A BAND THAT?
ROC LOBST
PEIRCE

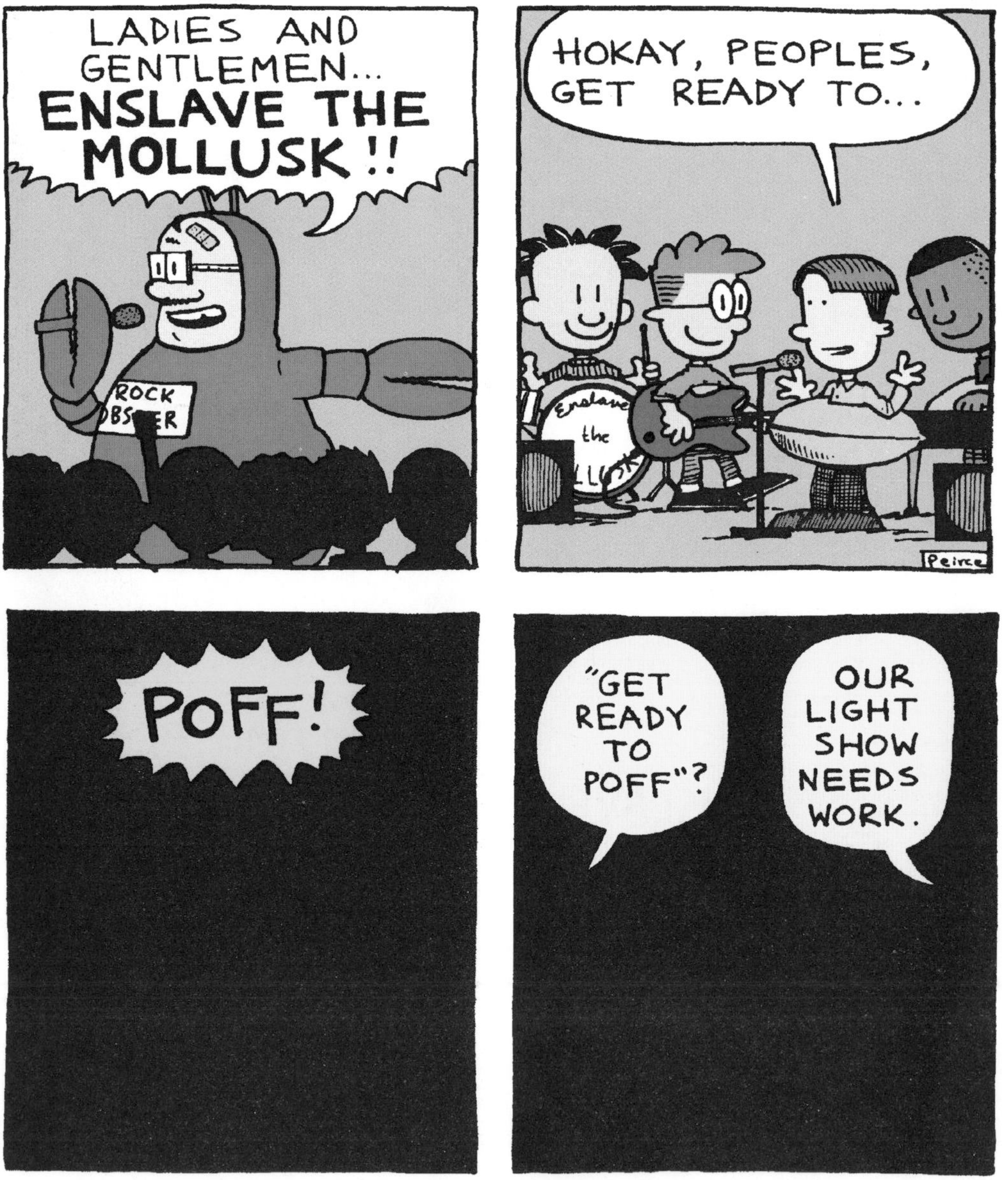
LADIES AND GENTLEMEN... ENSLAVE THE MOLLUSK!!
ROCK
HOKAY, PEOPLES, GET READY TO...
Enslave
the
Peirce
POFF!
"GET READY TO POFF"?
OUR LIGHT SHOW NEEDS WORK.

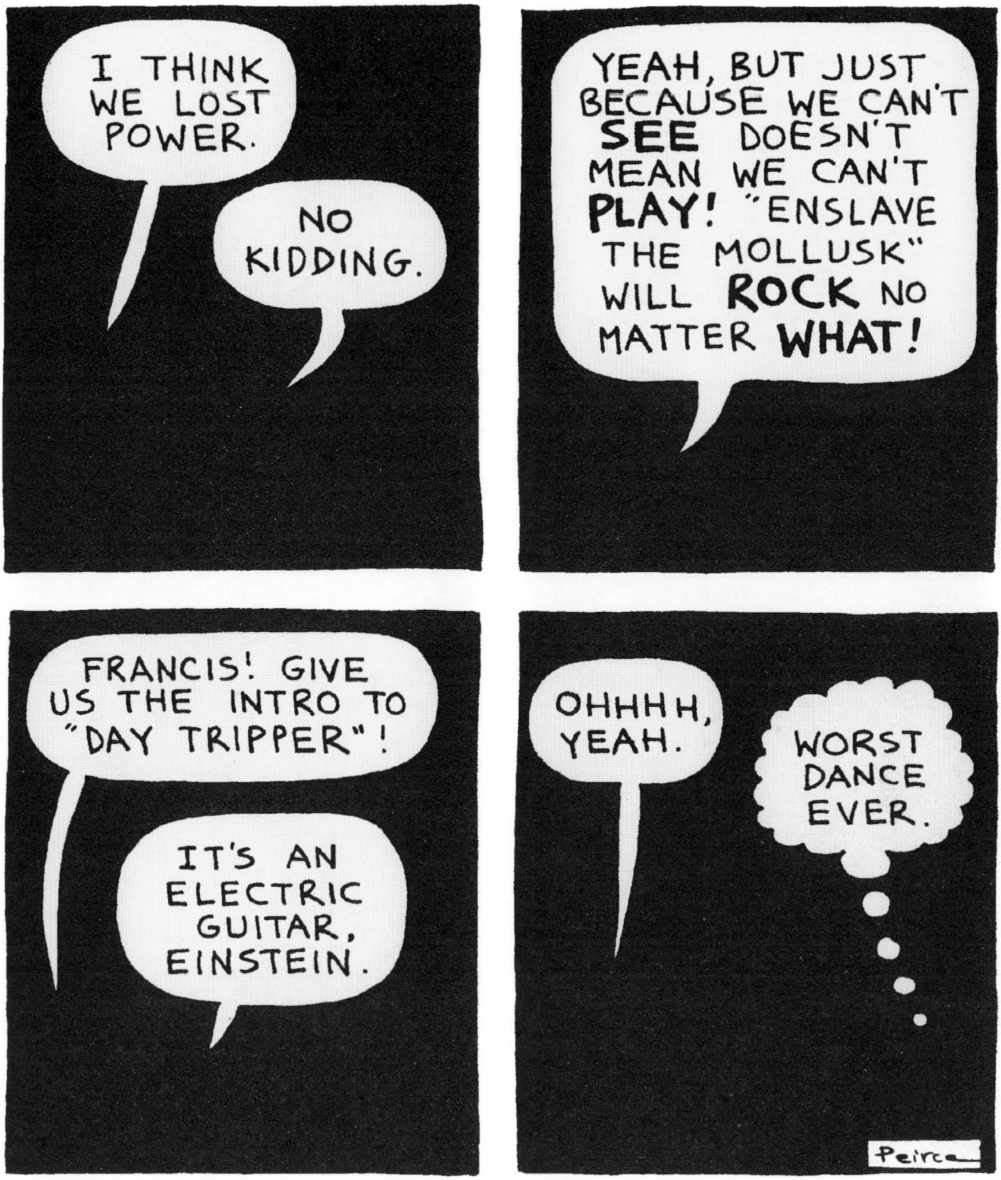
I THINK WE LOST POWER.
NO KIDDING.
YEAH, BUT JUST BECAUSE WE CAN'T SEE DOESN'T MEAN WE CAN'T PLAY! "ENSLAVE THE MOLLUSK" WILL ROCK NO MATTER WHAT!
FRANCIS! GIVE US THE INTRO TO "DAY TRIPPER"!
IT'S AN ELECTRIC GUITAR, EINSTEIN.
OHHHH, YEAH.
WORST DANCE EVER.
Peirce

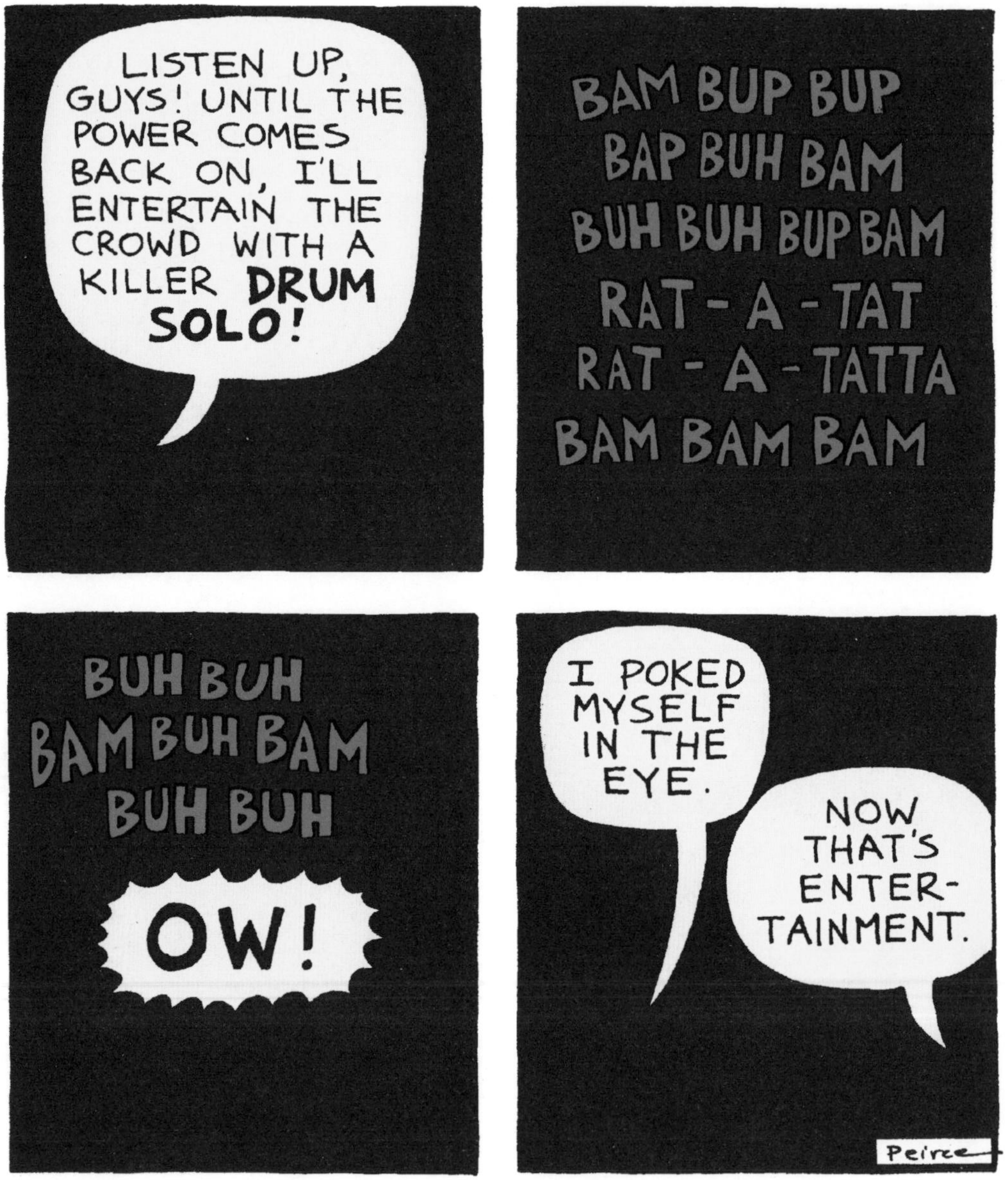
LISTEN UP, GUYS! UNTIL THE POWER COMES BACK ON, I'LL ENTERTAIN THE CROWD WITH A KILLER DRUM SOLO!
BAM BUP BUP BAP BUH BAM BUH BUH BUP BAM RAT-A-TAT RAT-A-TATTA BAM BAM BAM
BUH BUH BAM BUH BAM BUH BUH
OW!
I POKED MYSELF IN THE EYE.
NOW THAT'S ENTER-TAINMENT.
Peirce

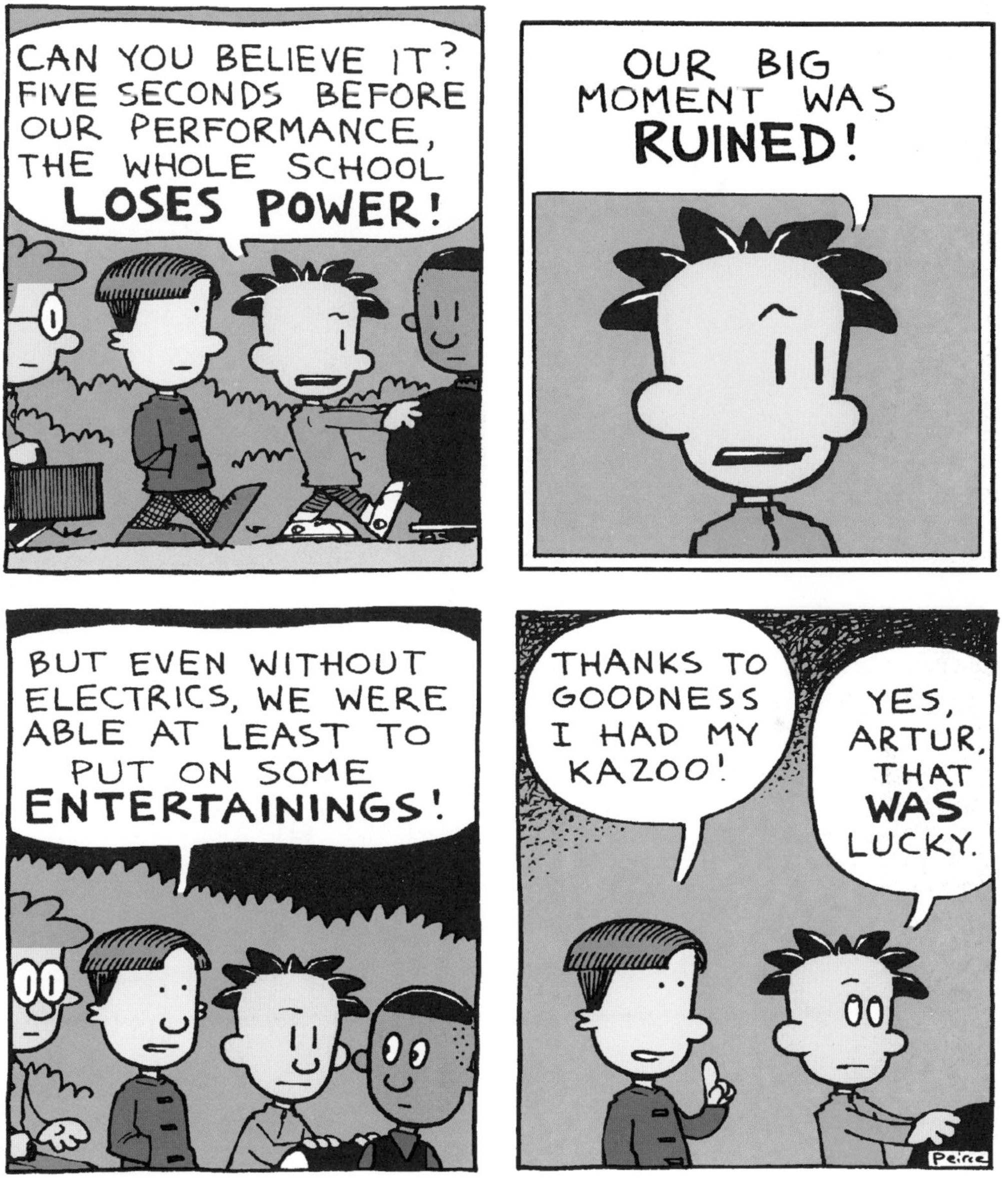
CAN YOU BELIEVE IT? FIVE SECONDS BEFORE OUR PERFORMANCE, THE WHOLE SCHOOL LOSES POWER!
OUR BIG MOMENT WAS RUINED!
BUT EVEN WITHOUT ELECTRICS, WE WERE ABLE AT LEAST TO PUT ON SOME ENTERTAININGS!
THANKS TO GOODNESS I HAD MY KAZOO!
YES, ARTUR, THAT WAS LUCKY.
Peirce

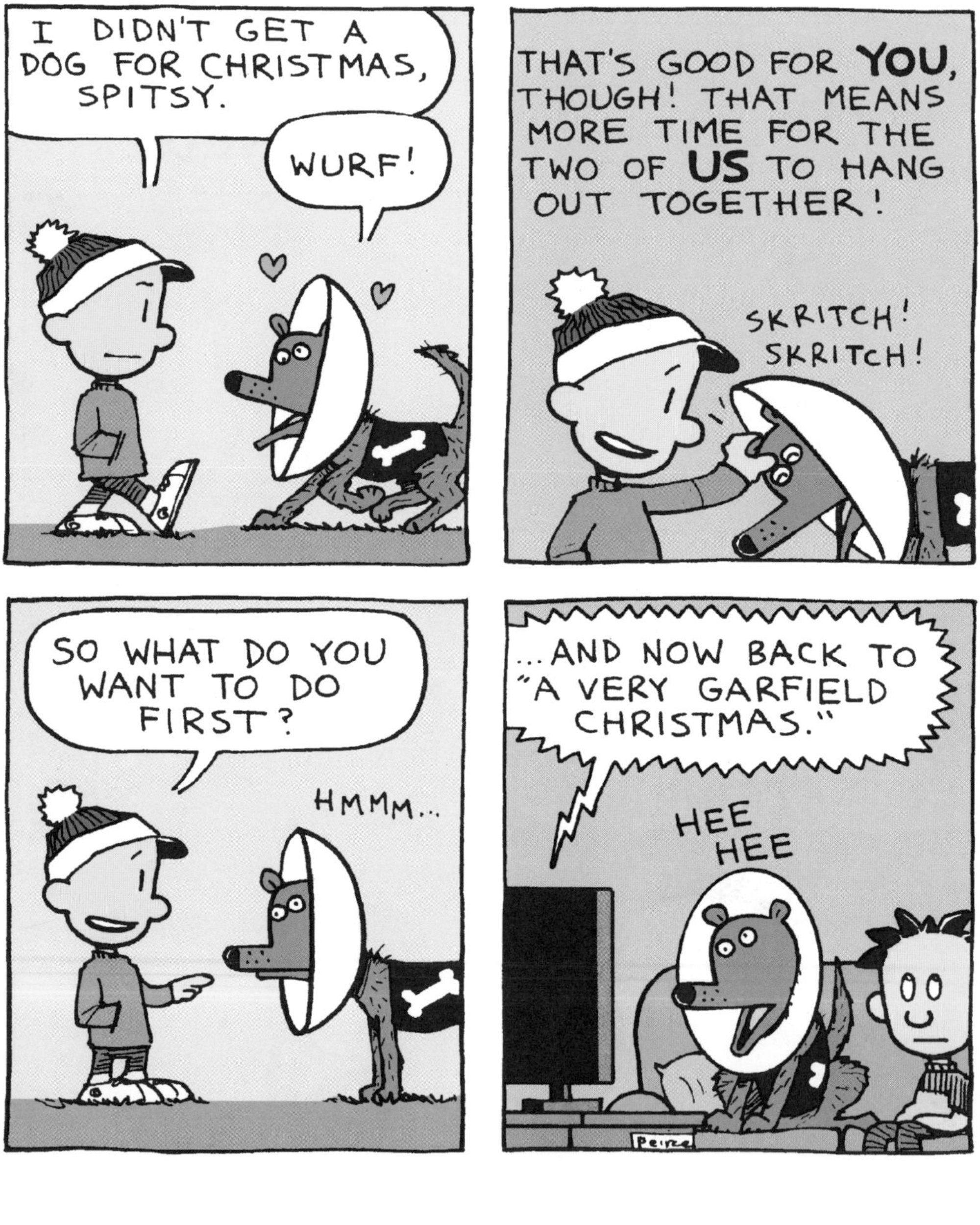
I DIDN'T GET A DOG FOR CHRISTMAS, SPITSY.
WURF!
THAT'S GOOD FOR **YOU**, THOUGH! THAT MEANS MORE TIME FOR THE TWO OF **US** TO HANG OUT TOGETHER!
SKRITCH! SKRITCH!
SO WHAT DO YOU WANT TO DO FIRST?
HMMM...
...AND NOW BACK TO "A VERY GARFIELD CHRISTMAS."
HEE HEE
Peirce

HOW MUCH WILL YOU GIVE ME IF I CAN HIT THAT STOP SIGN?

WAY OVER THERE?

YEAH! WILL YOU GIVE ME TEN DOLLARS?

ABSOLUTELY.

JUST SO WE'RE CLEAR: YOU'LL PAY ME TEN DOLLARS IF I HIT **THAT** STOP SIGN WITH **THIS** SNOWBALL?

YES.

oKAY!

CLANG!

I DIDN'T TELL YOU **WHERE** I'D THROW IT FROM! HA!

YOU OWE ME TEN BUCKS, DAD!

UH-HUH. EVENTUALLY.

I DIDN'T TELL YOU **WHEN** I'D PAY YOU! HA!

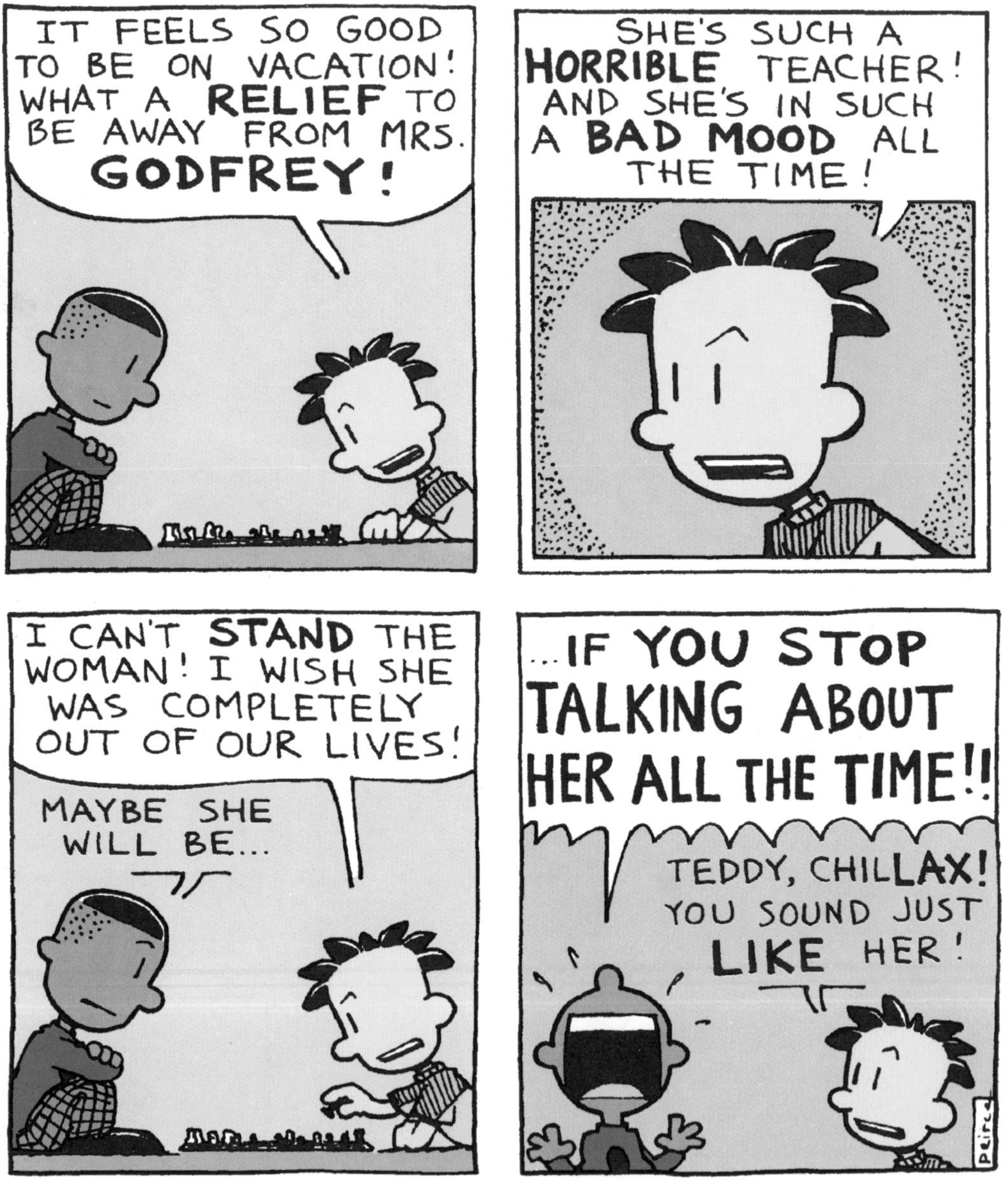
IT FEELS SO GOOD TO BE ON VACATION! WHAT A RELIEF TO BE AWAY FROM MRS. GODFREY!
SHE'S SUCH A HORRIBLE TEACHER! AND SHE'S IN SUCH A BAD MOOD ALL THE TIME!
I CAN'T STAND THE WOMAN! I WISH SHE WAS COMPLETELY OUT OF OUR LIVES!
MAYBE SHE WILL BE...
...IF YOU STOP TALKING ABOUT HER ALL THE TIME!!
TEDDY, CHILLAX! YOU SOUND JUST LIKE HER!
PEIRCE

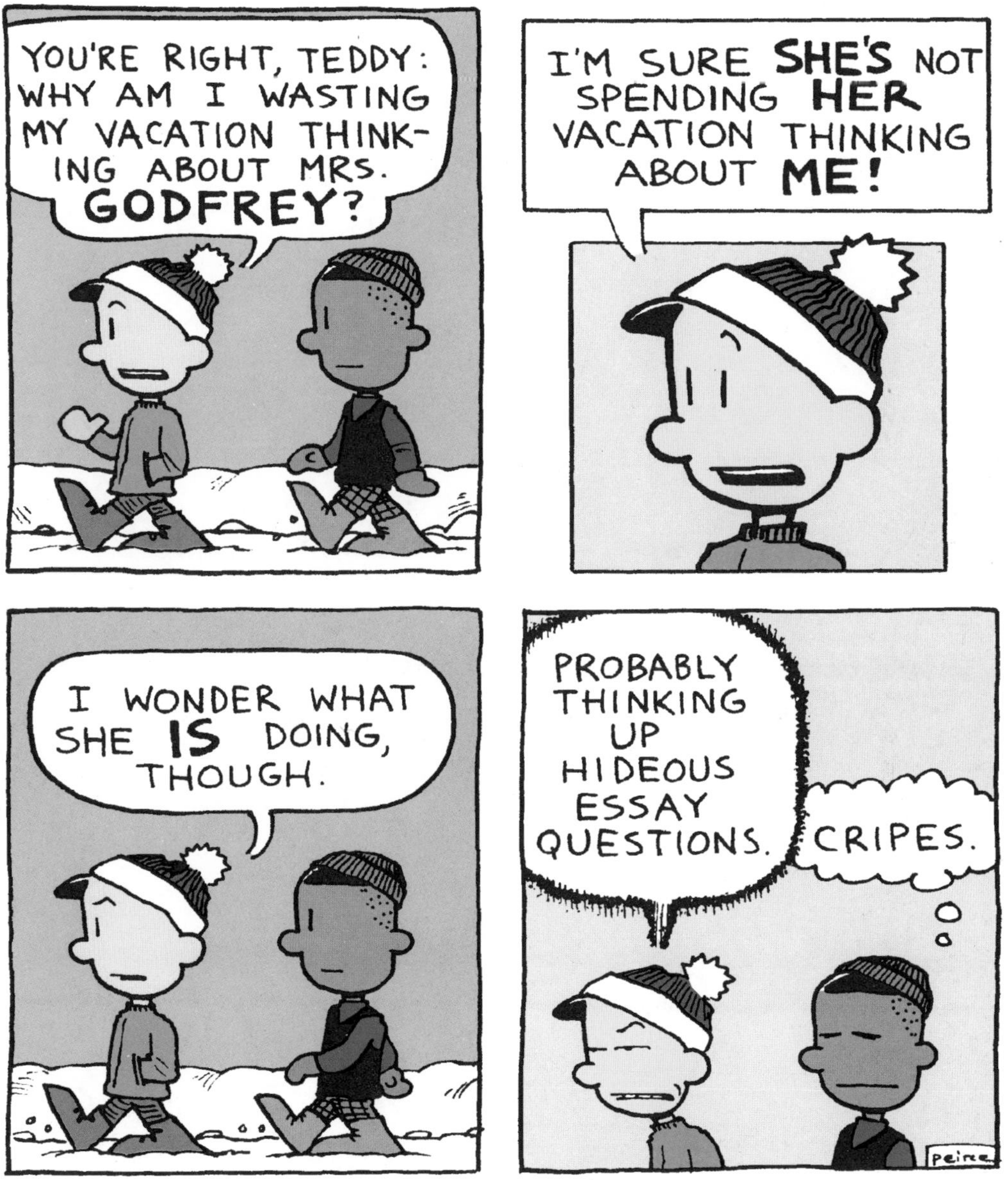

YOU'RE RIGHT, TEDDY: WHY AM I WASTING MY VACATION THINKING ABOUT MRS. GODFREY?
I'M SURE SHE'S NOT SPENDING HER VACATION THINKING ABOUT ME!
I WONDER WHAT SHE IS DOING, THOUGH.
PROBABLY THINKING UP HIDEOUS ESSAY QUESTIONS.
CRIPES.
peirce

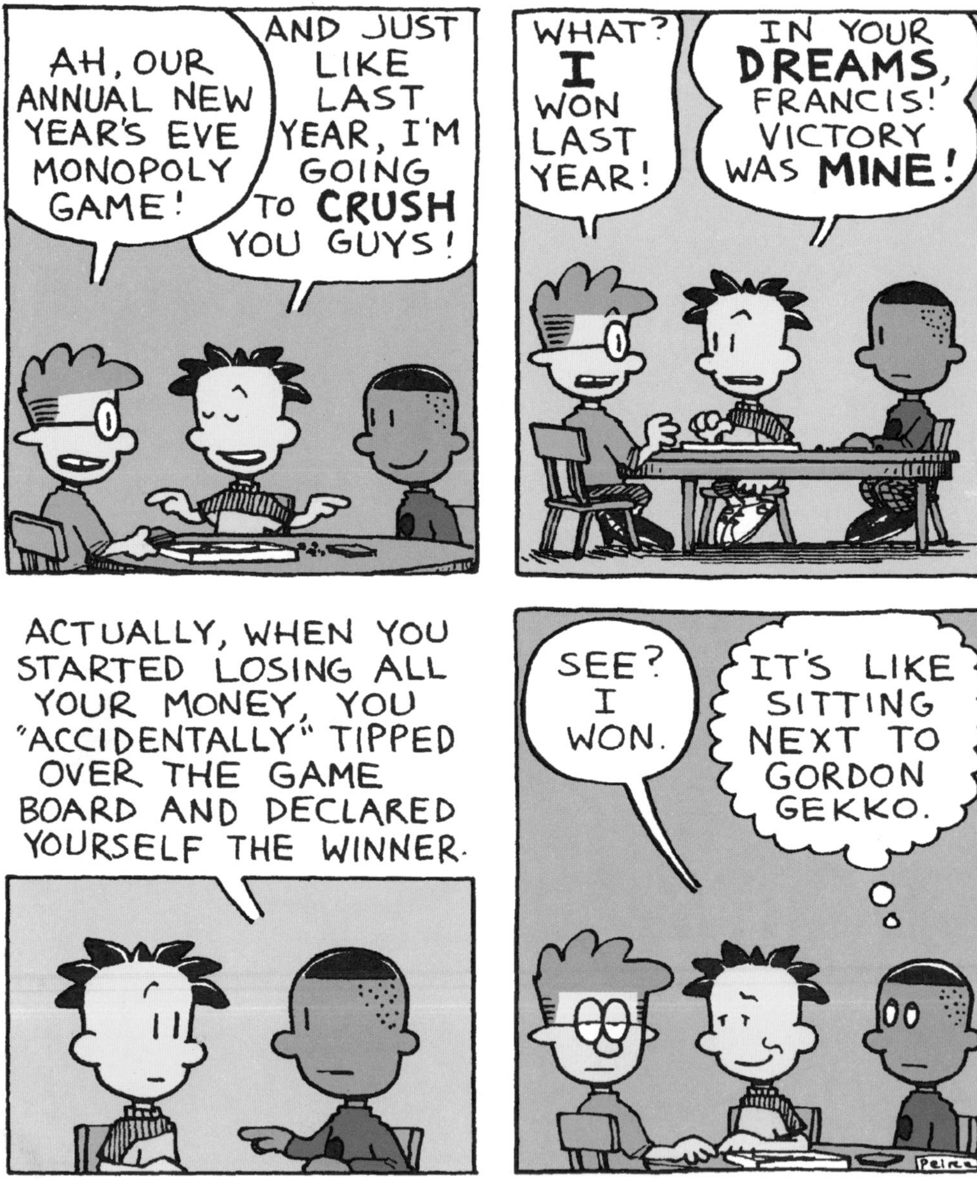
AH, OUR ANNUAL NEW YEAR'S EVE MONOPOLY GAME!
AND JUST LIKE LAST YEAR, I'M GOING TO CRUSH YOU GUYS!
WHAT? I WON LAST YEAR!
IN YOUR DREAMS, FRANCIS! VICTORY WAS MINE!
ACTUALLY, WHEN YOU STARTED LOSING ALL YOUR MONEY, YOU "ACCIDENTALLY" TIPPED OVER THE GAME BOARD AND DECLARED YOURSELF THE WINNER.
SEE? I WON.
IT'S LIKE SITTING NEXT TO GORDON GEKKO.
Peirce

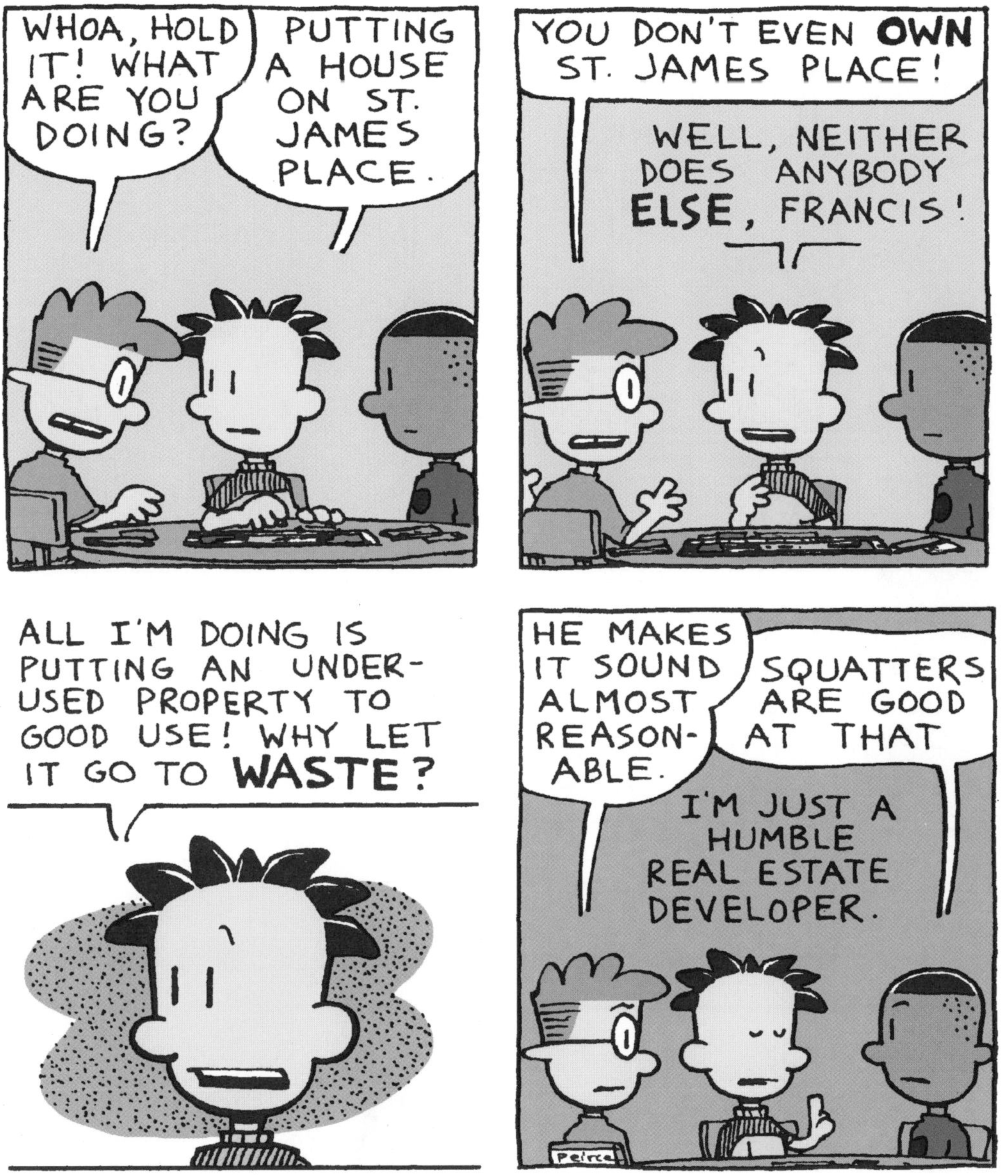
WHOA, HOLD IT! WHAT ARE YOU DOING?
PUTTING A HOUSE ON ST. JAMES PLACE.
YOU DON'T EVEN OWN ST. JAMES PLACE!
WELL, NEITHER DOES ANYBODY ELSE, FRANCIS!
ALL I'M DOING IS PUTTING AN UNDER-USED PROPERTY TO GOOD USE! WHY LET IT GO TO WASTE?
HE MAKES IT SOUND ALMOST REASON-ABLE.
SQUATTERS ARE GOOD AT THAT
I'M JUST A HUMBLE REAL ESTATE DEVELOPER.
Peirce

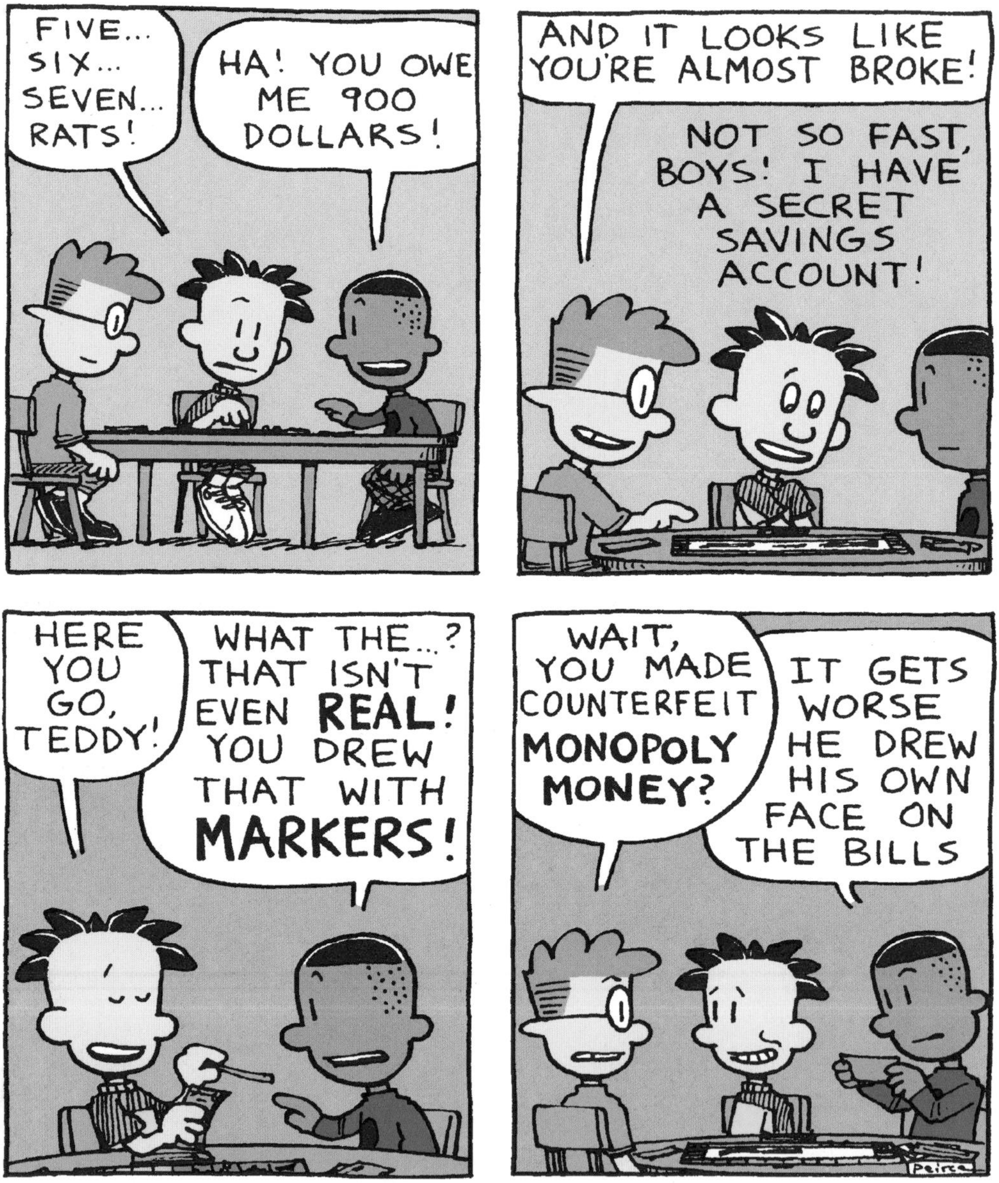
FIVE... SIX... SEVEN... RATS!
HA! YOU OWE ME 900 DOLLARS!
AND IT LOOKS LIKE YOU'RE ALMOST BROKE!
NOT SO FAST, BOYS! I HAVE A SECRET SAVINGS ACCOUNT!
HERE YOU GO, TEDDY!
WHAT THE...? THAT ISN'T EVEN REAL! YOU DREW THAT WITH MARKERS!
WAIT, YOU MADE COUNTERFEIT MONOPOLY MONEY?
IT GETS WORSE HE DREW HIS OWN FACE ON THE BILLS
Peirce

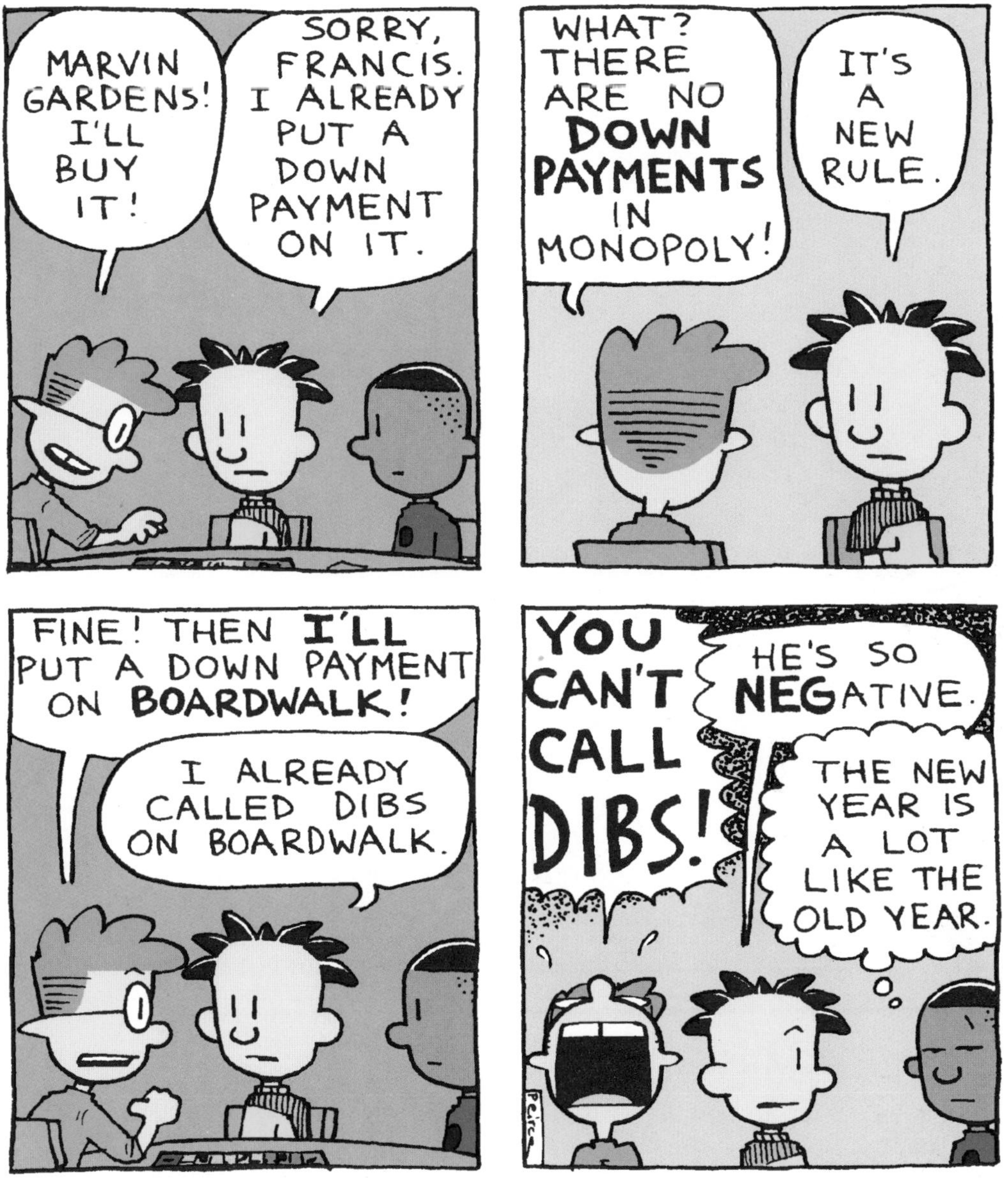
MARVIN GARDENS! I'LL BUY IT!
SORRY, FRANCIS. I ALREADY PUT A DOWN PAYMENT ON IT.
WHAT? THERE ARE NO **DOWN PAYMENTS** IN MONOPOLY!
IT'S A NEW RULE.
FINE! THEN **I'LL** PUT A DOWN PAYMENT ON **BOARDWALK!**
I ALREADY CALLED DIBS ON BOARDWALK.
YOU CAN'T CALL DIBS!
HE'S SO **NEG**ATIVE.
THE NEW YEAR IS A LOT LIKE THE OLD YEAR.
Peirce

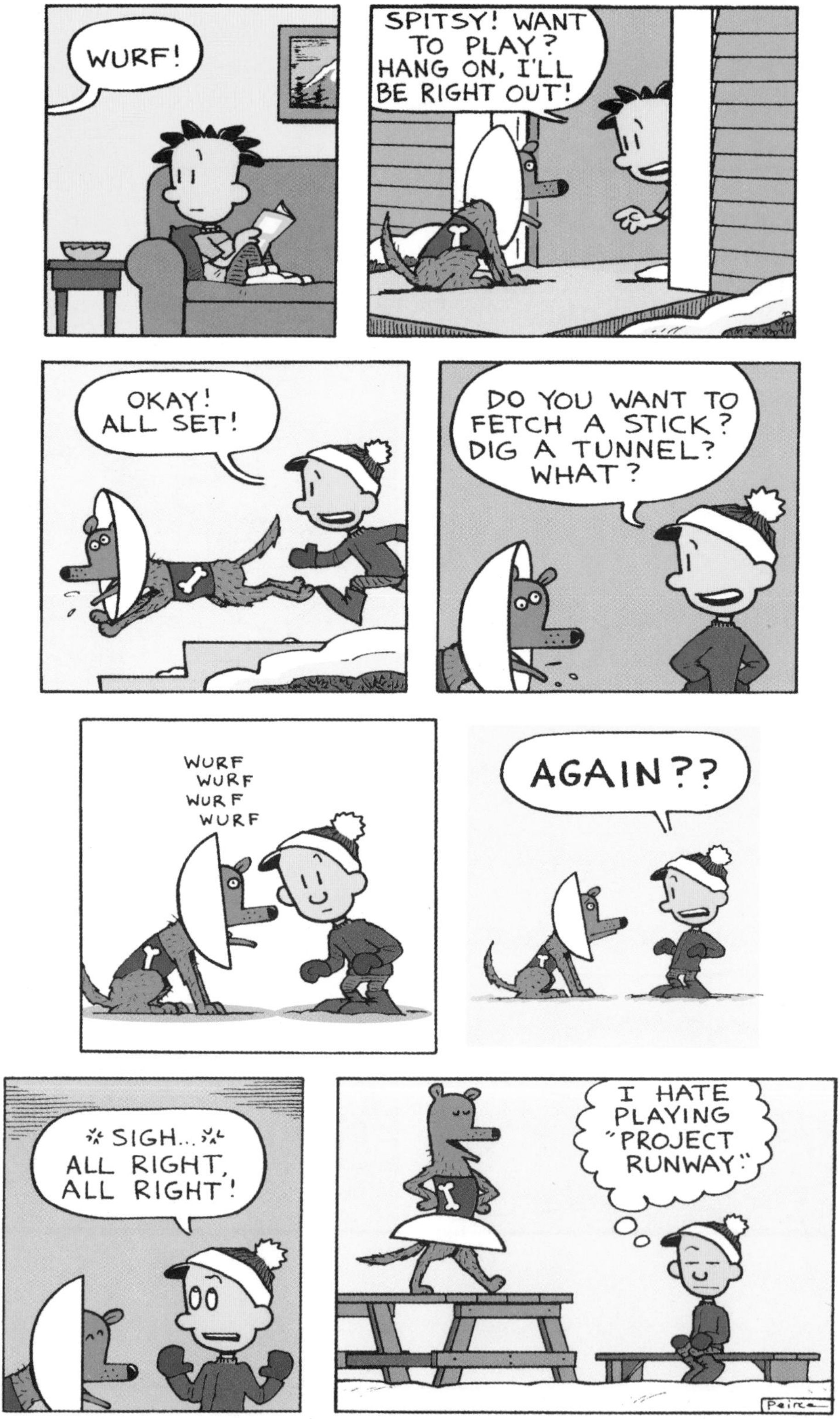
WURF!
SPITSY! WANT TO PLAY? HANG ON, I'LL BE RIGHT OUT!
OKAY! ALL SET!
DO YOU WANT TO FETCH A STICK? DIG A TUNNEL? WHAT?
WURF WURF WURF WURF
AGAIN??
SIGH... ALL RIGHT, ALL RIGHT!
I HATE PLAYING "PROJECT RUNWAY."
Peirce

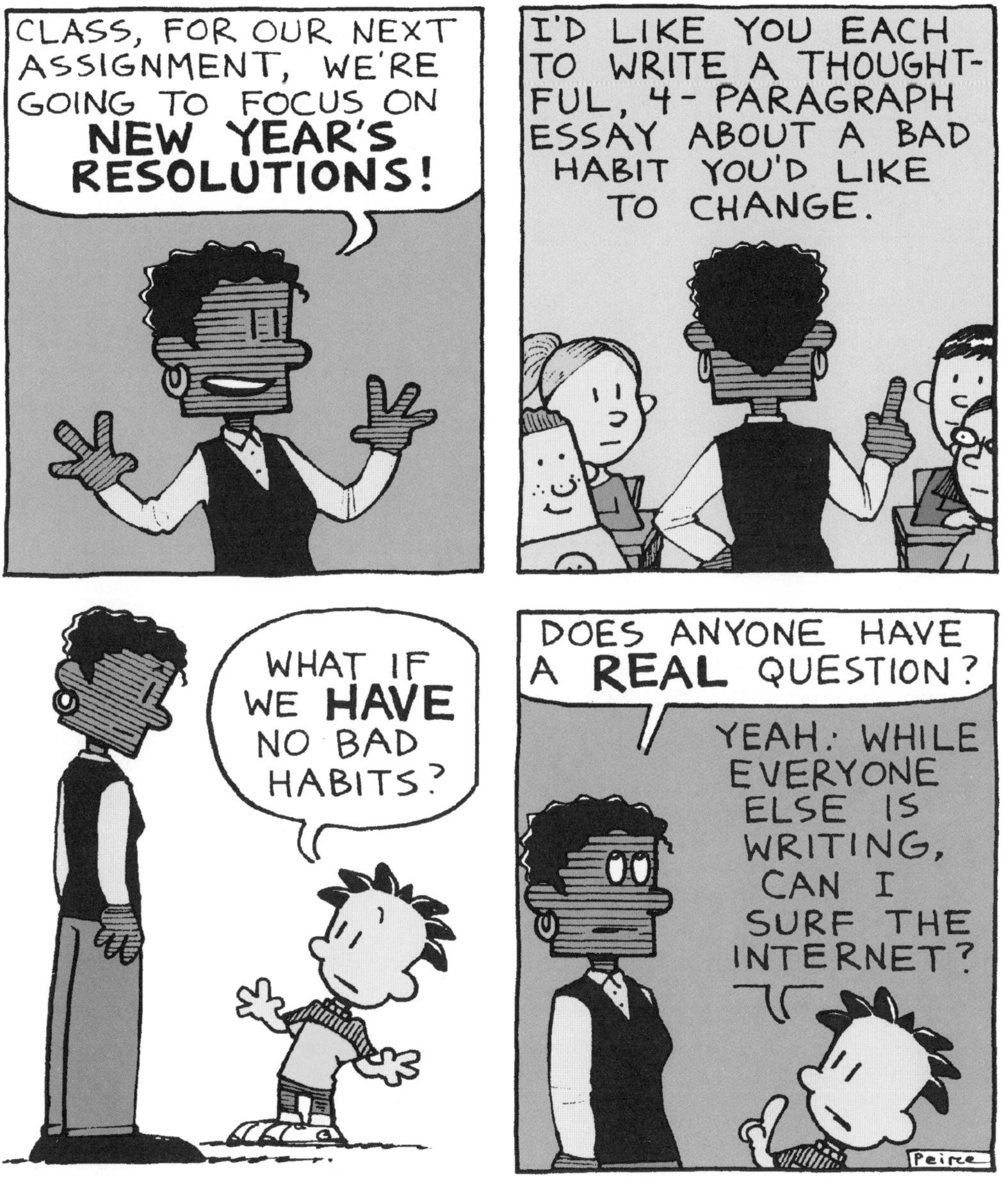
CLASS, FOR OUR NEXT ASSIGNMENT, WE'RE GOING TO FOCUS ON **NEW YEAR'S RESOLUTIONS!**
I'D LIKE YOU EACH TO WRITE A THOUGHT-FUL, 4-PARAGRAPH ESSAY ABOUT A BAD HABIT YOU'D LIKE TO CHANGE.
WHAT IF WE **HAVE** NO BAD HABITS?
DOES ANYONE HAVE A **REAL** QUESTION?
YEAH: WHILE EVERYONE ELSE IS WRITING, CAN I SURF THE INTERNET?
Peirce

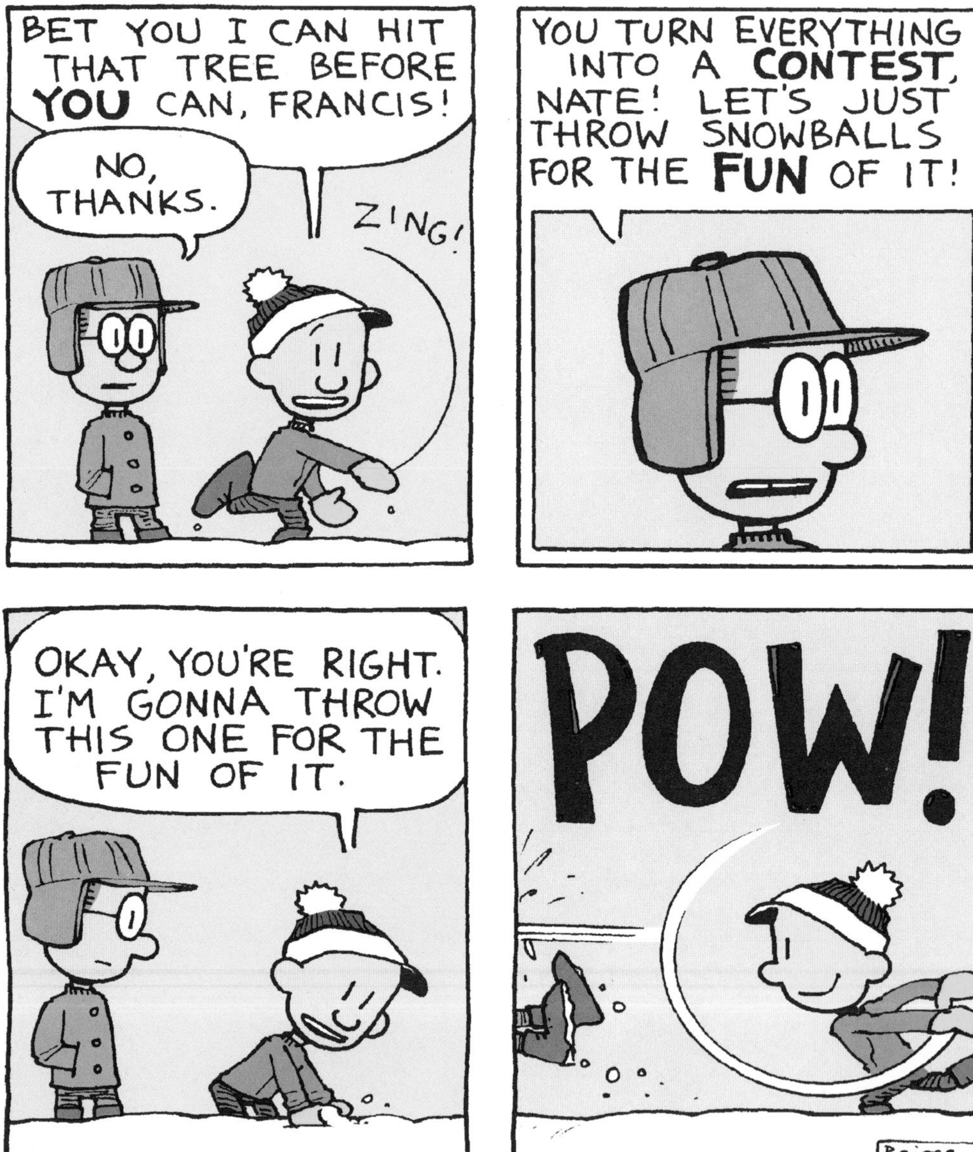
BET YOU I CAN HIT THAT TREE BEFORE YOU CAN, FRANCIS!
NO, THANKS.
ZING!
YOU TURN EVERYTHING INTO A CONTEST, NATE! LET'S JUST THROW SNOWBALLS FOR THE FUN OF IT!
OKAY, YOU'RE RIGHT. I'M GONNA THROW THIS ONE FOR THE FUN OF IT.
POW!
Peirce

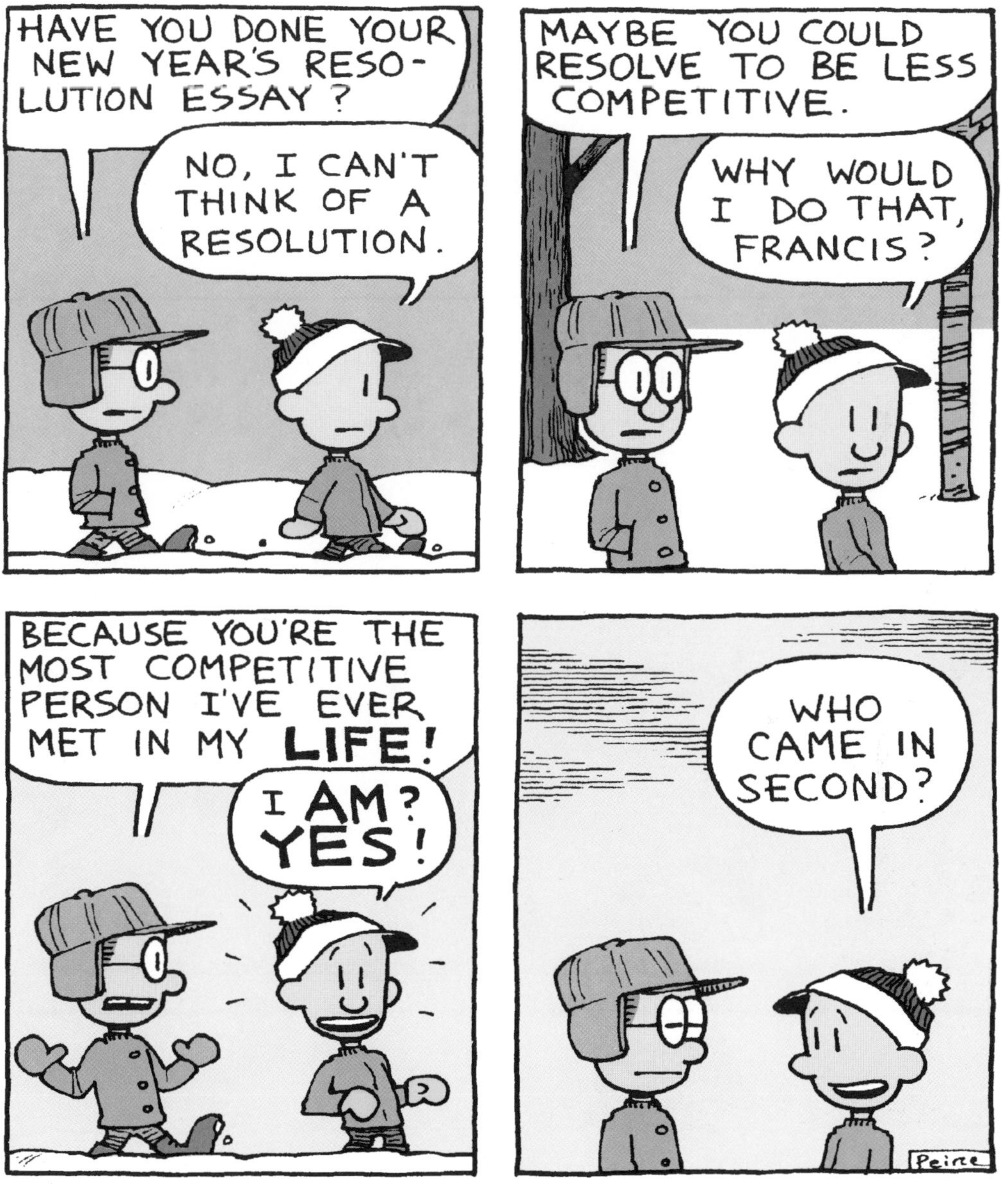
HAVE YOU DONE YOUR NEW YEAR'S RESO-LUTION ESSAY?
NO, I CAN'T THINK OF A RESOLUTION.
MAYBE YOU COULD RESOLVE TO BE LESS COMPETITIVE.
WHY WOULD I DO THAT, FRANCIS?
BECAUSE YOU'RE THE MOST COMPETITIVE PERSON I'VE EVER MET IN MY LIFE!
I AM? YES!
WHO CAME IN SECOND?
Peirce

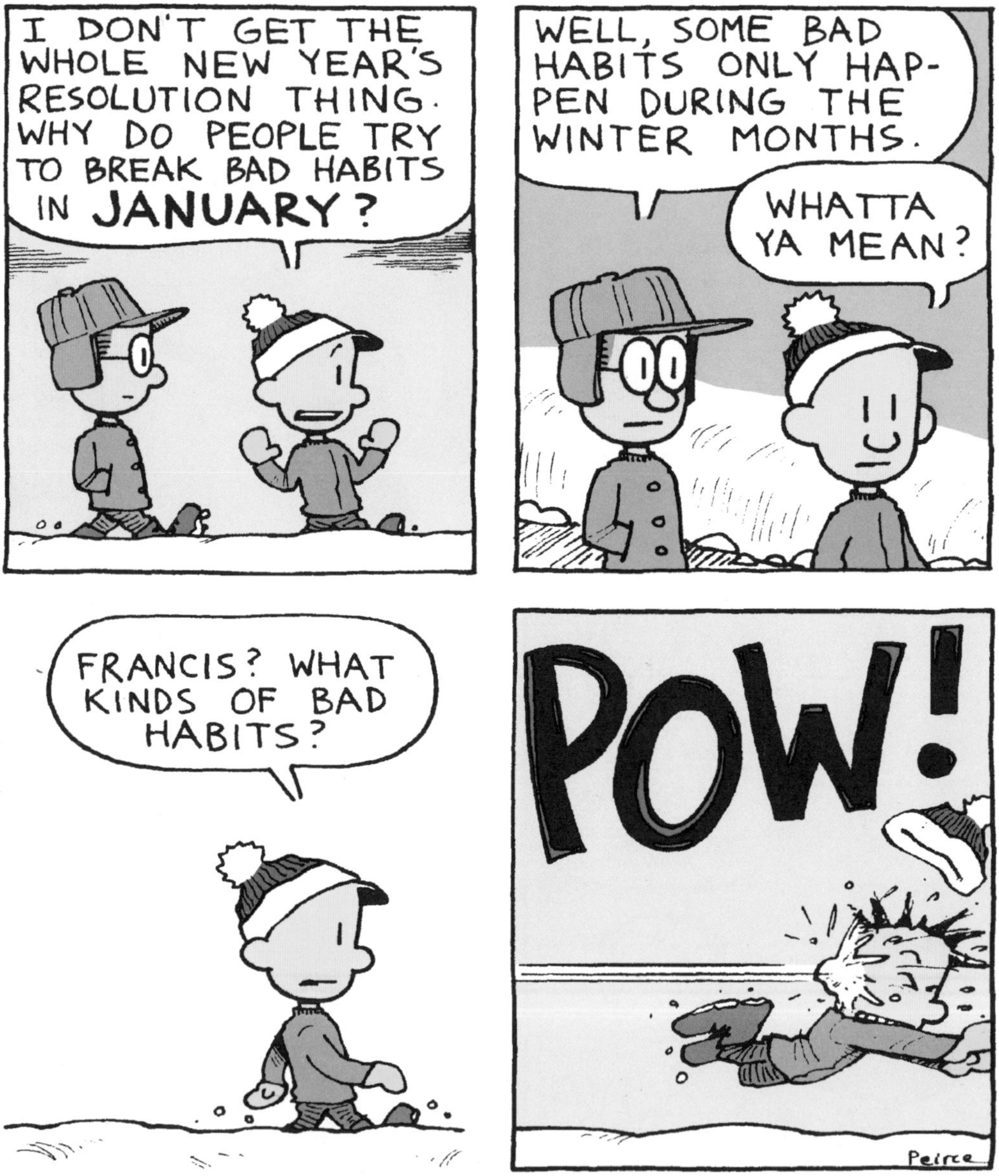
I DON'T GET THE WHOLE NEW YEAR'S RESOLUTION THING. WHY DO PEOPLE TRY TO BREAK BAD HABITS IN JANUARY?
WELL, SOME BAD HABITS ONLY HAPPEN DURING THE WINTER MONTHS.
WHATTA YA MEAN?
FRANCIS? WHAT KINDS OF BAD HABITS?
POW!
Peirce

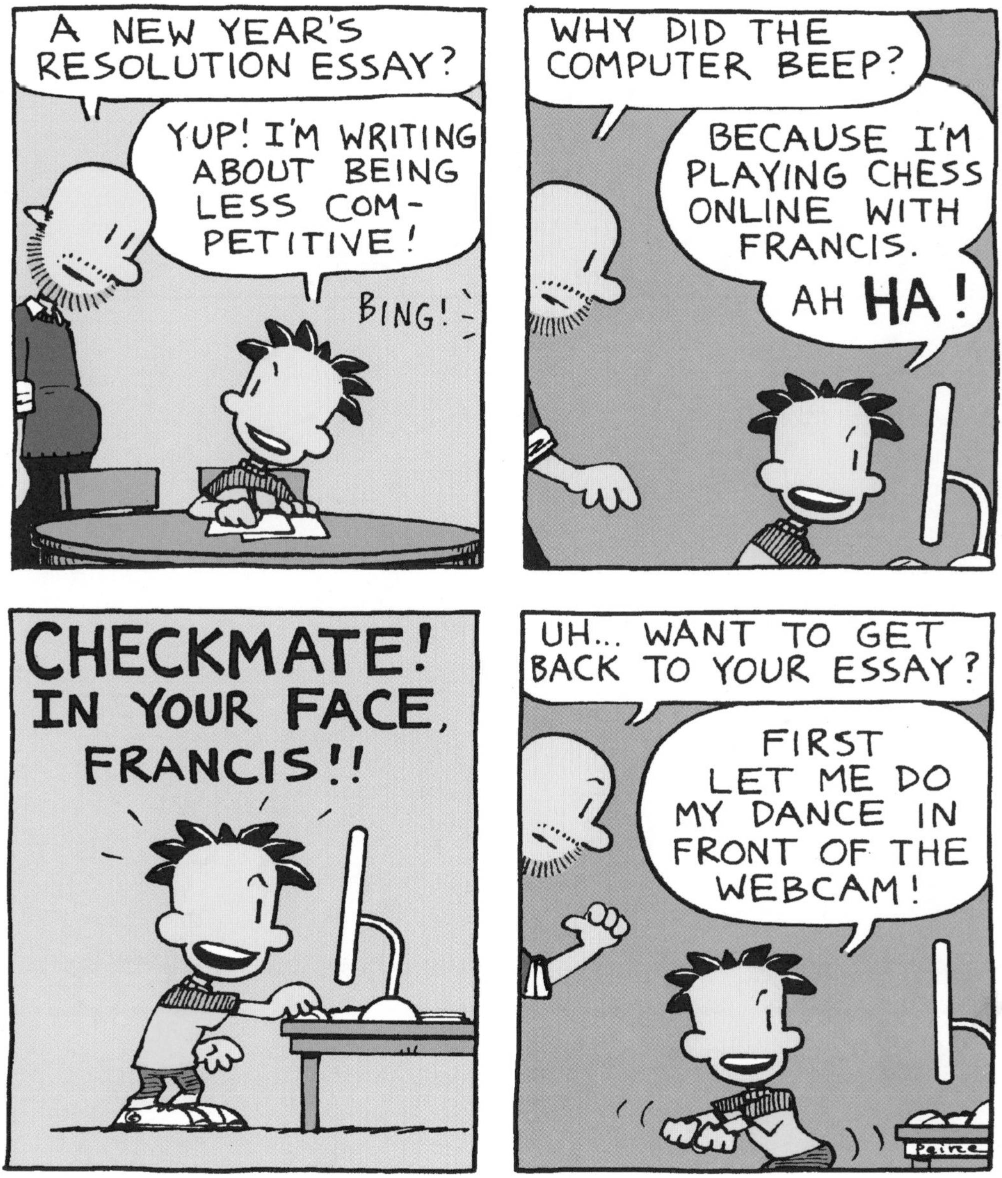

A NEW YEAR'S RESOLUTION ESSAY?
YUP! I'M WRITING ABOUT BEING LESS COM-PETITIVE!
BING!
WHY DID THE COMPUTER BEEP?
BECAUSE I'M PLAYING CHESS ONLINE WITH FRANCIS.
AH HA!
CHECKMATE! IN YOUR FACE, FRANCIS!!
UH... WANT TO GET BACK TO YOUR ESSAY?
FIRST LET ME DO MY DANCE IN FRONT OF THE WEBCAM!

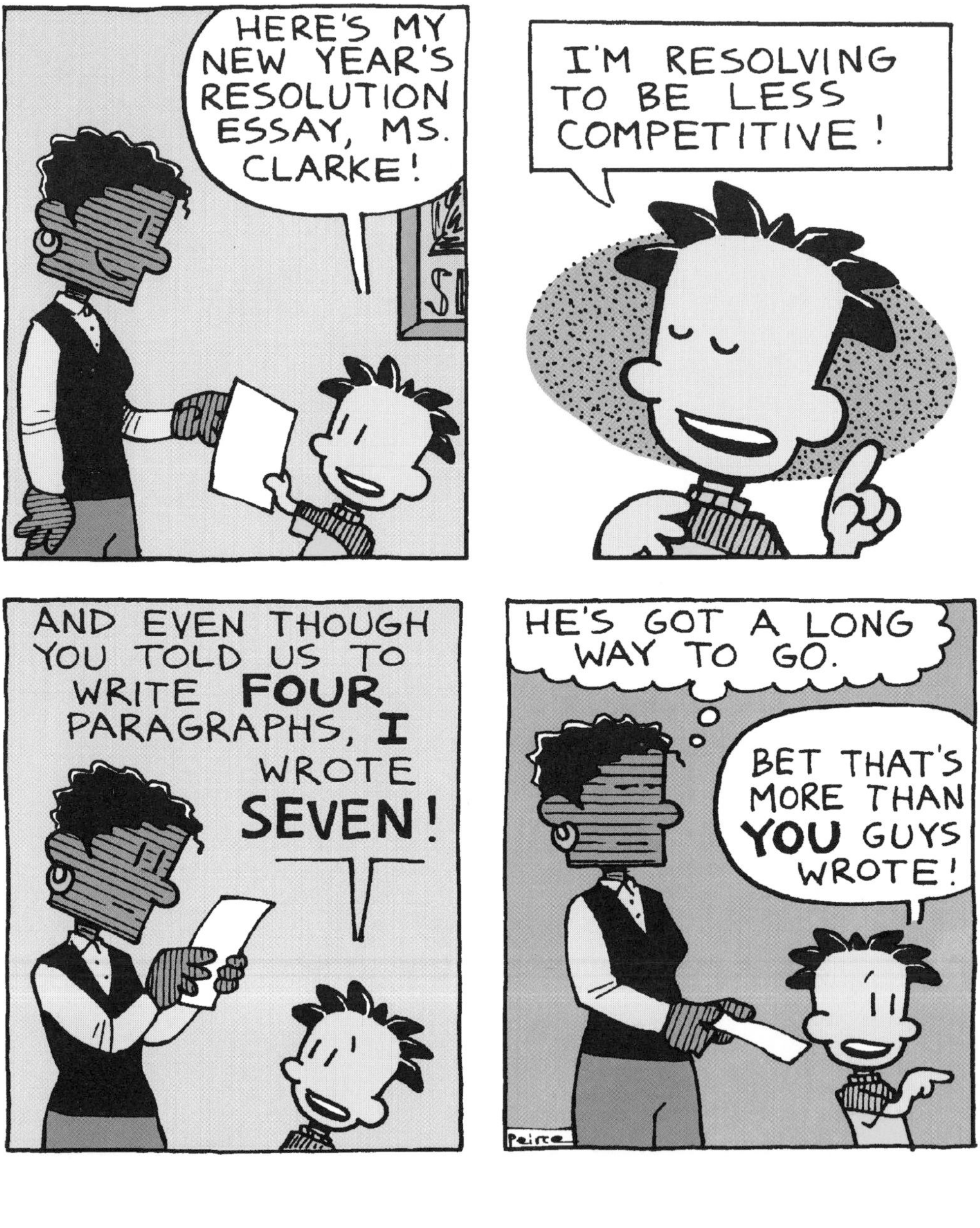
HERE'S MY NEW YEAR'S RESOLUTION ESSAY, MS. CLARKE!
I'M RESOLVING TO BE LESS COMPETITIVE!
AND EVEN THOUGH YOU TOLD US TO WRITE FOUR PARAGRAPHS, I WROTE SEVEN!
HE'S GOT A LONG WAY TO GO.
BET THAT'S MORE THAN YOU GUYS WROTE!
Peirce

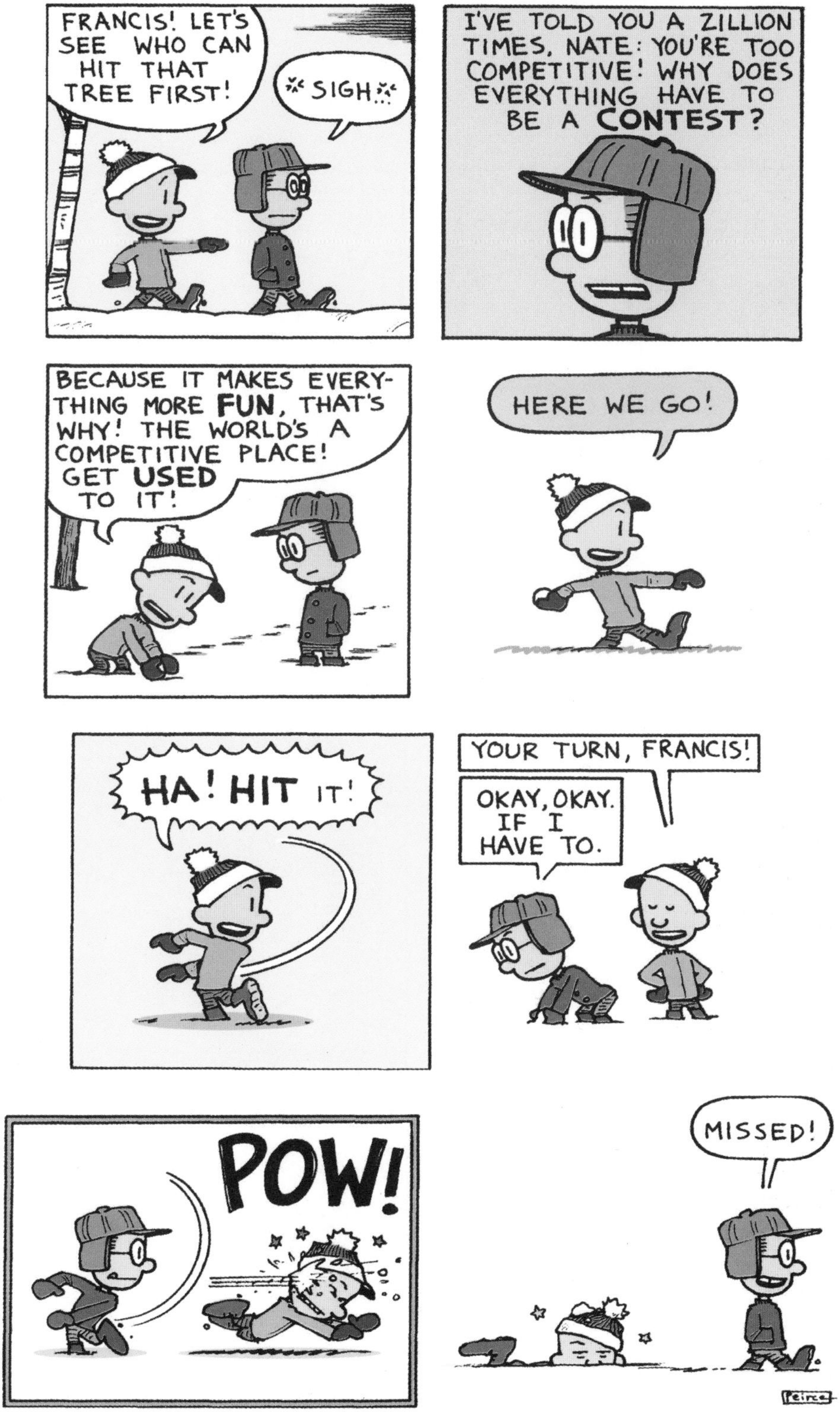
FRANCIS! LET'S SEE WHO CAN HIT THAT TREE FIRST!
SIGH
I'VE TOLD YOU A ZILLION TIMES, NATE: YOU'RE TOO COMPETITIVE! WHY DOES EVERYTHING HAVE TO BE A CONTEST?
BECAUSE IT MAKES EVERYTHING MORE FUN, THAT'S WHY! THE WORLD'S A COMPETITIVE PLACE! GET USED TO IT!
HERE WE GO!
HA! HIT IT!
YOUR TURN, FRANCIS!
OKAY, OKAY. IF I HAVE TO.
POW!
MISSED!
Peirce

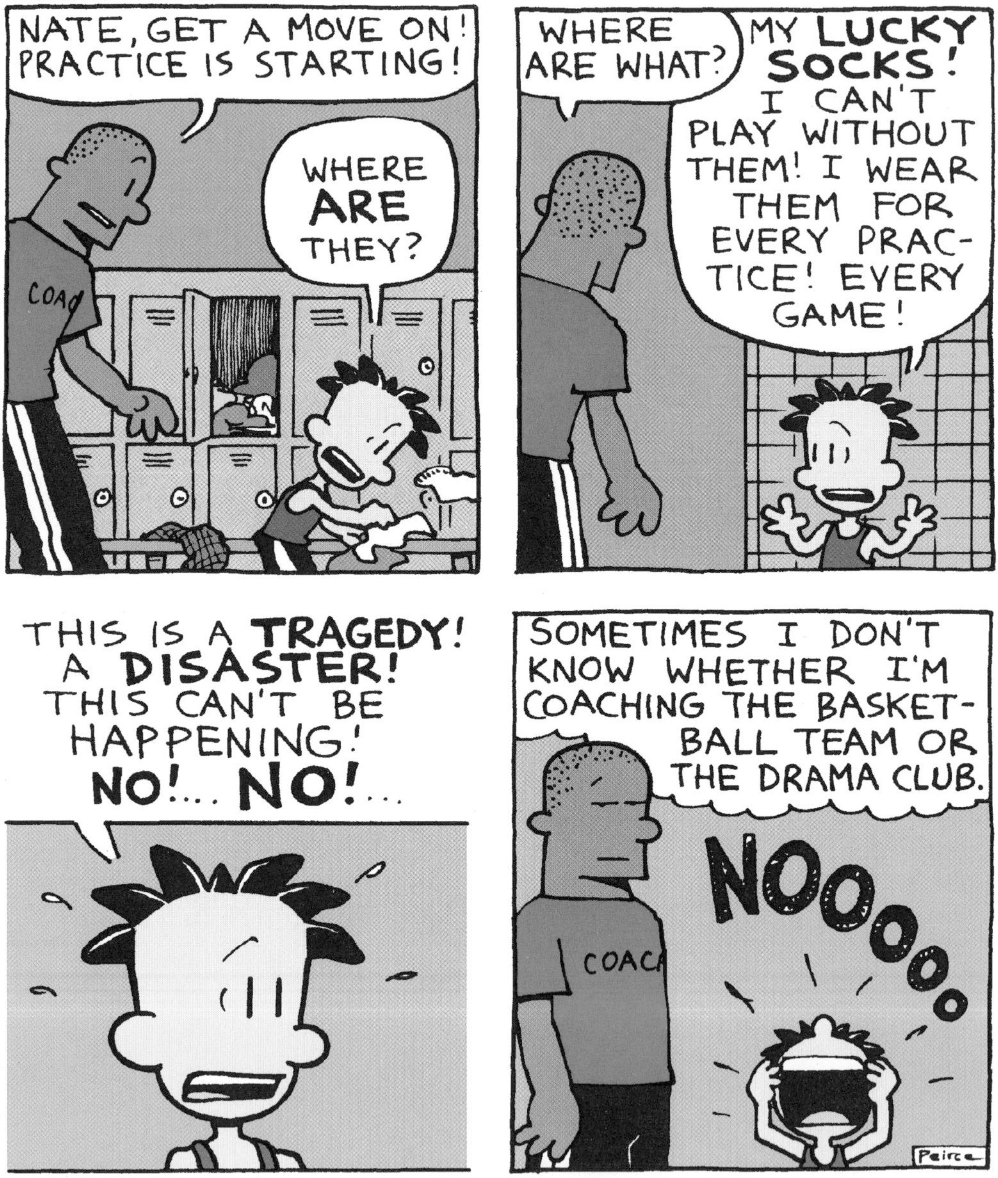
NATE, GET A MOVE ON! PRACTICE IS STARTING!
WHERE **ARE** THEY?
COAC
WHERE ARE WHAT?
MY **LUCKY SOCKS!** I CAN'T PLAY WITHOUT THEM! I WEAR THEM FOR EVERY PRACTICE! EVERY GAME!
THIS IS A **TRAGEDY!** A **DISASTER!** THIS CAN'T BE HAPPENING! **NO!... NO!...**
SOMETIMES I DON'T KNOW WHETHER I'M COACHING THE BASKETBALL TEAM OR THE DRAMA CLUB.
COAC
NOOOOOO
Peirce

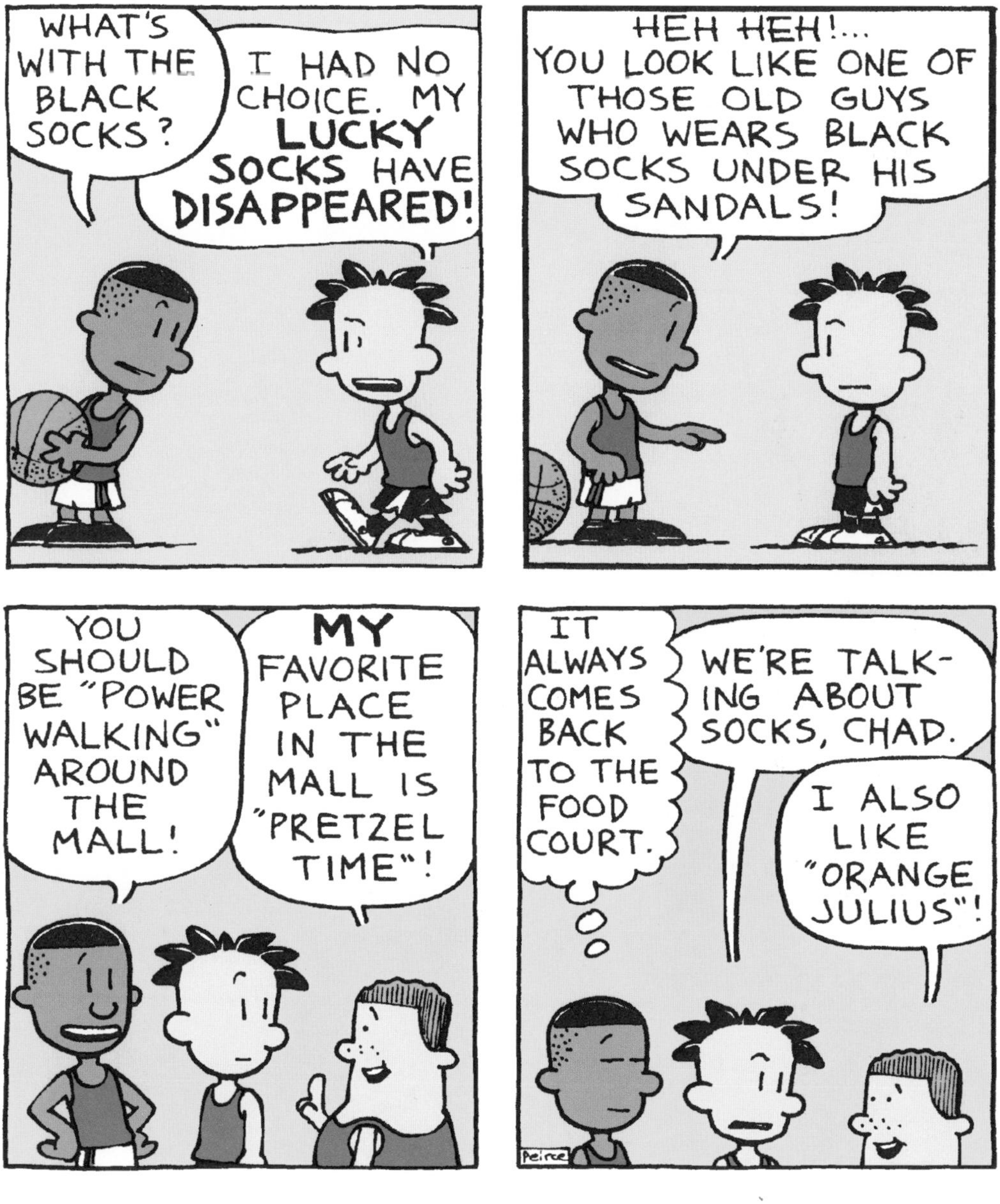
WHAT'S WITH THE BLACK SOCKS?
I HAD NO CHOICE. MY **LUCKY SOCKS** HAVE **DISAPPEARED!**
HEH HEH!... YOU LOOK LIKE ONE OF THOSE OLD GUYS WHO WEARS BLACK SOCKS UNDER HIS SANDALS!
YOU SHOULD BE "POWER WALKING" AROUND THE MALL!
MY FAVORITE PLACE IN THE MALL IS "PRETZEL TIME"!
IT ALWAYS COMES BACK TO THE FOOD COURT.
WE'RE TALKING ABOUT SOCKS, CHAD.
I ALSO LIKE "ORANGE JULIUS"!
Peirce

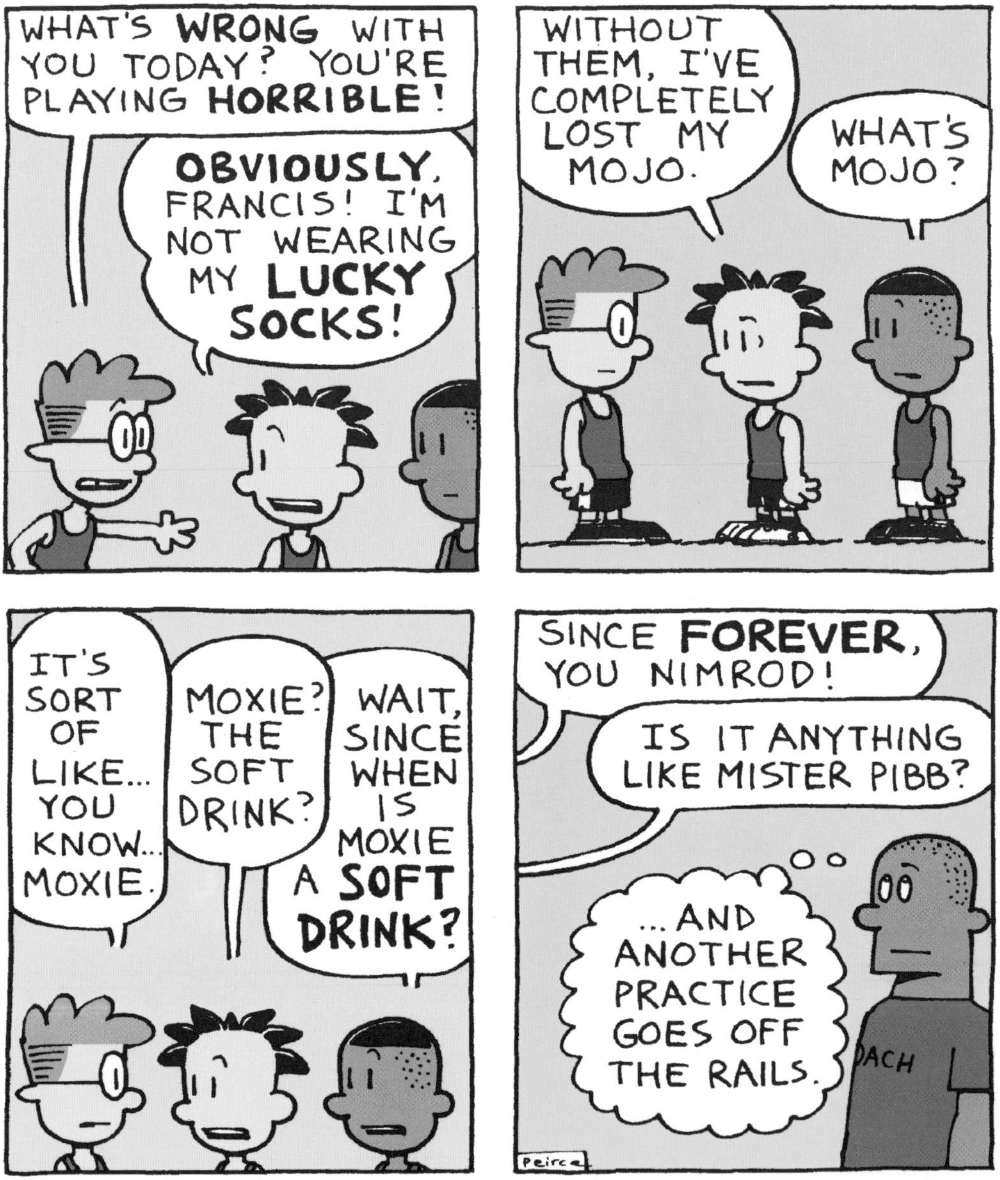
WHAT'S WRONG WITH YOU TODAY? YOU'RE PLAYING HORRIBLE!
OBVIOUSLY, FRANCIS! I'M NOT WEARING MY LUCKY SOCKS!
WITHOUT THEM, I'VE COMPLETELY LOST MY MOJO.
WHAT'S MOJO?
IT'S SORT OF LIKE... YOU KNOW... MOXIE.
MOXIE? THE SOFT DRINK?
WAIT, SINCE WHEN IS MOXIE A SOFT DRINK?
SINCE FOREVER, YOU NIMROD!
IS IT ANYTHING LIKE MISTER PIBB?
...AND ANOTHER PRACTICE GOES OFF THE RAILS.
ACH
Peirce

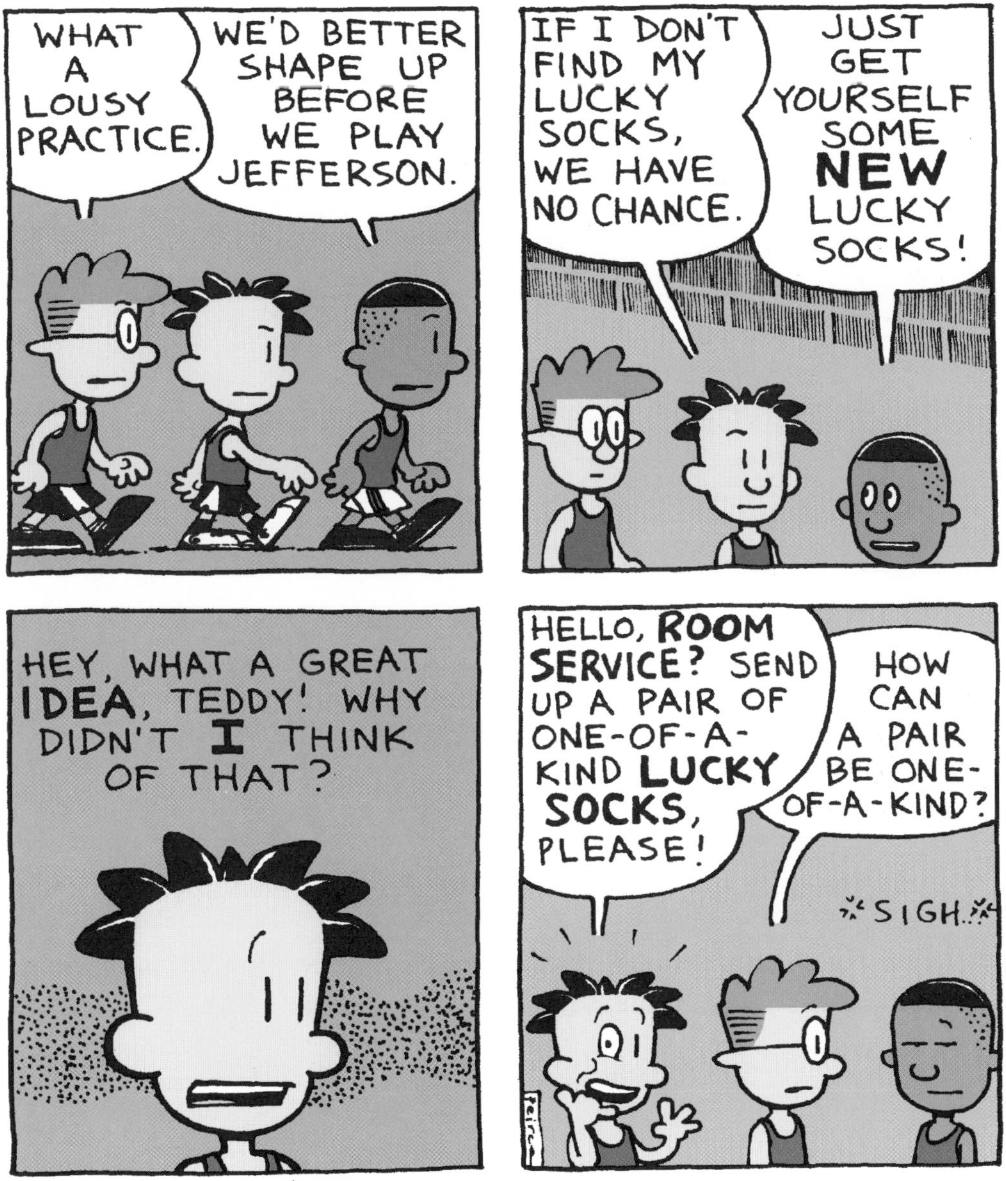
WHAT A LOUSY PRACTICE.
WE'D BETTER SHAPE UP BEFORE WE PLAY JEFFERSON.
IF I DON'T FIND MY LUCKY SOCKS, WE HAVE NO CHANCE.
JUST GET YOURSELF SOME NEW LUCKY SOCKS!
HEY, WHAT A GREAT IDEA, TEDDY! WHY DIDN'T I THINK OF THAT?
HELLO, ROOM SERVICE? SEND UP A PAIR OF ONE-OF-A-KIND LUCKY SOCKS, PLEASE!
HOW CAN A PAIR BE ONE-OF-A-KIND?
SIGH
peirce

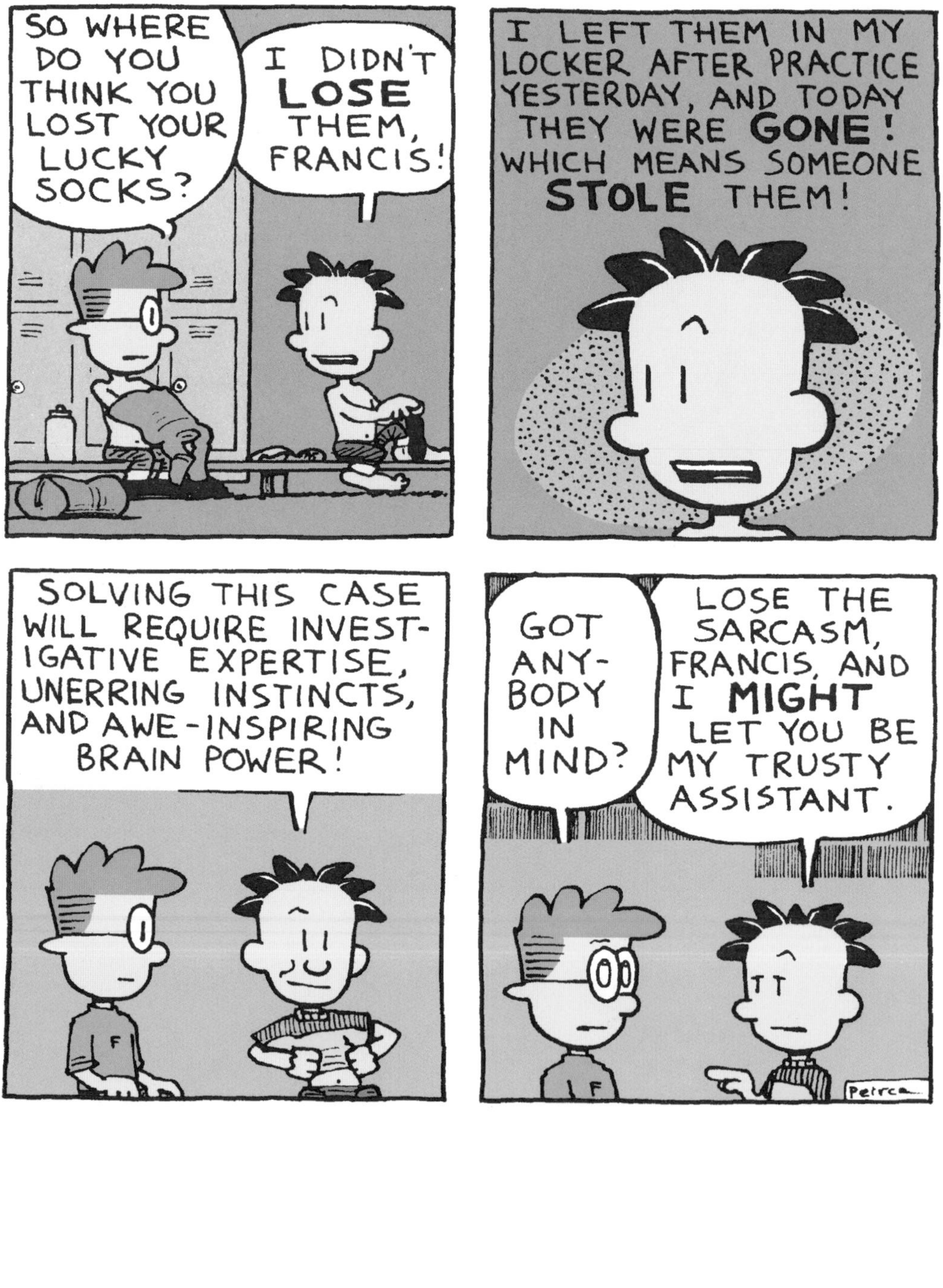
SO WHERE DO YOU THINK YOU LOST YOUR LUCKY SOCKS?
I DIDN'T **LOSE** THEM, FRANCIS!
I LEFT THEM IN MY LOCKER AFTER PRACTICE YESTERDAY, AND TODAY THEY WERE **GONE!** WHICH MEANS SOMEONE **STOLE** THEM!
SOLVING THIS CASE WILL REQUIRE INVESTIGATIVE EXPERTISE, UNERRING INSTINCTS, AND AWE-INSPIRING BRAIN POWER!
GOT ANYBODY IN MIND?
LOSE THE SARCASM, FRANCIS, AND I **MIGHT** LET YOU BE MY TRUSTY ASSISTANT.
Peirce

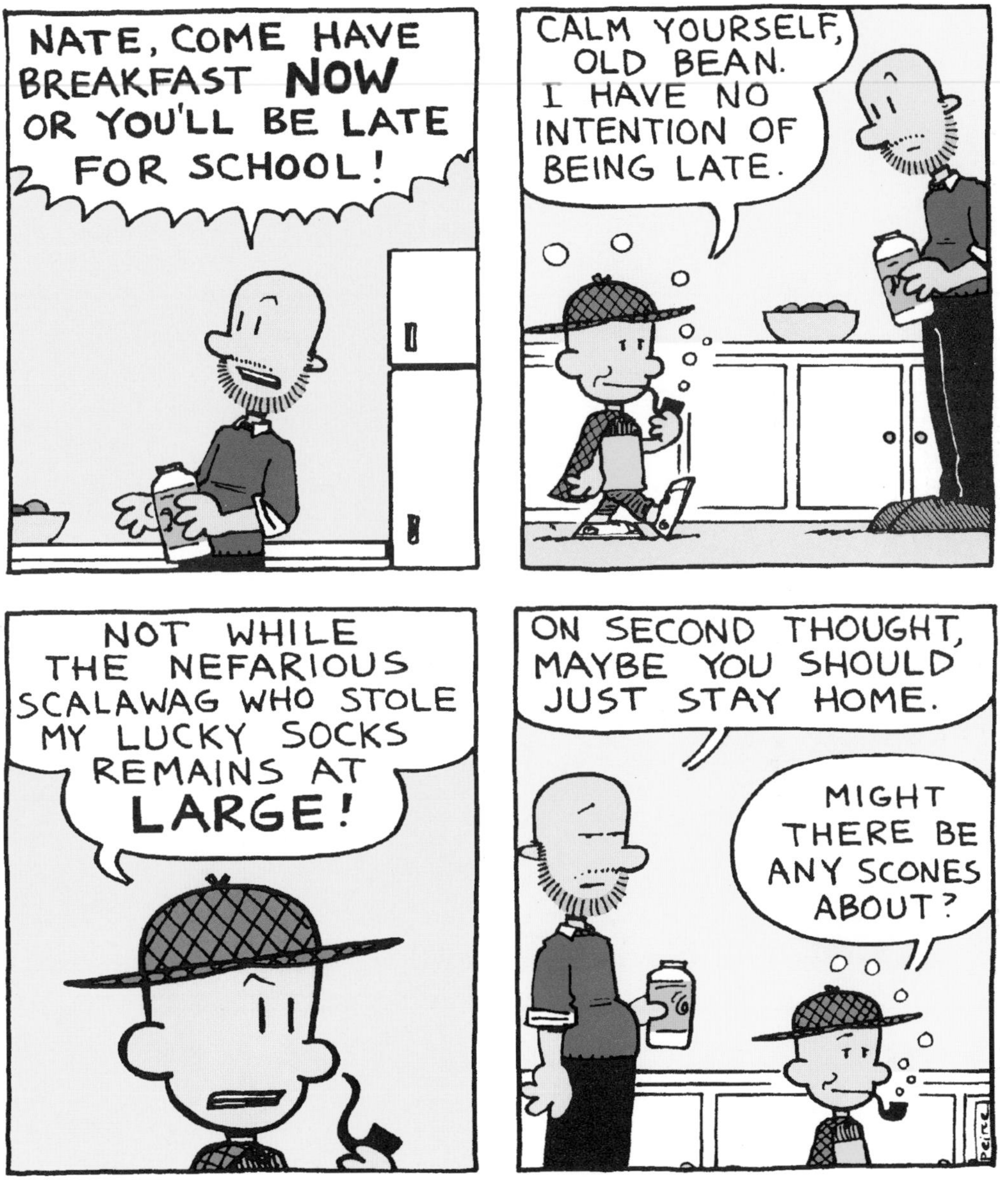
NATE, COME HAVE BREAKFAST **NOW** OR YOU'LL BE LATE FOR SCHOOL!
CALM YOURSELF, OLD BEAN. I HAVE NO INTENTION OF BEING LATE.
NOT WHILE THE NEFARIOUS SCALAWAG WHO STOLE MY LUCKY SOCKS REMAINS AT **LARGE!**
ON SECOND THOUGHT, MAYBE YOU SHOULD JUST STAY HOME.
MIGHT THERE BE ANY SCONES ABOUT?
PEIRCE

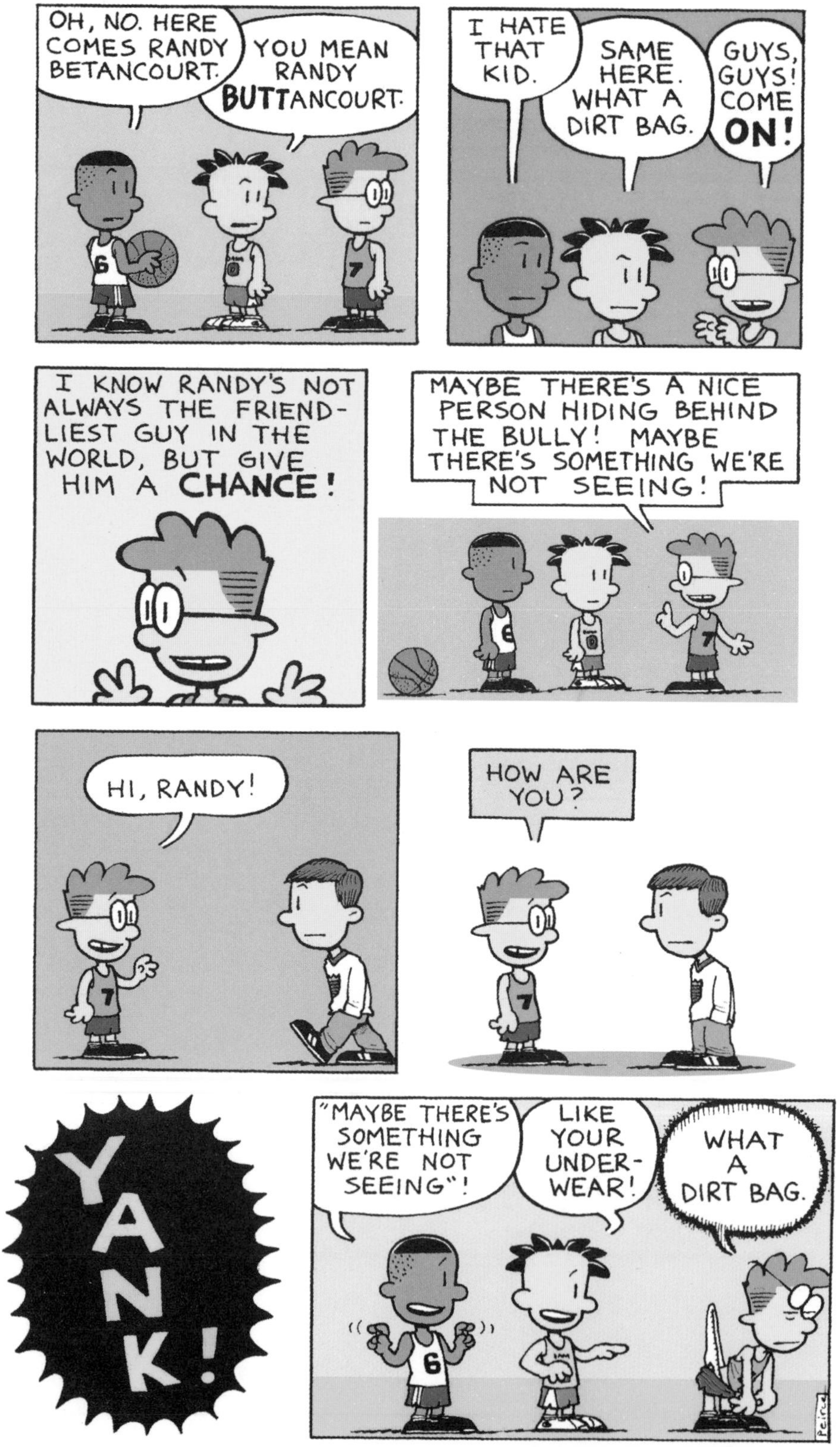
OH, NO. HERE COMES RANDY BETANCOURT.
YOU MEAN RANDY BUTTANCOURT.
I HATE THAT KID.
SAME HERE. WHAT A DIRT BAG.
GUYS, GUYS! COME ON!
I KNOW RANDY'S NOT ALWAYS THE FRIEND-LIEST GUY IN THE WORLD, BUT GIVE HIM A CHANCE!
MAYBE THERE'S A NICE PERSON HIDING BEHIND THE BULLY! MAYBE THERE'S SOMETHING WE'RE NOT SEEING!
HI, RANDY!
HOW ARE YOU?
YANK!
"MAYBE THERE'S SOMETHING WE'RE NOT SEEING"!
LIKE YOUR UNDER-WEAR!
WHAT A DIRT BAG.
Peirce

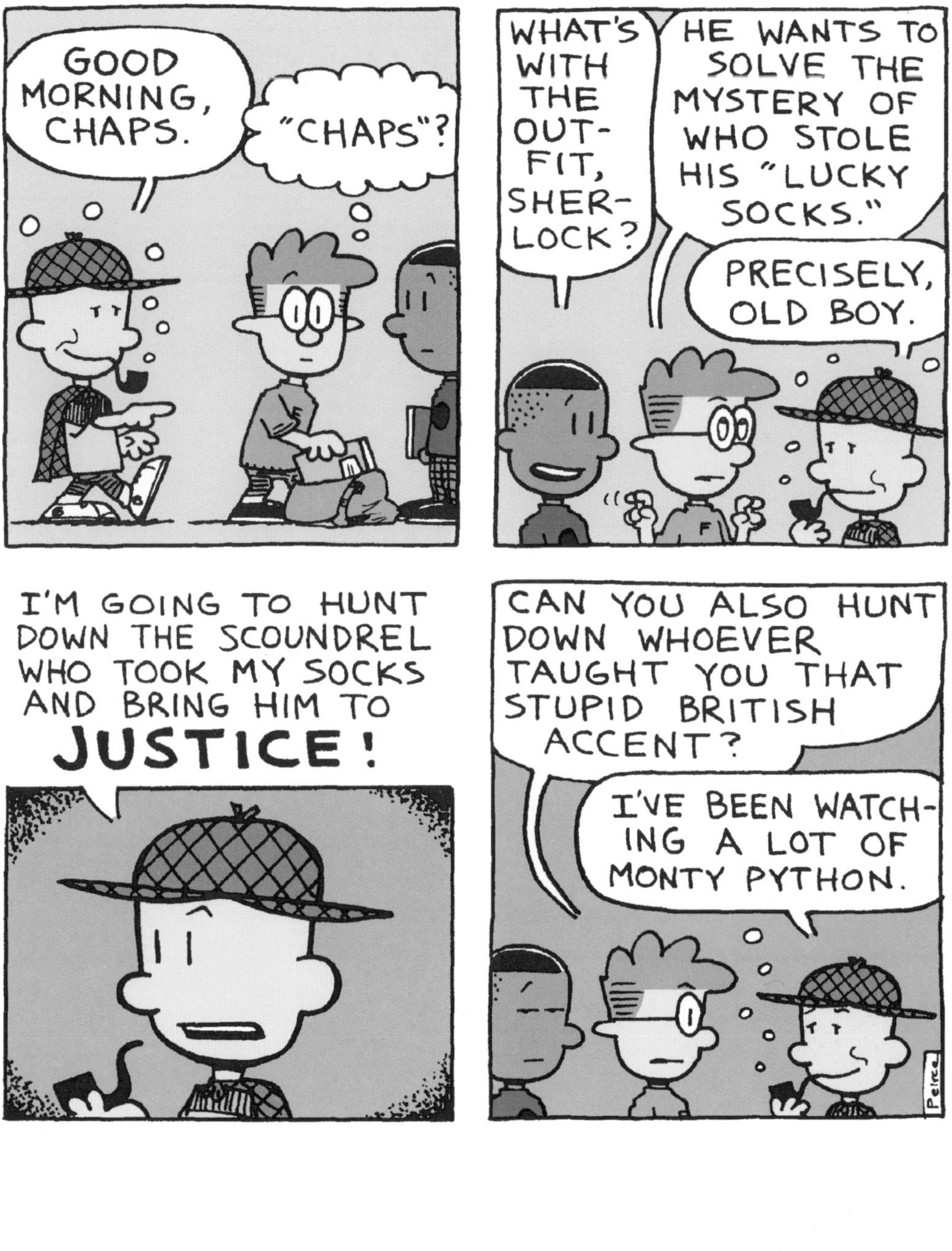
GOOD MORNING, CHAPS.
"CHAPS"?
WHAT'S WITH THE OUT-FIT, SHER-LOCK?
HE WANTS TO SOLVE THE MYSTERY OF WHO STOLE HIS "LUCKY SOCKS."
PRECISELY, OLD BOY.
I'M GOING TO HUNT DOWN THE SCOUNDREL WHO TOOK MY SOCKS AND BRING HIM TO JUSTICE!
CAN YOU ALSO HUNT DOWN WHOEVER TAUGHT YOU THAT STUPID BRITISH ACCENT?
I'VE BEEN WATCH-ING A LOT OF MONTY PYTHON.
Peirce

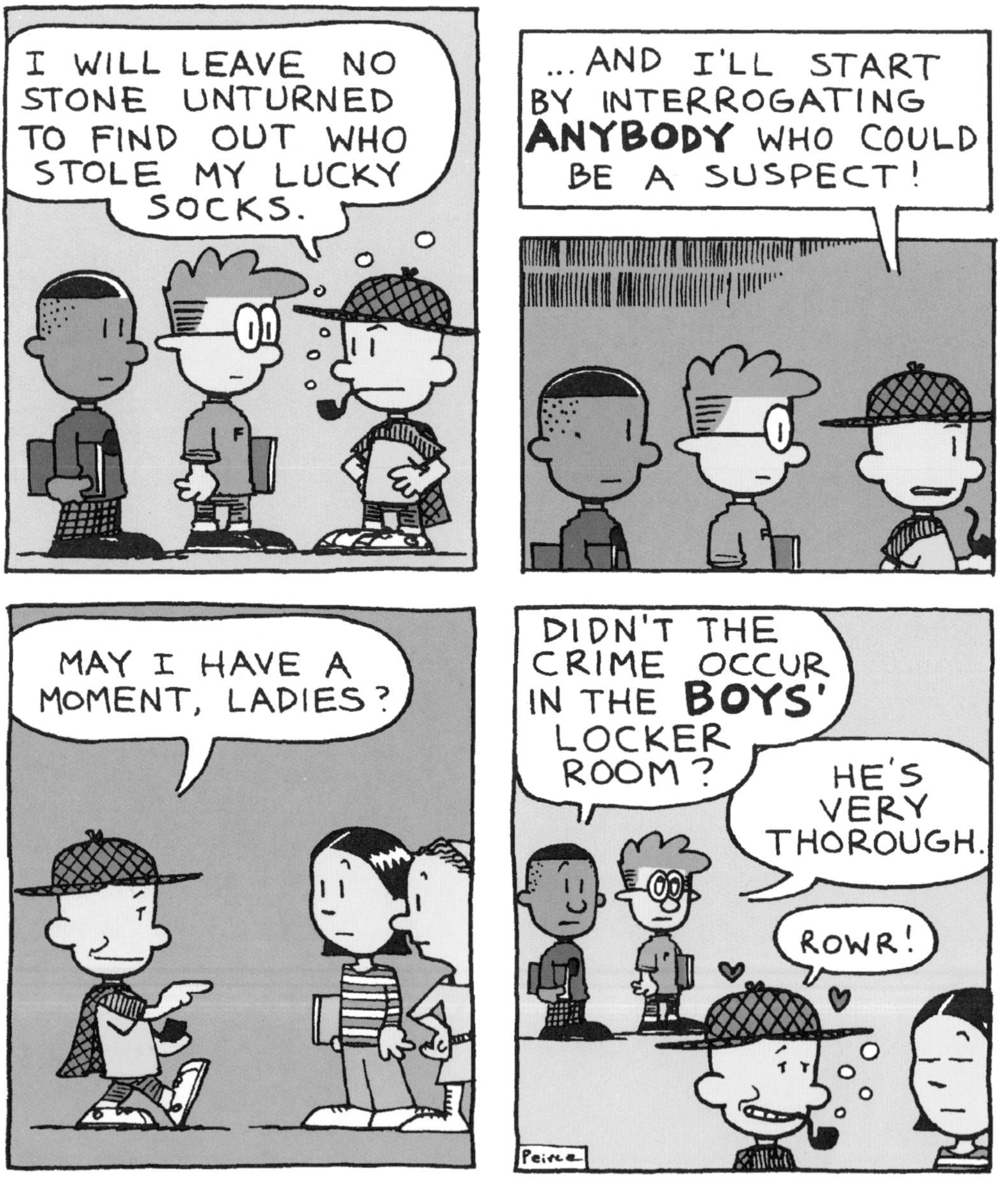
I WILL LEAVE NO STONE UNTURNED TO FIND OUT WHO STOLE MY LUCKY SOCKS.
...AND I'LL START BY INTERROGATING **ANYBODY** WHO COULD BE A SUSPECT!
MAY I HAVE A MOMENT, LADIES?
DIDN'T THE CRIME OCCUR IN THE **BOYS'** LOCKER ROOM?
HE'S VERY THOROUGH.
ROWR!
Peirce

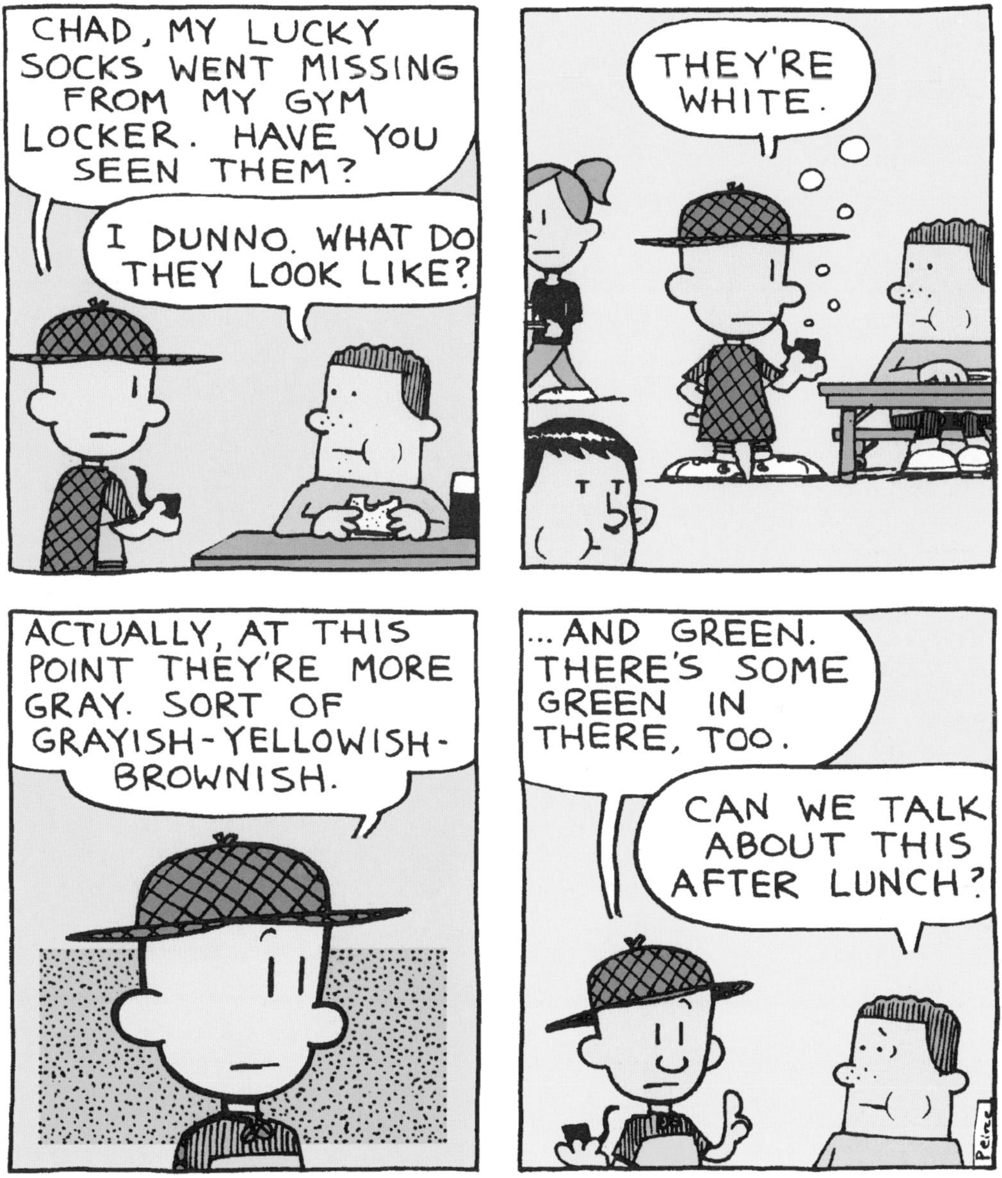
CHAD, MY LUCKY SOCKS WENT MISSING FROM MY GYM LOCKER. HAVE YOU SEEN THEM?
I DUNNO. WHAT DO THEY LOOK LIKE?
THEY'RE WHITE.
ACTUALLY, AT THIS POINT THEY'RE MORE GRAY. SORT OF GRAYISH-YELLOWISH-BROWNISH.
...AND GREEN. THERE'S SOME GREEN IN THERE, TOO.
CAN WE TALK ABOUT THIS AFTER LUNCH?
Peirce

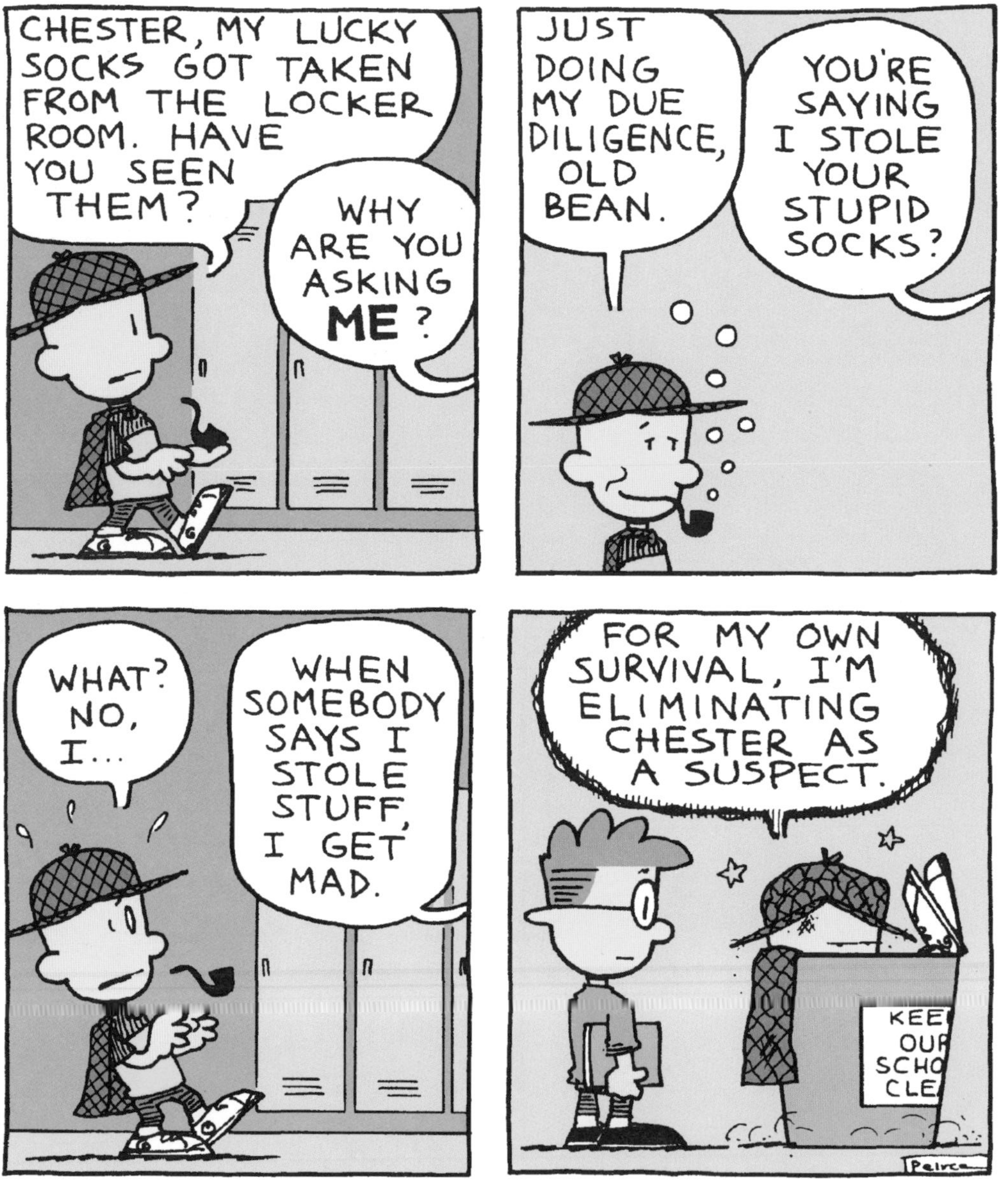
CHESTER, MY LUCKY SOCKS GOT TAKEN FROM THE LOCKER ROOM. HAVE YOU SEEN THEM?
WHY ARE YOU ASKING **ME**?
JUST DOING MY DUE DILIGENCE, OLD BEAN.
YOU'RE SAYING I STOLE YOUR STUPID SOCKS?
WHAT? NO, I...
WHEN SOMEBODY SAYS I STOLE STUFF, I GET MAD.
FOR MY OWN SURVIVAL, I'M ELIMINATING CHESTER AS A SUSPECT.
KEE
OUR
SCHO
CLE
Peirce

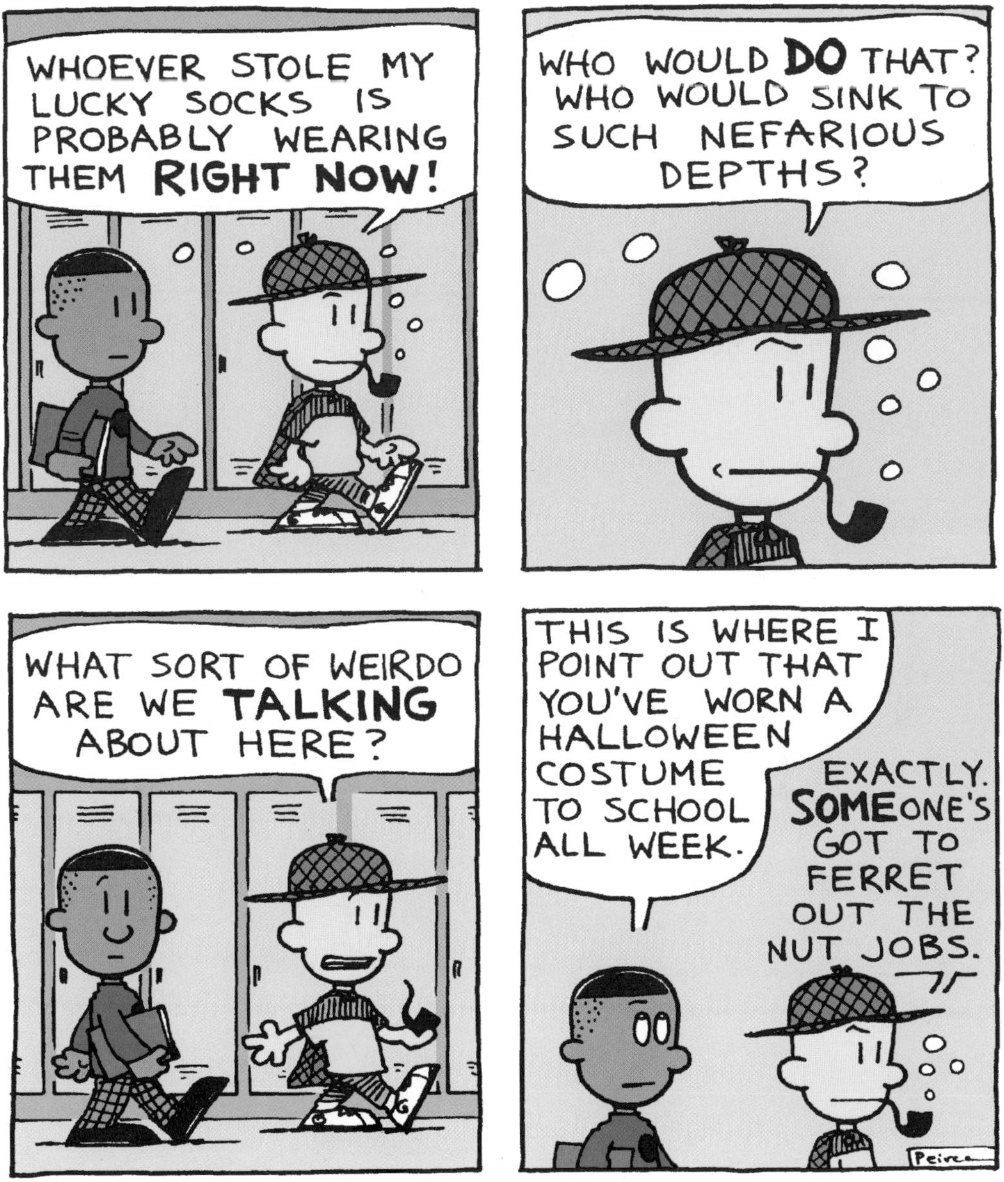
WHOEVER STOLE MY LUCKY SOCKS IS PROBABLY WEARING THEM RIGHT NOW!
WHO WOULD DO THAT? WHO WOULD SINK TO SUCH NEFARIOUS DEPTHS?
WHAT SORT OF WEIRDO ARE WE TALKING ABOUT HERE?
THIS IS WHERE I POINT OUT THAT YOU'VE WORN A HALLOWEEN COSTUME TO SCHOOL ALL WEEK.
EXACTLY. SOMEONE'S GOT TO FERRET OUT THE NUT JOBS.
Peirce

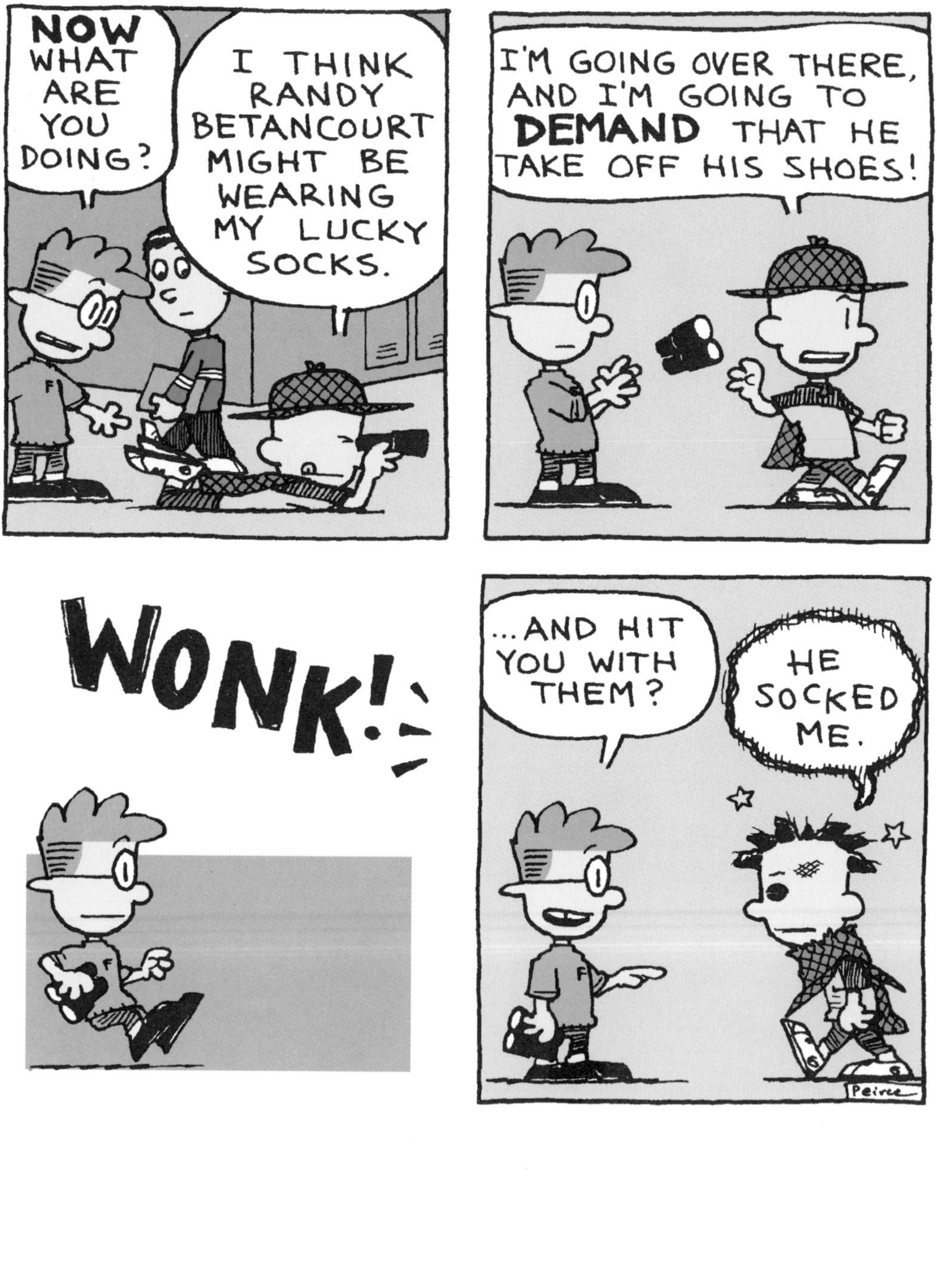
NOW WHAT ARE YOU DOING?
I THINK RANDY BETANCOURT MIGHT BE WEARING MY LUCKY SOCKS.
I'M GOING OVER THERE, AND I'M GOING TO **DEMAND** THAT HE TAKE OFF HIS SHOES!
WONK!
...AND HIT YOU WITH THEM?
HE SOCKED ME.
Peirce

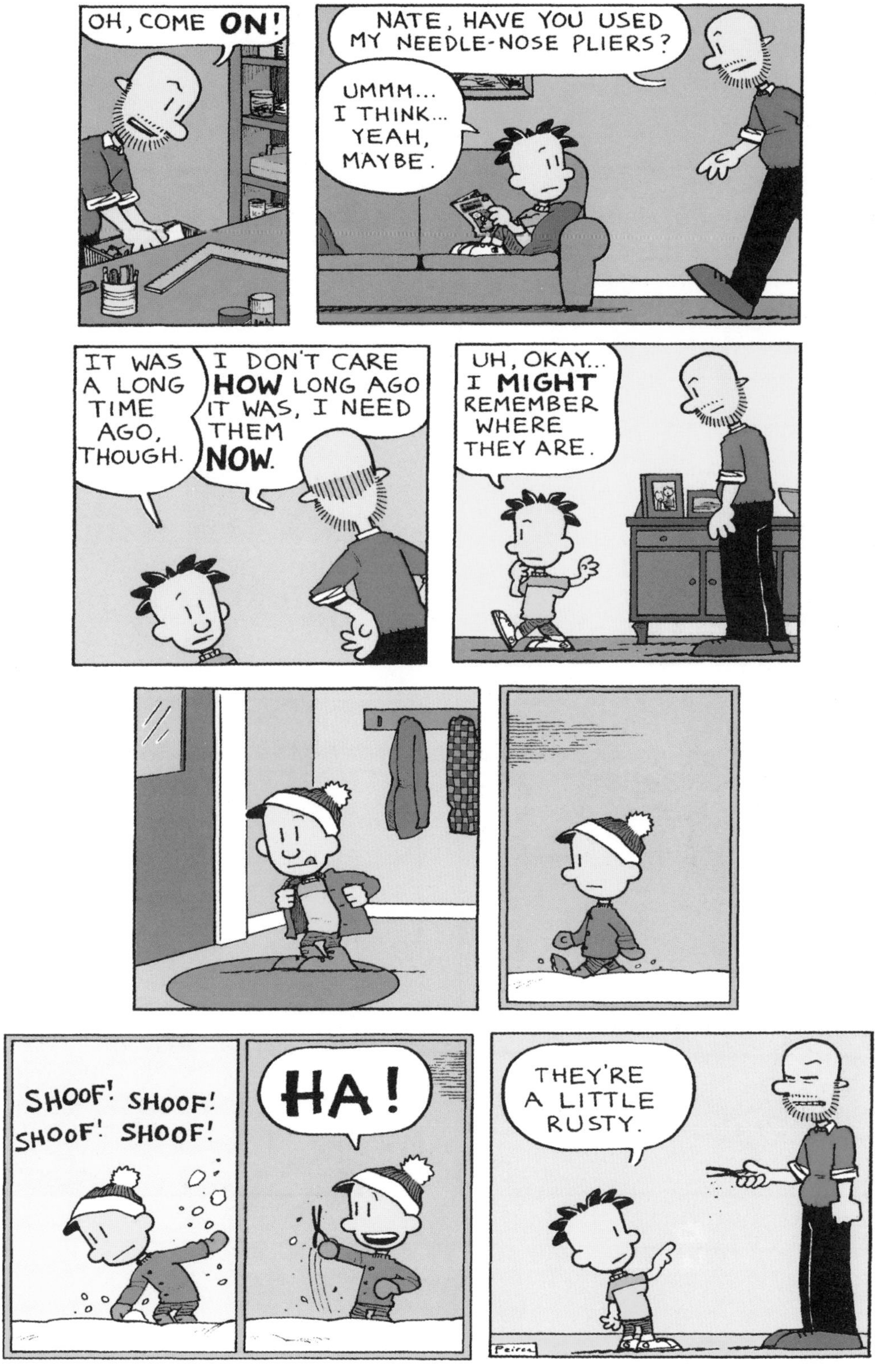
OH, COME ON!
NATE, HAVE YOU USED MY NEEDLE-NOSE PLIERS?
UMMM... I THINK... YEAH, MAYBE.
IT WAS A LONG TIME AGO, THOUGH.
I DON'T CARE HOW LONG AGO IT WAS, I NEED THEM NOW.
UH, OKAY... I MIGHT REMEMBER WHERE THEY ARE.
SHOOF! SHOOF! SHOOF! SHOOF!
HA!
THEY'RE A LITTLE RUSTY.
Peirce

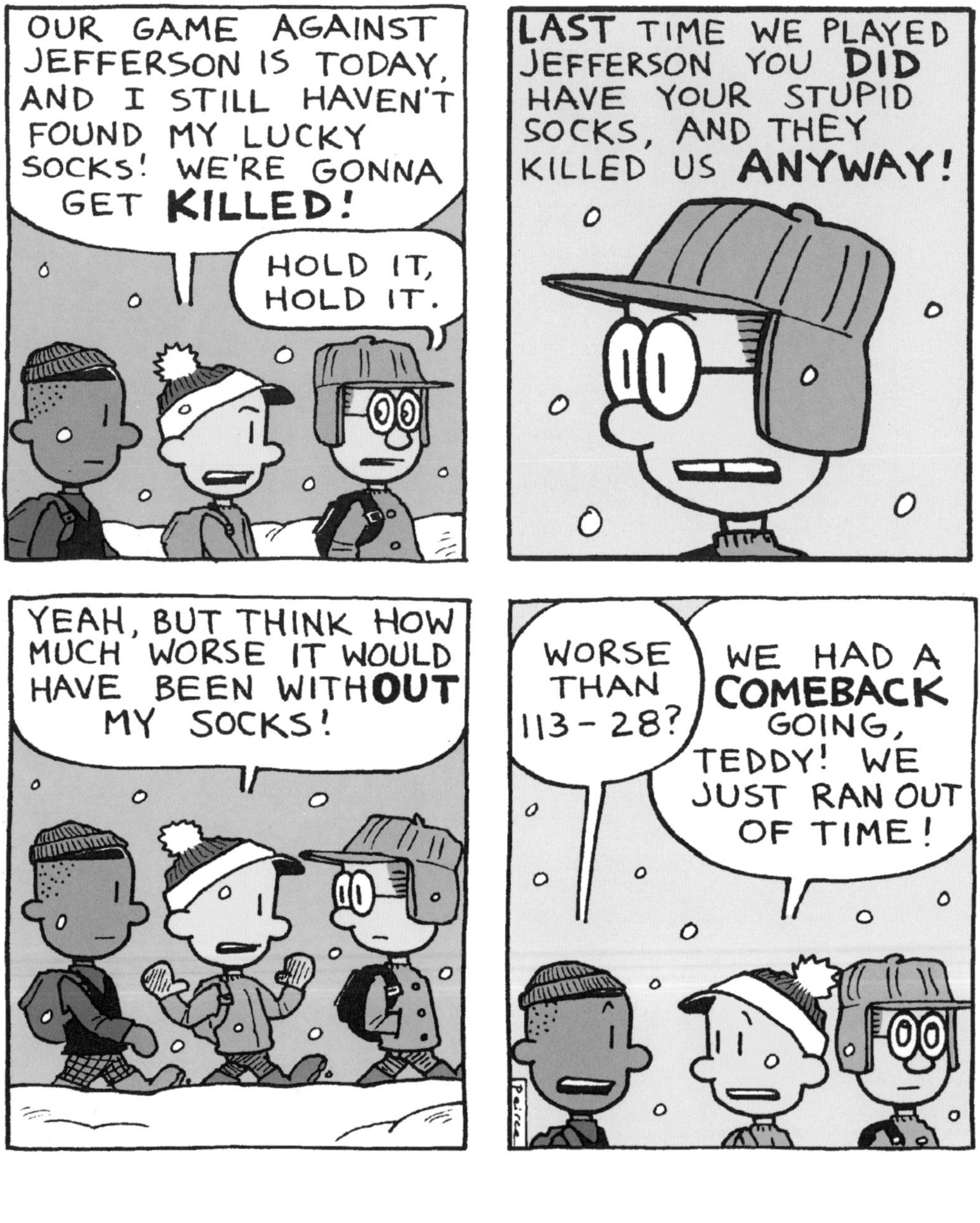
OUR GAME AGAINST JEFFERSON IS TODAY, AND I STILL HAVEN'T FOUND MY LUCKY SOCKS! WE'RE GONNA GET **KILLED!**
HOLD IT, HOLD IT.
LAST TIME WE PLAYED JEFFERSON YOU **DID** HAVE YOUR STUPID SOCKS, AND THEY KILLED US **ANYWAY!**
YEAH, BUT THINK HOW MUCH WORSE IT WOULD HAVE BEEN WITH**OUT** MY SOCKS!
WORSE THAN 113-28?
WE HAD A **COMEBACK** GOING, TEDDY! WE JUST RAN OUT OF TIME!

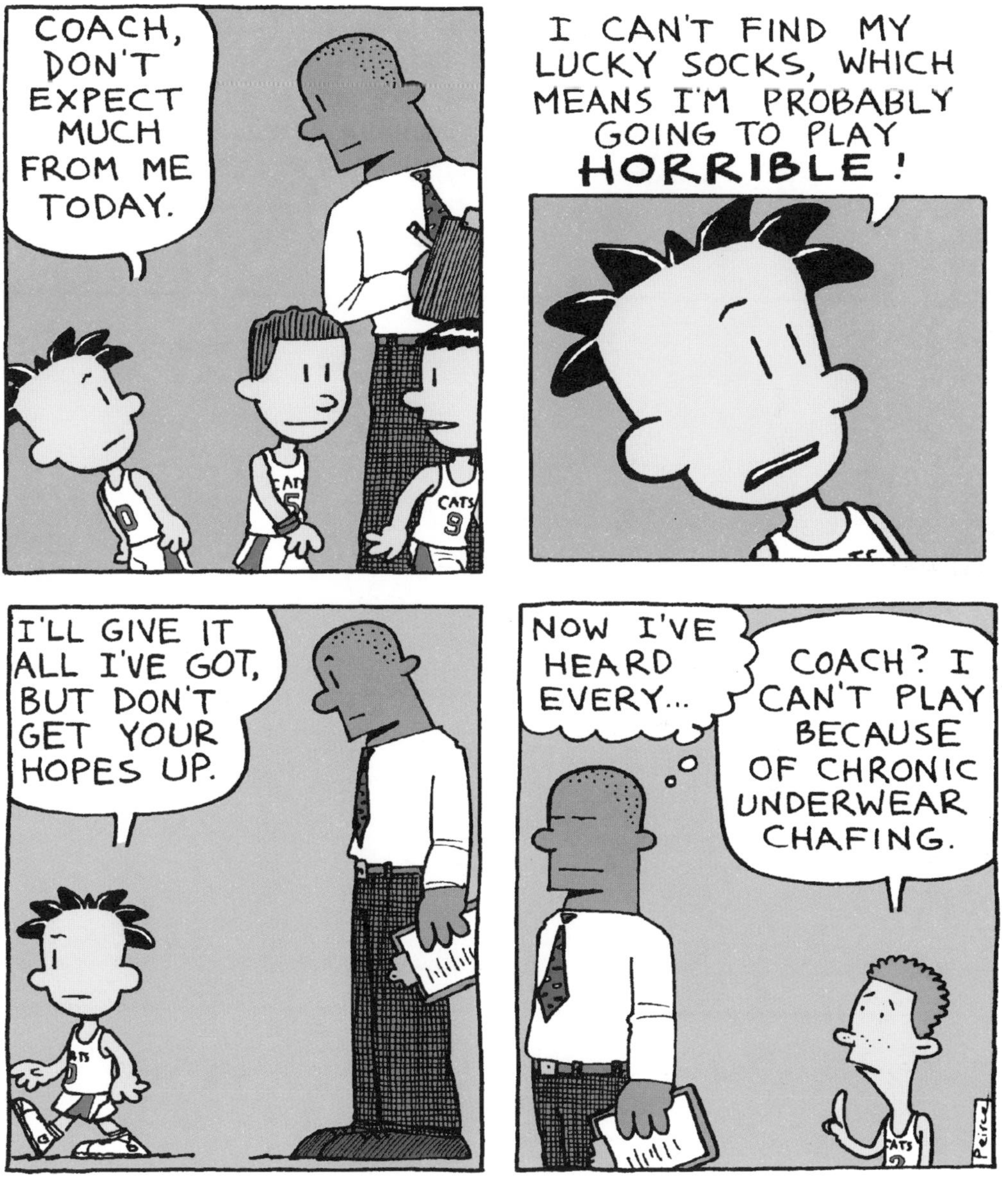
COACH, DON'T EXPECT MUCH FROM ME TODAY.
I CAN'T FIND MY LUCKY SOCKS, WHICH MEANS I'M PROBABLY GOING TO PLAY **HORRIBLE**!
I'LL GIVE IT ALL I'VE GOT, BUT DON'T GET YOUR HOPES UP.
NOW I'VE HEARD EVERY...
COACH? I CAN'T PLAY BECAUSE OF CHRONIC UNDERWEAR CHAFING.
Peirce

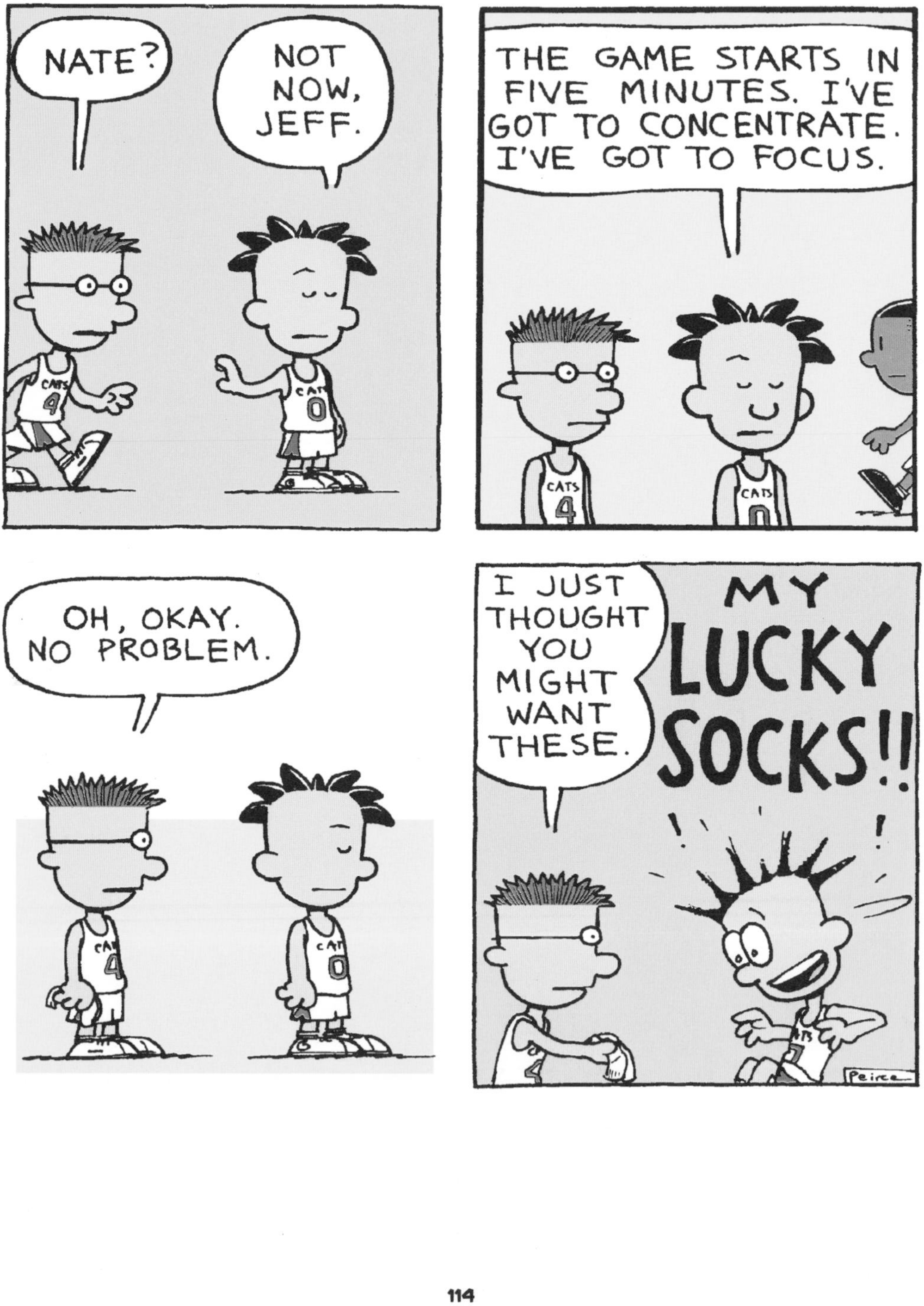
NATE?
NOT NOW, JEFF.
THE GAME STARTS IN FIVE MINUTES. I'VE GOT TO CONCENTRATE. I'VE GOT TO FOCUS.
CATS
4
CATS
OH, OKAY. NO PROBLEM.
I JUST THOUGHT YOU MIGHT WANT THESE.
MY LUCKY SOCKS!!
Peirce

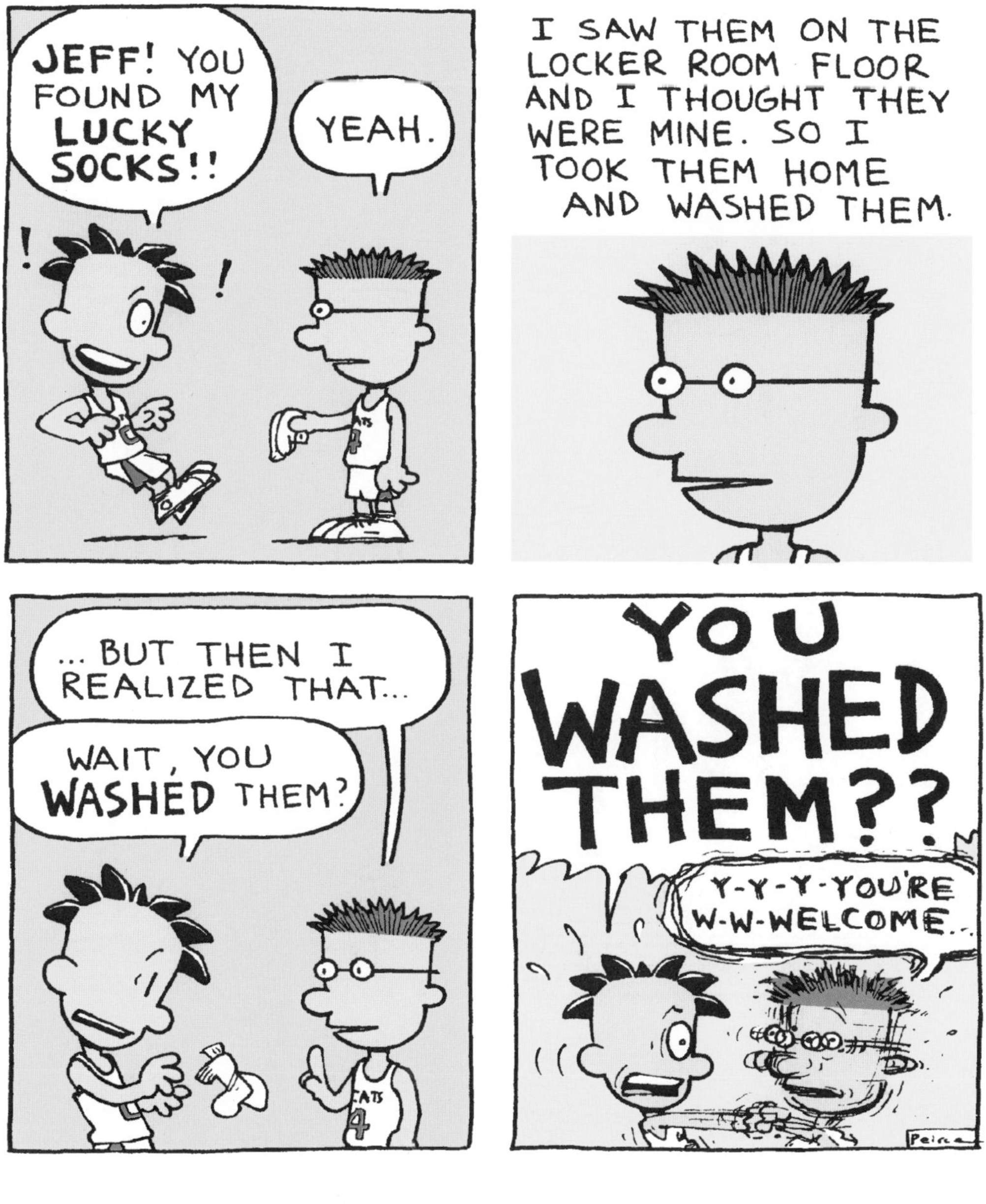
JEFF! YOU FOUND MY LUCKY SOCKS!!
YEAH.
I SAW THEM ON THE LOCKER ROOM FLOOR AND I THOUGHT THEY WERE MINE. SO I TOOK THEM HOME AND WASHED THEM.
... BUT THEN I REALIZED THAT...
WAIT, YOU WASHED THEM?
YOU WASHED THEM??
Y-Y-Y-YOU'RE W-W-WELCOME...
Peirce

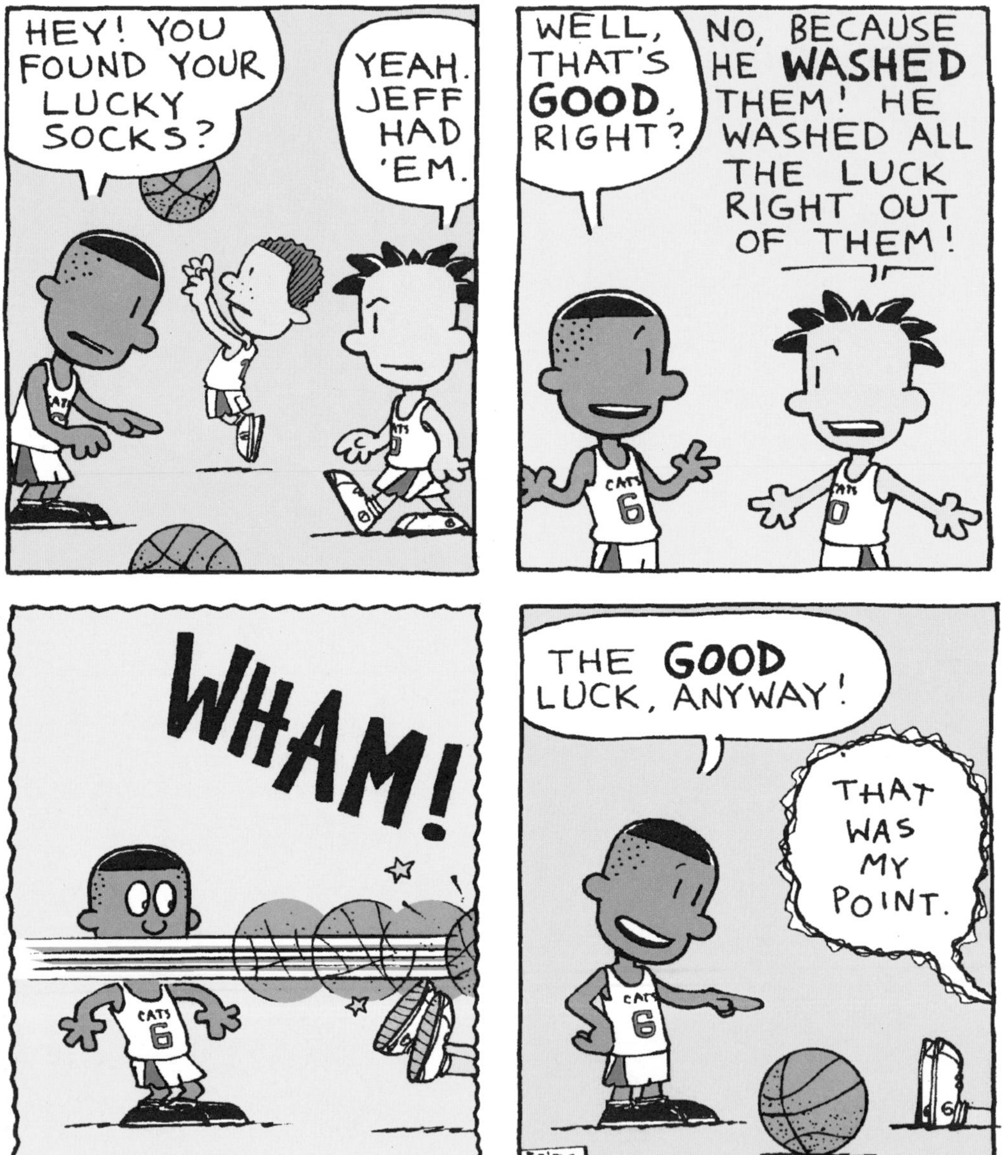
HEY! YOU FOUND YOUR LUCKY SOCKS?
YEAH. JEFF HAD 'EM.
WELL, THAT'S **GOOD**, RIGHT?
NO, BECAUSE HE **WASHED** THEM! HE WASHED ALL THE LUCK RIGHT OUT OF THEM!
WHAM!
THE **GOOD** LUCK, ANYWAY!
THAT WAS MY POINT.
Peirce

TOUGH GAME, SPORT.
YES, THANKS TO JEFF.
JEFF? BUT HE BARELY PLAYED!
HE WASHED MY SOCKS, DAD! HE WASHED ALL THE GOOD LUCK OUT OF 'EM!
NOW WE'VE GOT TO GO TO THE ENORMOUS EXPENSE OF RE-LUCKIFYING THEM!
BOBCATS
SON, "ENORMOUS EXPENSE" AND "SOCKS" DON'T GO TOGETHER.
LOOK, WE'LL START SLOW. WE'LL GO OUT FOR ICE CREAM.
Peirce

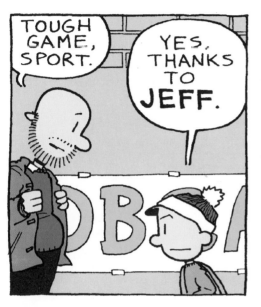

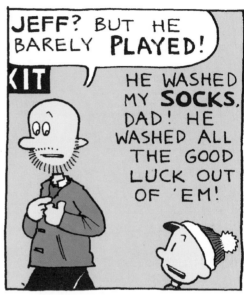

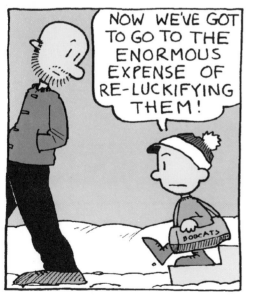

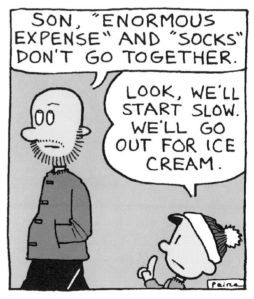

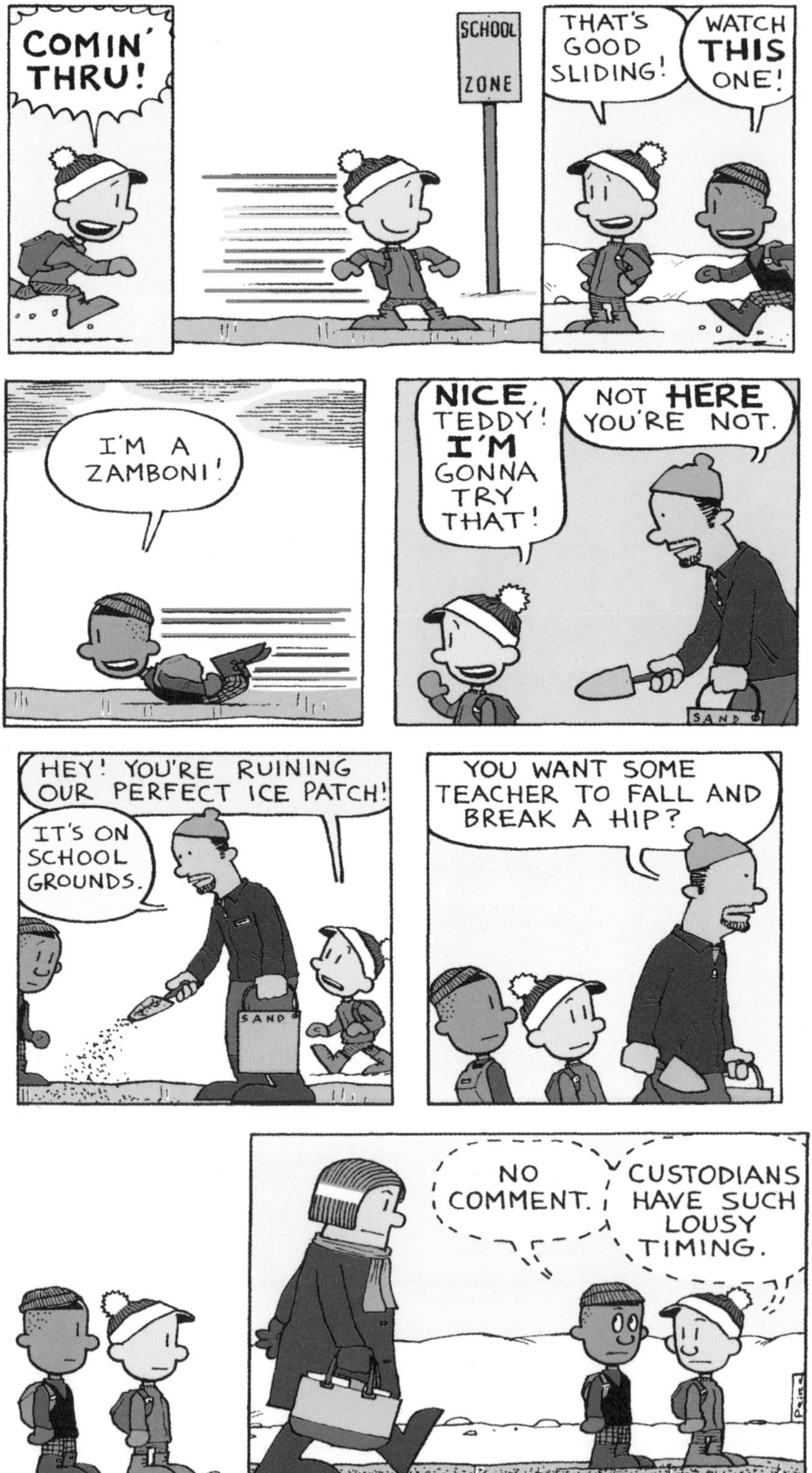
COMIN' THRU!
SCHOOL ZONE
THAT'S GOOD SLIDING!
WATCH THIS ONE!
I'M A ZAMBONI!
NICE, TEDDY! I'M GONNA TRY THAT!
NOT HERE YOU'RE NOT.
SAND
HEY! YOU'RE RUINING OUR PERFECT ICE PATCH!
IT'S ON SCHOOL GROUNDS.
SAND
YOU WANT SOME TEACHER TO FALL AND BREAK A HIP?
NO COMMENT.
CUSTODIANS HAVE SUCH LOUSY TIMING.

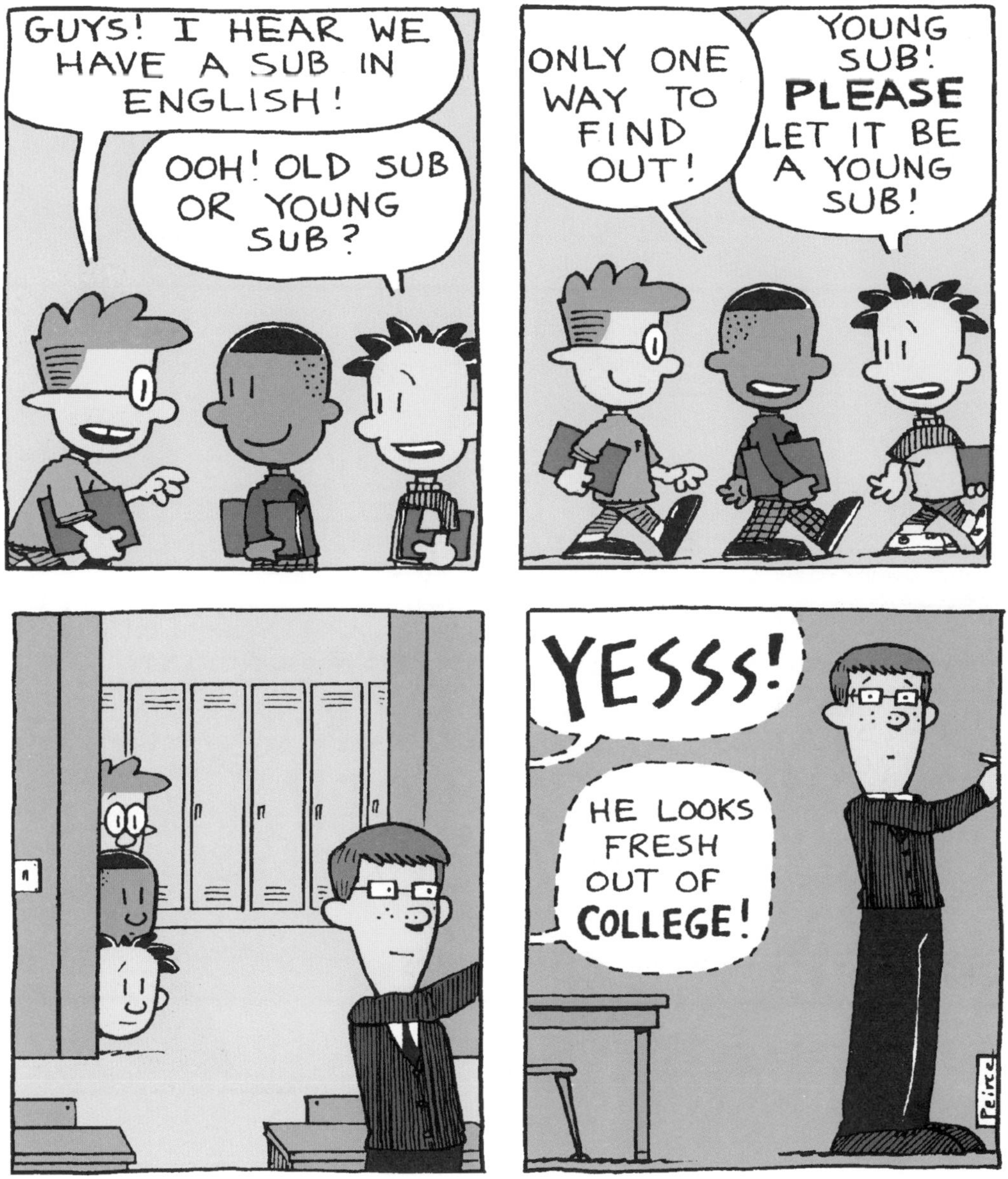
GUYS! I HEAR WE HAVE A SUB IN ENGLISH!
OOH! OLD SUB OR YOUNG SUB?
ONLY ONE WAY TO FIND OUT!
YOUNG SUB! **PLEASE** LET IT BE A YOUNG SUB!
YESSS!
HE LOOKS FRESH OUT OF **COLLEGE**!
Peirce

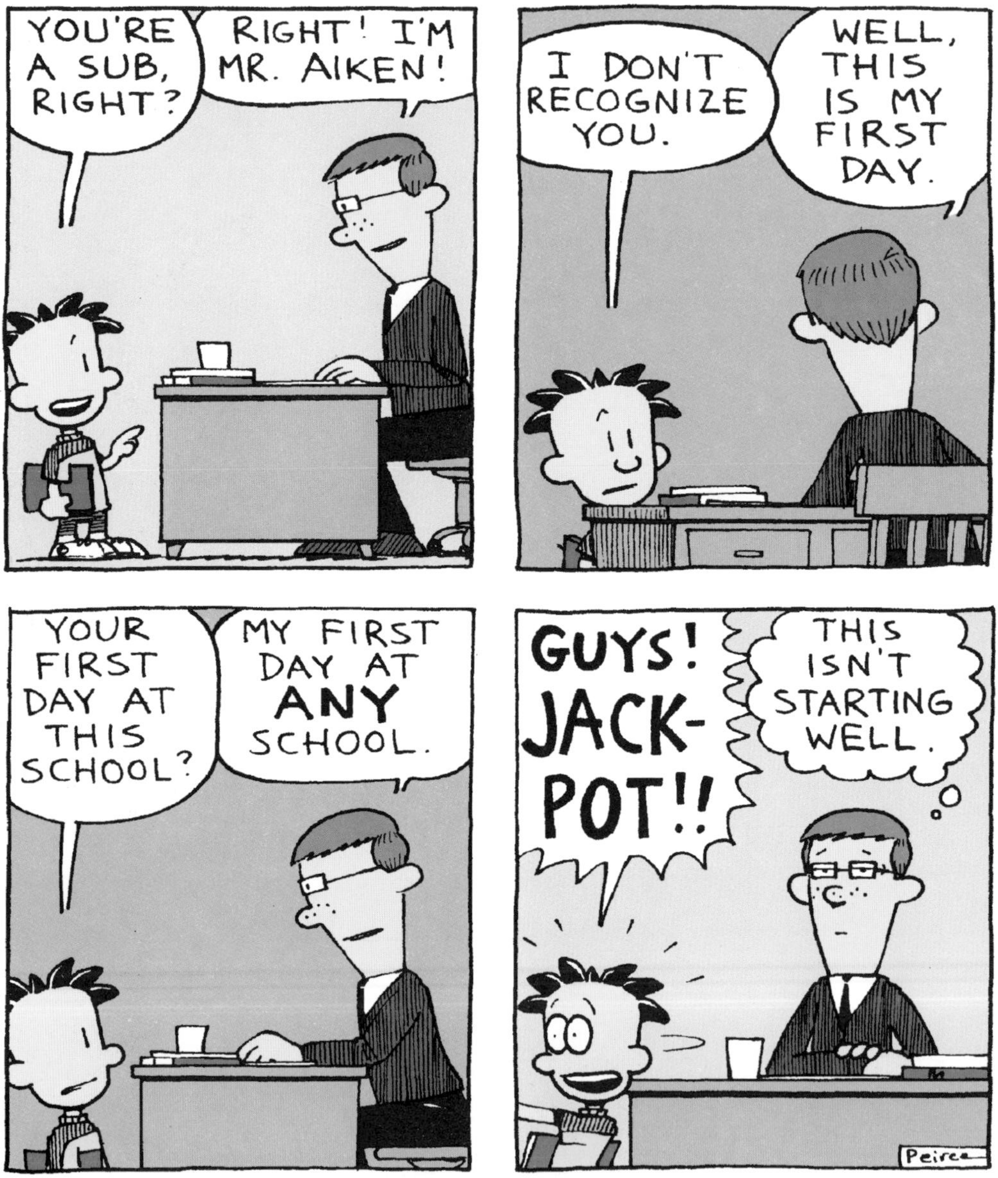
YOU'RE A SUB, RIGHT?
RIGHT! I'M MR. AIKEN!
I DON'T RECOGNIZE YOU.
WELL, THIS IS MY FIRST DAY.
YOUR FIRST DAY AT THIS SCHOOL?
MY FIRST DAY AT **ANY** SCHOOL.
GUYS! JACK-POT!!
THIS ISN'T STARTING WELL.
Peirce

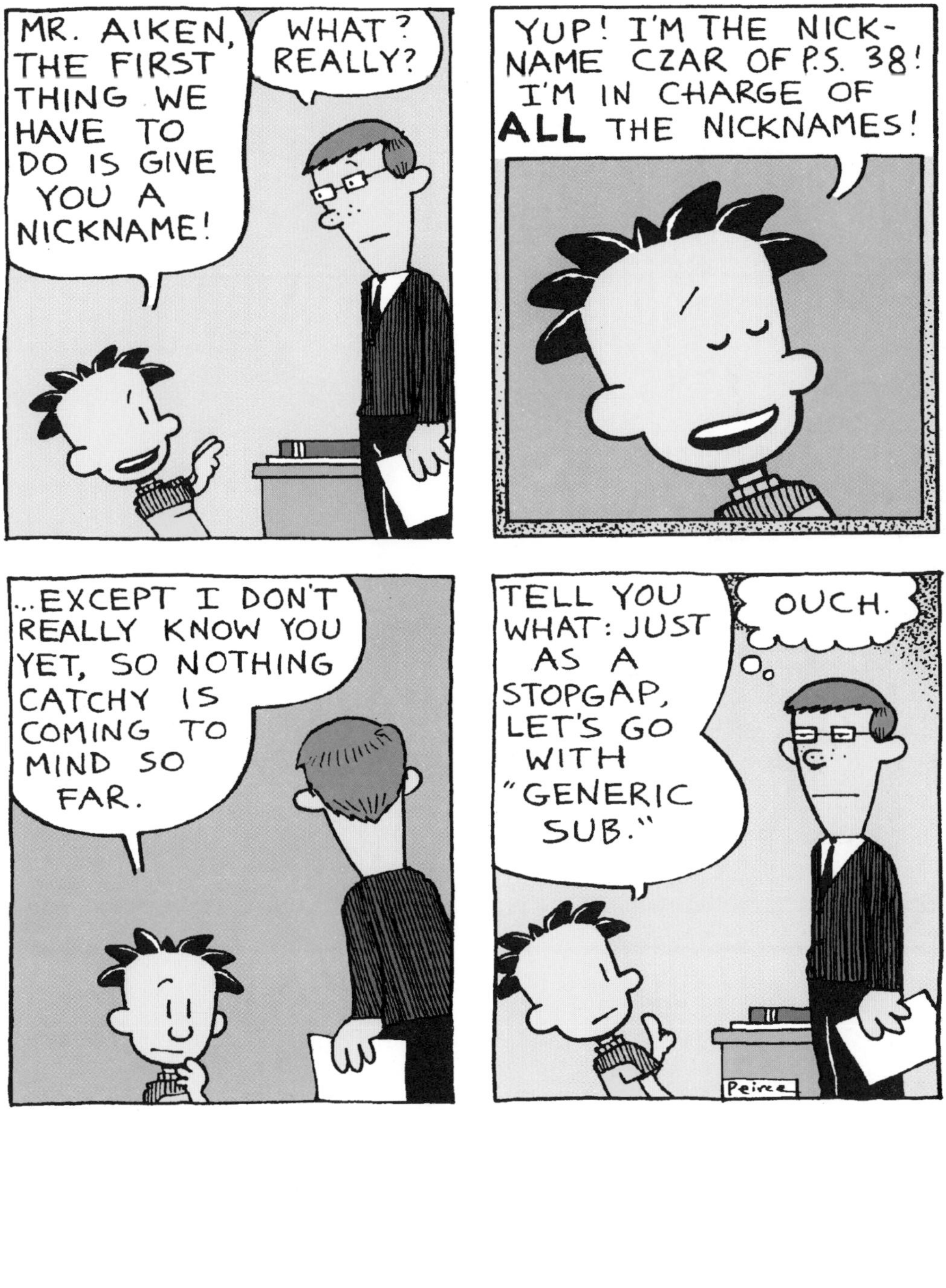
MR. AIKEN, THE FIRST THING WE HAVE TO DO IS GIVE YOU A NICKNAME!
WHAT? REALLY?
YUP! I'M THE NICK-NAME CZAR OF P.S. 38! I'M IN CHARGE OF **ALL** THE NICKNAMES!
...EXCEPT I DON'T REALLY KNOW YOU YET, SO NOTHING CATCHY IS COMING TO MIND SO FAR.
TELL YOU WHAT: JUST AS A STOPGAP, LET'S GO WITH "GENERIC SUB."
OUCH.
Peirce

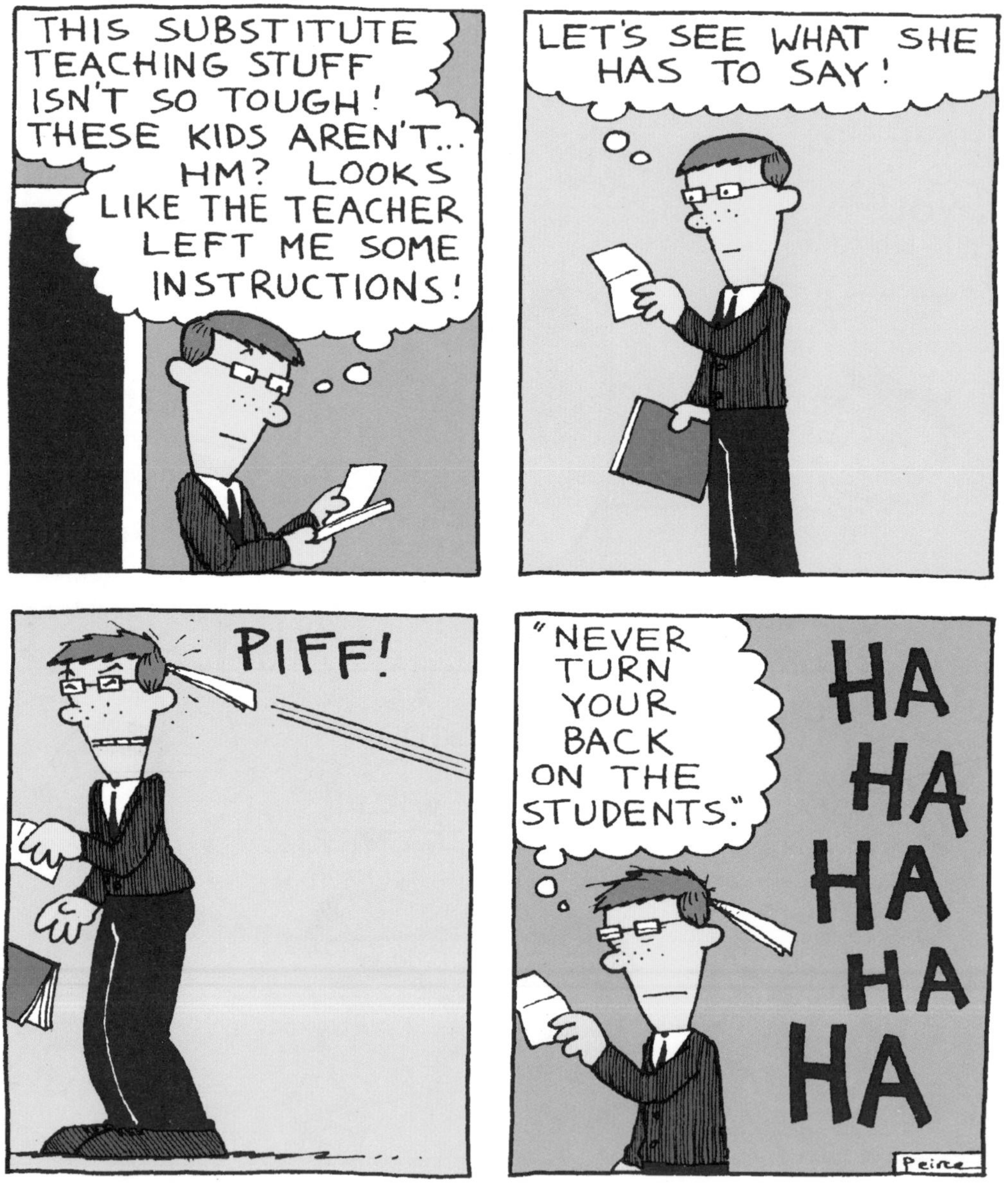
THIS SUBSTITUTE TEACHING STUFF ISN'T SO TOUGH! THESE KIDS AREN'T... HM? LOOKS LIKE THE TEACHER LEFT ME SOME INSTRUCTIONS!
LET'S SEE WHAT SHE HAS TO SAY!
PIFF!
"NEVER TURN YOUR BACK ON THE STUDENTS."
HA HA HA HA HA
Peirce

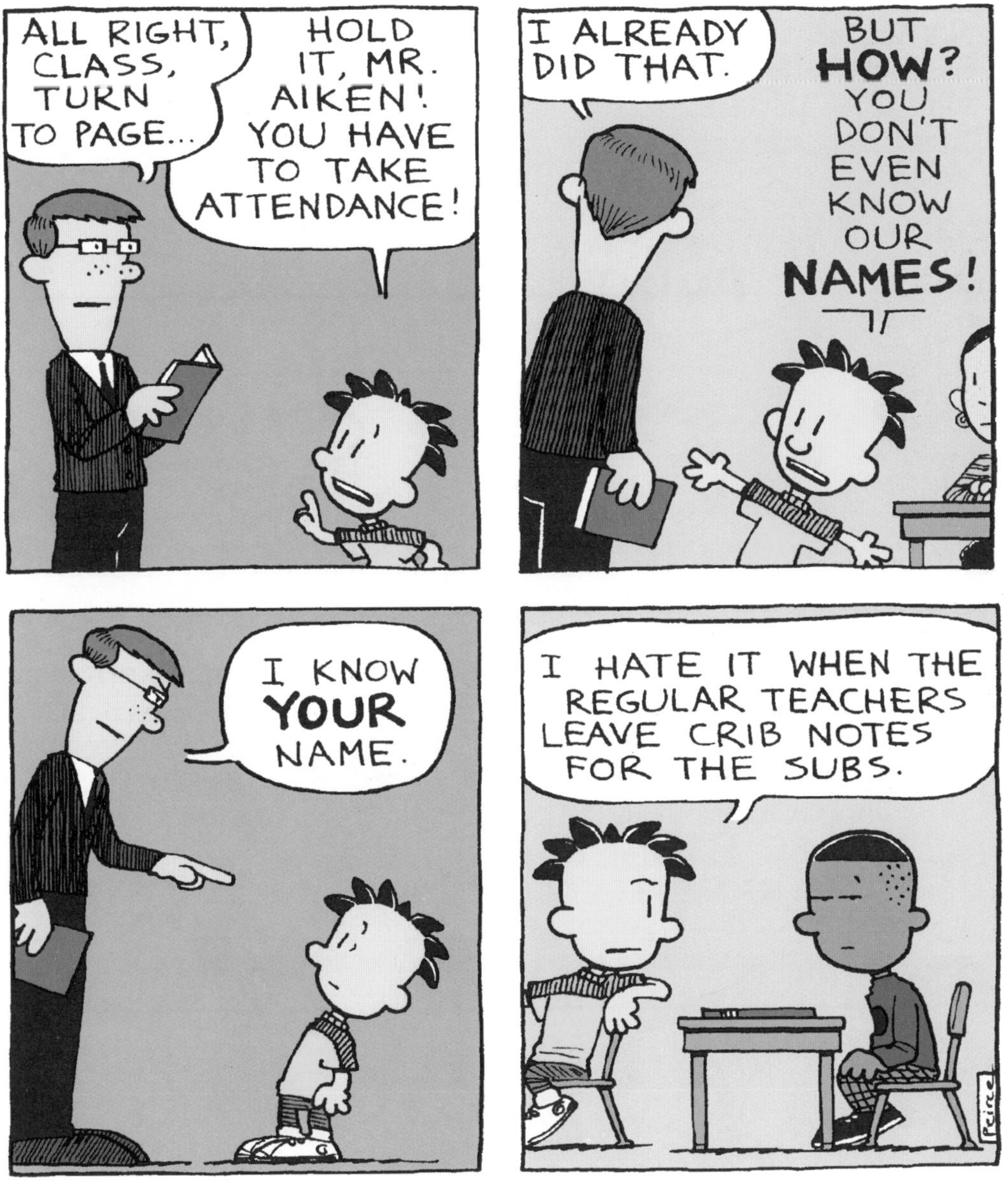
ALL RIGHT, CLASS, TURN TO PAGE...
HOLD IT, MR. AIKEN! YOU HAVE TO TAKE ATTENDANCE!
I ALREADY DID THAT.
BUT **HOW**? YOU DON'T EVEN KNOW OUR **NAMES**!
I KNOW **YOUR** NAME.
I HATE IT WHEN THE REGULAR TEACHERS LEAVE CRIB NOTES FOR THE SUBS.
Peirce

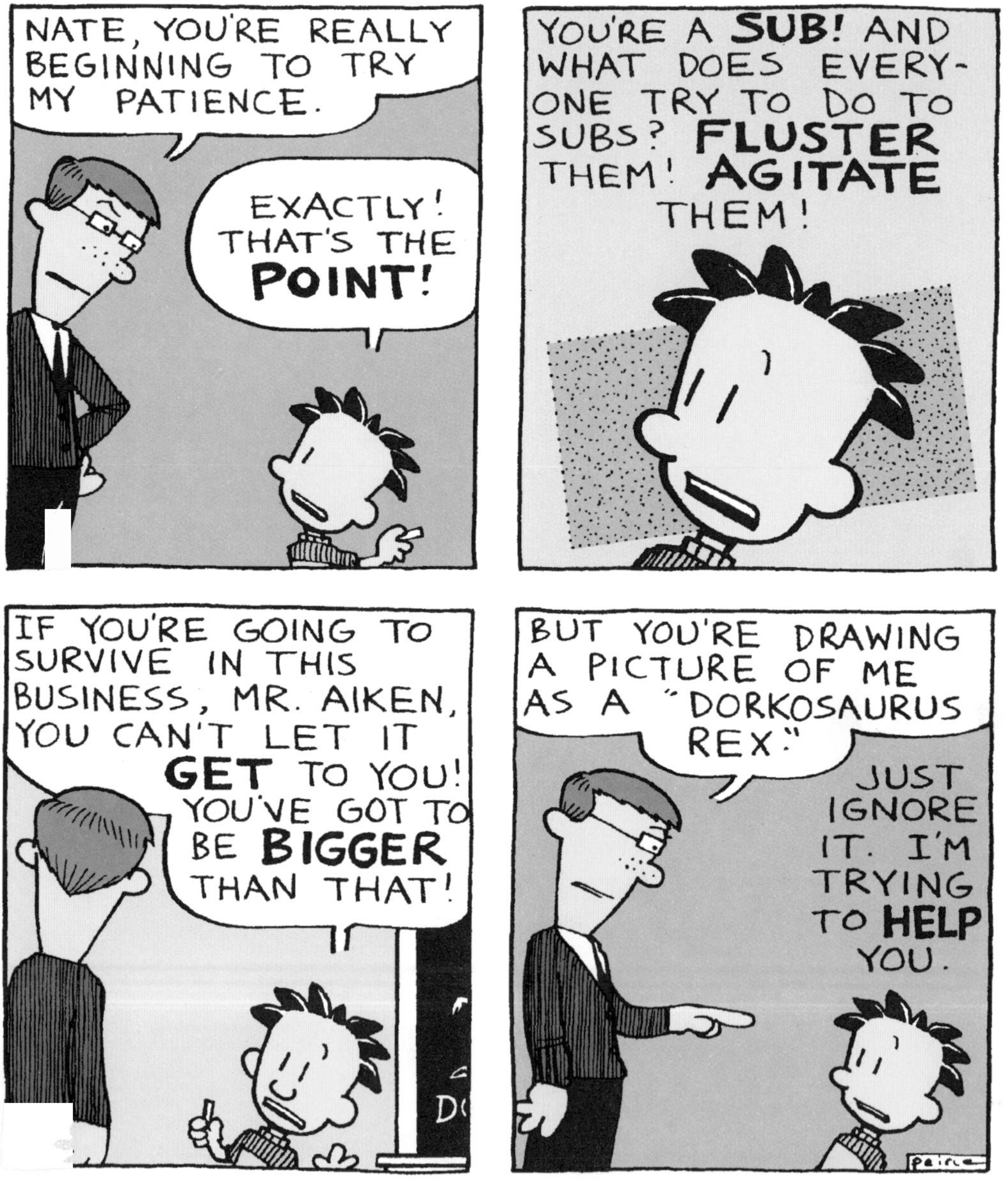

NATE, YOU'RE REALLY BEGINNING TO TRY MY PATIENCE.
EXACTLY! THAT'S THE **POINT**!
YOU'RE A **SUB**! AND WHAT DOES EVERYONE TRY TO DO TO SUBS? **FLUSTER** THEM! **AGITATE** THEM!
IF YOU'RE GOING TO SURVIVE IN THIS BUSINESS, MR. AIKEN, YOU CAN'T LET IT **GET** TO YOU! YOU'VE GOT TO BE **BIGGER** THAN THAT!
BUT YOU'RE DRAWING A PICTURE OF ME AS A "DORKOSAURUS REX."
JUST IGNORE IT. I'M TRYING TO **HELP** YOU.

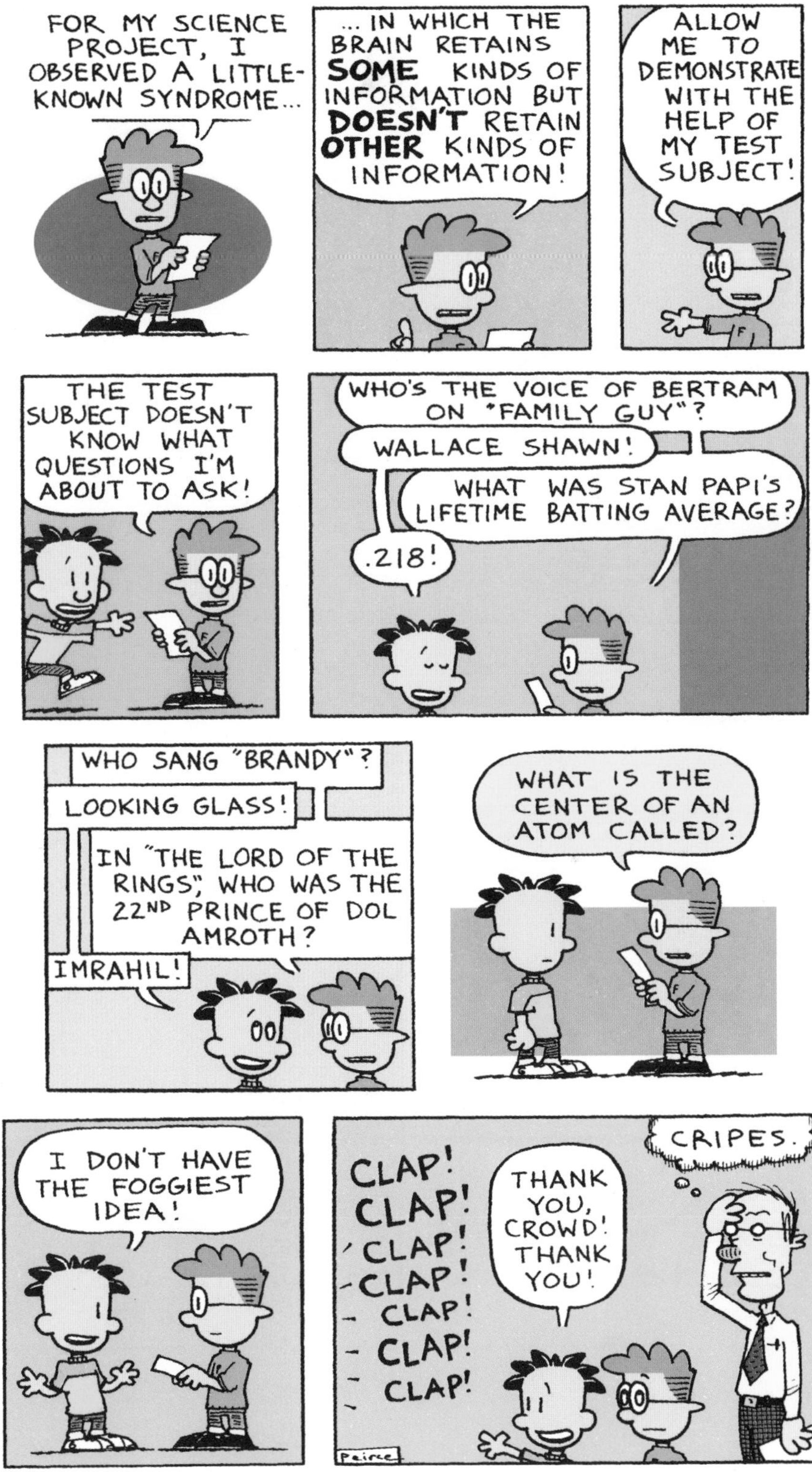
FOR MY SCIENCE PROJECT, I OBSERVED A LITTLE-KNOWN SYNDROME...
... IN WHICH THE BRAIN RETAINS SOME KINDS OF INFORMATION BUT DOESN'T RETAIN OTHER KINDS OF INFORMATION!
ALLOW ME TO DEMONSTRATE WITH THE HELP OF MY TEST SUBJECT!
THE TEST SUBJECT DOESN'T KNOW WHAT QUESTIONS I'M ABOUT TO ASK!
WHO'S THE VOICE OF BERTRAM ON "FAMILY GUY"?
WALLACE SHAWN!
WHAT WAS STAN PAPI'S LIFETIME BATTING AVERAGE?
.218!
WHO SANG "BRANDY"?
LOOKING GLASS!
IN "THE LORD OF THE RINGS," WHO WAS THE 22ND PRINCE OF DOL AMROTH?
IMRAHIL!
WHAT IS THE CENTER OF AN ATOM CALLED?
I DON'T HAVE THE FOGGIEST IDEA!
CLAP! CLAP! CLAP! CLAP! CLAP! CLAP! CLAP!
THANK YOU, CROWD! THANK YOU!
CRIPES.
Peirce

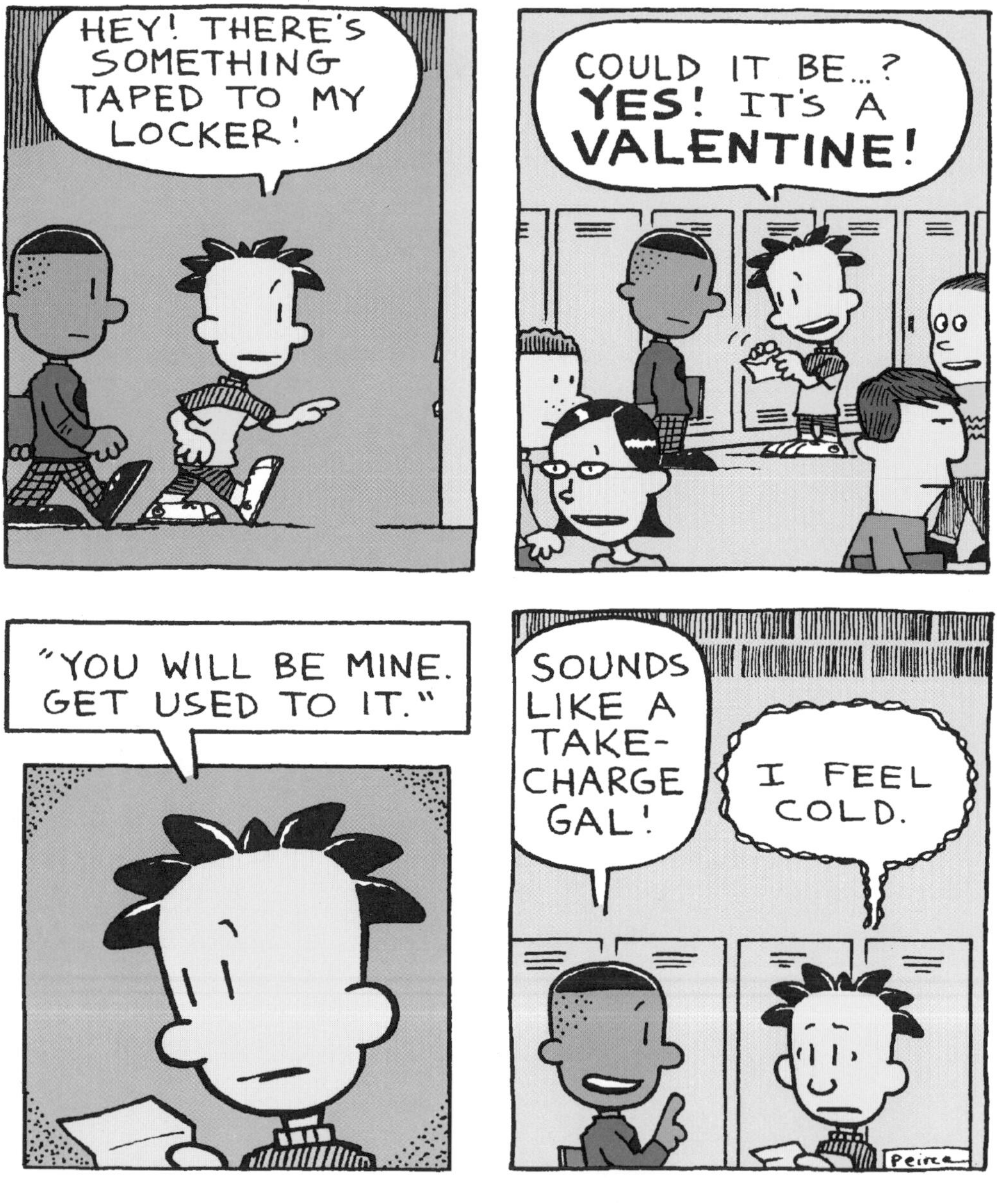
HEY! THERE'S SOMETHING TAPED TO MY LOCKER!
COULD IT BE...? YES! IT'S A VALENTINE!
"YOU WILL BE MINE. GET USED TO IT."
SOUNDS LIKE A TAKE-CHARGE GAL!
I FEEL COLD.
Peirce

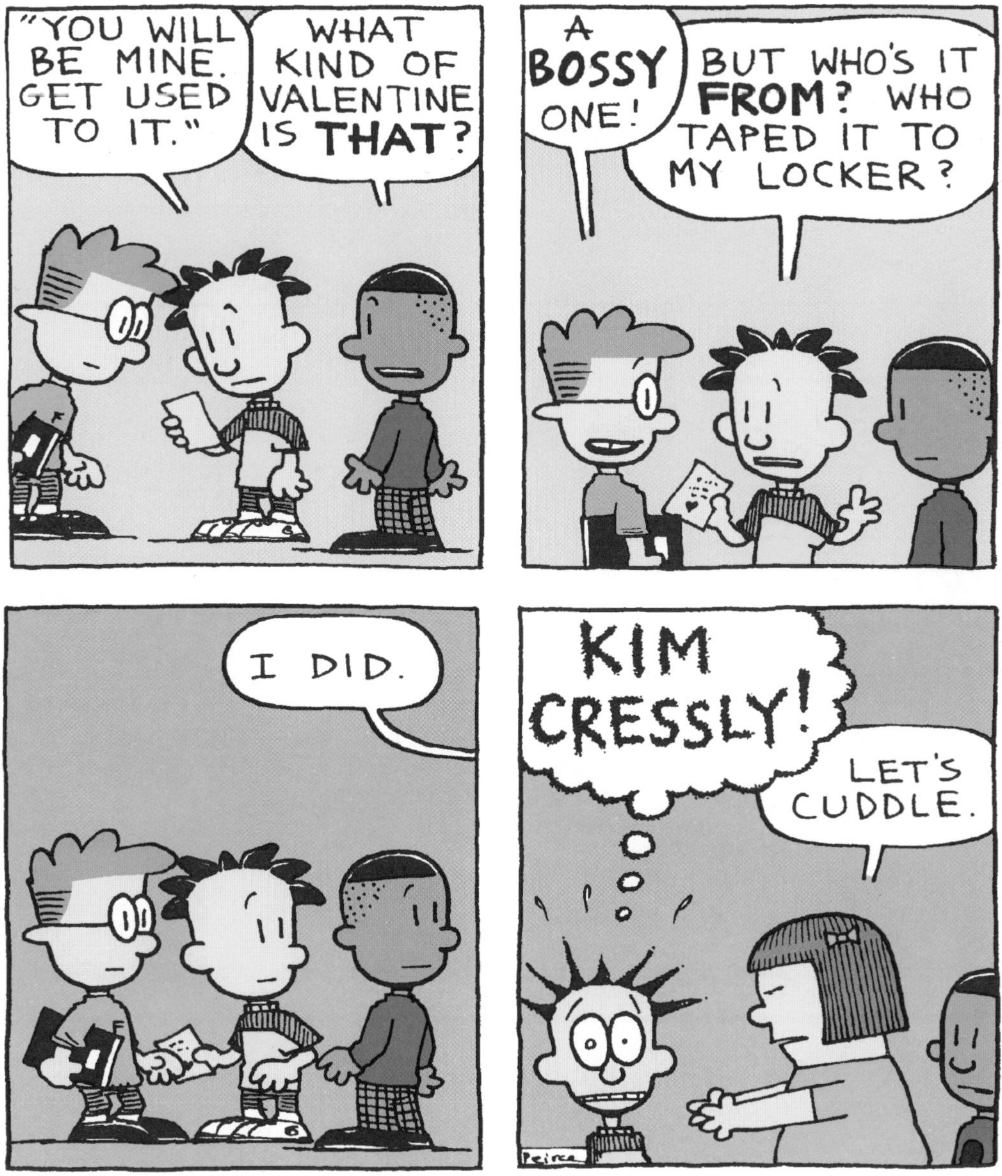
"YOU WILL BE MINE. GET USED TO IT."
WHAT KIND OF VALENTINE IS **THAT**?
A **BOSSY** ONE!
BUT WHO'S IT **FROM**? WHO TAPED IT TO MY LOCKER?
I DID.
KIM CRESSLY!
LET'S CUDDLE.
Peirce

K-**KIM! YOU** GAVE ME THIS VALENTINE?

YEAH.

I WANT A BOYFRIEND, AND ALL THE GOOD ONES ARE TAKEN ALREADY. SO I'M CHOOSING YOU.

LET'S GO HANG OUT IN THE CAFETORIUM.

THIS IS SO ROMANTIC!

YOU CAN BUY ME A TWINKIE.

URK!

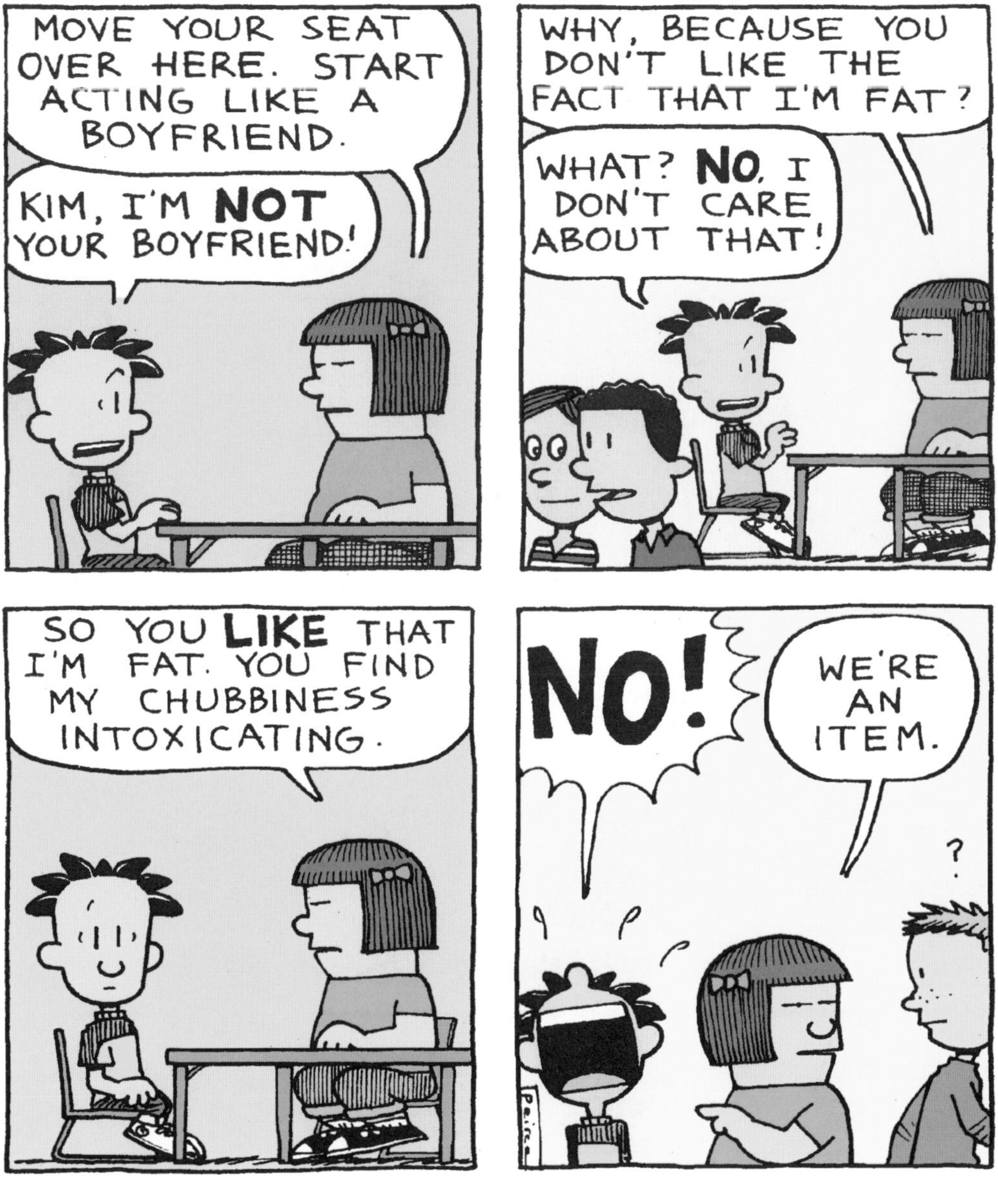
MOVE YOUR SEAT OVER HERE. START ACTING LIKE A BOYFRIEND.
KIM, I'M **NOT** YOUR BOYFRIEND!
WHY, BECAUSE YOU DON'T LIKE THE FACT THAT I'M FAT?
WHAT? **NO**, I DON'T CARE ABOUT THAT!
SO YOU **LIKE** THAT I'M FAT. YOU FIND MY CHUBBINESS INTOXICATING.
NO!
WE'RE AN ITEM.
?

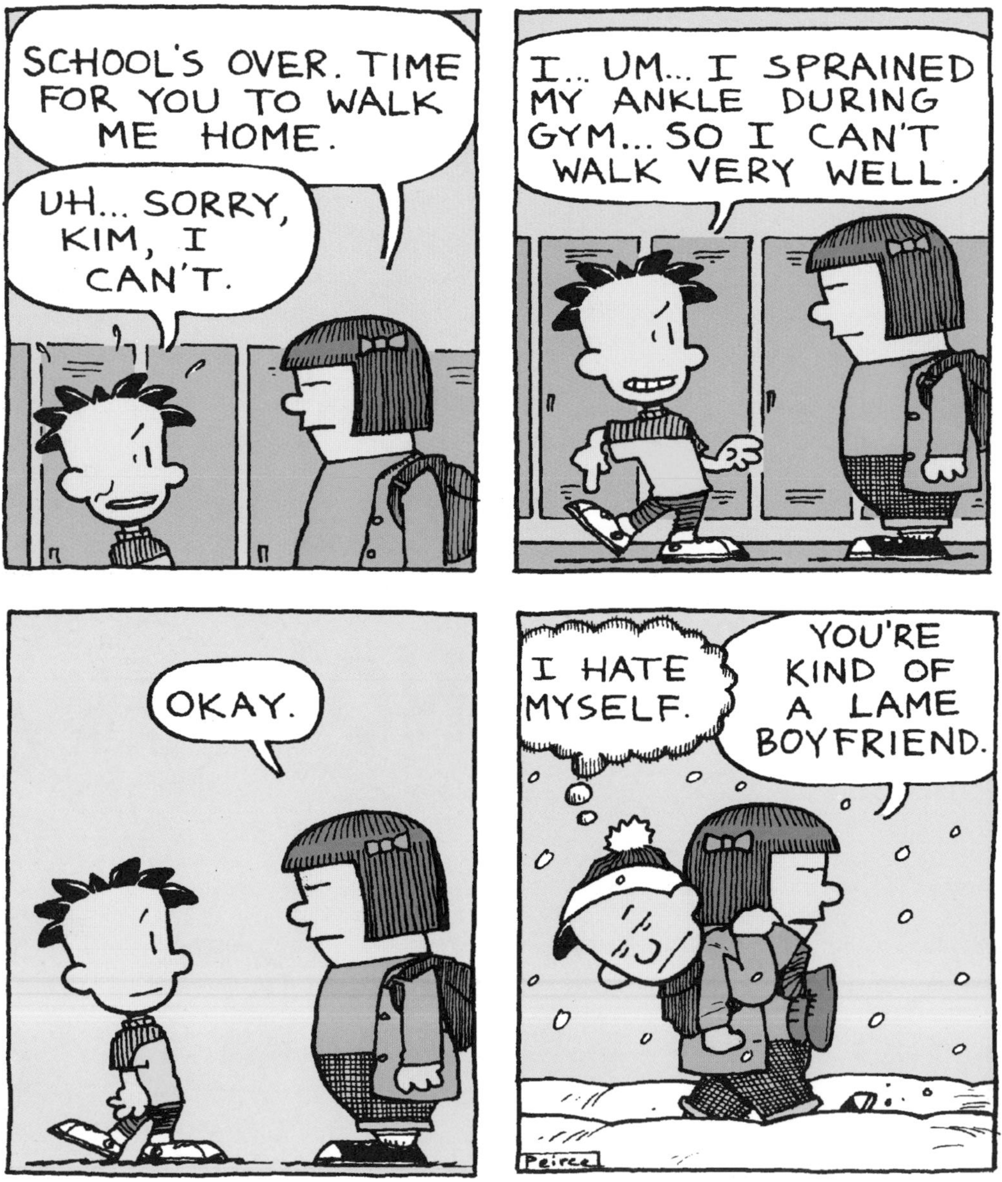
SCHOOL'S OVER. TIME FOR YOU TO WALK ME HOME.
UH... SORRY, KIM, I CAN'T.
I... UM... I SPRAINED MY ANKLE DURING GYM... SO I CAN'T WALK VERY WELL.
OKAY.
I HATE MYSELF.
YOU'RE KIND OF A LAME BOYFRIEND.
Peirce

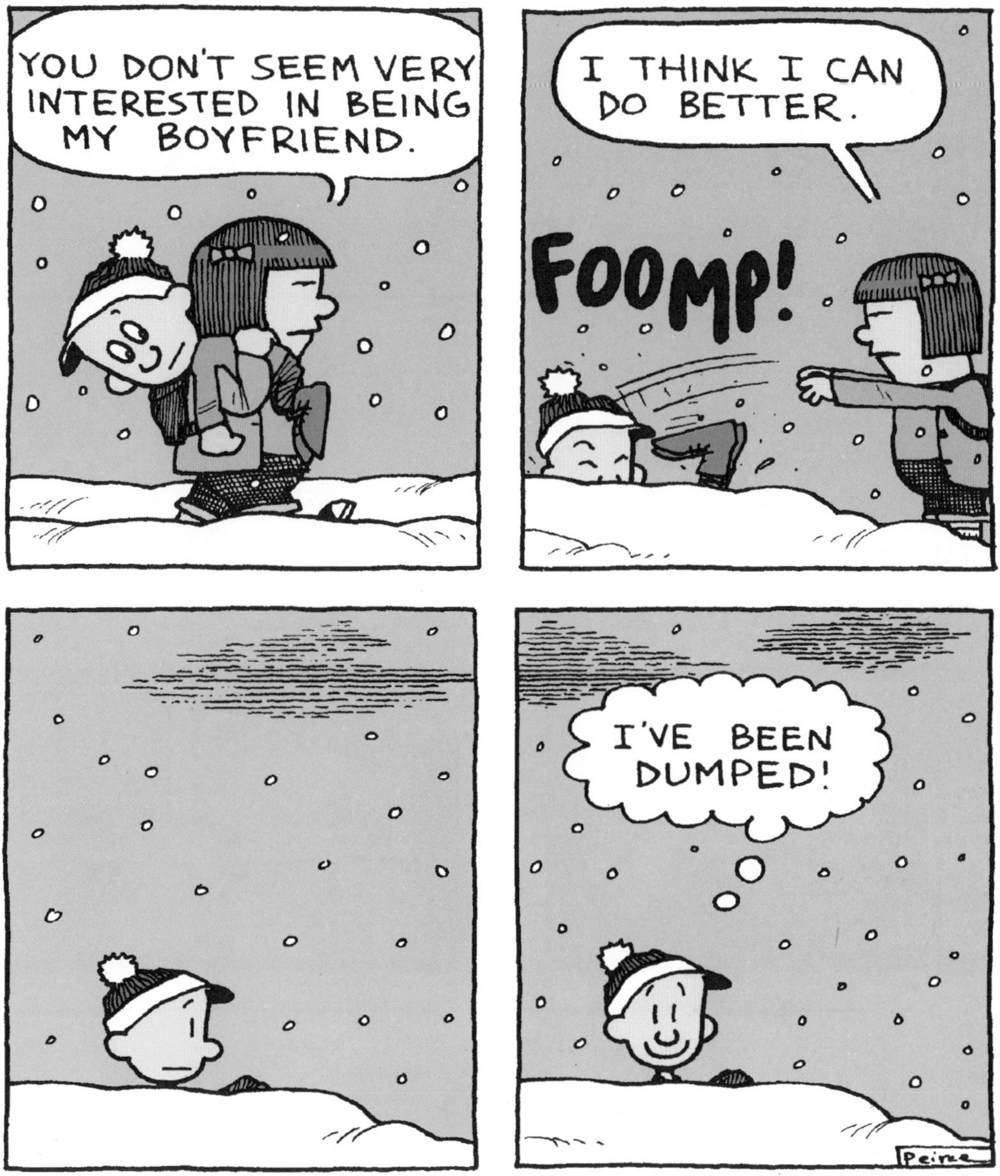
YOU DON'T SEEM VERY INTERESTED IN BEING MY BOYFRIEND.
I THINK I CAN DO BETTER.
FOOMP!
I'VE BEEN DUMPED!
Peirce

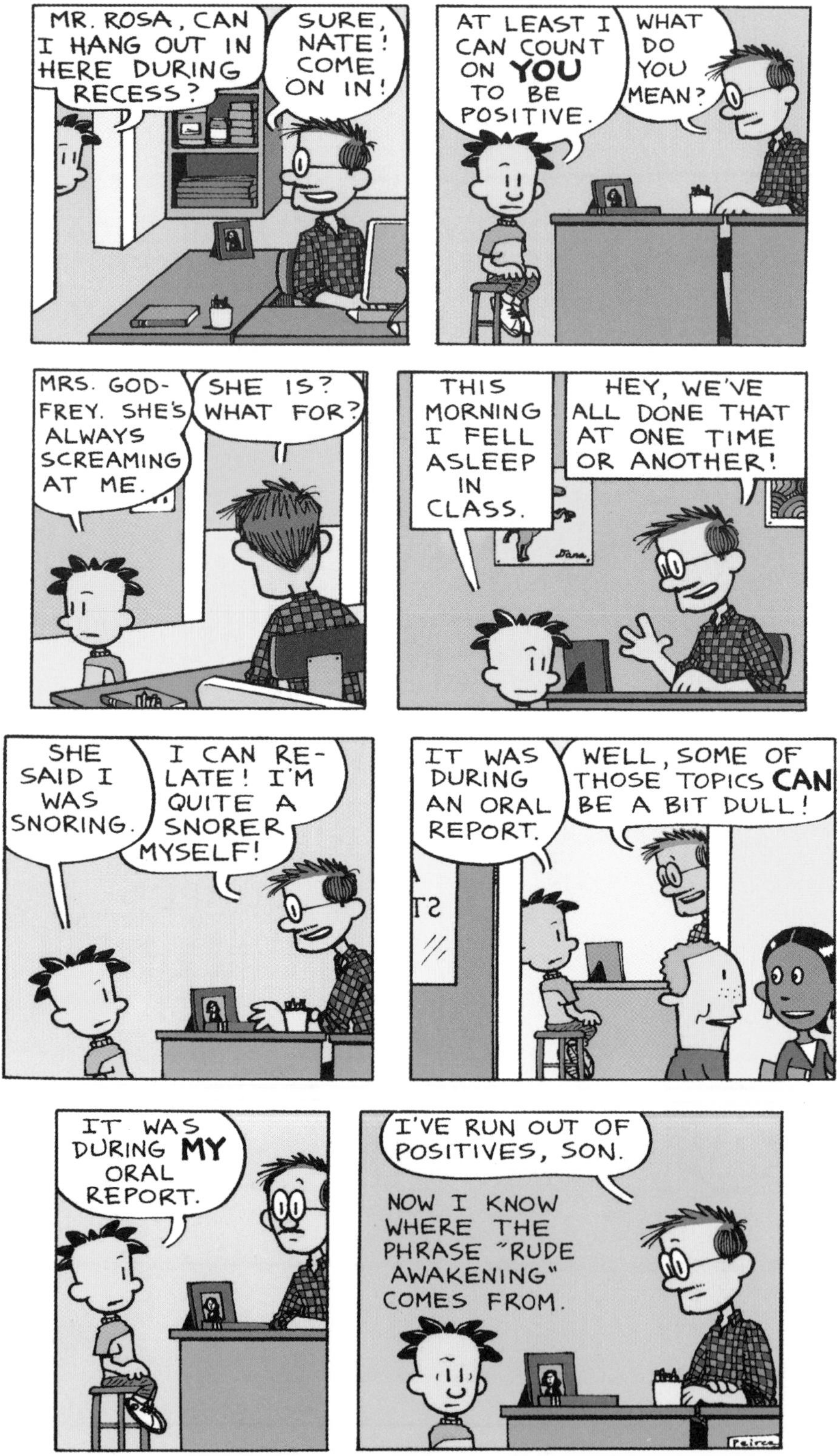
MR. ROSA, CAN I HANG OUT IN HERE DURING RECESS?
SURE, NATE! COME ON IN!
AT LEAST I CAN COUNT ON **YOU** TO BE POSITIVE.
WHAT DO YOU MEAN?
MRS. GOD-FREY. SHE'S ALWAYS SCREAMING AT ME.
SHE IS? WHAT FOR?
THIS MORNING I FELL ASLEEP IN CLASS.
HEY, WE'VE ALL DONE THAT AT ONE TIME OR ANOTHER!
SHE SAID I WAS SNORING.
I CAN RE-LATE! I'M QUITE A SNORER MYSELF!
IT WAS DURING AN ORAL REPORT.
WELL, SOME OF THOSE TOPICS **CAN** BE A BIT DULL!
IT WAS DURING **MY** ORAL REPORT.
I'VE RUN OUT OF POSITIVES, SON.
NOW I KNOW WHERE THE PHRASE "RUDE AWAKENING" COMES FROM.

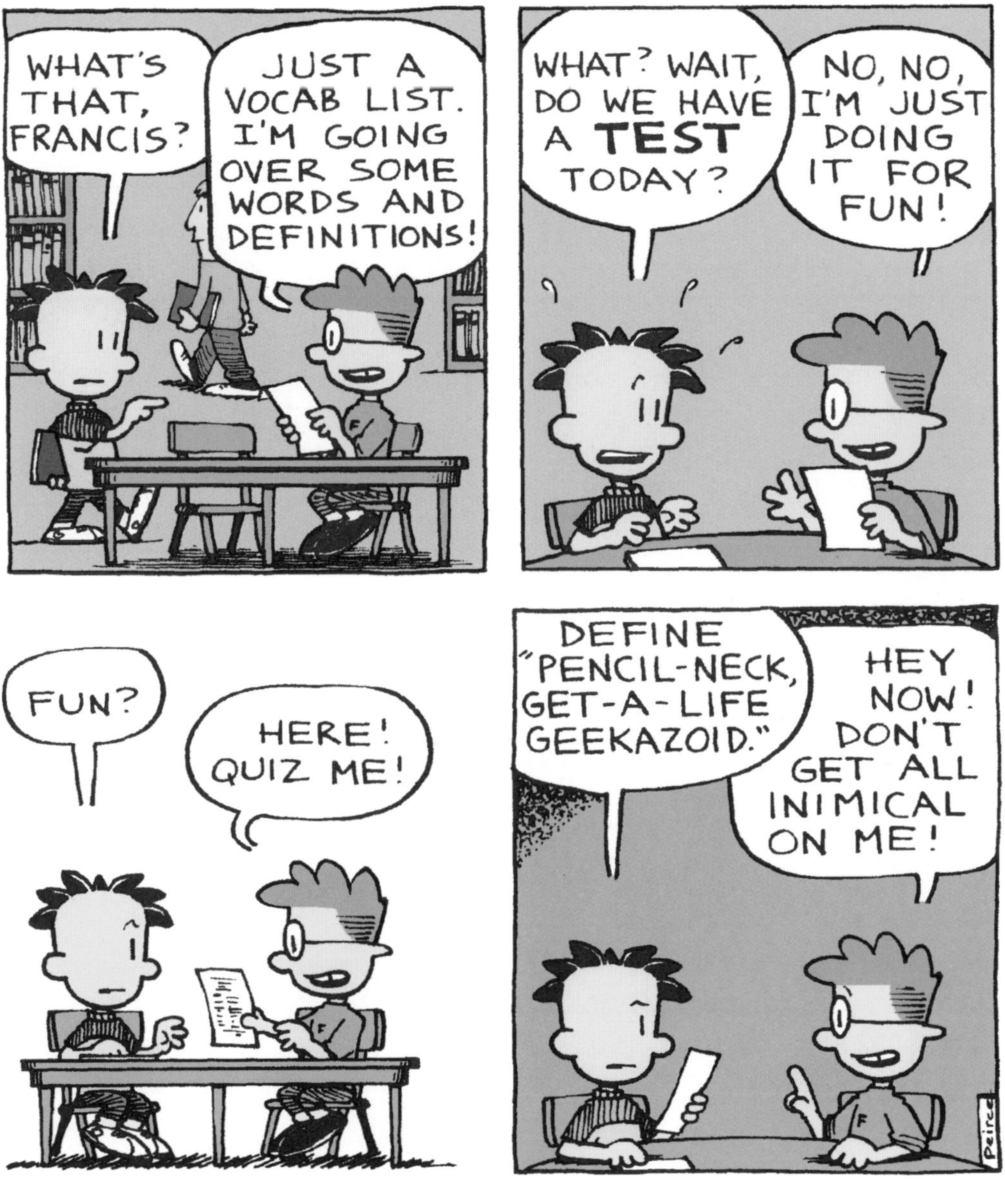
WHAT'S THAT, FRANCIS?
JUST A VOCAB LIST. I'M GOING OVER SOME WORDS AND DEFINITIONS!
WHAT? WAIT, DO WE HAVE A **TEST** TODAY?
NO, NO, I'M JUST DOING IT FOR FUN!
FUN?
HERE! QUIZ ME!
DEFINE "PENCIL-NECK, GET-A-LIFE GEEKAZOID."
HEY NOW! DON'T GET ALL INIMICAL ON ME!
Peirce

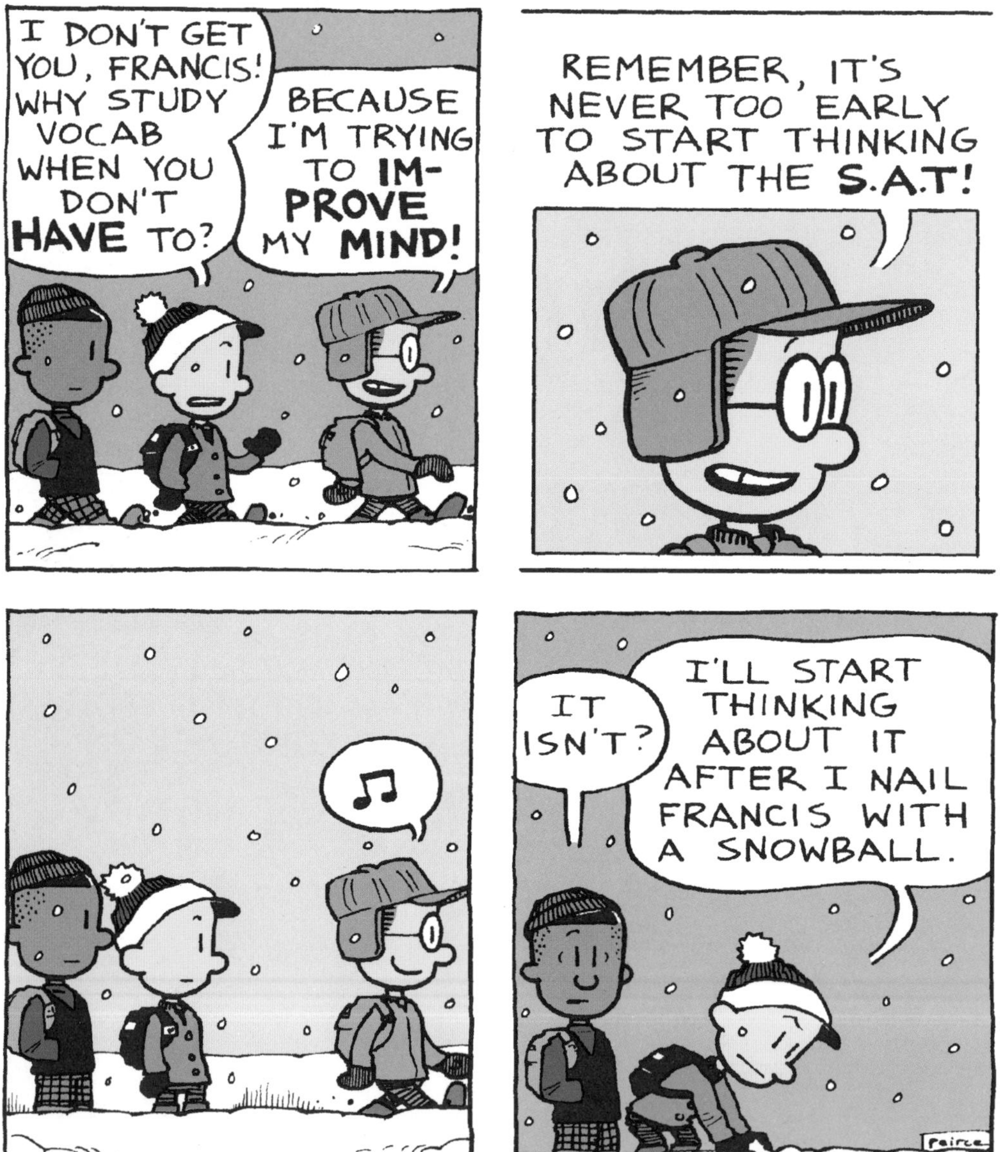
I DON'T GET YOU, FRANCIS! WHY STUDY VOCAB WHEN YOU DON'T **HAVE** TO?
BECAUSE I'M TRYING TO **IM-PROVE** MY **MIND**!
REMEMBER, IT'S NEVER TOO EARLY TO START THINKING ABOUT THE **S.A.T**!
♫
IT ISN'T?
I'LL START THINKING ABOUT IT AFTER I NAIL FRANCIS WITH A SNOWBALL.
Peirce

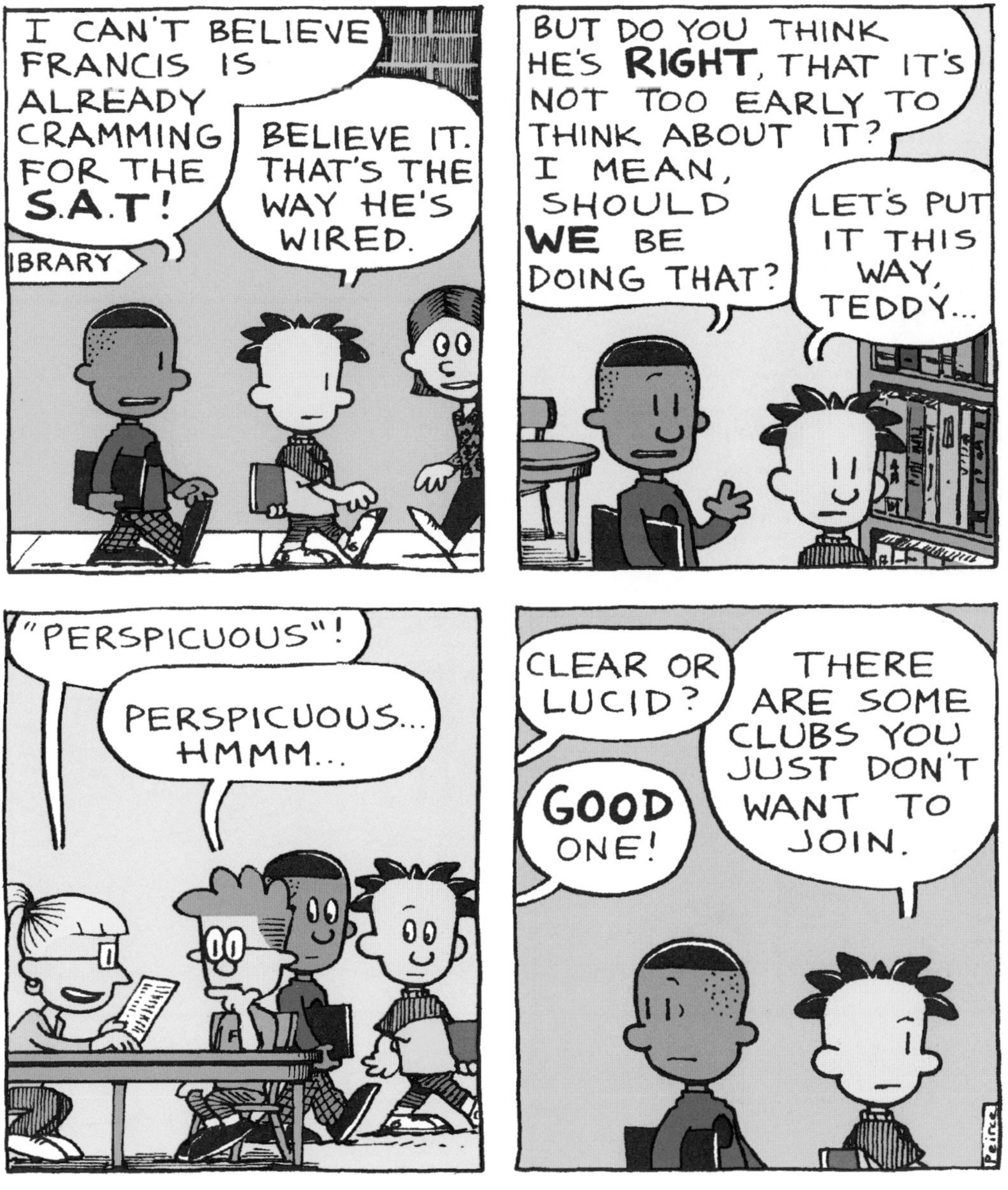
I CAN'T BELIEVE FRANCIS IS ALREADY CRAMMING FOR THE S.A.T!
BELIEVE IT. THAT'S THE WAY HE'S WIRED.
IBRARY
BUT DO YOU THINK HE'S RIGHT, THAT IT'S NOT TOO EARLY TO THINK ABOUT IT? I MEAN, SHOULD WE BE DOING THAT?
LET'S PUT IT THIS WAY, TEDDY...
"PERSPICUOUS"!
PERSPICUOUS... HMMM...
CLEAR OR LUCID?
GOOD ONE!
THERE ARE SOME CLUBS YOU JUST DON'T WANT TO JOIN.
Peirce

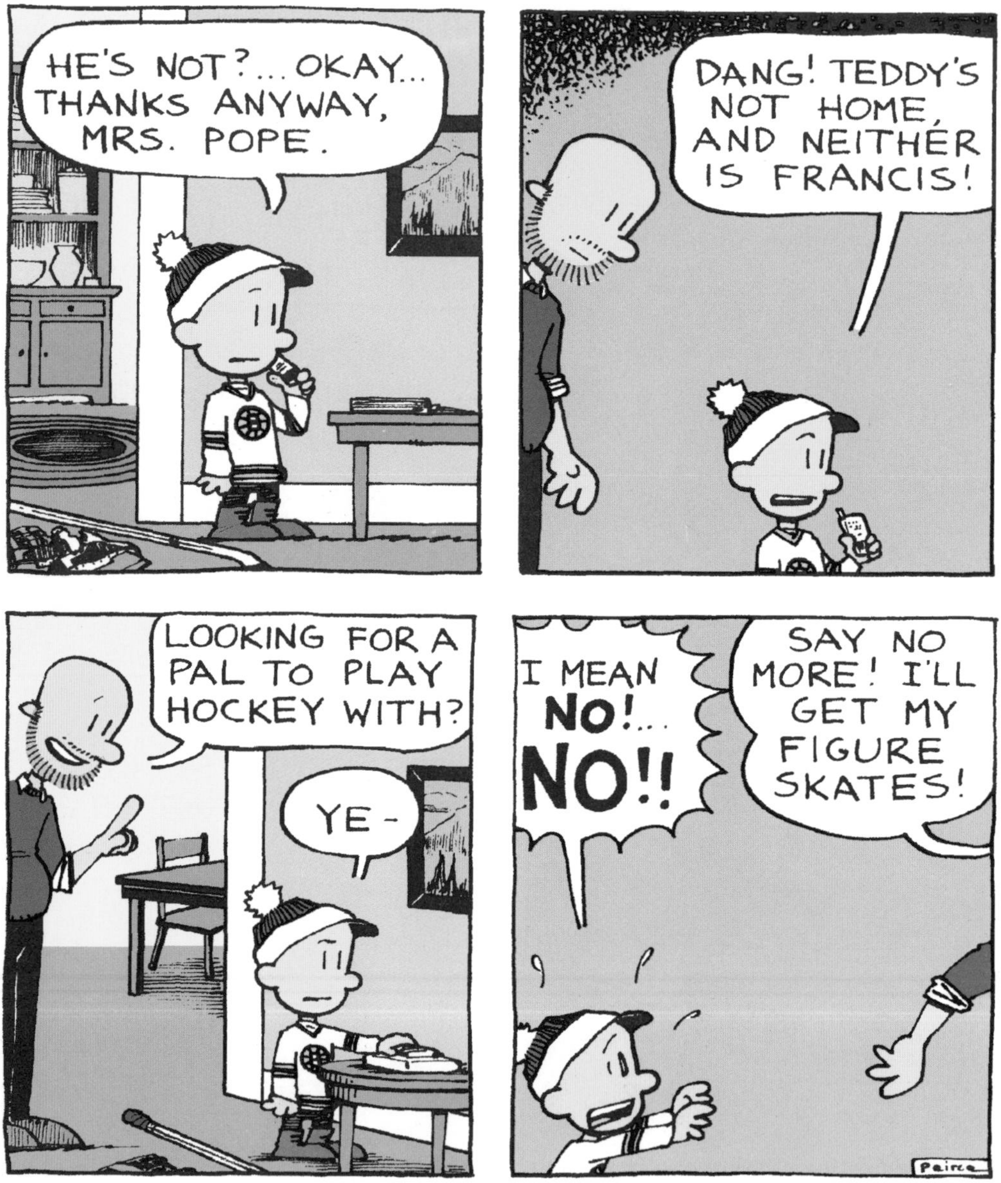
HE'S NOT?... OKAY... THANKS ANYWAY, MRS. POPE.
DANG! TEDDY'S NOT HOME, AND NEITHER IS FRANCIS!
LOOKING FOR A PAL TO PLAY HOCKEY WITH?
YE-
SAY NO MORE! I'LL GET MY FIGURE SKATES!
I MEAN NO!... NO!!
Peirce

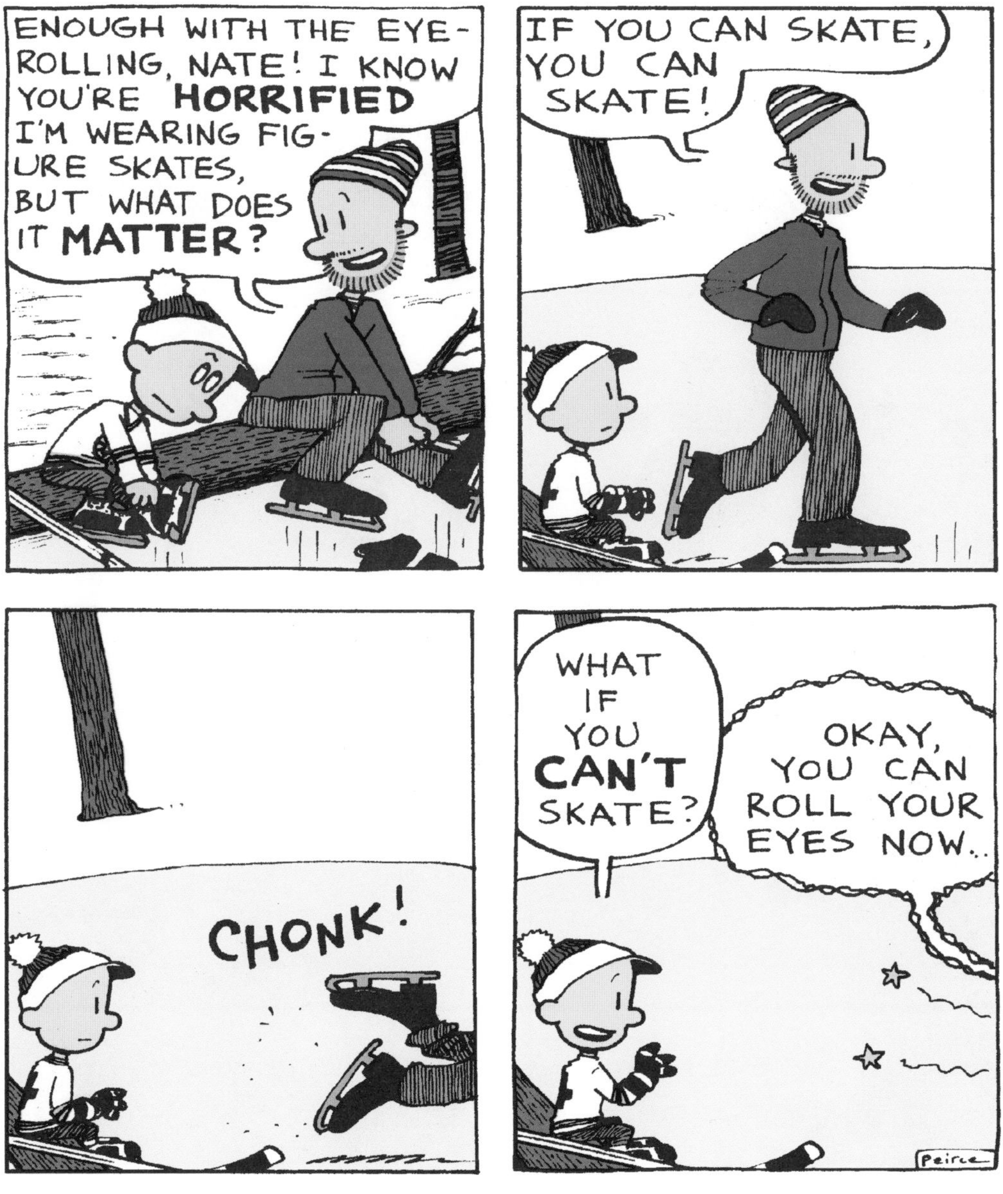
ENOUGH WITH THE EYE-ROLLING, NATE! I KNOW YOU'RE **HORRIFIED** I'M WEARING FIG-URE SKATES, BUT WHAT DOES IT **MATTER**?
IF YOU CAN SKATE, YOU CAN SKATE!
CHONK!
WHAT IF YOU **CAN'T** SKATE?
OKAY, YOU CAN ROLL YOUR EYES NOW...
Peirce

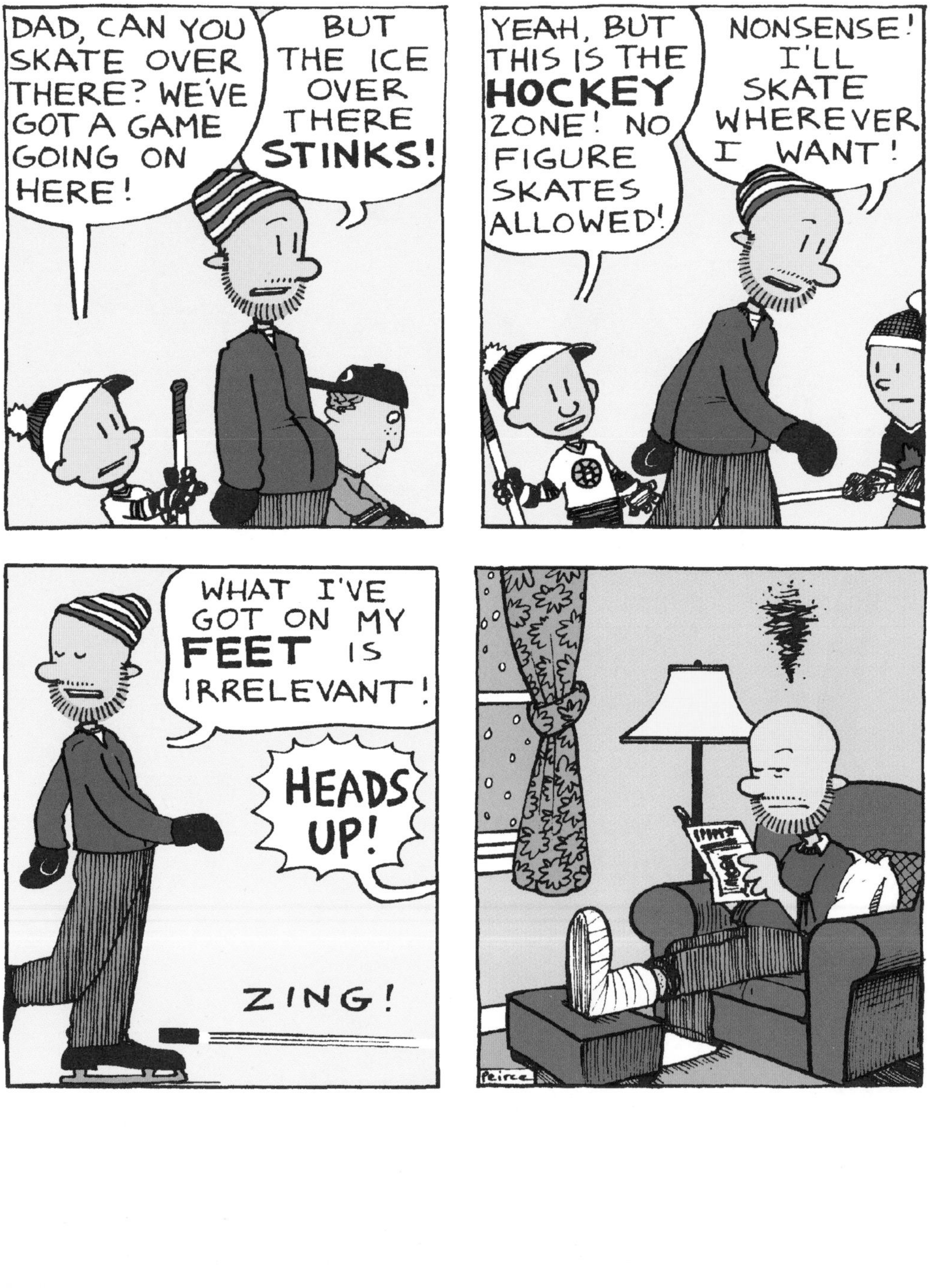
DAD, CAN YOU SKATE OVER THERE? WE'VE GOT A GAME GOING ON HERE!
BUT THE ICE OVER THERE **STINKS!**
YEAH, BUT THIS IS THE **HOCKEY** ZONE! NO FIGURE SKATES ALLOWED!
NONSENSE! I'LL SKATE WHEREVER I WANT!
WHAT I'VE GOT ON MY **FEET** IS IRRELEVANT!
HEADS UP!
ZING!
Peirce

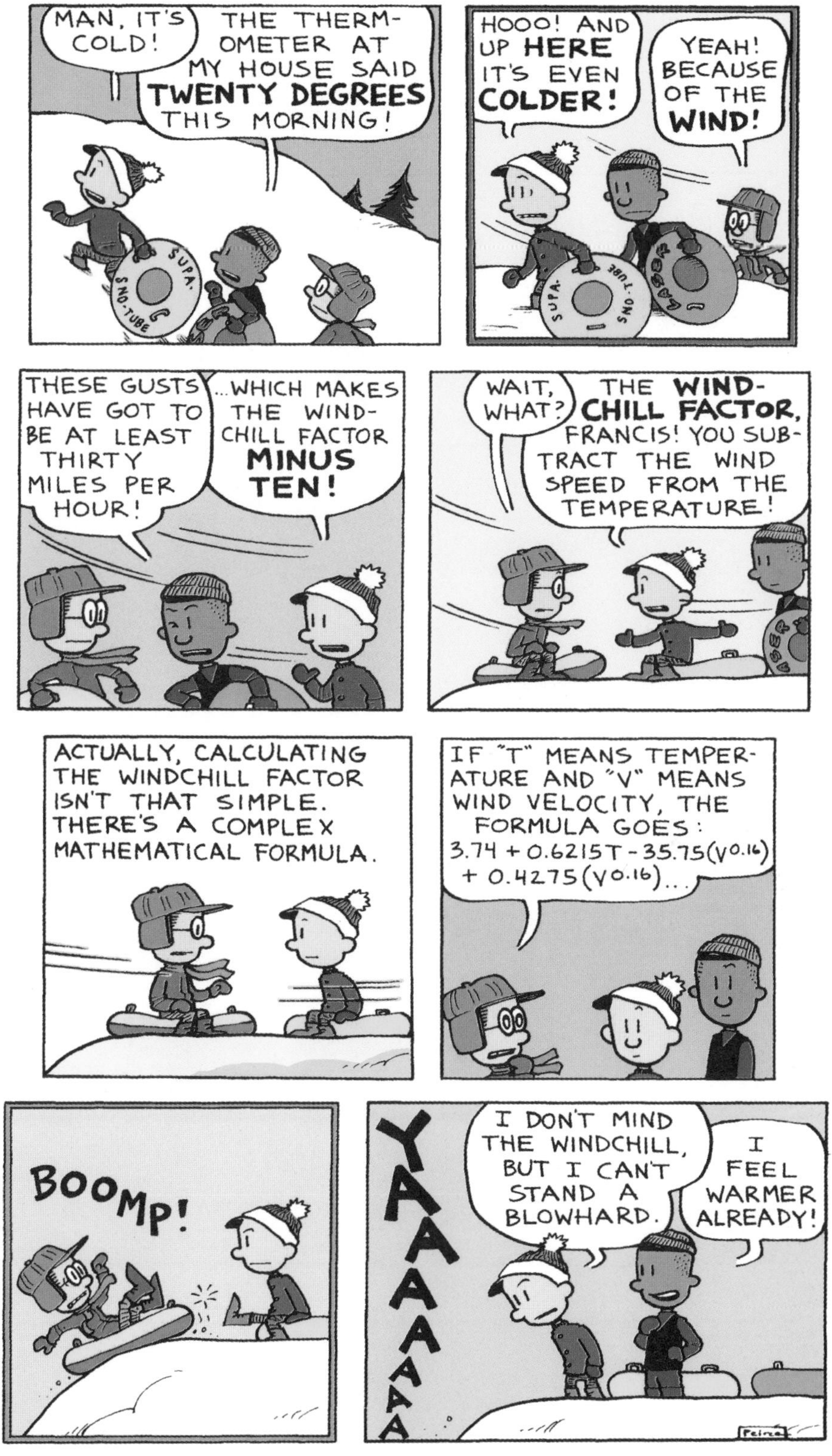

MAN, IT'S COLD!
THE THERMOMETER AT MY HOUSE SAID **TWENTY DEGREES** THIS MORNING!
SUPA. SNO-TUBE
HOOO! AND UP **HERE** IT'S EVEN **COLDER!**
YEAH! BECAUSE OF THE **WIND!**
THESE GUSTS HAVE GOT TO BE AT LEAST THIRTY MILES PER HOUR!
...WHICH MAKES THE WIND-CHILL FACTOR **MINUS TEN!**
WAIT, WHAT?
THE **WIND-CHILL FACTOR,** FRANCIS! YOU SUBTRACT THE WIND SPEED FROM THE TEMPERATURE!
ACTUALLY, CALCULATING THE WINDCHILL FACTOR ISN'T THAT SIMPLE. THERE'S A COMPLEX MATHEMATICAL FORMULA.
IF "T" MEANS TEMPERATURE AND "V" MEANS WIND VELOCITY, THE FORMULA GOES:
3.74 + 0.6215T - 35.75(V0.16) + 0.4275(V0.16)...
BOOMP!
YAAAAAAA
I DON'T MIND THE WINDCHILL, BUT I CAN'T STAND A BLOWHARD.
I FEEL WARMER ALREADY!

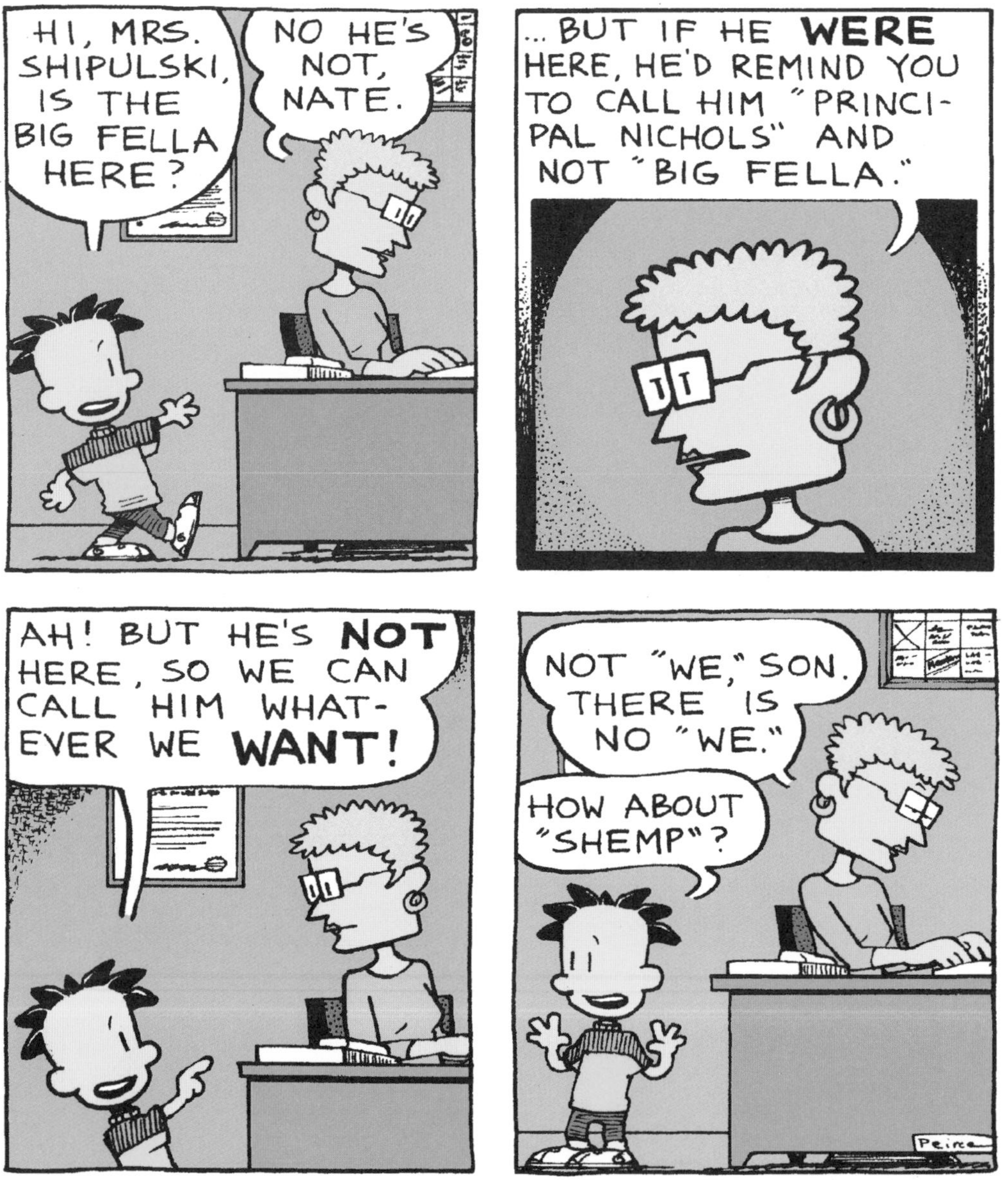
HI, MRS. SHIPULSKI, IS THE BIG FELLA HERE?
NO HE'S NOT, NATE.
...BUT IF HE WERE HERE, HE'D REMIND YOU TO CALL HIM "PRINCIPAL NICHOLS" AND NOT "BIG FELLA."
AH! BUT HE'S NOT HERE, SO WE CAN CALL HIM WHATEVER WE WANT!
NOT "WE," SON. THERE IS NO "WE."
HOW ABOUT "SHEMP"?
Peirce

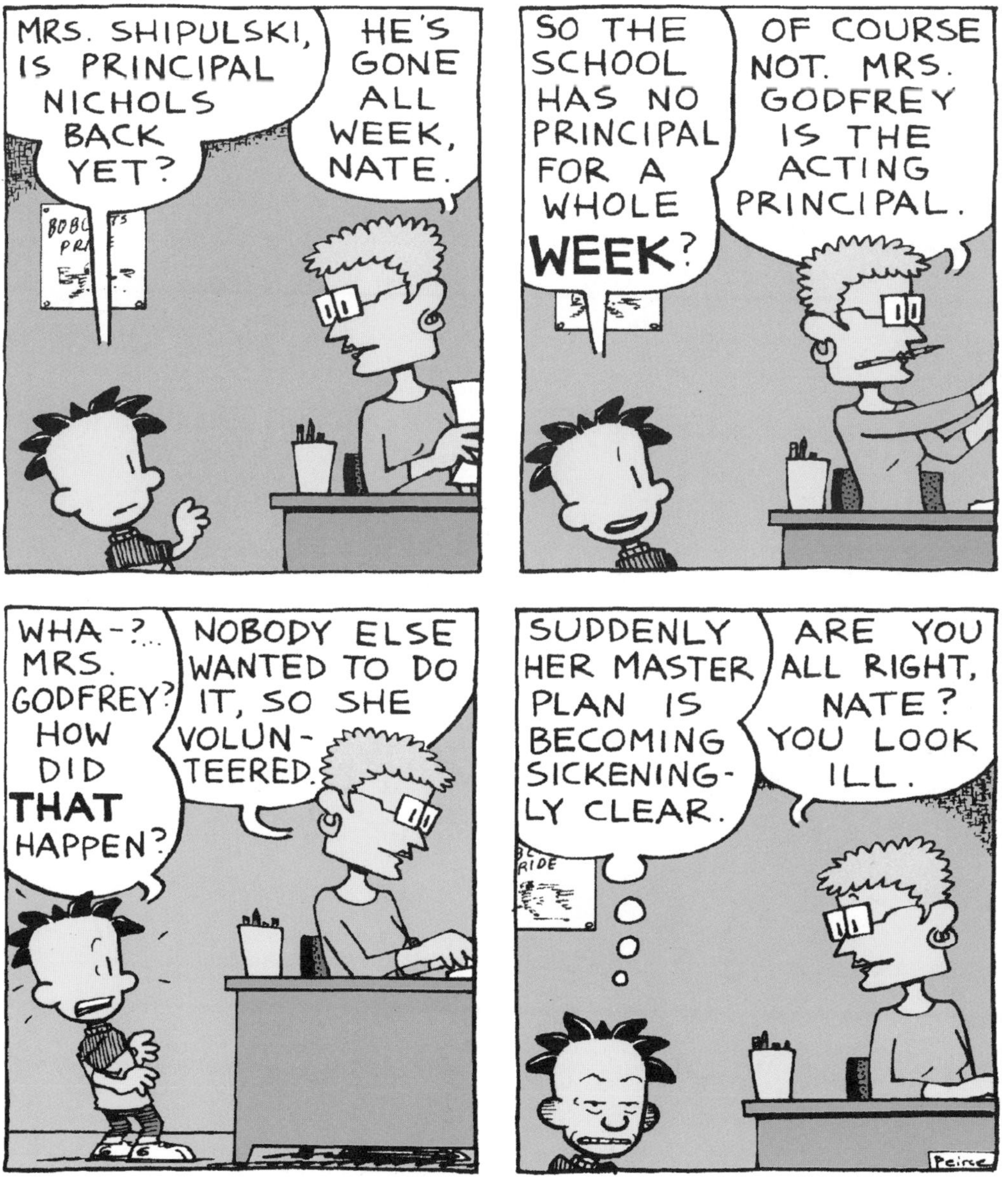
MRS. SHIPULSKI, IS PRINCIPAL NICHOLS BACK YET?
HE'S GONE ALL WEEK, NATE.
SO THE SCHOOL HAS NO PRINCIPAL FOR A WHOLE WEEK?
OF COURSE NOT. MRS. GODFREY IS THE ACTING PRINCIPAL.
WHA-?.. MRS. GODFREY? HOW DID THAT HAPPEN?
NOBODY ELSE WANTED TO DO IT, SO SHE VOLUNTEERED.
SUDDENLY HER MASTER PLAN IS BECOMING SICKENINGLY CLEAR.
ARE YOU ALL RIGHT, NATE? YOU LOOK ILL.
Peirce

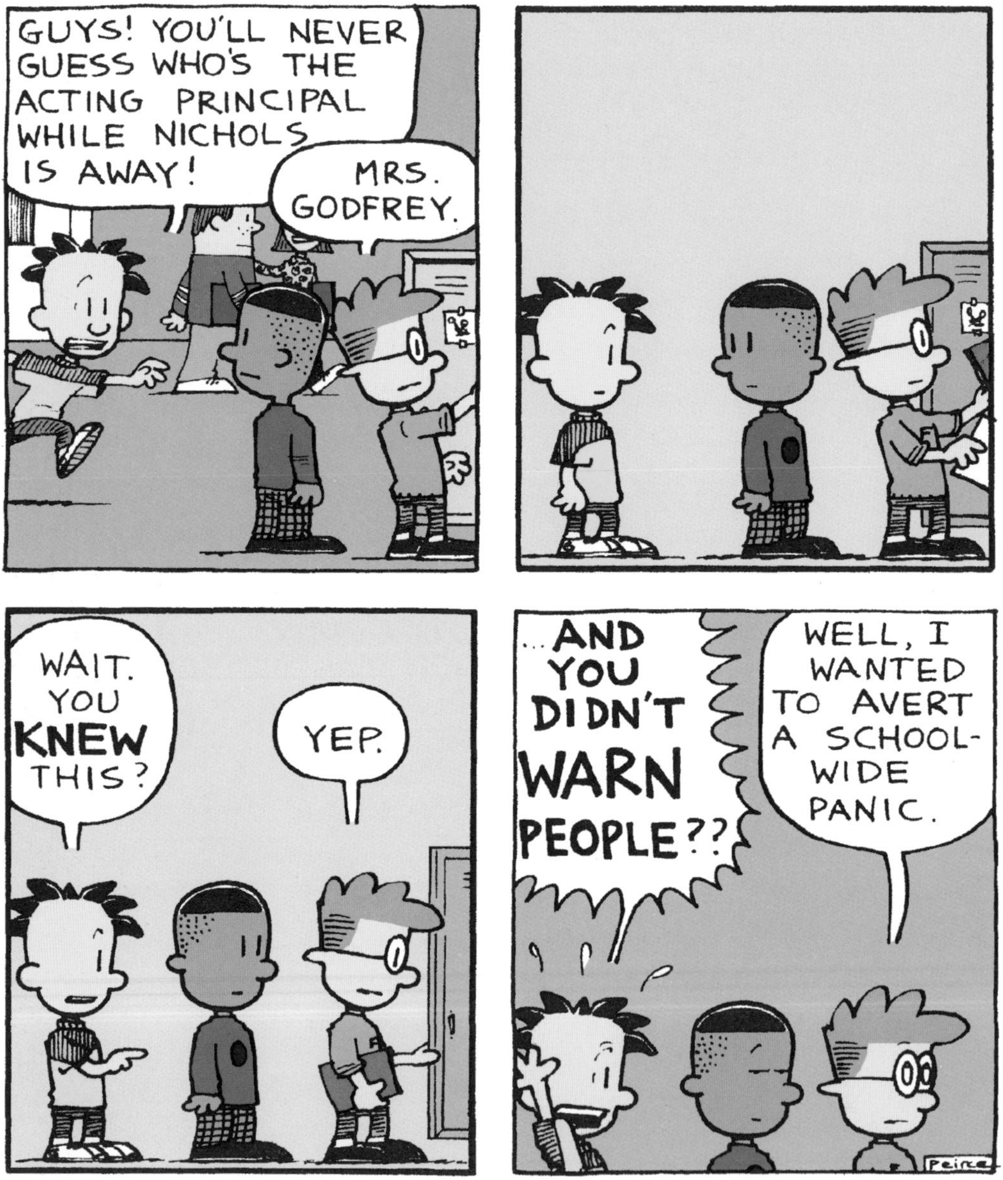
GUYS! YOU'LL NEVER GUESS WHO'S THE ACTING PRINCIPAL WHILE NICHOLS IS AWAY!
MRS. GODFREY.
WAIT. YOU KNEW THIS?
YEP.
...AND YOU DIDN'T WARN PEOPLE??
WELL, I WANTED TO AVERT A SCHOOL-WIDE PANIC.
Peirce

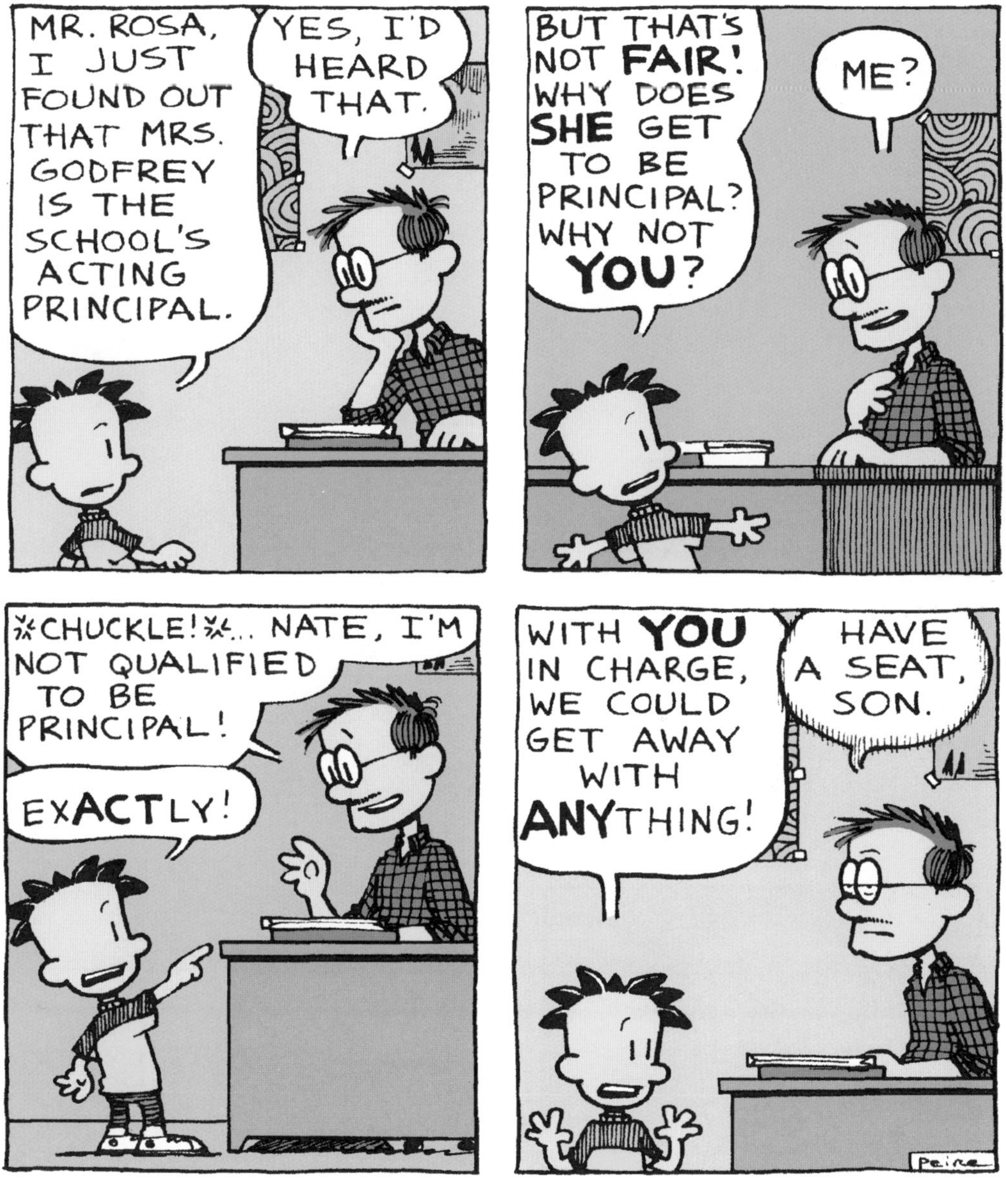
MR. ROSA, I JUST FOUND OUT THAT MRS. GODFREY IS THE SCHOOL'S ACTING PRINCIPAL.
YES, I'D HEARD THAT.
BUT THAT'S NOT FAIR! WHY DOES SHE GET TO BE PRINCIPAL? WHY NOT YOU?
ME?
CHUCKLE! ... NATE, I'M NOT QUALIFIED TO BE PRINCIPAL!
EXACTLY!
WITH YOU IN CHARGE, WE COULD GET AWAY WITH ANYTHING!
HAVE A SEAT, SON.
Peirce

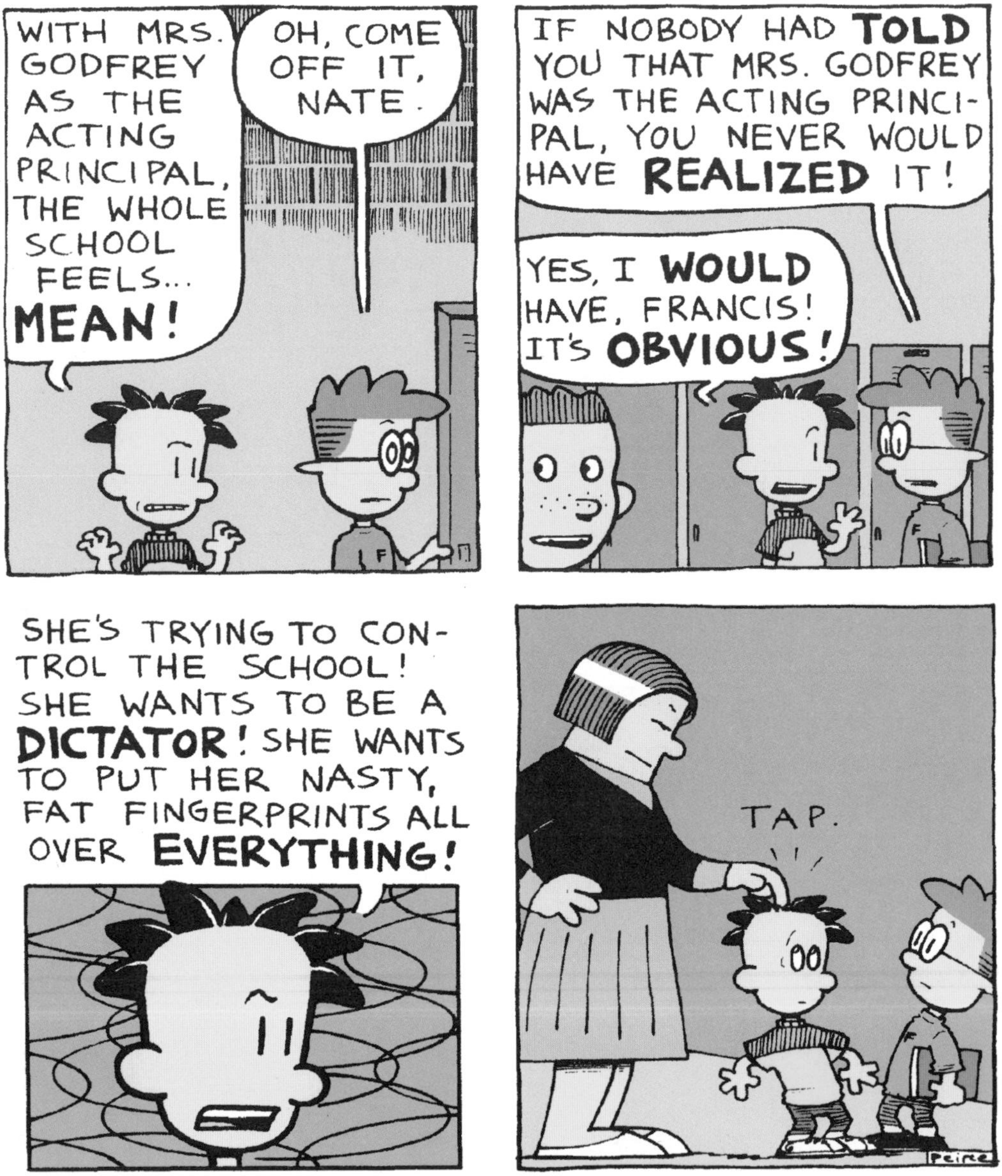

WITH MRS. GODFREY AS THE ACTING PRINCIPAL, THE WHOLE SCHOOL FEELS... MEAN!
OH, COME OFF IT, NATE.
IF NOBODY HAD TOLD YOU THAT MRS. GODFREY WAS THE ACTING PRINCIPAL, YOU NEVER WOULD HAVE REALIZED IT!
YES, I WOULD HAVE, FRANCIS! IT'S OBVIOUS!
SHE'S TRYING TO CONTROL THE SCHOOL! SHE WANTS TO BE A DICTATOR! SHE WANTS TO PUT HER NASTY, FAT FINGERPRINTS ALL OVER EVERYTHING!
TAP.
Peirce

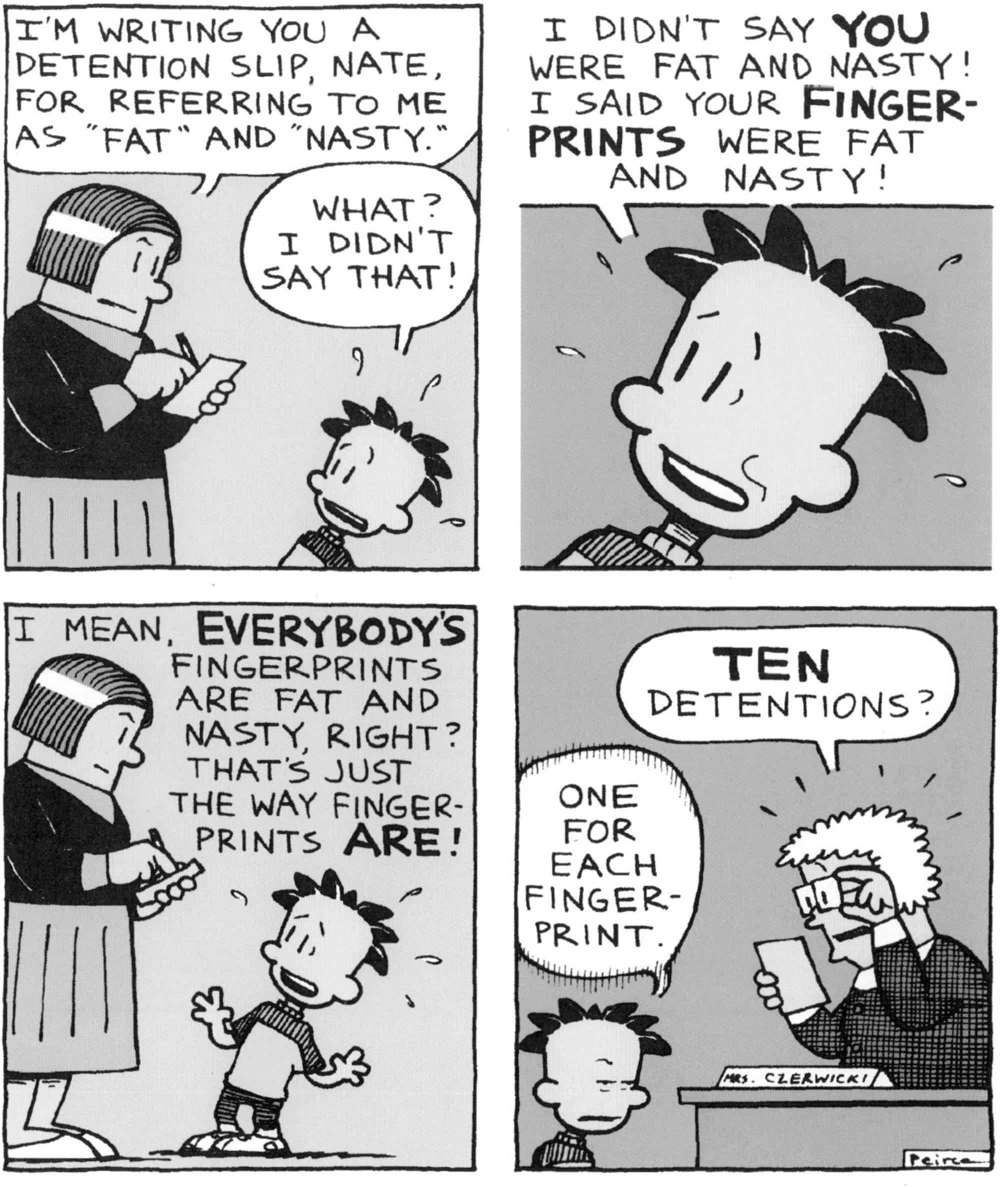
I'M WRITING YOU A DETENTION SLIP, NATE, FOR REFERRING TO ME AS "FAT" AND "NASTY."
WHAT? I DIDN'T SAY THAT!
I DIDN'T SAY YOU WERE FAT AND NASTY! I SAID YOUR FINGER-PRINTS WERE FAT AND NASTY!
I MEAN, EVERYBODY'S FINGERPRINTS ARE FAT AND NASTY, RIGHT? THAT'S JUST THE WAY FINGER-PRINTS ARE!
TEN DETENTIONS?
ONE FOR EACH FINGER-PRINT.
MRS. CZERWICKI
Peirce

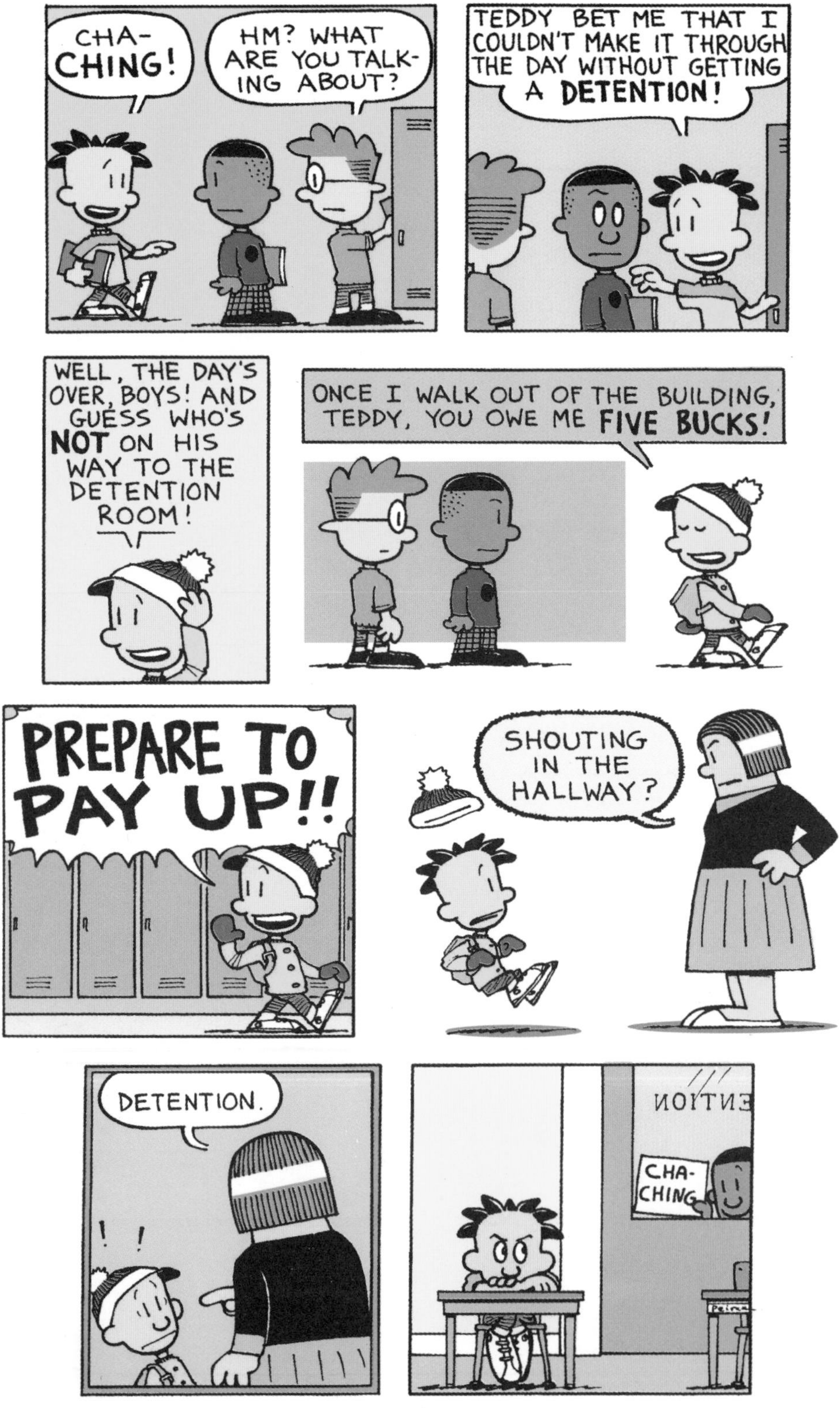
CHA-CHING!
HM? WHAT ARE YOU TALKING ABOUT?
TEDDY BET ME THAT I COULDN'T MAKE IT THROUGH THE DAY WITHOUT GETTING A DETENTION!
WELL, THE DAY'S OVER, BOYS! AND GUESS WHO'S NOT ON HIS WAY TO THE DETENTION ROOM!
ONCE I WALK OUT OF THE BUILDING, TEDDY, YOU OWE ME FIVE BUCKS!
PREPARE TO PAY UP!!
SHOUTING IN THE HALLWAY?
DETENTION.
! !
CHA-CHING

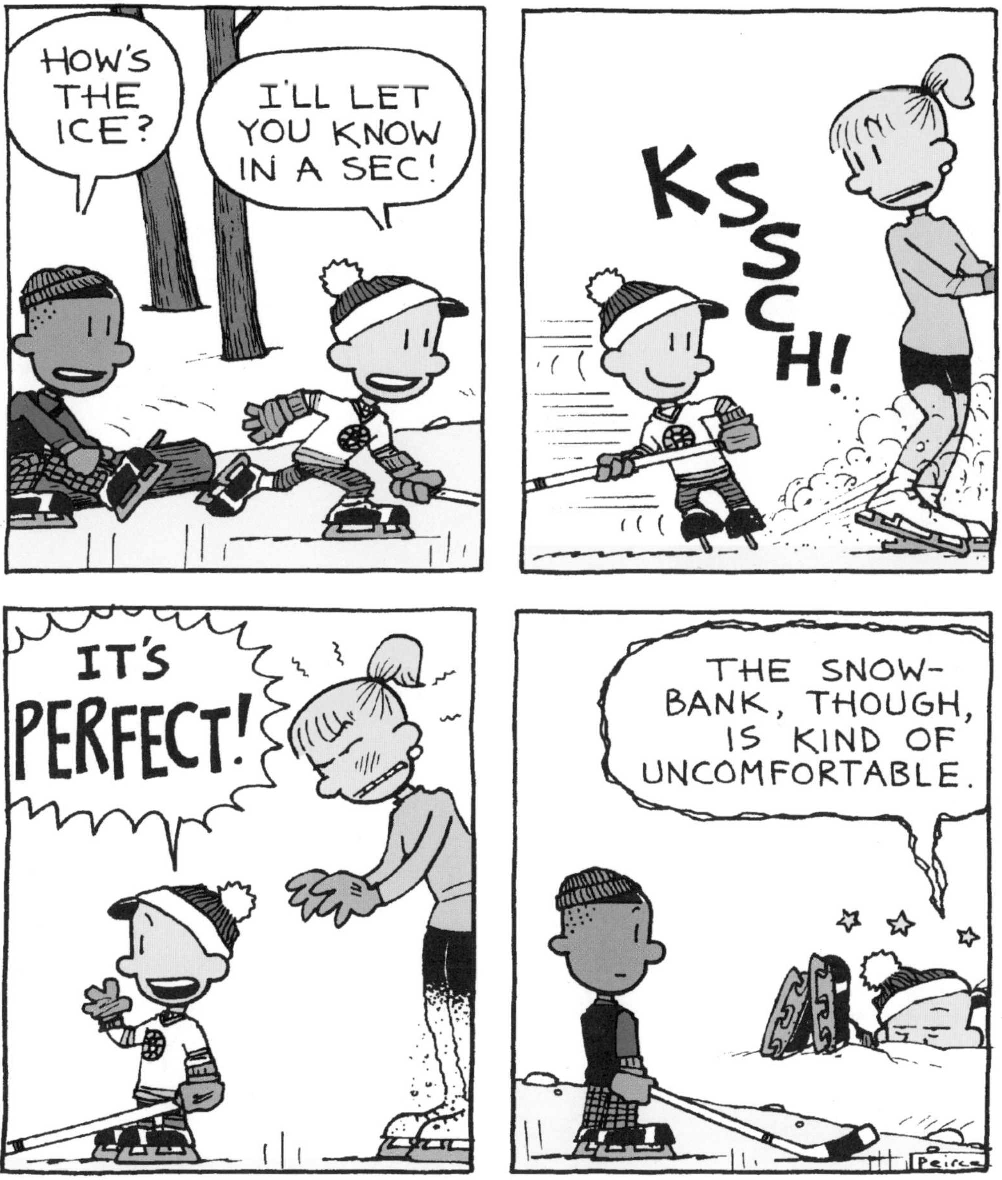
HOW'S THE ICE?
I'LL LET YOU KNOW IN A SEC!
KSSCH!
IT'S PERFECT!
THE SNOW-BANK, THOUGH, IS KIND OF UNCOMFORTABLE.
Peirce

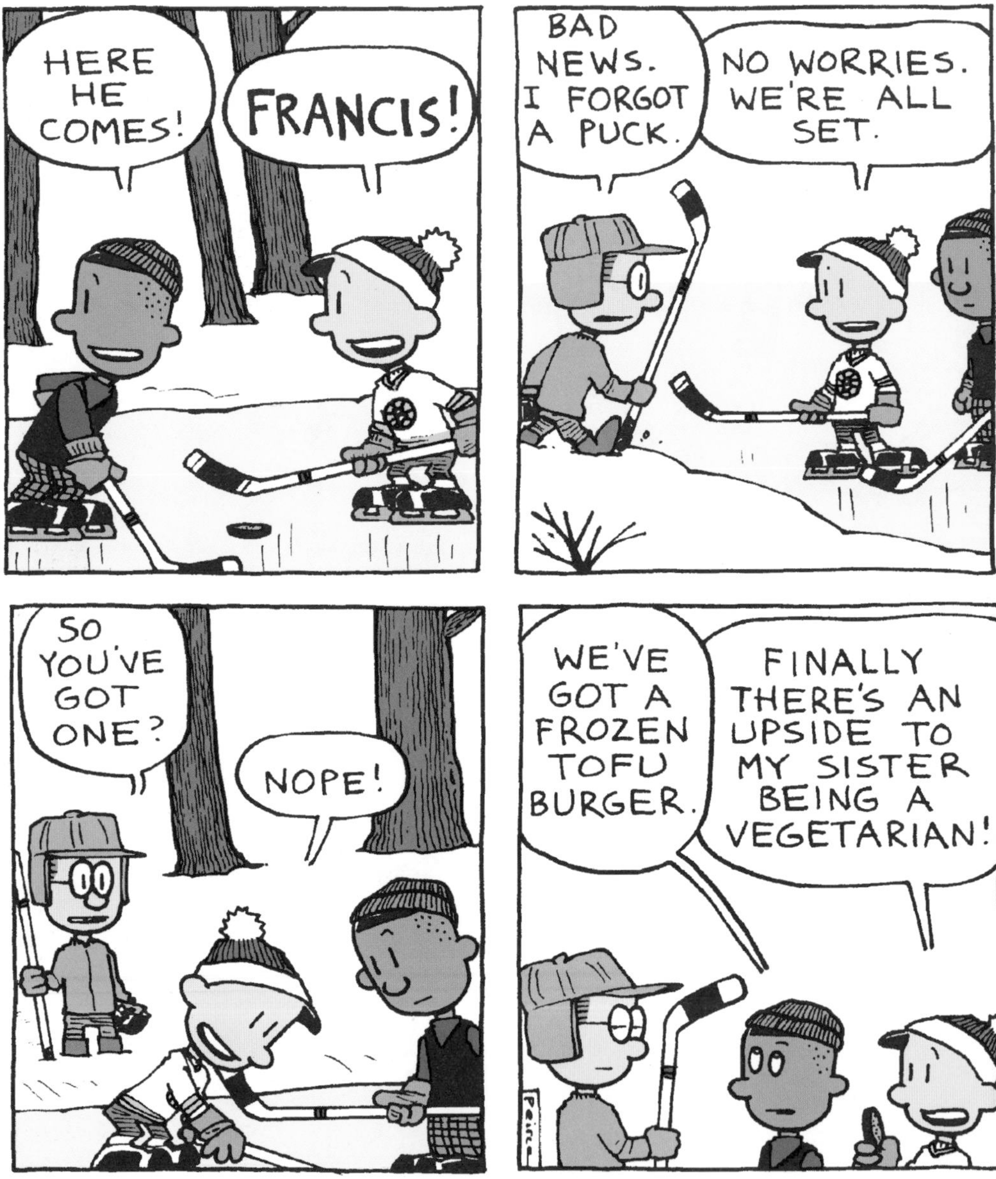
HERE HE COMES!
FRANCIS!
BAD NEWS. I FORGOT A PUCK.
NO WORRIES. WE'RE ALL SET.
SO YOU'VE GOT ONE?
NOPE!
WE'VE GOT A FROZEN TOFU BURGER.
FINALLY THERE'S AN UPSIDE TO MY SISTER BEING A VEGETARIAN!
Peirce

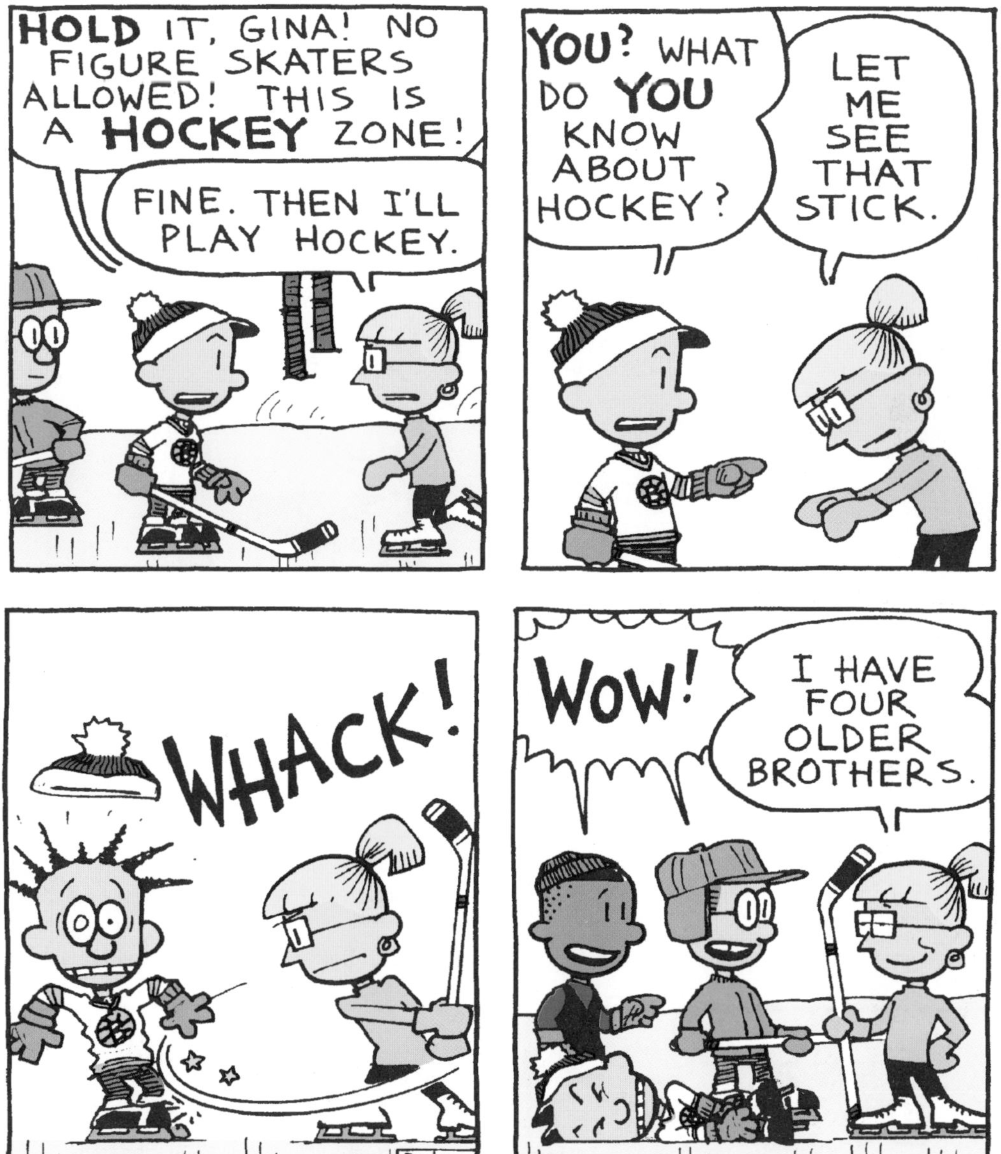
HOLD IT, GINA! NO FIGURE SKATERS ALLOWED! THIS IS A HOCKEY ZONE!
FINE. THEN I'LL PLAY HOCKEY.
YOU? WHAT DO YOU KNOW ABOUT HOCKEY?
LET ME SEE THAT STICK.
WHACK!
Peirce
WOW!
I HAVE FOUR OLDER BROTHERS.

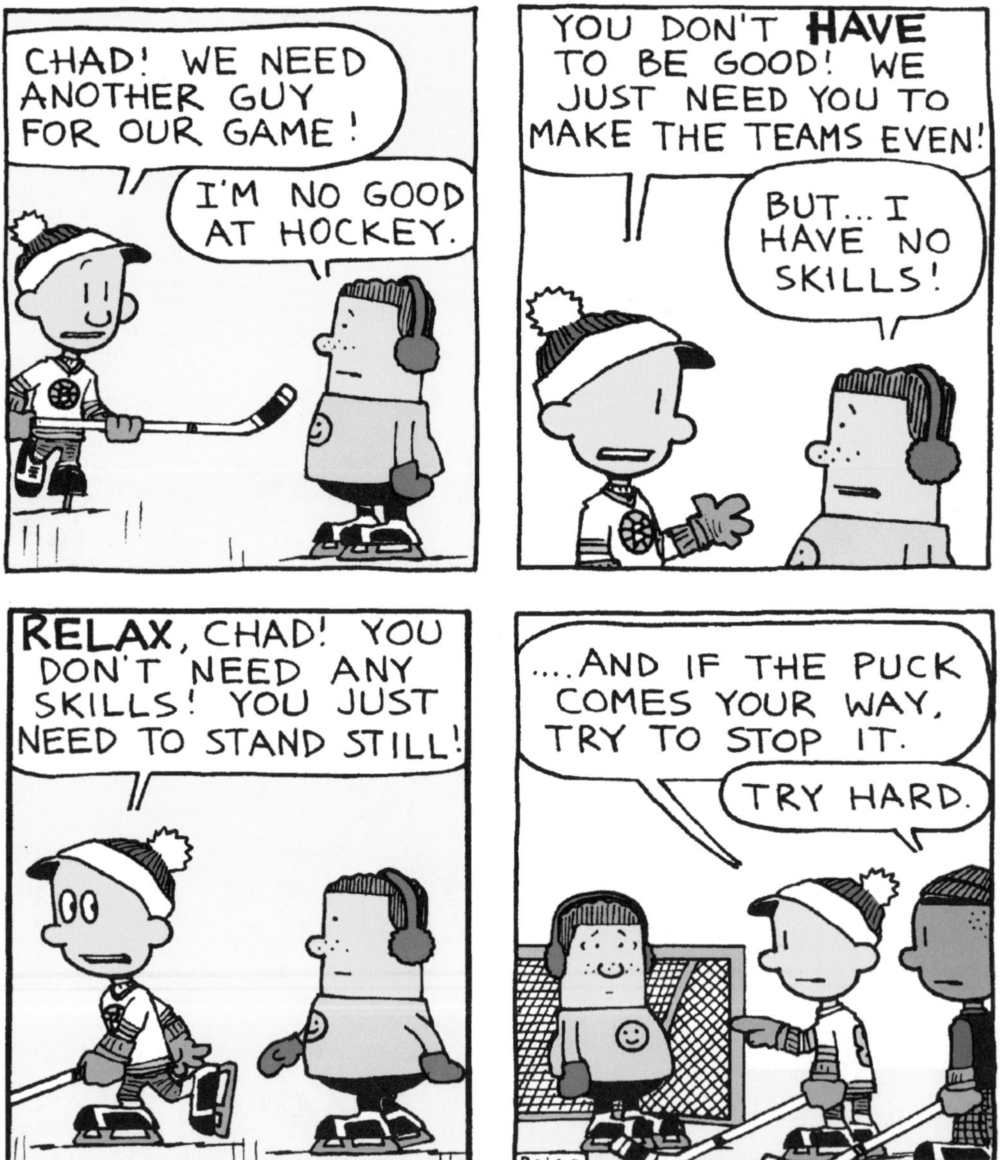
CHAD! WE NEED ANOTHER GUY FOR OUR GAME!
I'M NO GOOD AT HOCKEY.
YOU DON'T HAVE TO BE GOOD! WE JUST NEED YOU TO MAKE THE TEAMS EVEN!
BUT... I HAVE NO SKILLS!
RELAX, CHAD! YOU DON'T NEED ANY SKILLS! YOU JUST NEED TO STAND STILL!
....AND IF THE PUCK COMES YOUR WAY, TRY TO STOP IT.
TRY HARD.
Peirce

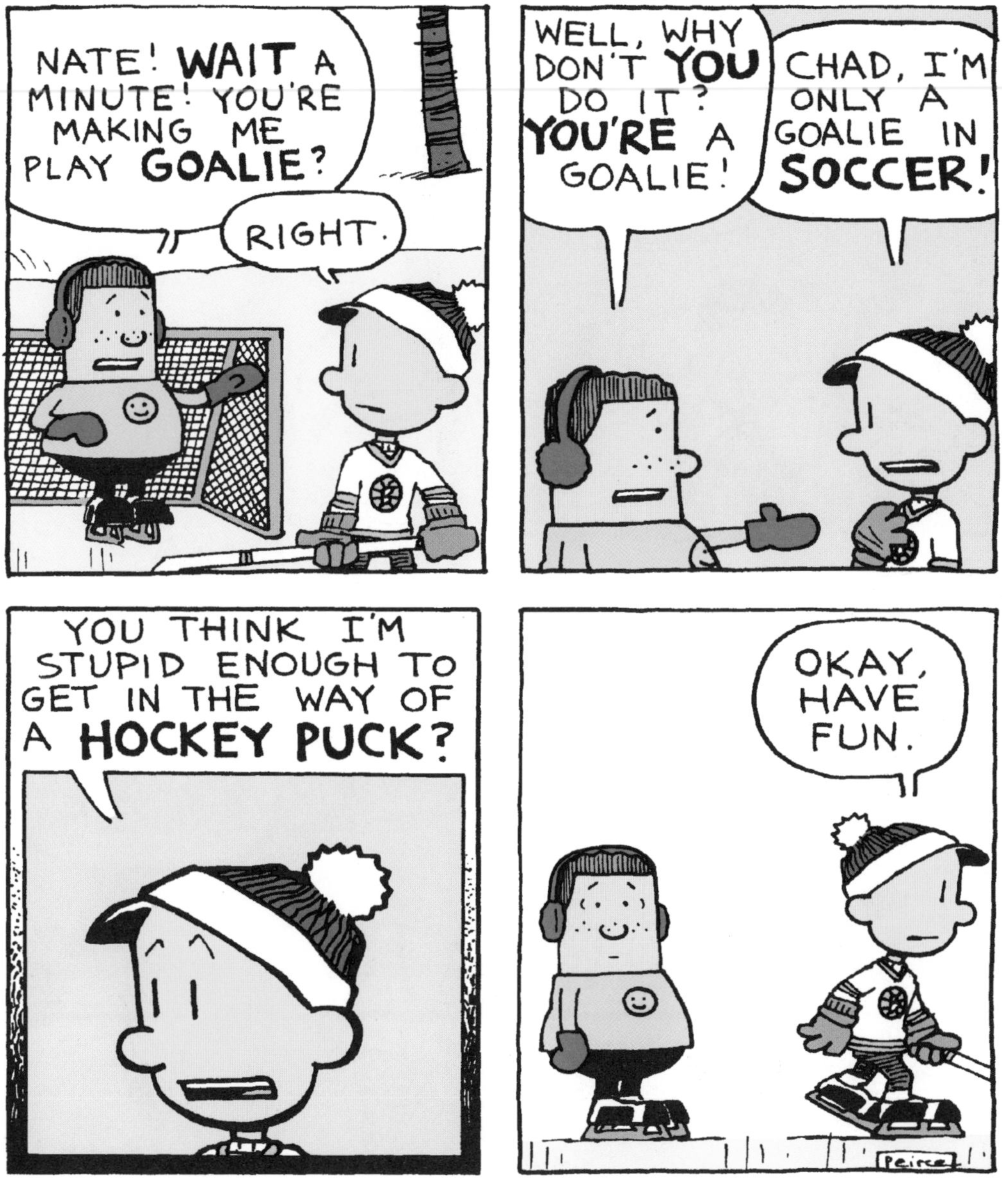
NATE! **WAIT** A MINUTE! YOU'RE MAKING ME PLAY **GOALIE**?
RIGHT.
WELL, WHY DON'T **YOU** DO IT? **YOU'RE** A GOALIE!
CHAD, I'M ONLY A GOALIE IN **SOCCER**!
YOU THINK I'M STUPID ENOUGH TO GET IN THE WAY OF A **HOCKEY PUCK**?
OKAY, HAVE FUN.
Peirce

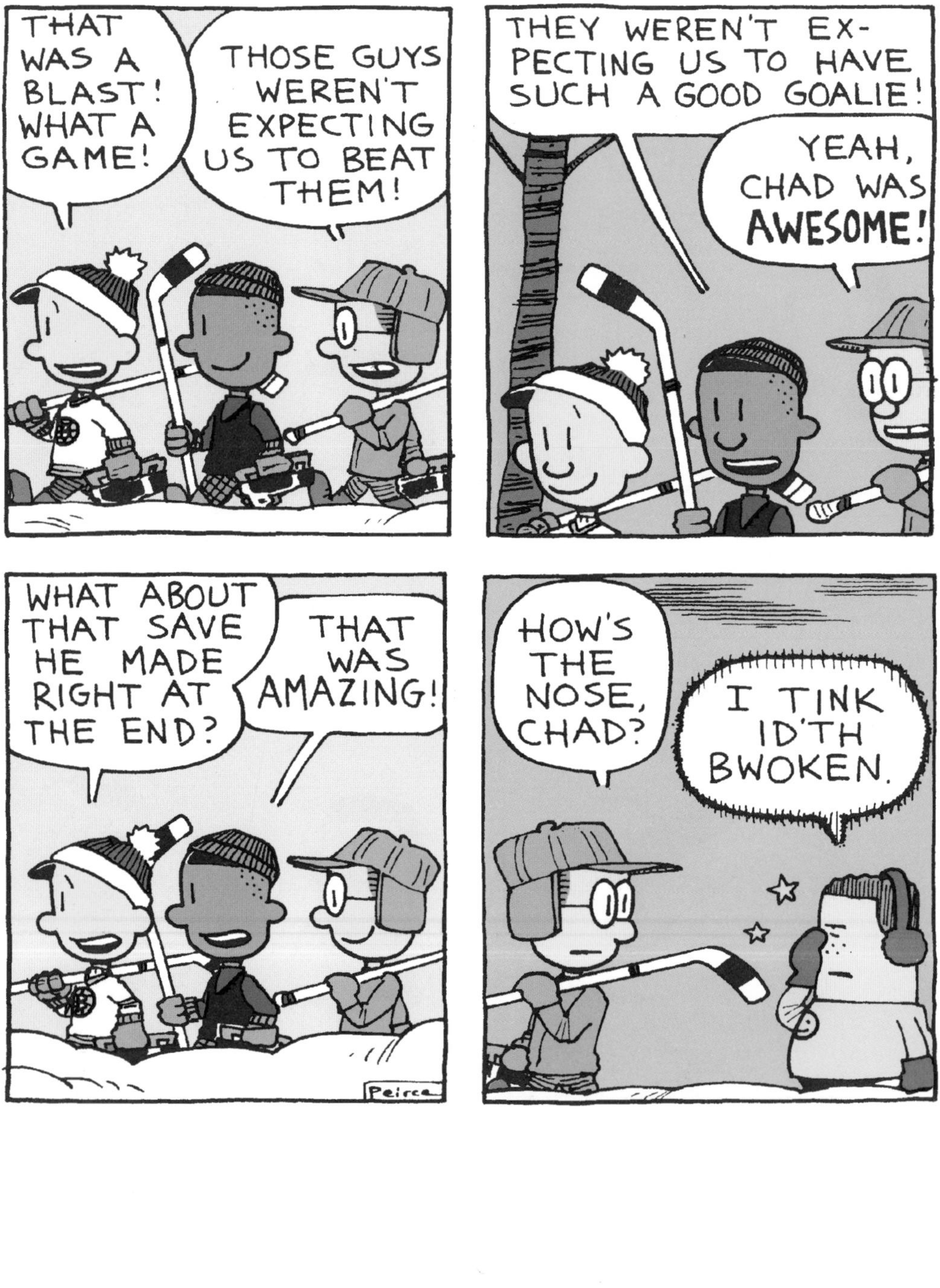
THAT WAS A BLAST! WHAT A GAME!
THOSE GUYS WEREN'T EXPECTING US TO BEAT THEM!
THEY WEREN'T EX-PECTING US TO HAVE SUCH A GOOD GOALIE!
YEAH, CHAD WAS **AWESOME!**
WHAT ABOUT THAT SAVE HE MADE RIGHT AT THE END?
THAT WAS AMAZING!
Peirce
HOW'S THE NOSE, CHAD?
I TINK ID'TH BWOKEN.

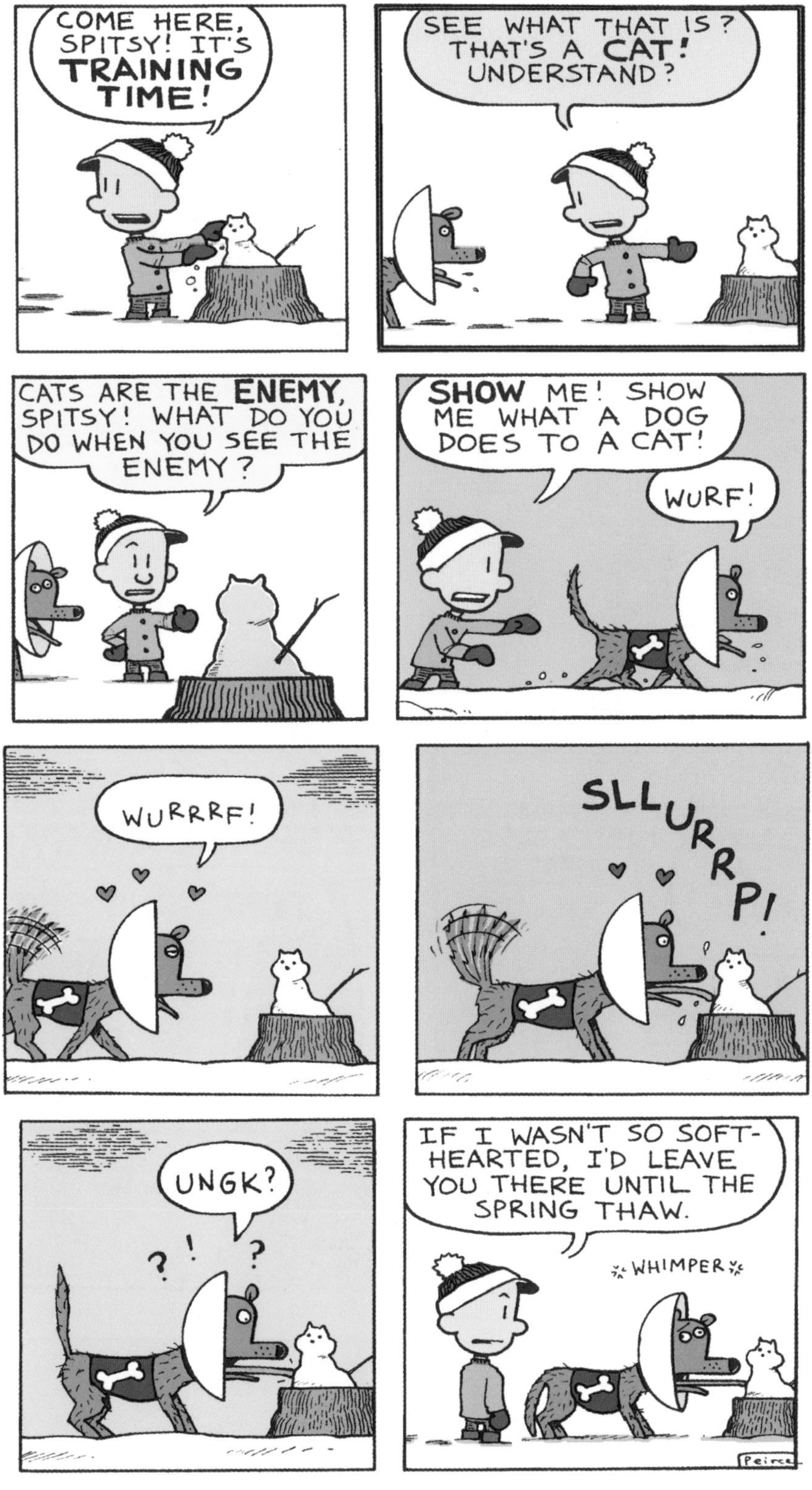
COME HERE, SPITSY! IT'S TRAINING TIME!
SEE WHAT THAT IS? THAT'S A CAT! UNDERSTAND?
CATS ARE THE ENEMY, SPITSY! WHAT DO YOU DO WHEN YOU SEE THE ENEMY?
SHOW ME! SHOW ME WHAT A DOG DOES TO A CAT!
WURF!
WURRRF!
SLLURRRP!
UNGK?
? ! ?
IF I WASN'T SO SOFT-HEARTED, I'D LEAVE YOU THERE UNTIL THE SPRING THAW.
WHIMPER
Peirce

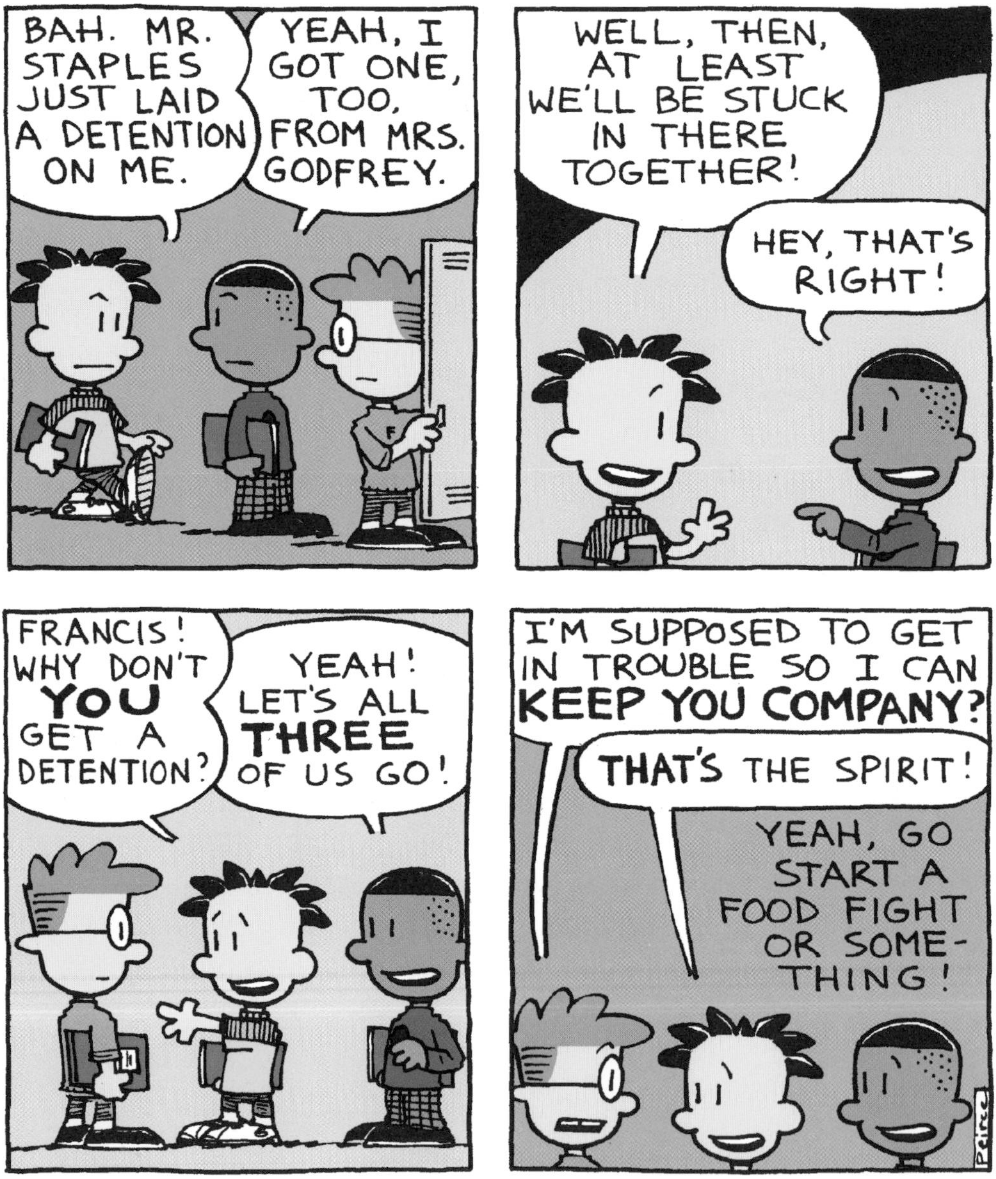
BAH. MR. STAPLES JUST LAID A DETENTION ON ME.
YEAH, I GOT ONE, TOO, FROM MRS. GODFREY.
WELL, THEN, AT LEAST WE'LL BE STUCK IN THERE TOGETHER!
HEY, THAT'S RIGHT!
FRANCIS! WHY DON'T **YOU** GET A DETENTION?
YEAH! LET'S ALL **THREE** OF US GO!
I'M SUPPOSED TO GET IN TROUBLE SO I CAN **KEEP YOU COMPANY?**
THAT'S THE SPIRIT!
YEAH, GO START A FOOD FIGHT OR SOME-THING!
PEIRCE

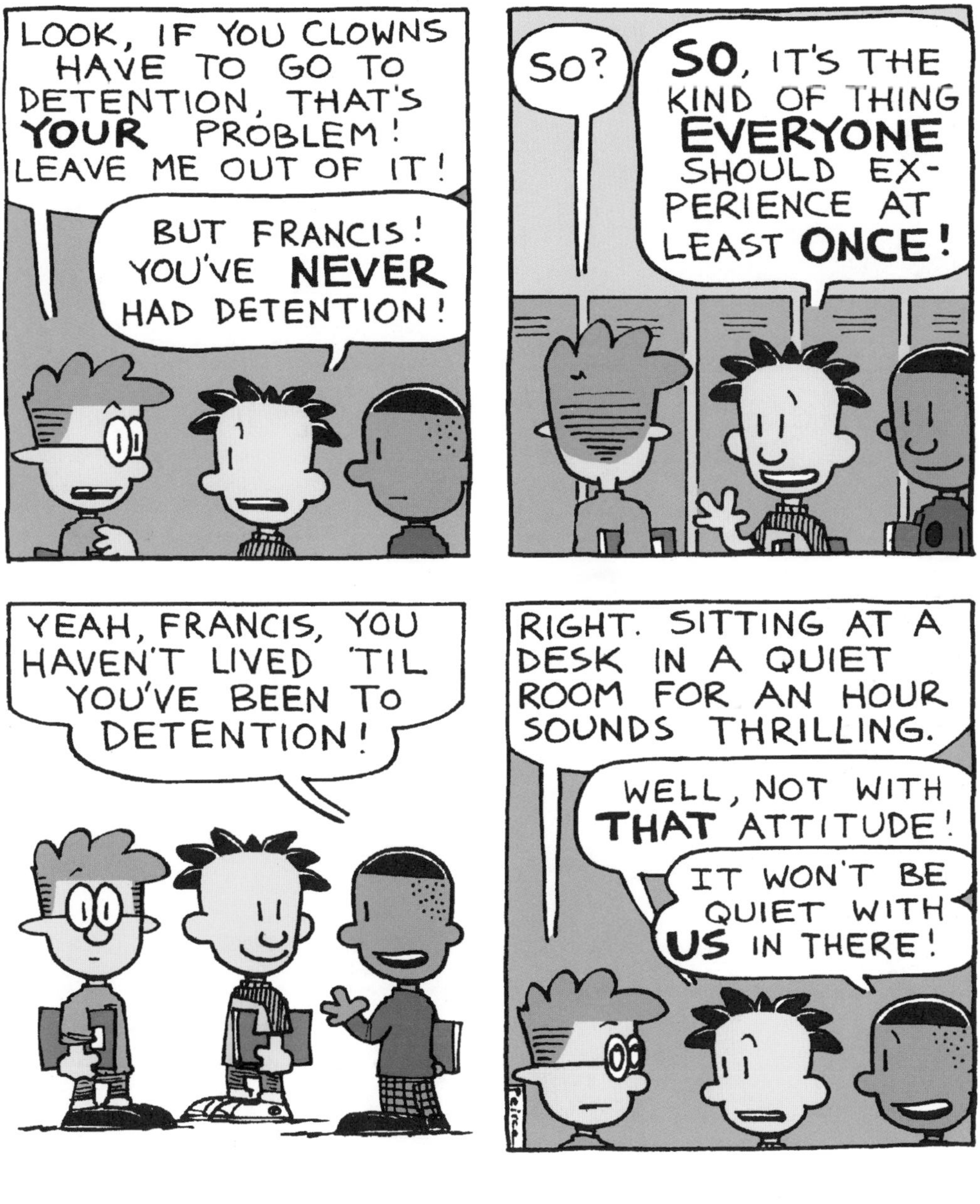
LOOK, IF YOU CLOWNS HAVE TO GO TO DETENTION, THAT'S YOUR PROBLEM! LEAVE ME OUT OF IT!
BUT FRANCIS! YOU'VE NEVER HAD DETENTION!
SO?
SO, IT'S THE KIND OF THING EVERYONE SHOULD EXPERIENCE AT LEAST ONCE!
YEAH, FRANCIS, YOU HAVEN'T LIVED 'TIL YOU'VE BEEN TO DETENTION!
RIGHT. SITTING AT A DESK IN A QUIET ROOM FOR AN HOUR SOUNDS THRILLING.
WELL, NOT WITH THAT ATTITUDE!
IT WON'T BE QUIET WITH US IN THERE!
Peirce

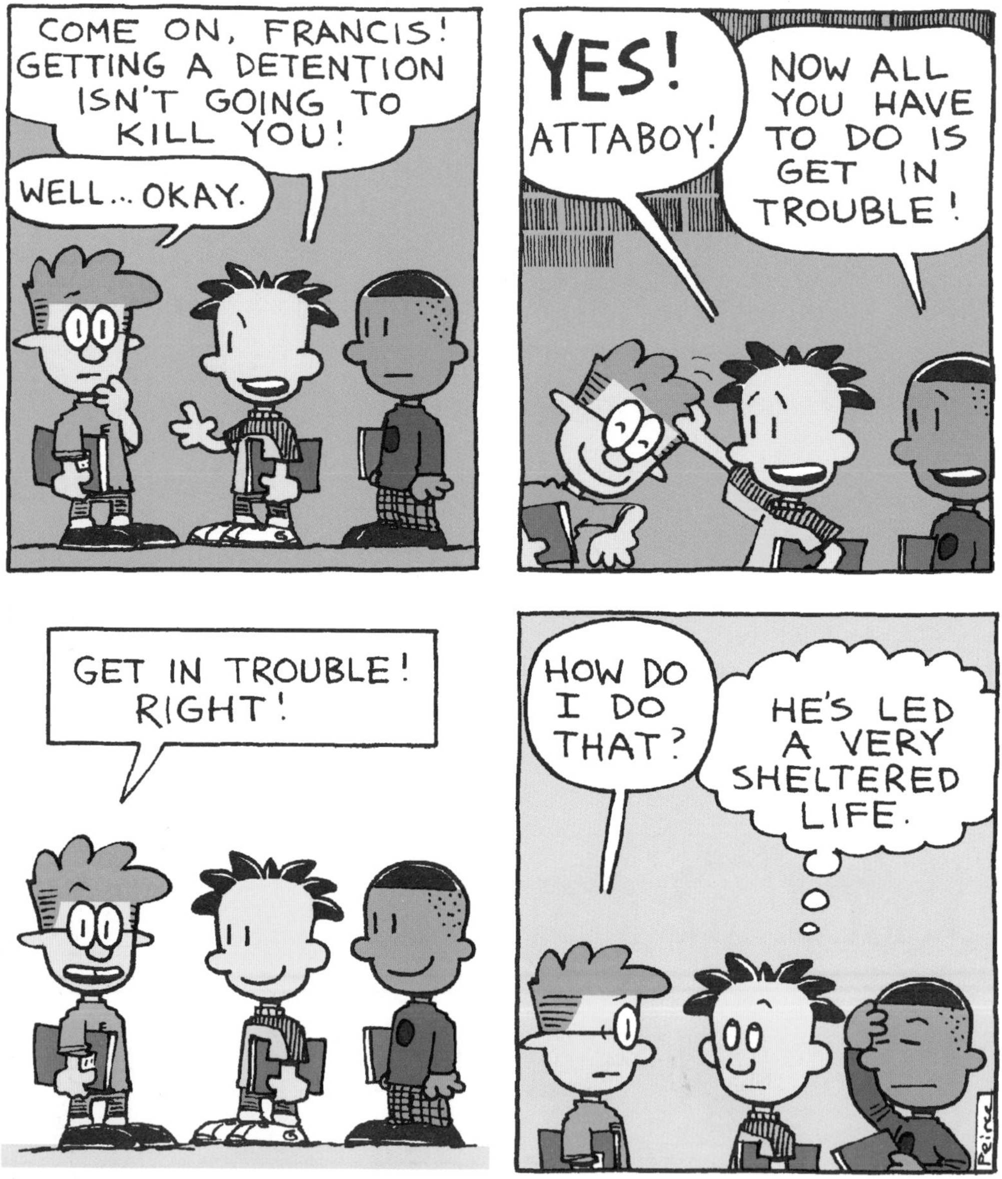
COME ON, FRANCIS! GETTING A DETENTION ISN'T GOING TO KILL YOU!
WELL... OKAY.
YES! ATTABOY!
NOW ALL YOU HAVE TO DO IS GET IN TROUBLE!
GET IN TROUBLE! RIGHT!
HOW DO I DO THAT?
HE'S LED A VERY SHELTERED LIFE.
Peirce

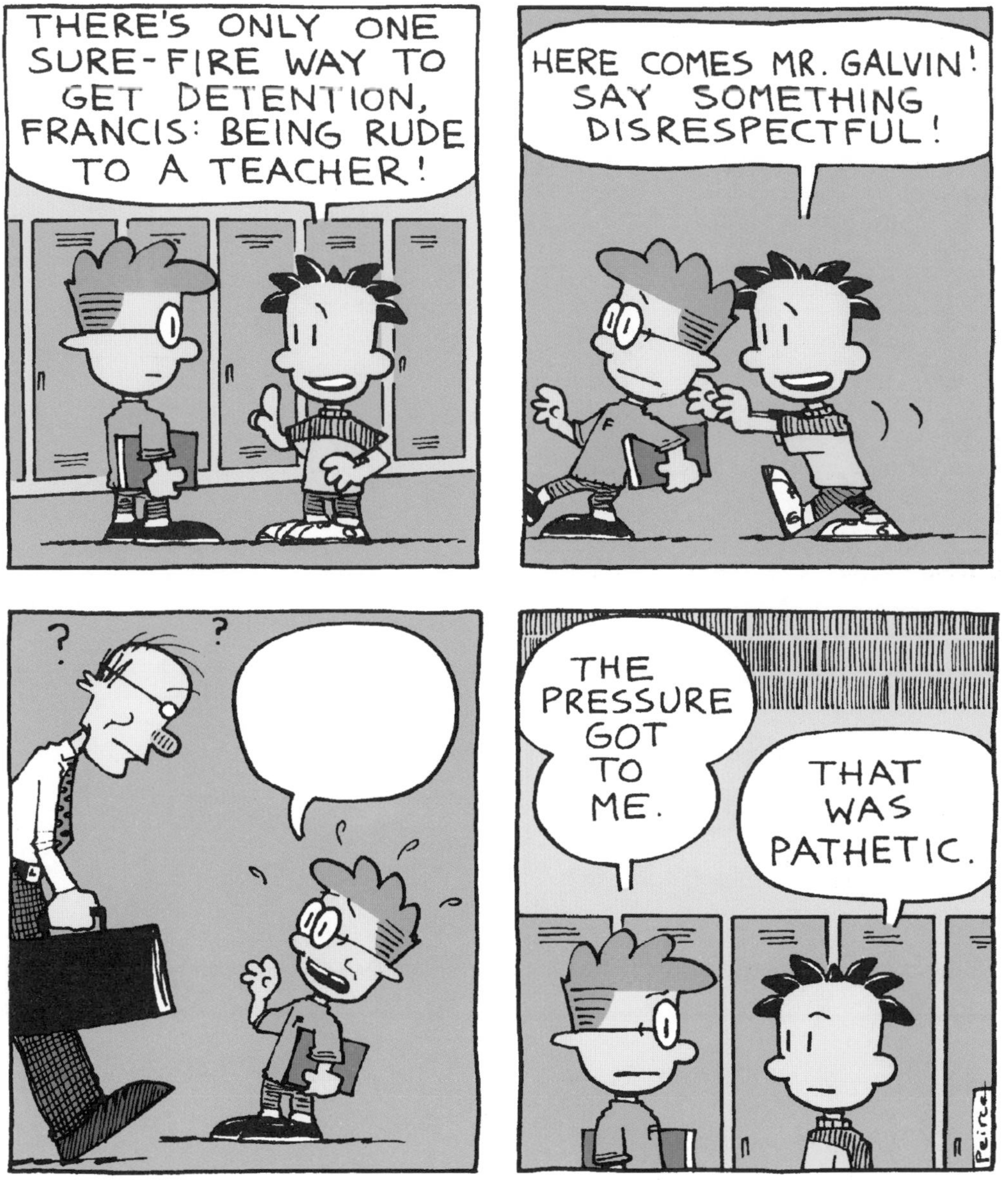
THERE'S ONLY ONE SURE-FIRE WAY TO GET DETENTION, FRANCIS: BEING RUDE TO A TEACHER!
HERE COMES MR. GALVIN! SAY SOMETHING DISRESPECTFUL!
?
?
THE PRESSURE GOT TO ME.
THAT WAS PATHETIC.
Peirce

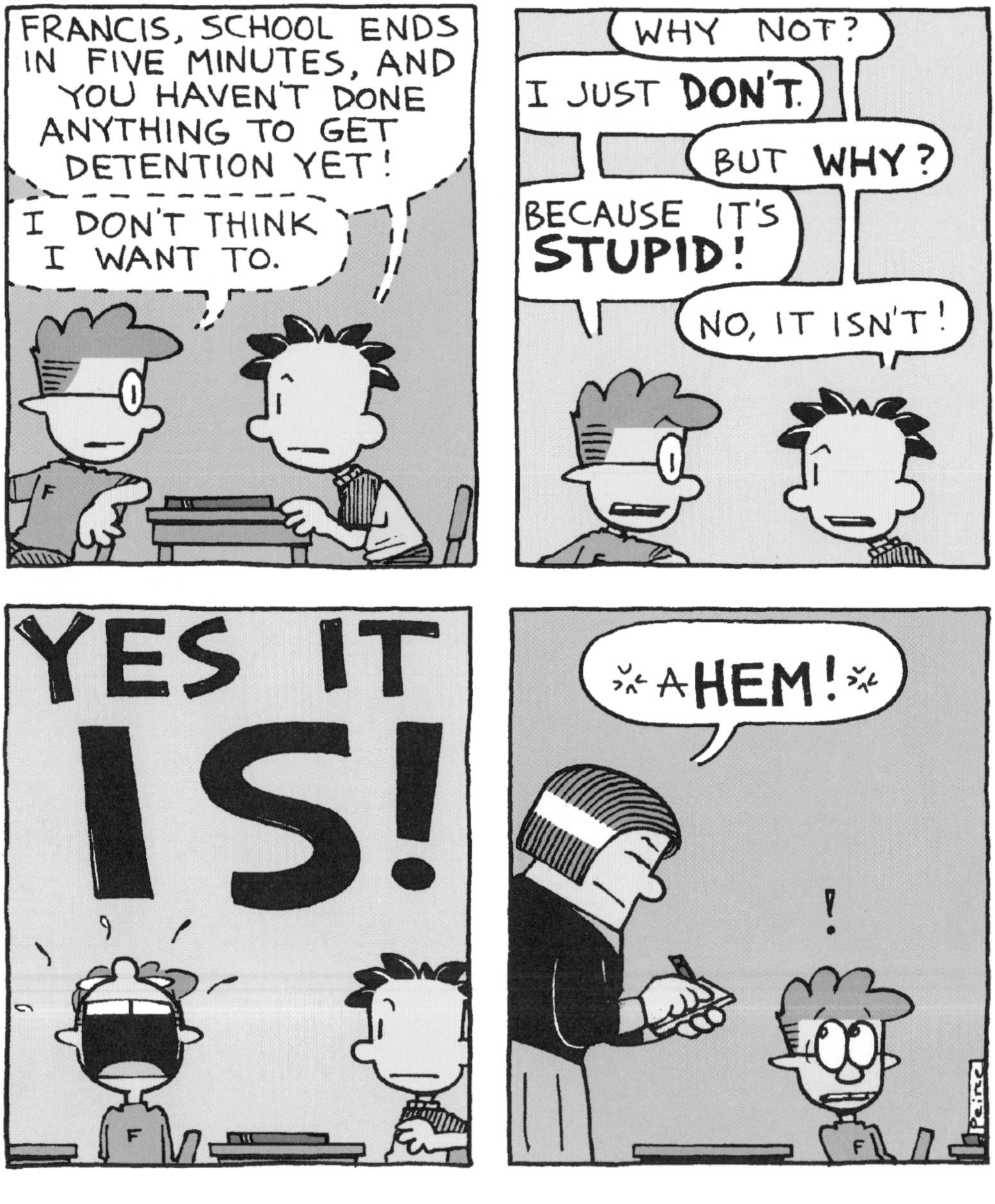
FRANCIS, SCHOOL ENDS IN FIVE MINUTES, AND YOU HAVEN'T DONE ANYTHING TO GET DETENTION YET!
I DON'T THINK I WANT TO.
WHY NOT?
I JUST DON'T.
BUT WHY?
BECAUSE IT'S STUPID!
NO, IT ISN'T!
YES IT IS!
AHEM!
!
Peirce

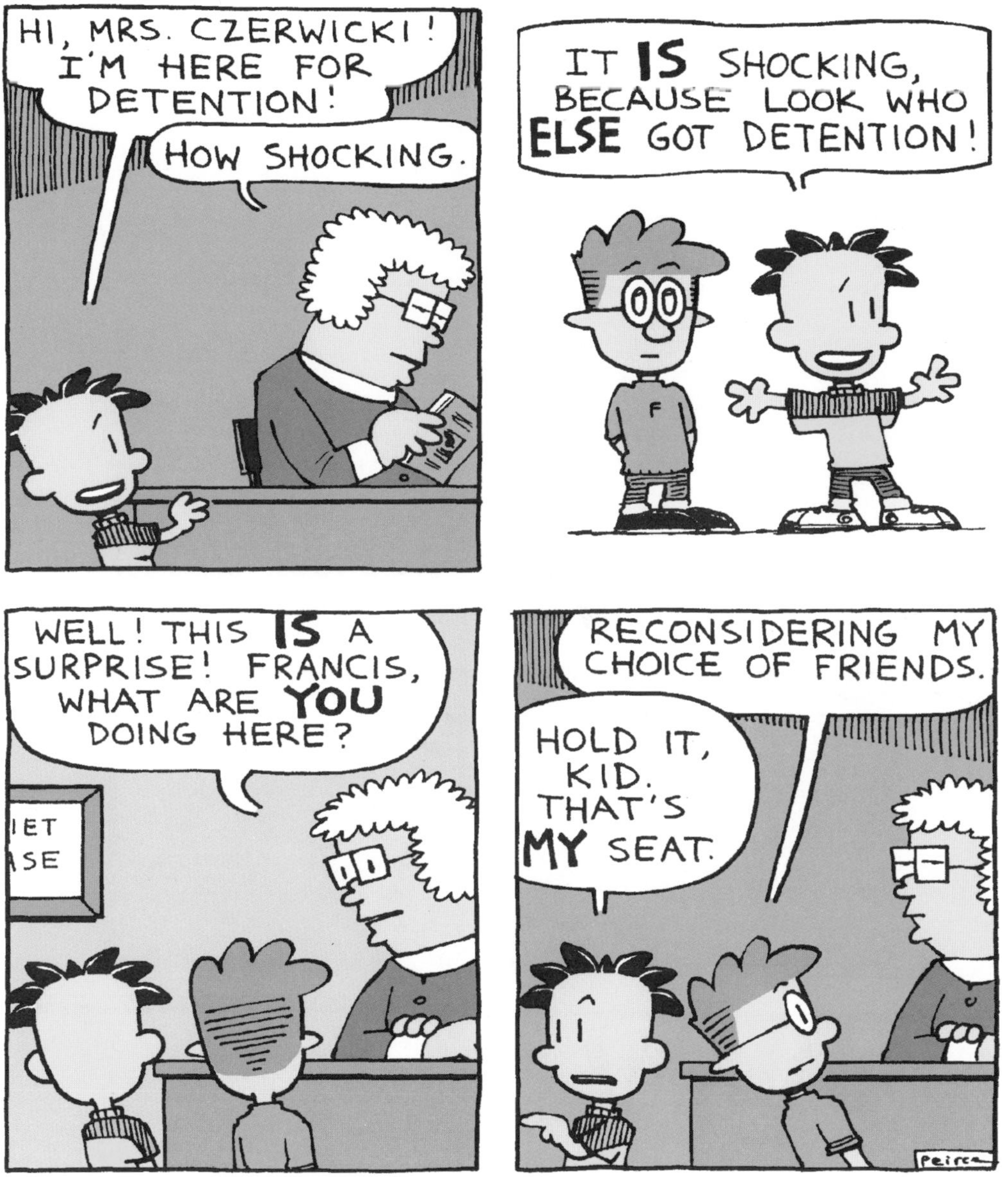
HI, MRS. CZERWICKI! I'M HERE FOR DETENTION!
HOW SHOCKING.
IT IS SHOCKING, BECAUSE LOOK WHO ELSE GOT DETENTION!
F
WELL! THIS IS A SURPRISE! FRANCIS, WHAT ARE YOU DOING HERE?
IET
ASE
RECONSIDERING MY CHOICE OF FRIENDS.
HOLD IT, KID. THAT'S MY SEAT.
Peirce

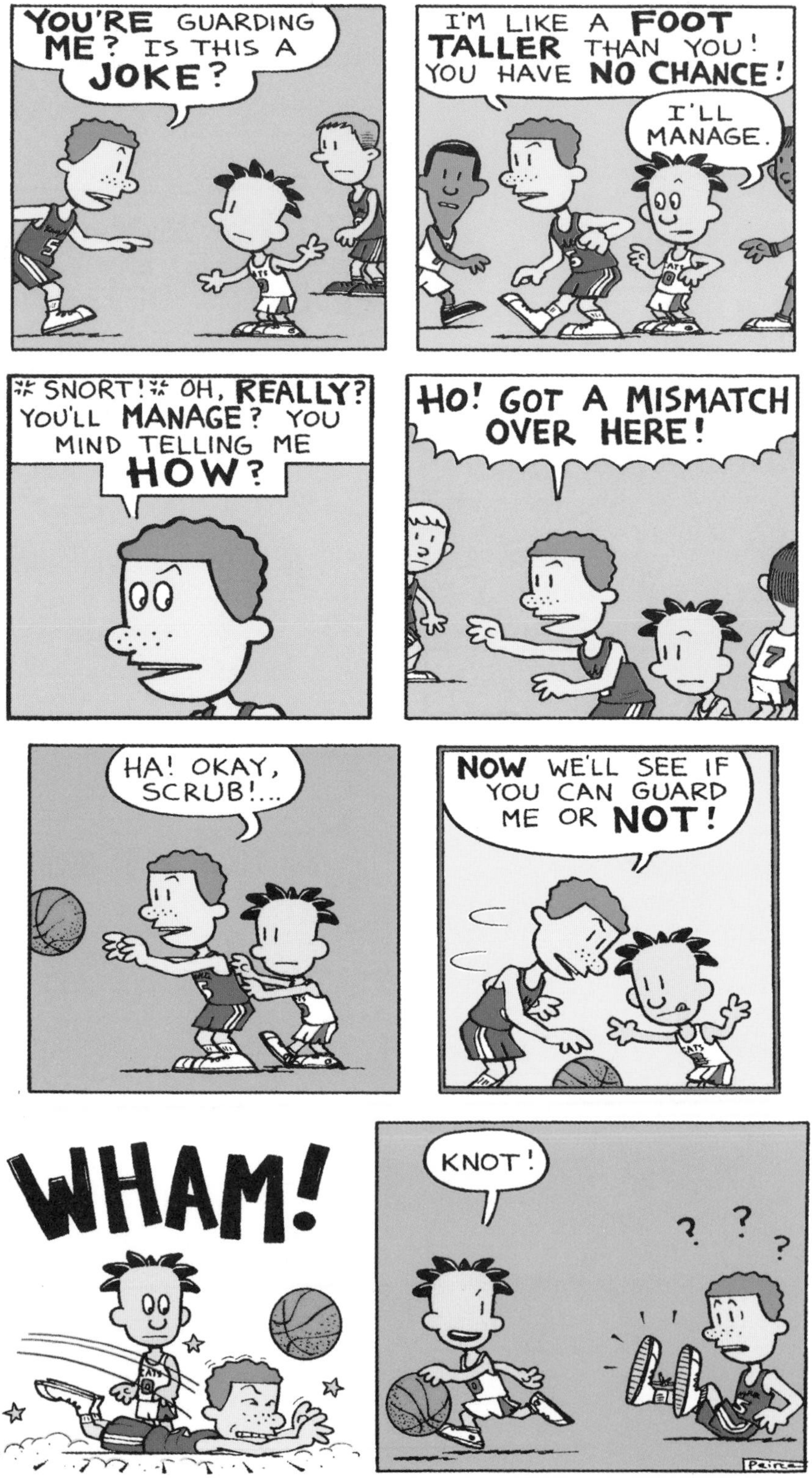
YOU'RE GUARDING ME? IS THIS A JOKE?
I'M LIKE A FOOT TALLER THAN YOU! YOU HAVE NO CHANCE!
I'LL MANAGE.
SNORT! OH, REALLY? YOU'LL MANAGE? YOU MIND TELLING ME HOW?
HO! GOT A MISMATCH OVER HERE!
HA! OKAY, SCRUB!...
NOW WE'LL SEE IF YOU CAN GUARD ME OR NOT!
WHAM!
KNOT!
? ? ?

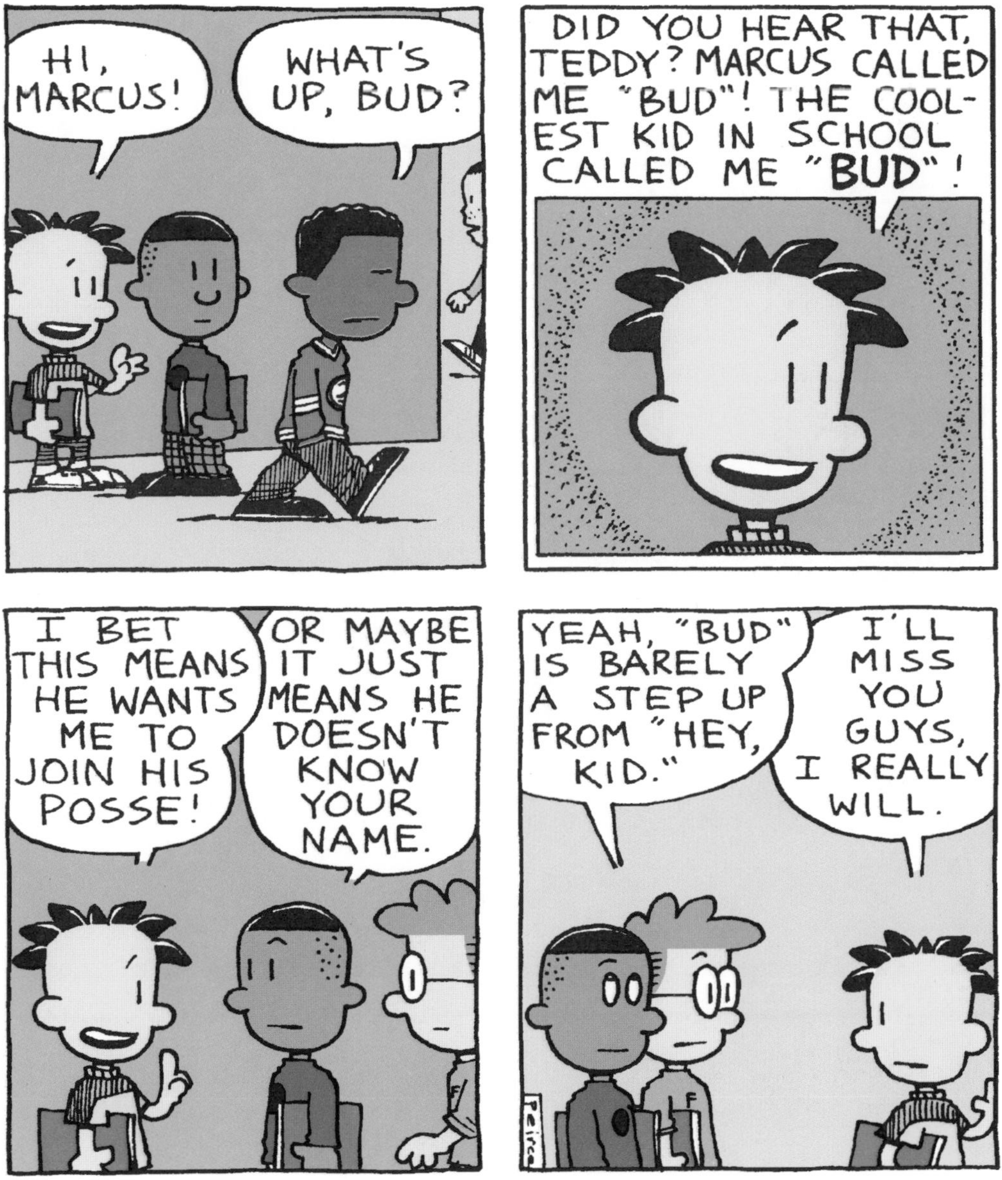
HI, MARCUS!
WHAT'S UP, BUD?
DID YOU HEAR THAT, TEDDY? MARCUS CALLED ME "BUD"! THE COOLEST KID IN SCHOOL CALLED ME "BUD"!
I BET THIS MEANS HE WANTS ME TO JOIN HIS POSSE!
OR MAYBE IT JUST MEANS HE DOESN'T KNOW YOUR NAME.
YEAH, "BUD" IS BARELY A STEP UP FROM "HEY, KID."
I'LL MISS YOU GUYS, I REALLY WILL.
Peirce

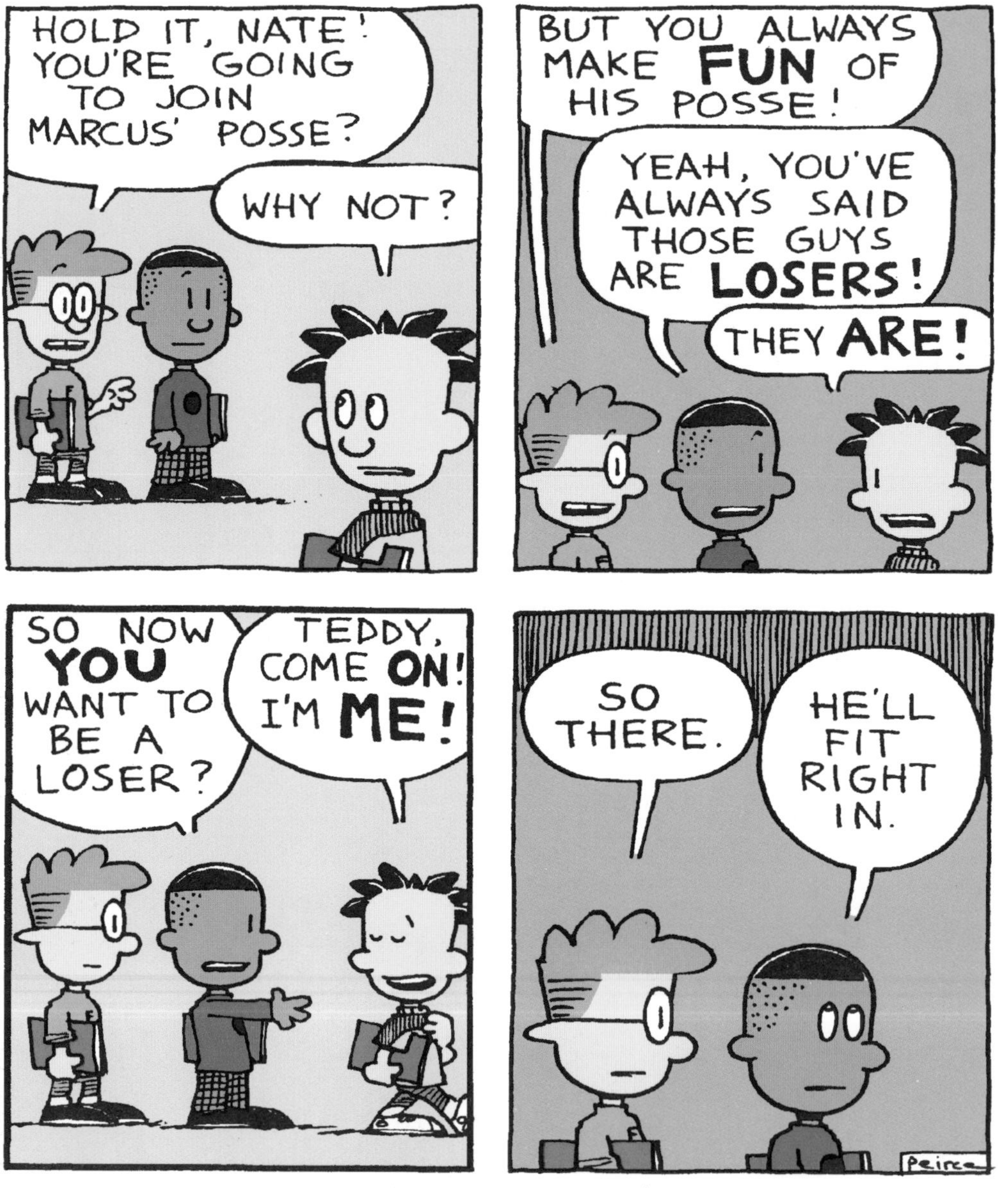
HOLD IT, NATE! YOU'RE GOING TO JOIN MARCUS' POSSE?
WHY NOT?
BUT YOU ALWAYS MAKE **FUN** OF HIS POSSE!
YEAH, YOU'VE ALWAYS SAID THOSE GUYS ARE **LOSERS**!
THEY **ARE**!
SO NOW **YOU** WANT TO BE A LOSER?
TEDDY, COME **ON**! I'M **ME**!
SO THERE.
HE'LL FIT RIGHT IN.
Peirce

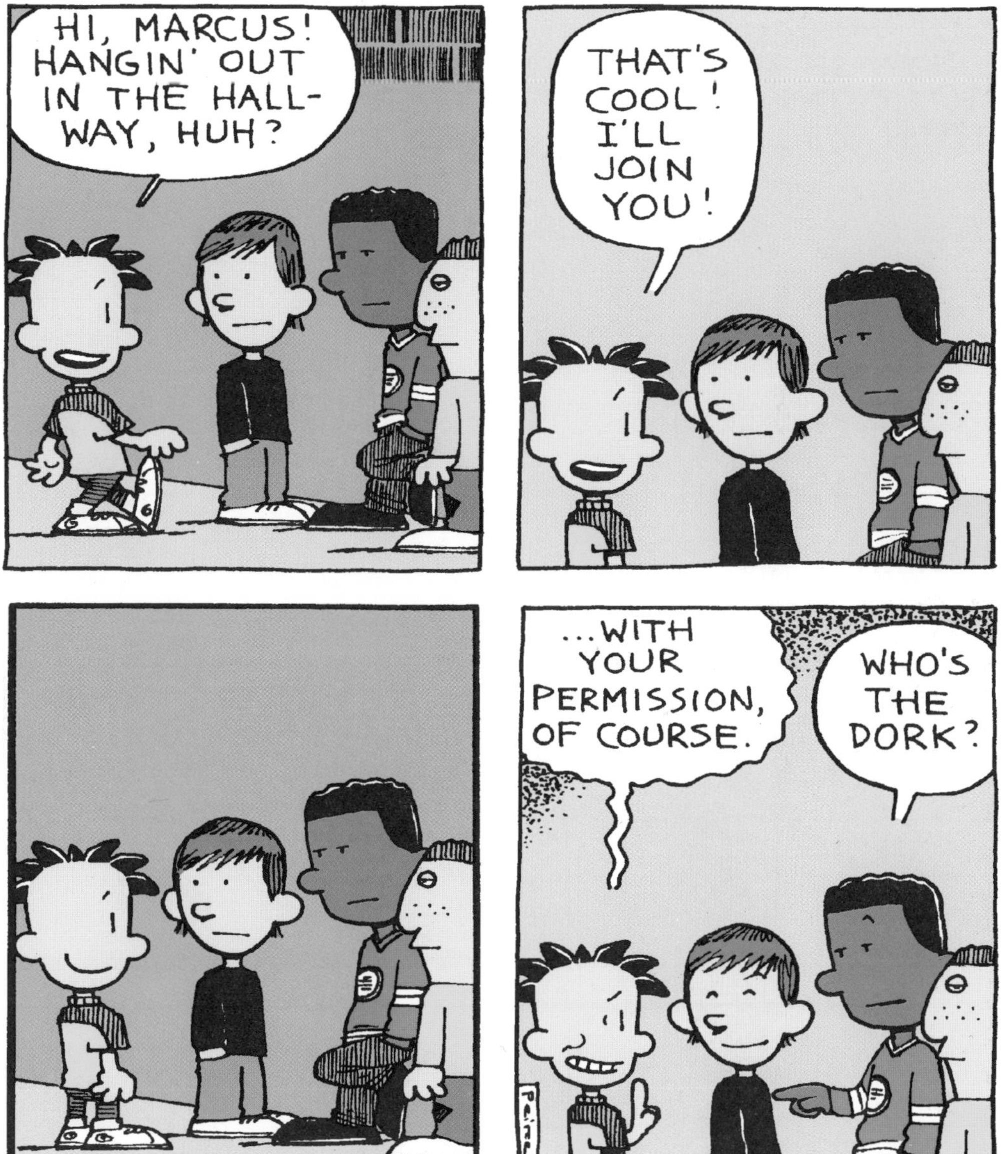
HI, MARCUS! HANGIN' OUT IN THE HALL-WAY, HUH?
THAT'S COOL! I'LL JOIN YOU!
...WITH YOUR PERMISSION, OF COURSE.
WHO'S THE DORK?

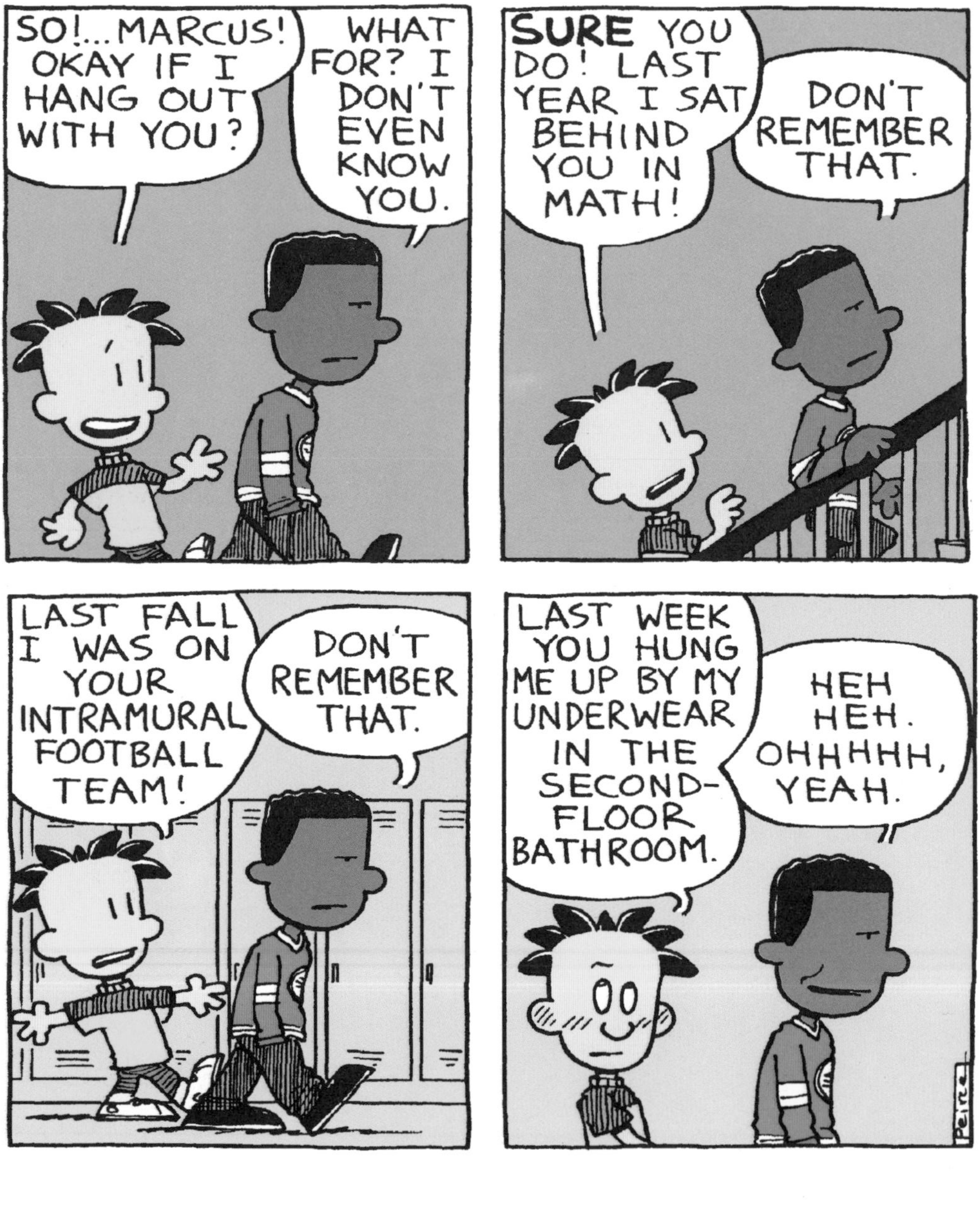
SO!...MARCUS! OKAY IF I HANG OUT WITH YOU?
WHAT FOR? I DON'T EVEN KNOW YOU.
SURE YOU DO! LAST YEAR I SAT BEHIND YOU IN MATH!
DON'T REMEMBER THAT.
LAST FALL I WAS ON YOUR INTRAMURAL FOOTBALL TEAM!
DON'T REMEMBER THAT.
LAST WEEK YOU HUNG ME UP BY MY UNDERWEAR IN THE SECOND-FLOOR BATHROOM.
HEH HEH. OHHHHH, YEAH.
Peirce

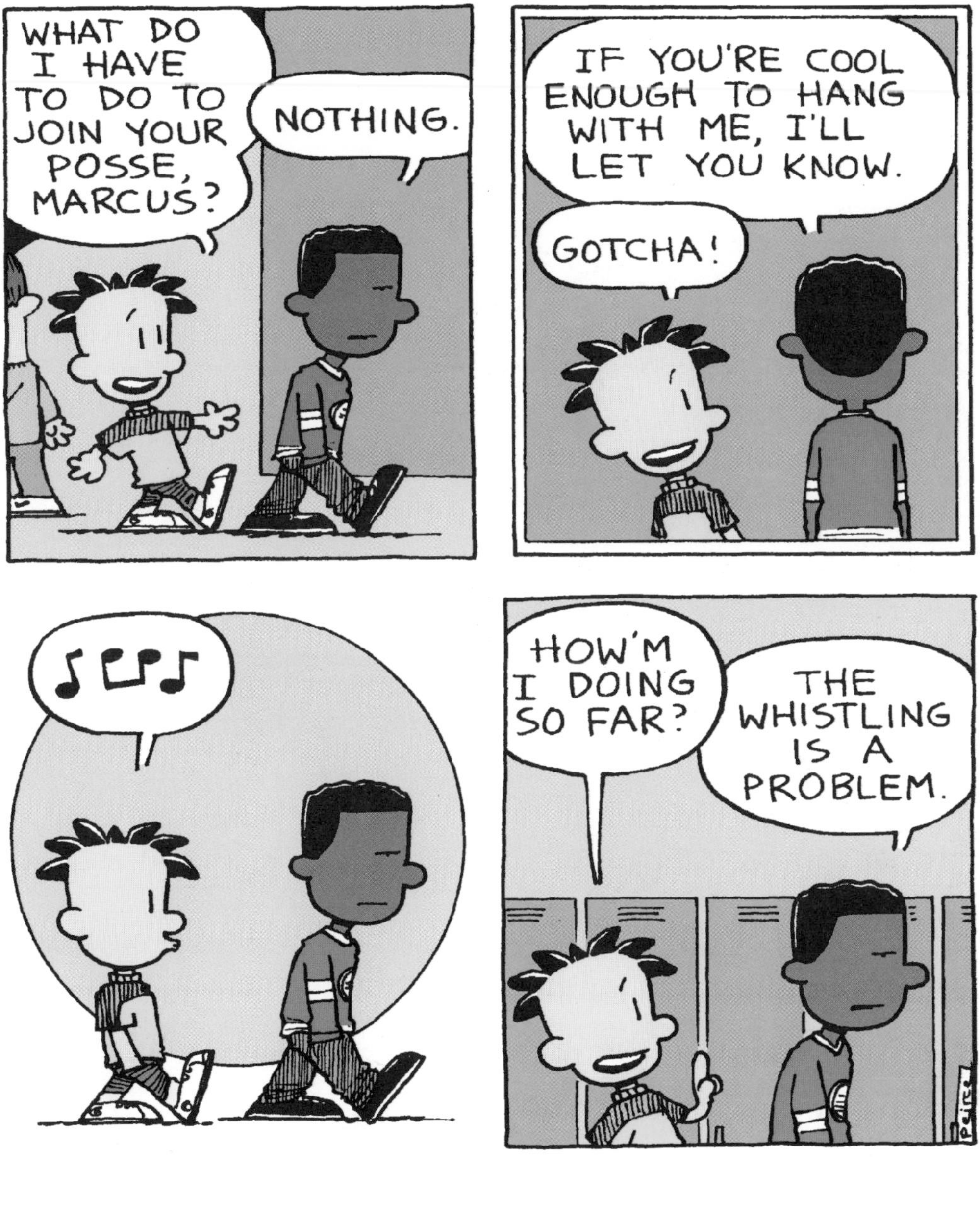
WHAT DO I HAVE TO DO TO JOIN YOUR POSSE, MARCUS?
NOTHING.
IF YOU'RE COOL ENOUGH TO HANG WITH ME, I'LL LET YOU KNOW.
GOTCHA!
HOW'M I DOING SO FAR?
THE WHISTLING IS A PROBLEM.
PEIRCE

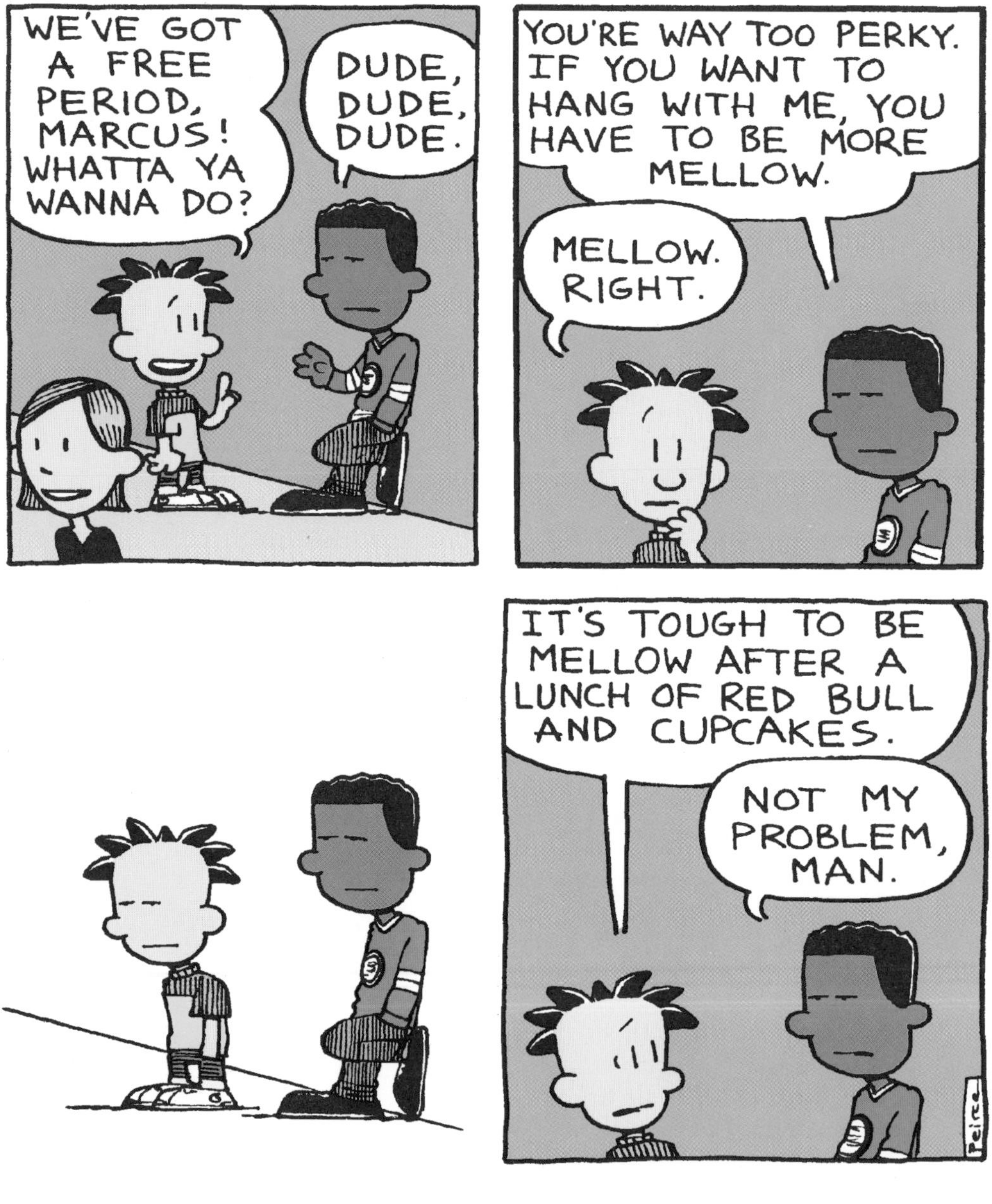
WE'VE GOT A FREE PERIOD, MARCUS! WHATTA YA WANNA DO?
DUDE, DUDE, DUDE.
YOU'RE WAY TOO PERKY. IF YOU WANT TO HANG WITH ME, YOU HAVE TO BE MORE MELLOW.
MELLOW. RIGHT.
IT'S TOUGH TO BE MELLOW AFTER A LUNCH OF RED BULL AND CUPCAKES.
NOT MY PROBLEM, MAN.
Peirce

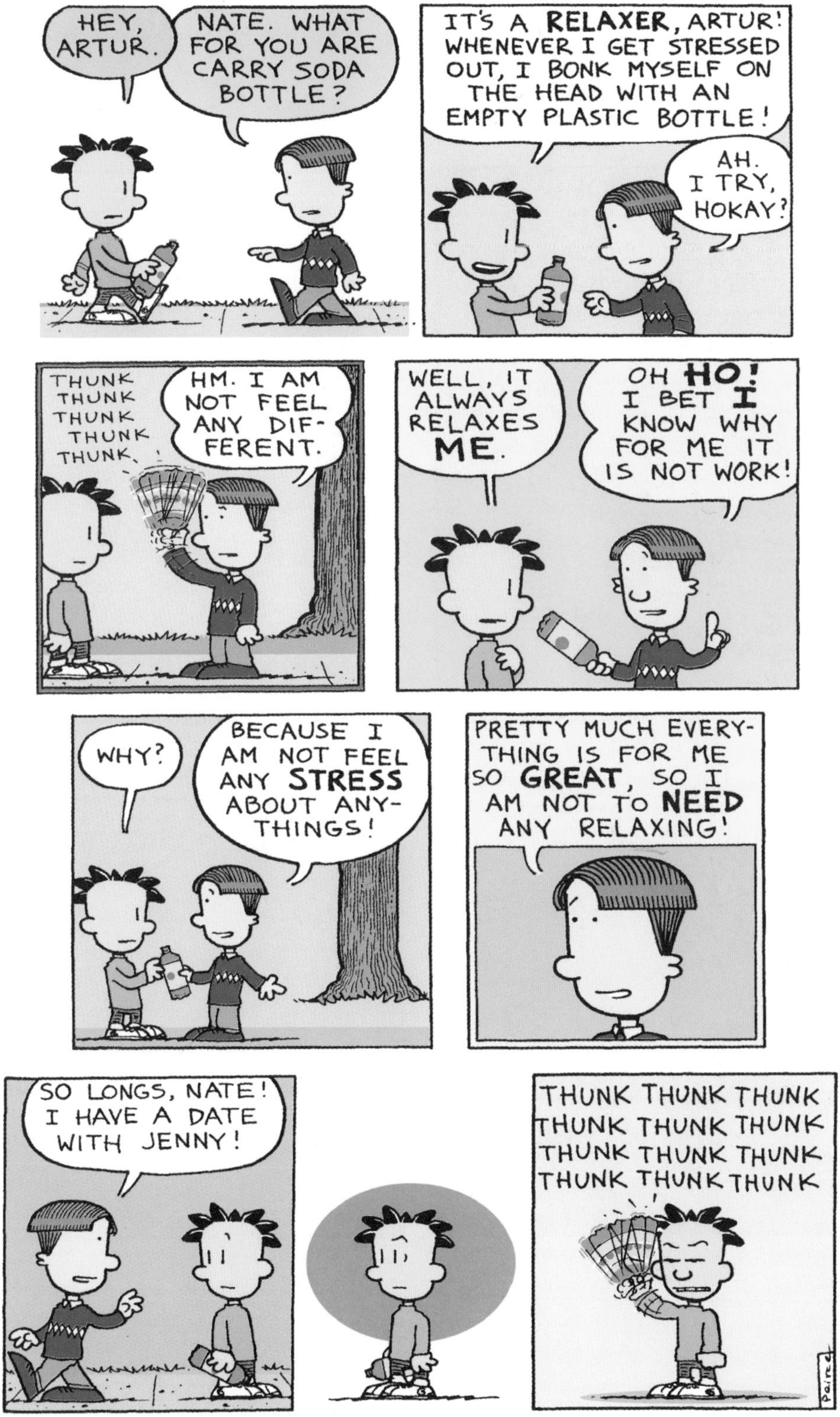
HEY, ARTUR.
NATE. WHAT FOR YOU ARE CARRY SODA BOTTLE?
IT'S A RELAXER, ARTUR! WHENEVER I GET STRESSED OUT, I BONK MYSELF ON THE HEAD WITH AN EMPTY PLASTIC BOTTLE!
AH. I TRY, HOKAY?
THUNK THUNK THUNK THUNK THUNK
HM. I AM NOT FEEL ANY DIF-FERENT.
WELL, IT ALWAYS RELAXES ME.
OH HO! I BET I KNOW WHY FOR ME IT IS NOT WORK!
WHY?
BECAUSE I AM NOT FEEL ANY STRESS ABOUT ANY-THINGS!
PRETTY MUCH EVERY-THING IS FOR ME SO GREAT, SO I AM NOT TO NEED ANY RELAXING!
SO LONGS, NATE! I HAVE A DATE WITH JENNY!
THUNK THUNK THUNK THUNK THUNK THUNK THUNK THUNK THUNK THUNK THUNK THUNK
Peirce

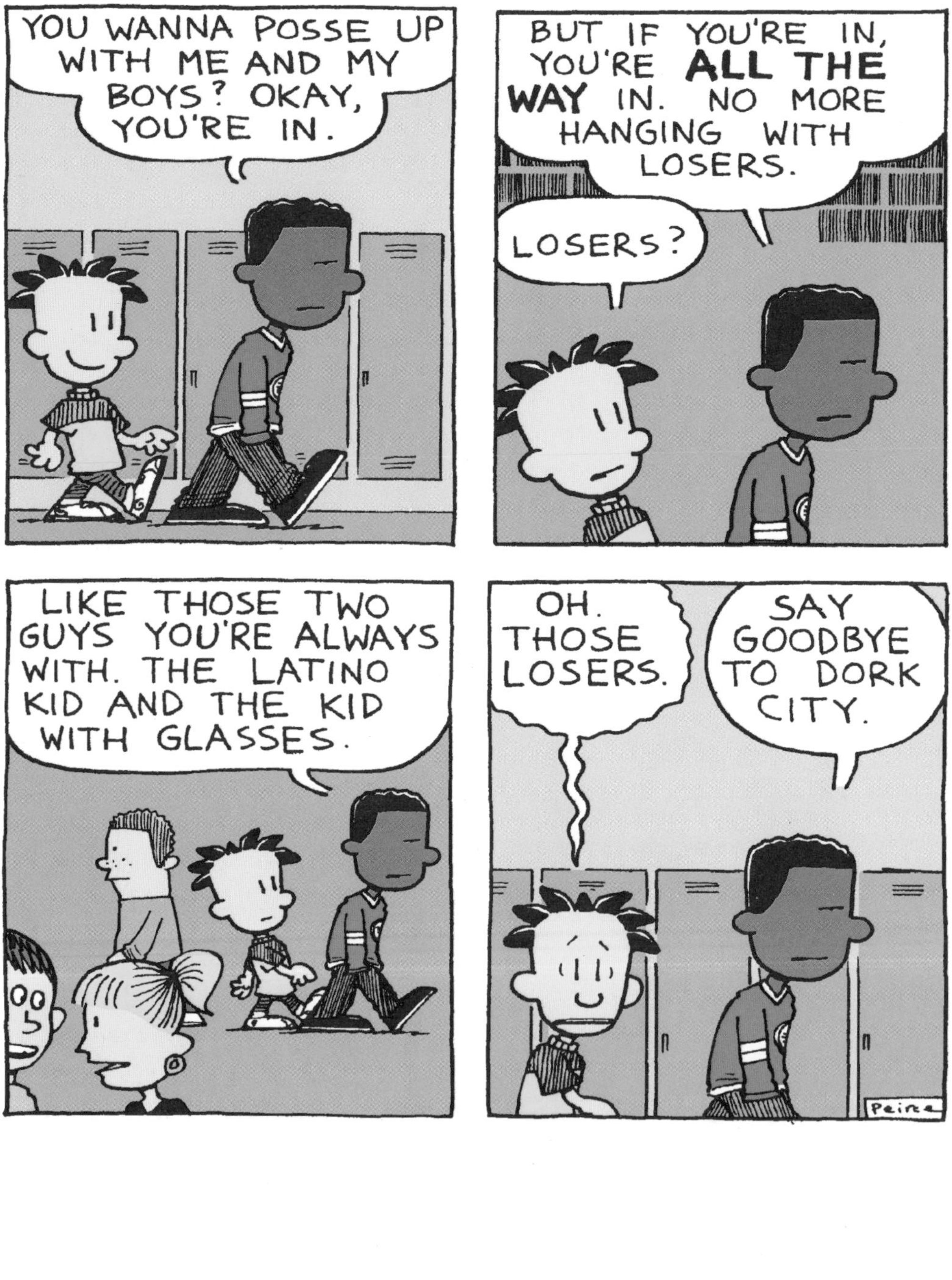
YOU WANNA POSSE UP WITH ME AND MY BOYS? OKAY, YOU'RE IN.
BUT IF YOU'RE IN, YOU'RE **ALL THE WAY** IN. NO MORE HANGING WITH LOSERS.
LOSERS?
LIKE THOSE TWO GUYS YOU'RE ALWAYS WITH. THE LATINO KID AND THE KID WITH GLASSES.
OH. THOSE LOSERS.
SAY GOODBYE TO DORK CITY.
Peirce

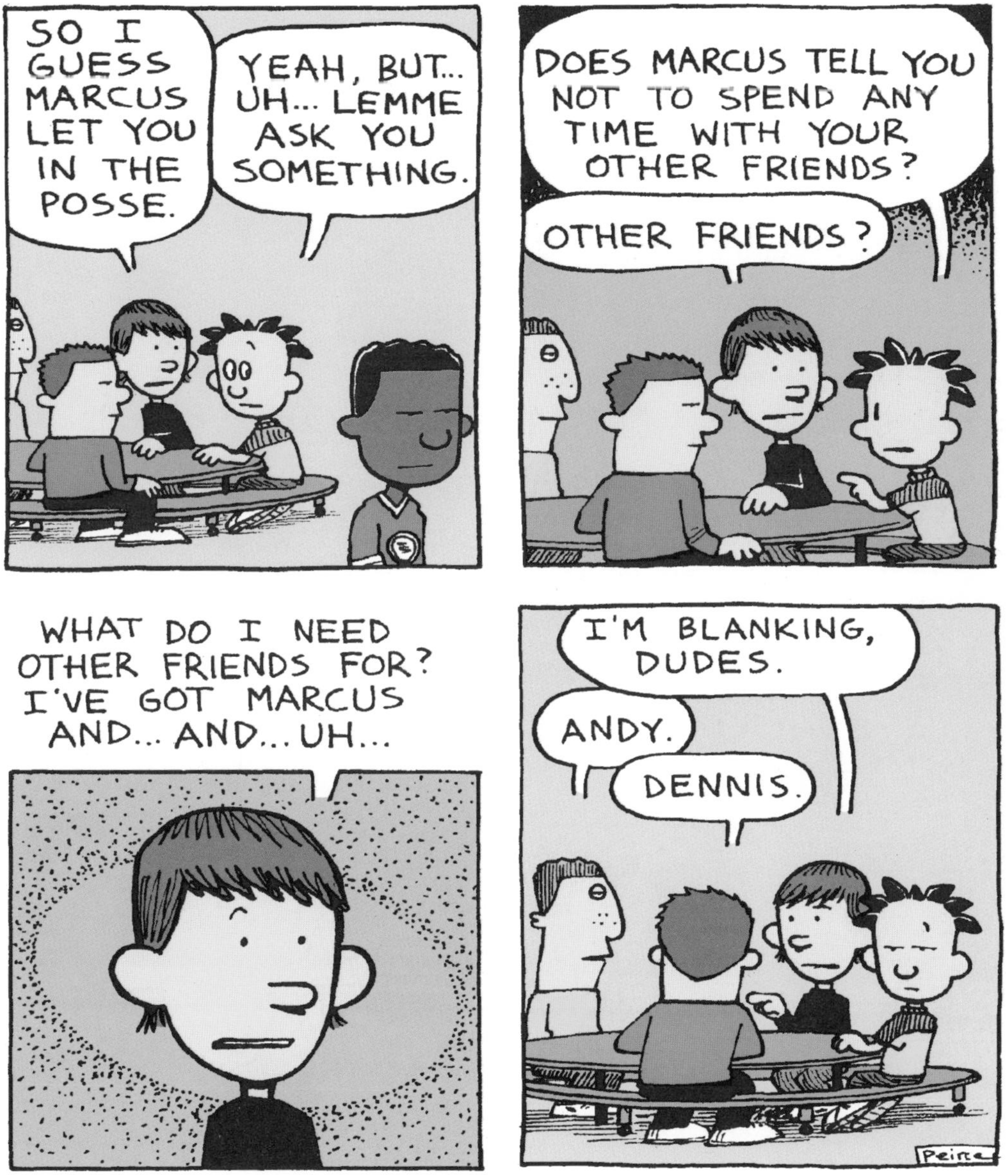
SO I GUESS MARCUS LET YOU IN THE POSSE.
YEAH, BUT... UH... LEMME ASK YOU SOMETHING.
DOES MARCUS TELL YOU NOT TO SPEND ANY TIME WITH YOUR OTHER FRIENDS?
OTHER FRIENDS?
WHAT DO I NEED OTHER FRIENDS FOR? I'VE GOT MARCUS AND... AND... UH...
I'M BLANKING, DUDES.
ANDY.
DENNIS.
Peirce

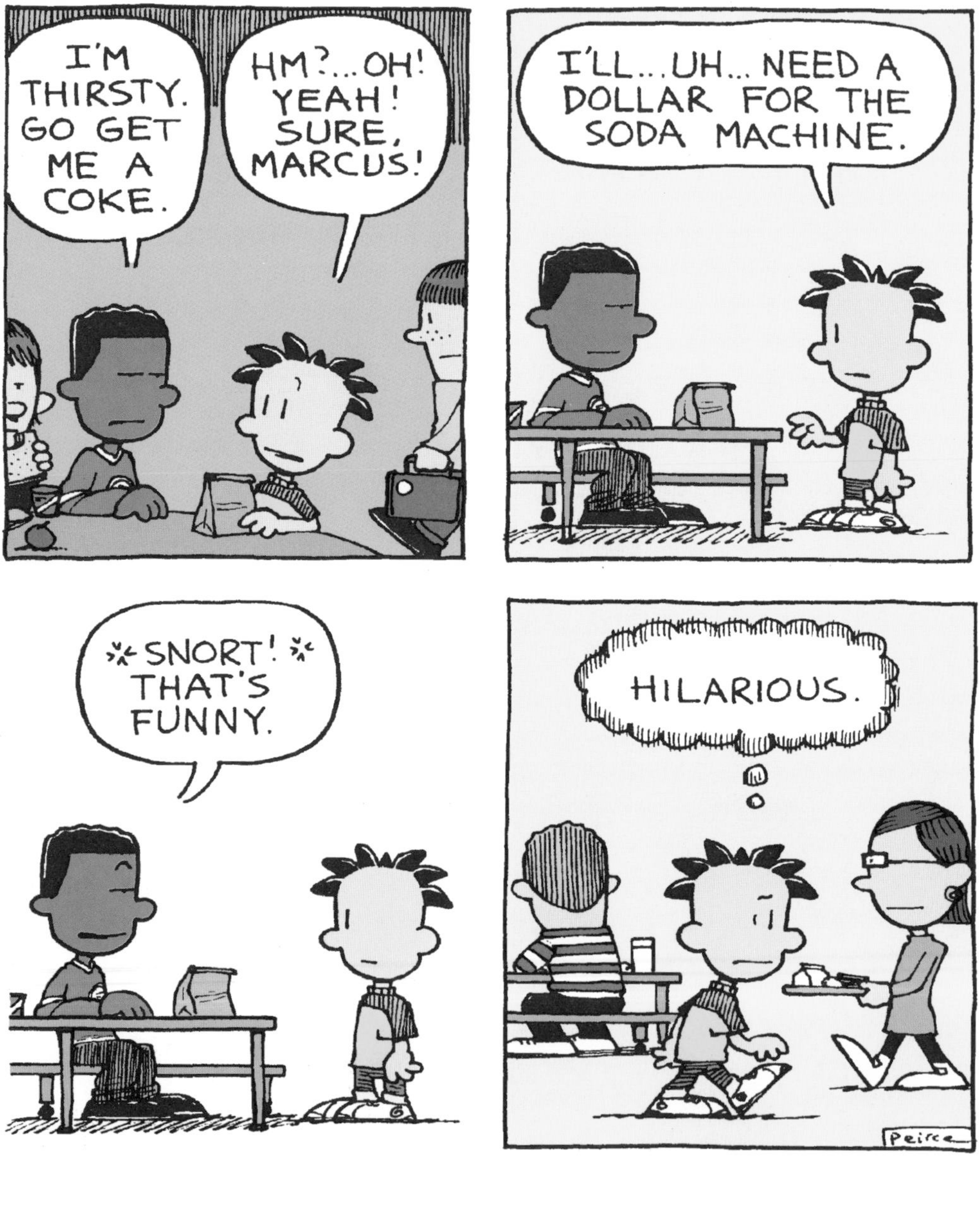
I'M THIRSTY. GO GET ME A COKE.
HM?...OH! YEAH! SURE, MARCUS!
I'LL...UH... NEED A DOLLAR FOR THE SODA MACHINE.
SNORT! THAT'S FUNNY.
HILARIOUS.
Peirce

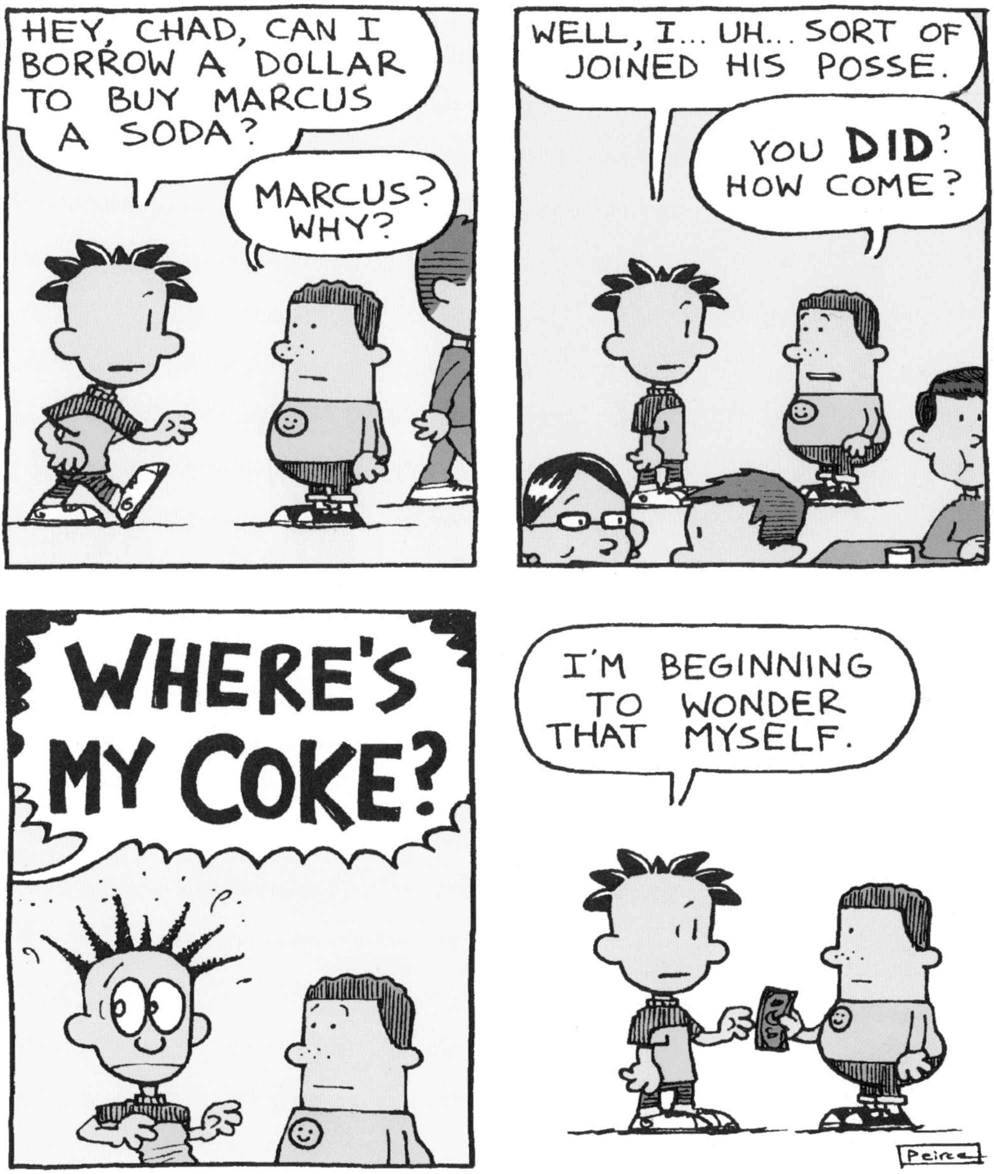
HEY, CHAD, CAN I BORROW A DOLLAR TO BUY MARCUS A SODA?
MARCUS? WHY?
WELL, I... UH... SORT OF JOINED HIS POSSE.
YOU **DID**? HOW COME?
WHERE'S MY COKE?
I'M BEGINNING TO WONDER THAT MYSELF.
Peirce

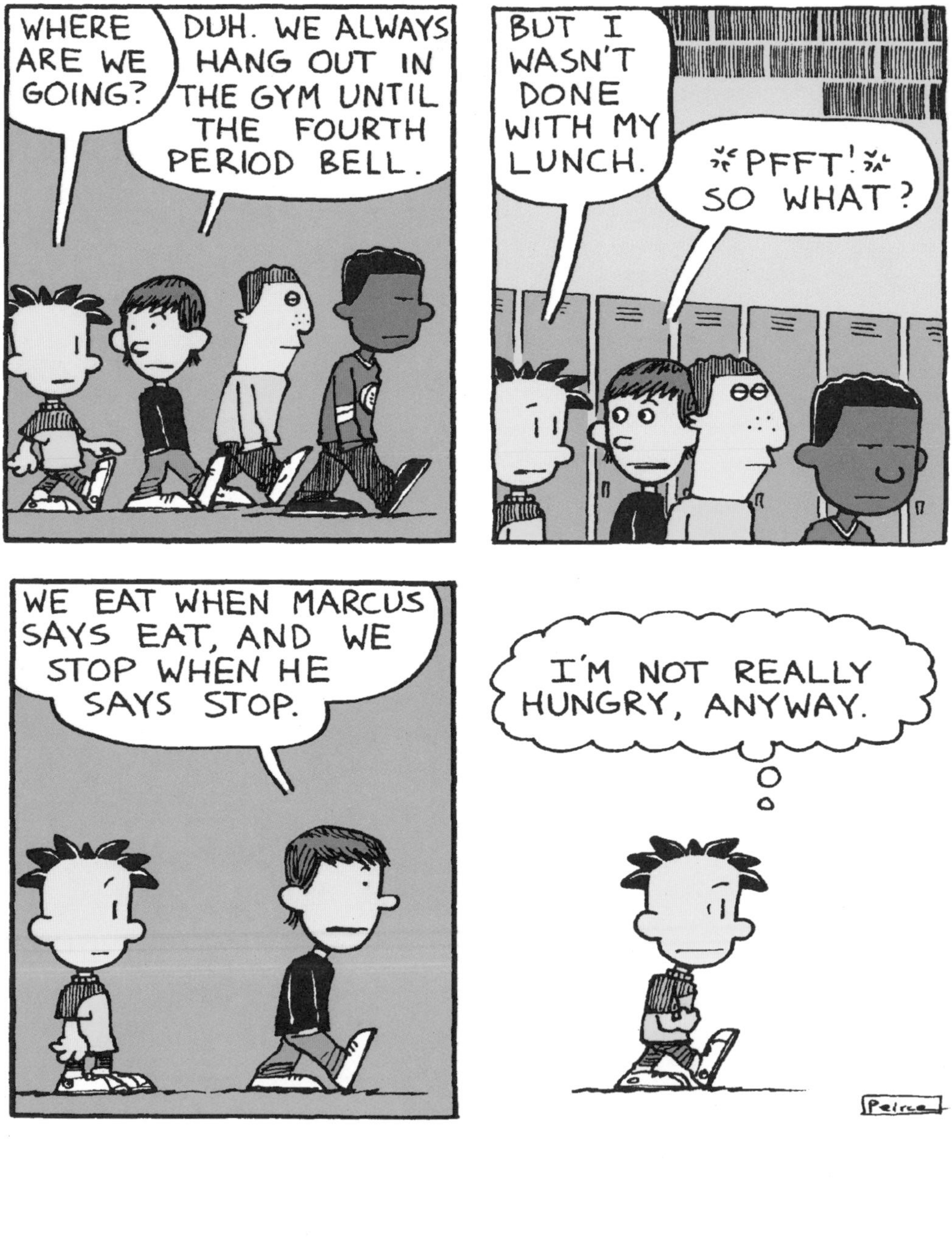
WHERE ARE WE GOING?
DUH. WE ALWAYS HANG OUT IN THE GYM UNTIL THE FOURTH PERIOD BELL.
BUT I WASN'T DONE WITH MY LUNCH.
PFFT! SO WHAT?
WE EAT WHEN MARCUS SAYS EAT, AND WE STOP WHEN HE SAYS STOP.
I'M NOT REALLY HUNGRY, ANYWAY.
Peirce

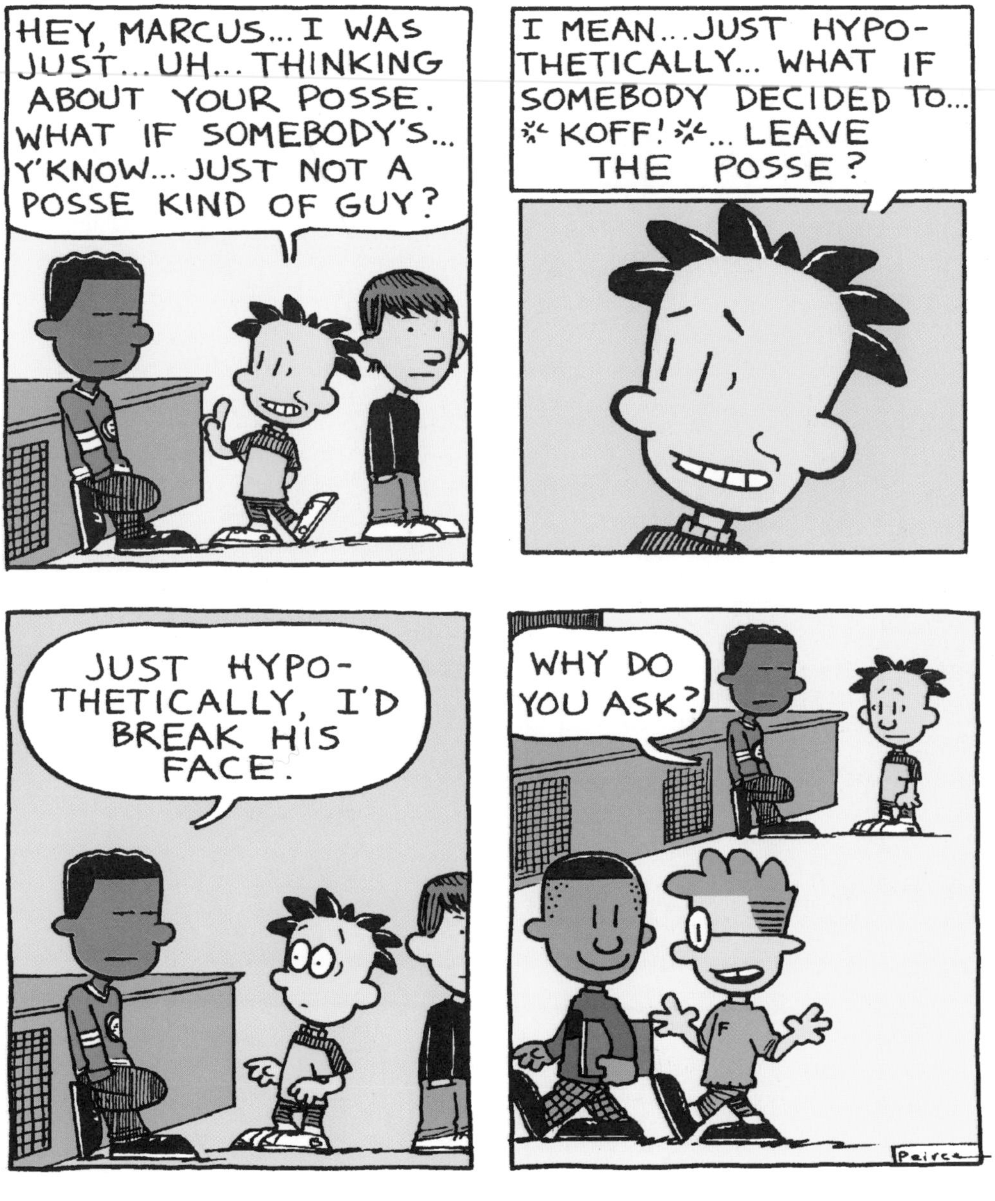
HEY, MARCUS... I WAS JUST... UH... THINKING ABOUT YOUR POSSE. WHAT IF SOMEBODY'S... Y'KNOW... JUST NOT A POSSE KIND OF GUY?
I MEAN... JUST HYPOTHETICALLY... WHAT IF SOMEBODY DECIDED TO... *KOFF!*... LEAVE THE POSSE?
JUST HYPOTHETICALLY, I'D BREAK HIS FACE.
WHY DO YOU ASK?
Peirce

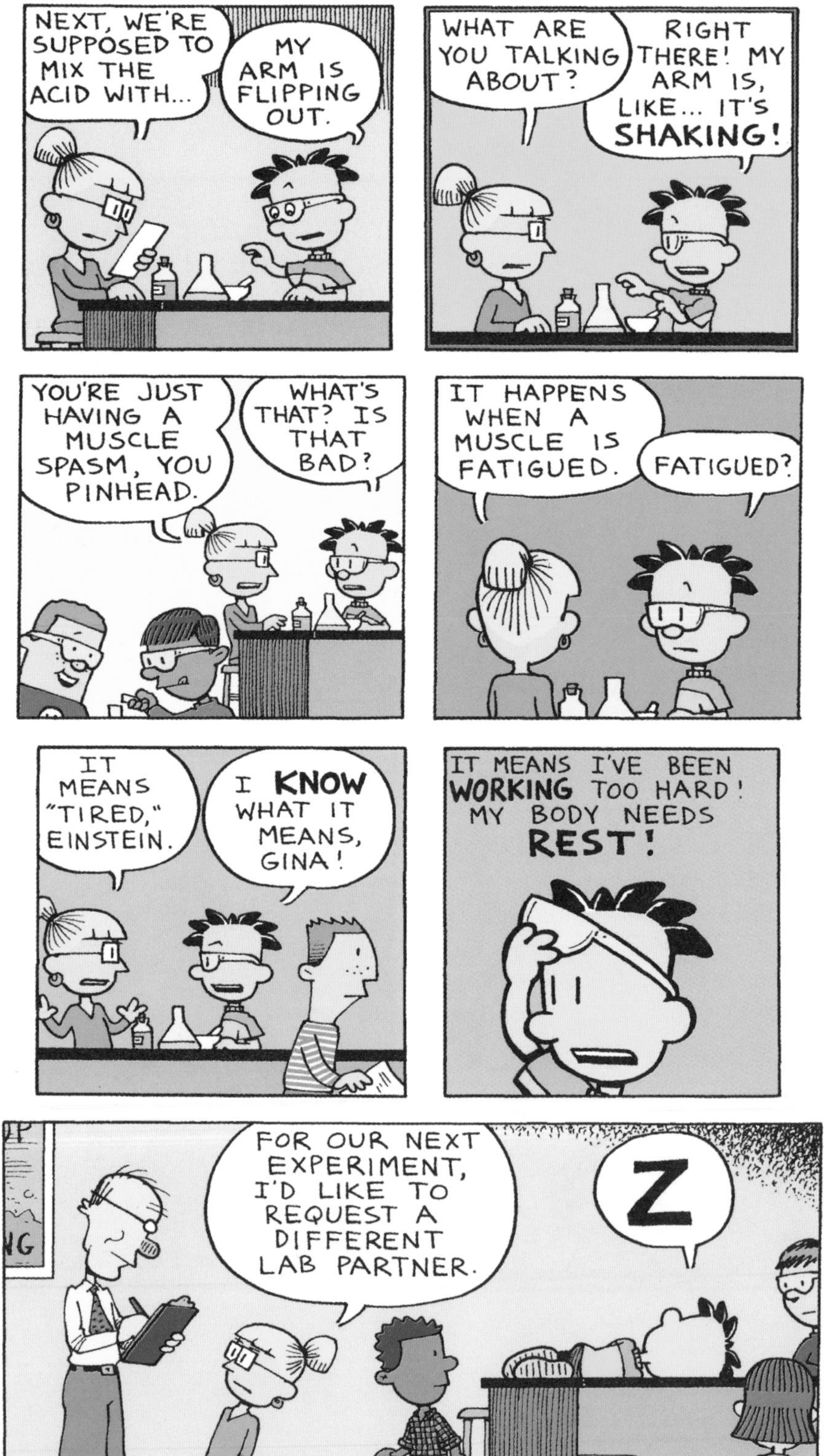
NEXT, WE'RE SUPPOSED TO MIX THE ACID WITH...
MY ARM IS FLIPPING OUT.
WHAT ARE YOU TALKING ABOUT?
RIGHT THERE! MY ARM IS, LIKE... IT'S **SHAKING!**
YOU'RE JUST HAVING A MUSCLE SPASM, YOU PINHEAD.
WHAT'S THAT? IS THAT BAD?
IT HAPPENS WHEN A MUSCLE IS FATIGUED.
FATIGUED?
IT MEANS "TIRED," EINSTEIN.
I **KNOW** WHAT IT MEANS, GINA!
IT MEANS I'VE BEEN **WORKING** TOO HARD! MY BODY NEEDS **REST!**
FOR OUR NEXT EXPERIMENT, I'D LIKE TO REQUEST A DIFFERENT LAB PARTNER.
Z
Peirce

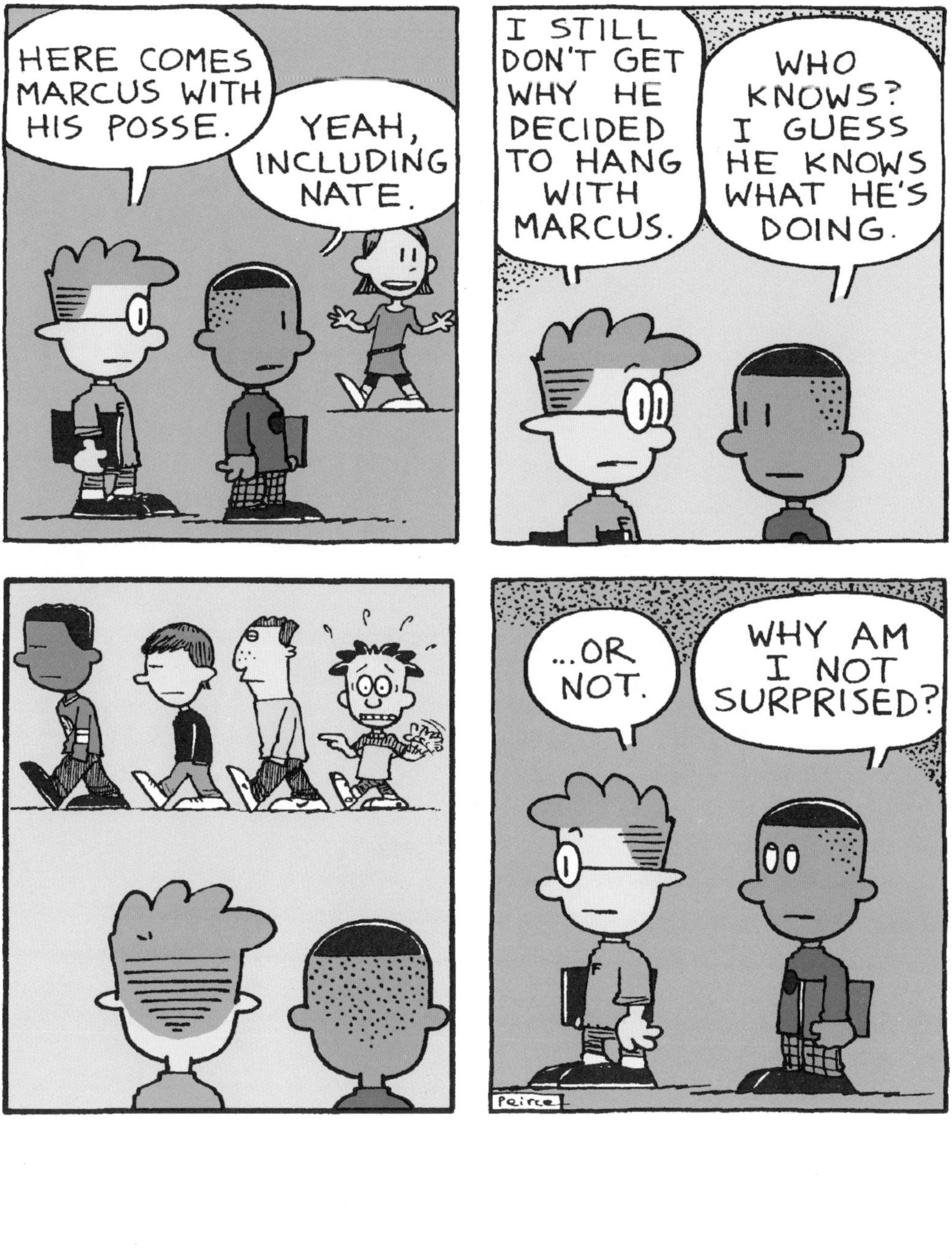

HERE COMES MARCUS WITH HIS POSSE.
YEAH, INCLUDING NATE.
I STILL DON'T GET WHY HE DECIDED TO HANG WITH MARCUS.
WHO KNOWS? I GUESS HE KNOWS WHAT HE'S DOING.
...OR NOT.
WHY AM I NOT SURPRISED?
Peirce

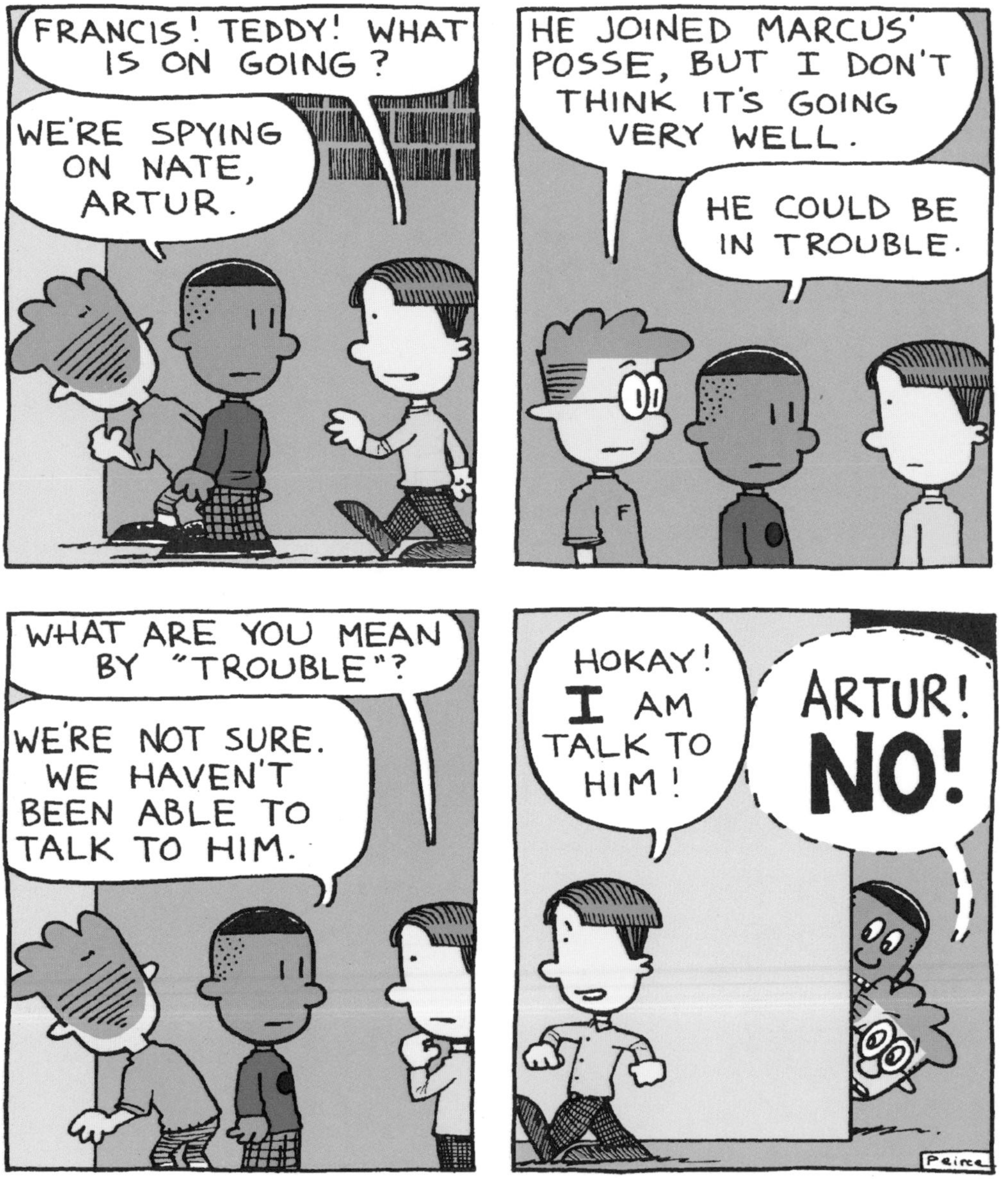
FRANCIS! TEDDY! WHAT IS ON GOING?
WE'RE SPYING ON NATE, ARTUR.
HE JOINED MARCUS' POSSE, BUT I DON'T THINK IT'S GOING VERY WELL.
HE COULD BE IN TROUBLE.
WHAT ARE YOU MEAN BY "TROUBLE"?
WE'RE NOT SURE. WE HAVEN'T BEEN ABLE TO TALK TO HIM.
HOKAY! I AM TALK TO HIM!
ARTUR! NO!
Peirce

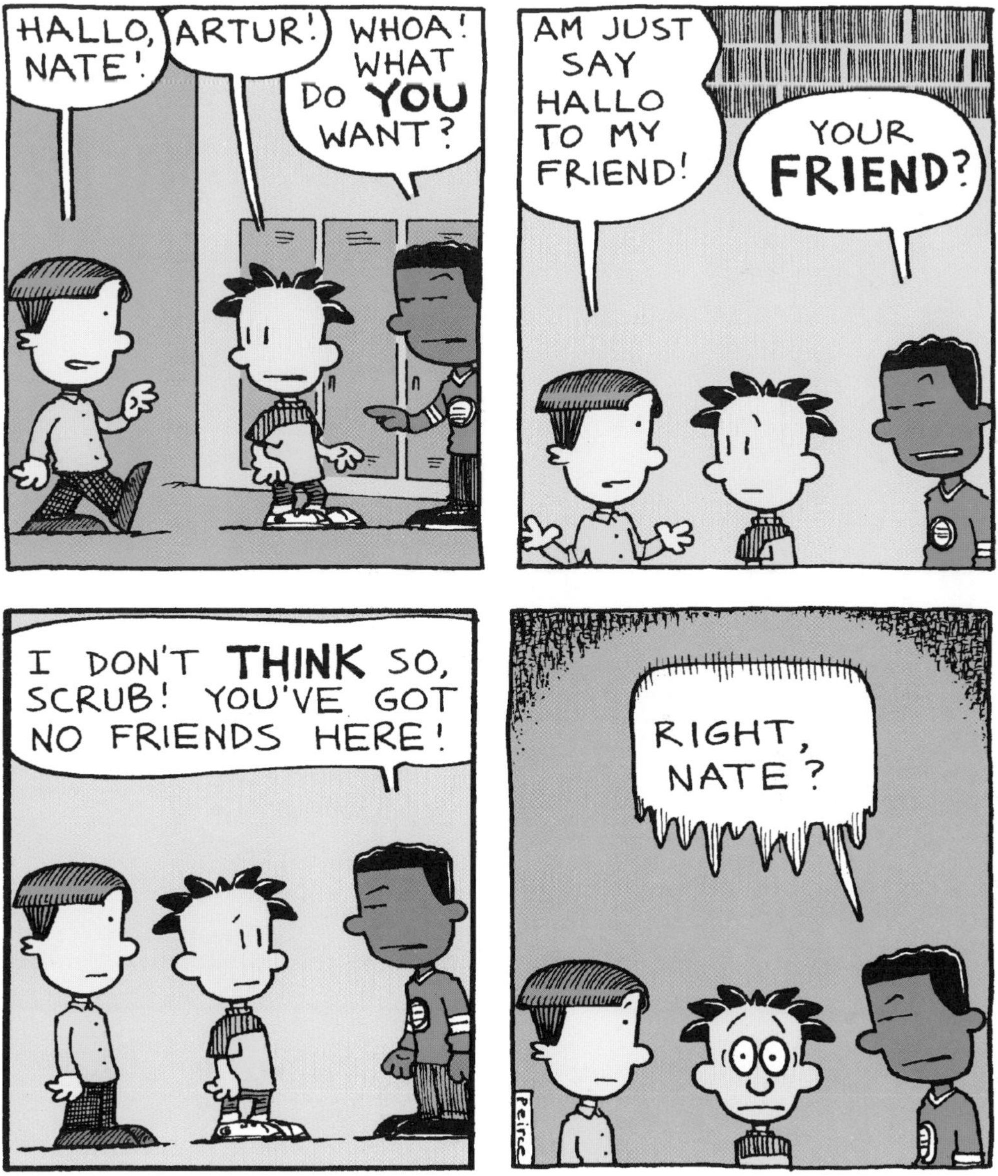
HALLO, NATE!
ARTUR!
WHOA! WHAT DO **YOU** WANT?
AM JUST SAY HALLO TO MY FRIEND!
YOUR **FRIEND**?
I DON'T **THINK** SO, SCRUB! YOU'VE GOT NO FRIENDS HERE!
RIGHT, NATE?
peirce

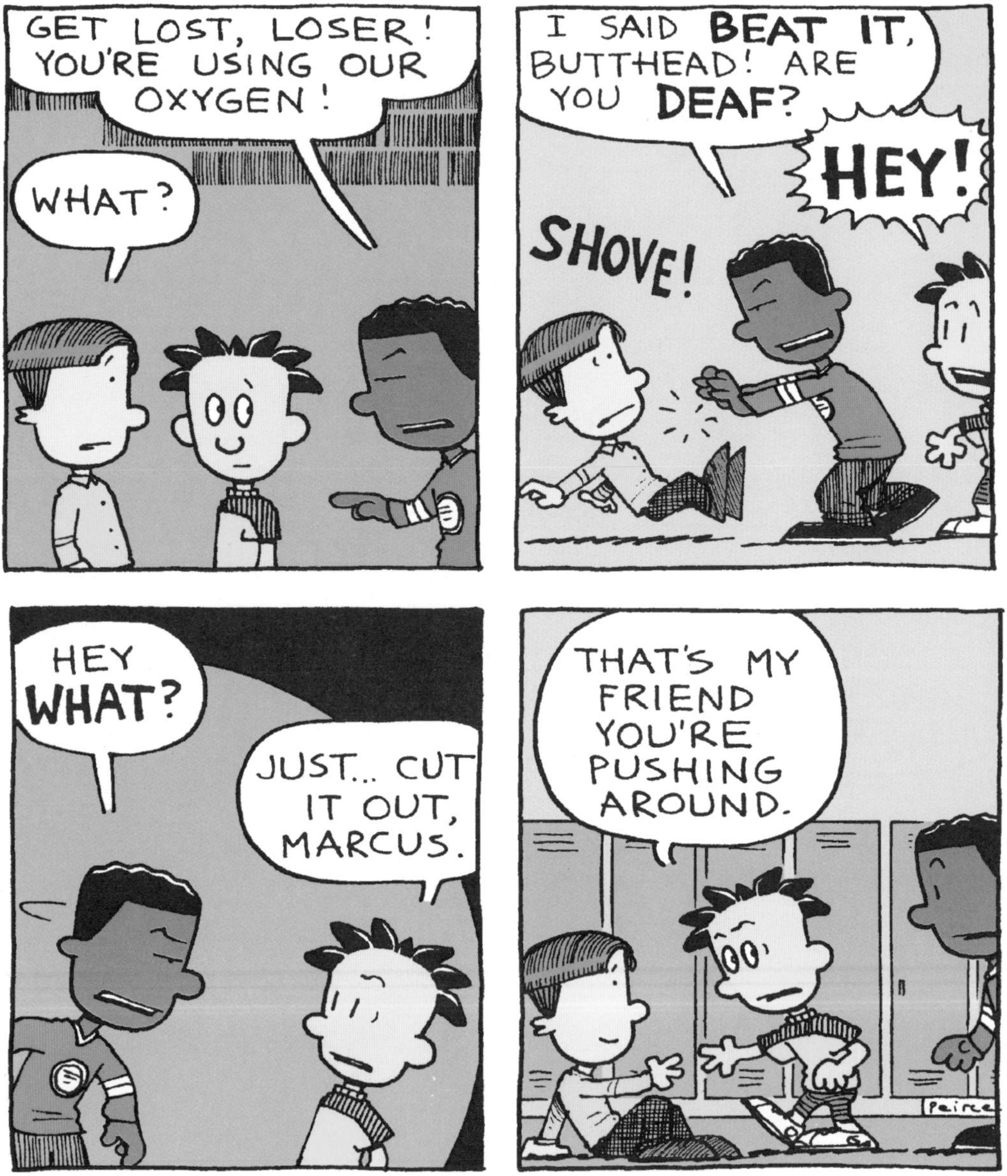
GET LOST, LOSER! YOU'RE USING OUR OXYGEN!
WHAT?
I SAID BEAT IT, BUTTHEAD! ARE YOU DEAF?
SHOVE!
HEY!
HEY WHAT?
JUST... CUT IT OUT, MARCUS.
THAT'S MY FRIEND YOU'RE PUSHING AROUND.
Peirce

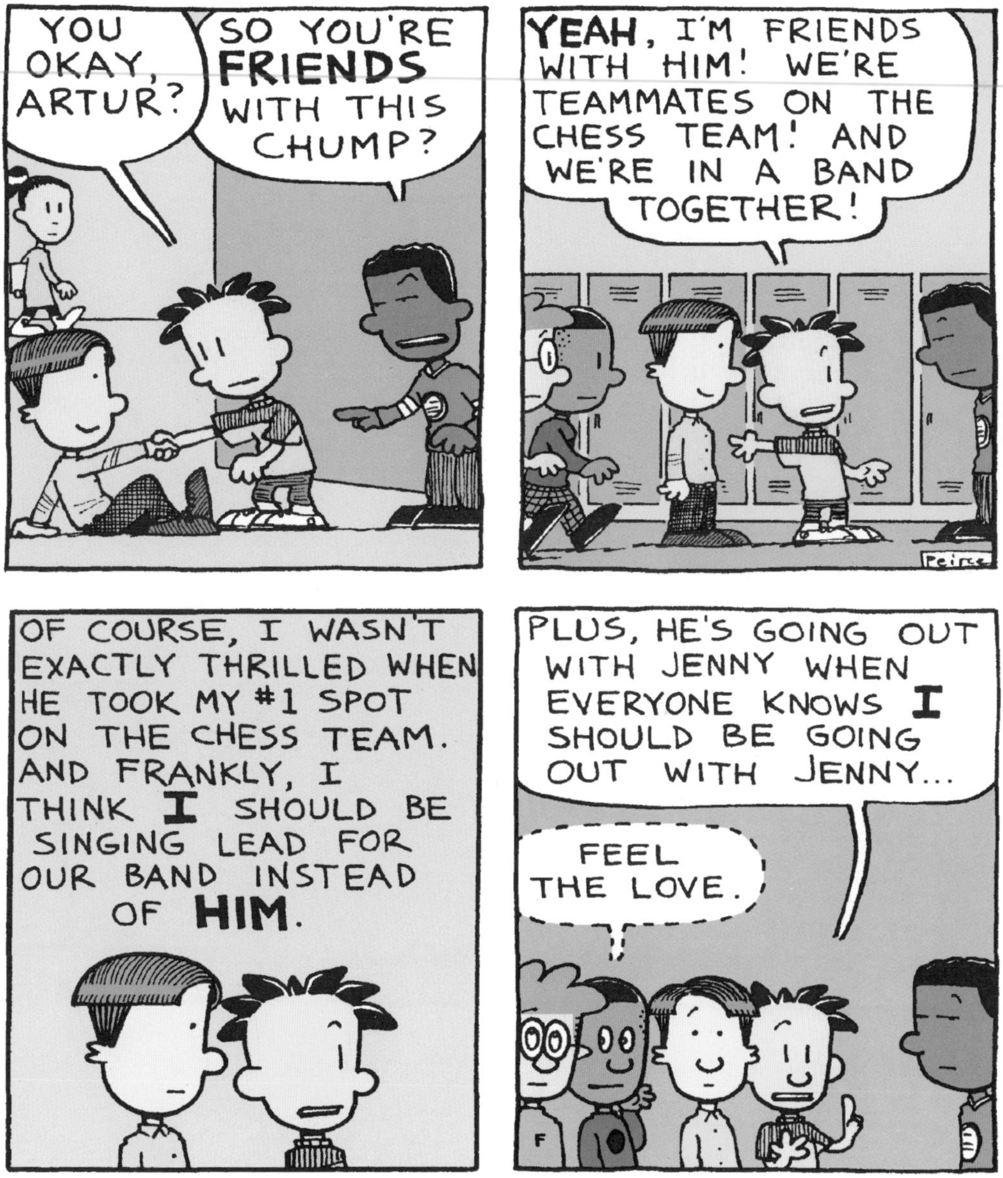
YOU OKAY, ARTUR?
SO YOU'RE **FRIENDS** WITH THIS CHUMP?
YEAH, I'M FRIENDS WITH HIM! WE'RE TEAMMATES ON THE CHESS TEAM! AND WE'RE IN A BAND TOGETHER!
Peirce
OF COURSE, I WASN'T EXACTLY THRILLED WHEN HE TOOK MY #1 SPOT ON THE CHESS TEAM. AND FRANKLY, I THINK **I** SHOULD BE SINGING LEAD FOR OUR BAND INSTEAD OF **HIM**.
PLUS, HE'S GOING OUT WITH JENNY WHEN EVERYONE KNOWS **I** SHOULD BE GOING OUT WITH JENNY...
FEEL THE LOVE.

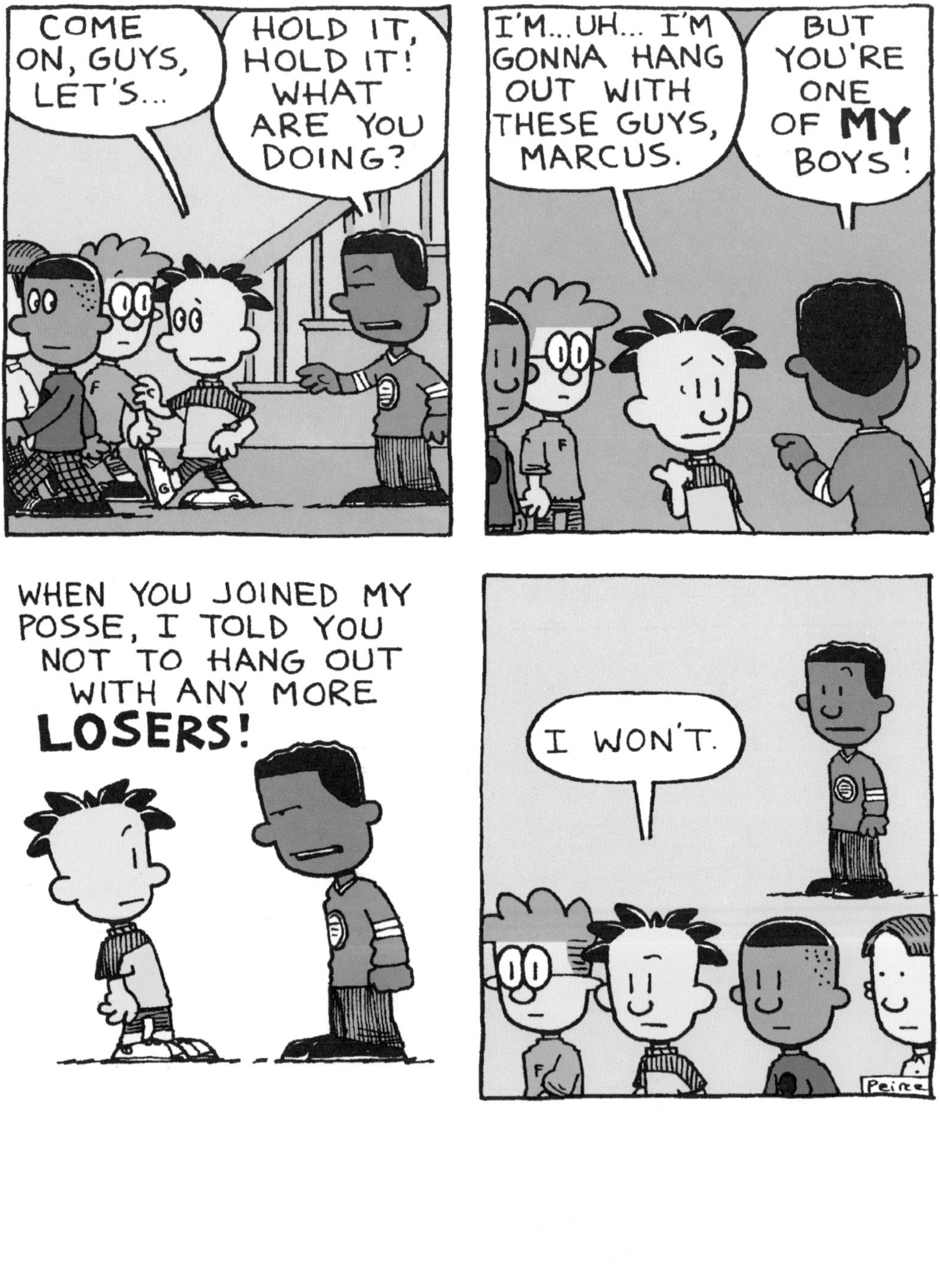
COME ON, GUYS, LET'S...
HOLD IT, HOLD IT! WHAT ARE YOU DOING?
I'M... UH... I'M GONNA HANG OUT WITH THESE GUYS, MARCUS.
BUT YOU'RE ONE OF **MY** BOYS!
WHEN YOU JOINED MY POSSE, I TOLD YOU NOT TO HANG OUT WITH ANY MORE **LOSERS!**
I WON'T.
Peirce

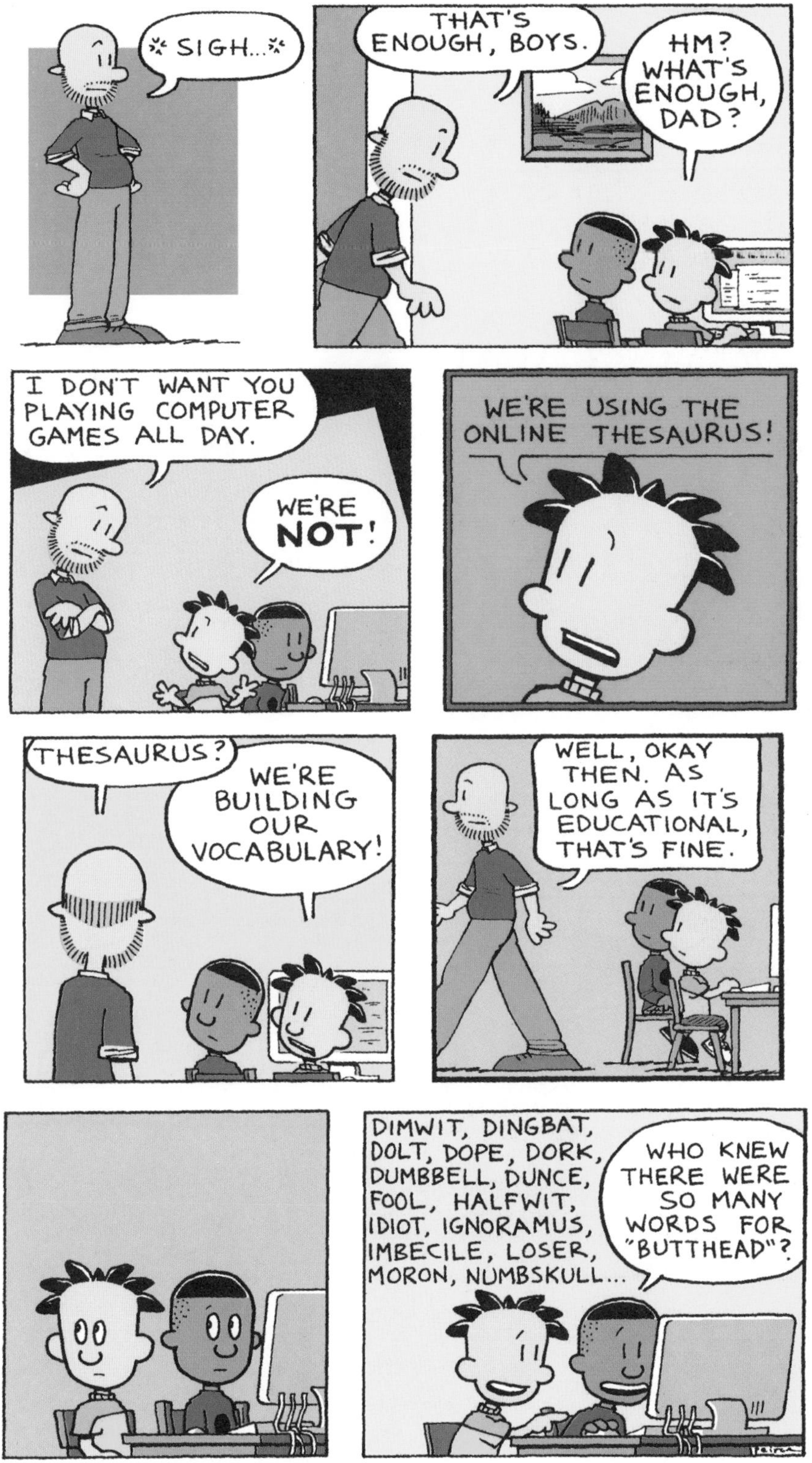

SIGH...
THAT'S ENOUGH, BOYS.
HM? WHAT'S ENOUGH, DAD?
I DON'T WANT YOU PLAYING COMPUTER GAMES ALL DAY.
WE'RE **NOT**!
WE'RE USING THE ONLINE THESAURUS!
THESAURUS?
WE'RE BUILDING OUR VOCABULARY!
WELL, OKAY THEN. AS LONG AS IT'S EDUCATIONAL, THAT'S FINE.
DIMWIT, DINGBAT, DOLT, DOPE, DORK, DUMBBELL, DUNCE, FOOL, HALFWIT, IDIOT, IGNORAMUS, IMBECILE, LOSER, MORON, NUMBSKULL...
WHO KNEW THERE WERE SO MANY WORDS FOR "BUTTHEAD"?

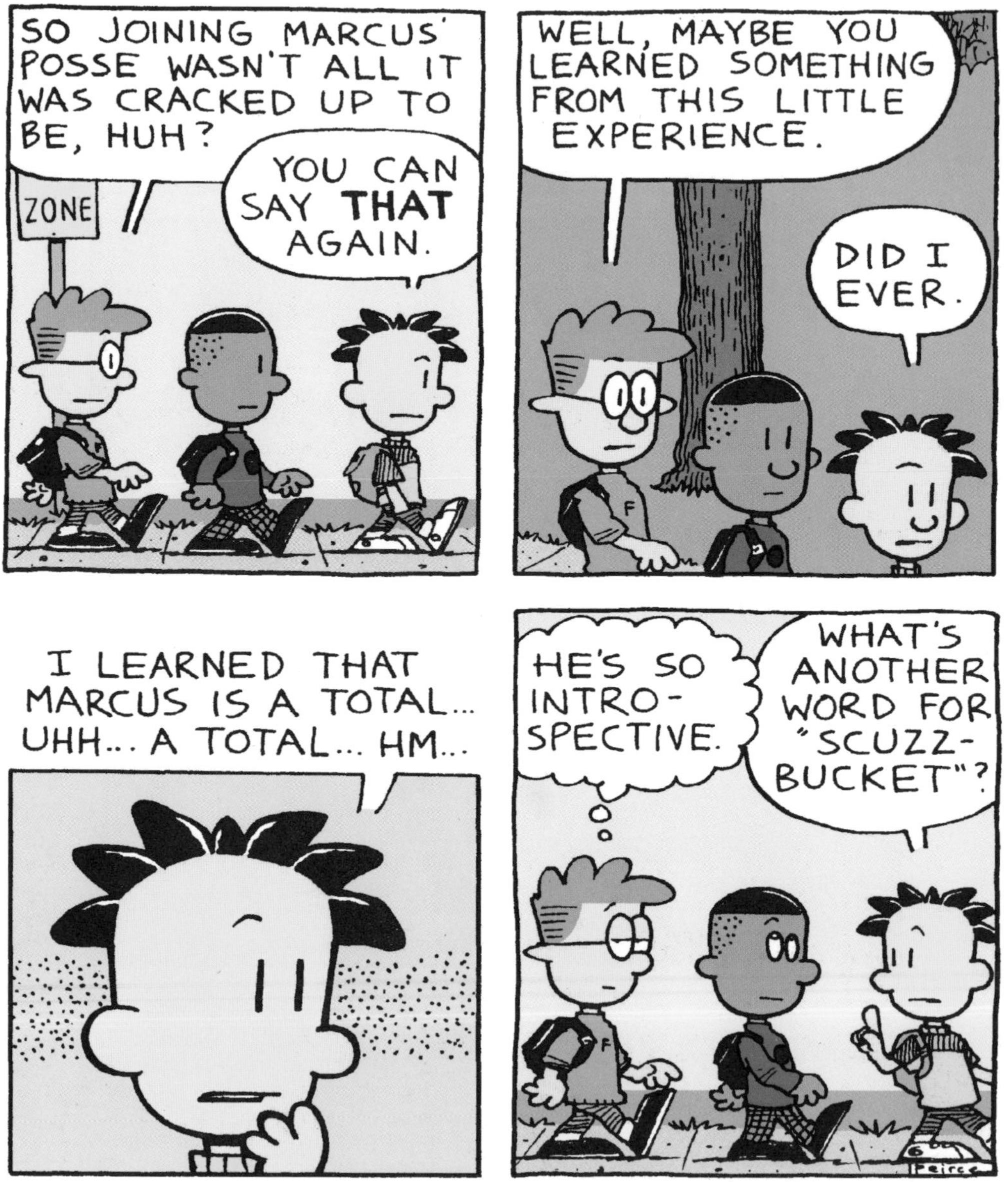
SO JOINING MARCUS' POSSE WASN'T ALL IT WAS CRACKED UP TO BE, HUH?
ZONE
YOU CAN SAY **THAT** AGAIN.
WELL, MAYBE YOU LEARNED SOMETHING FROM THIS LITTLE EXPERIENCE.
DID I EVER.
I LEARNED THAT MARCUS IS A TOTAL... UHH... A TOTAL... HM...
HE'S SO INTRO-SPECTIVE.
WHAT'S ANOTHER WORD FOR "SCUZZ-BUCKET"?
Peirce

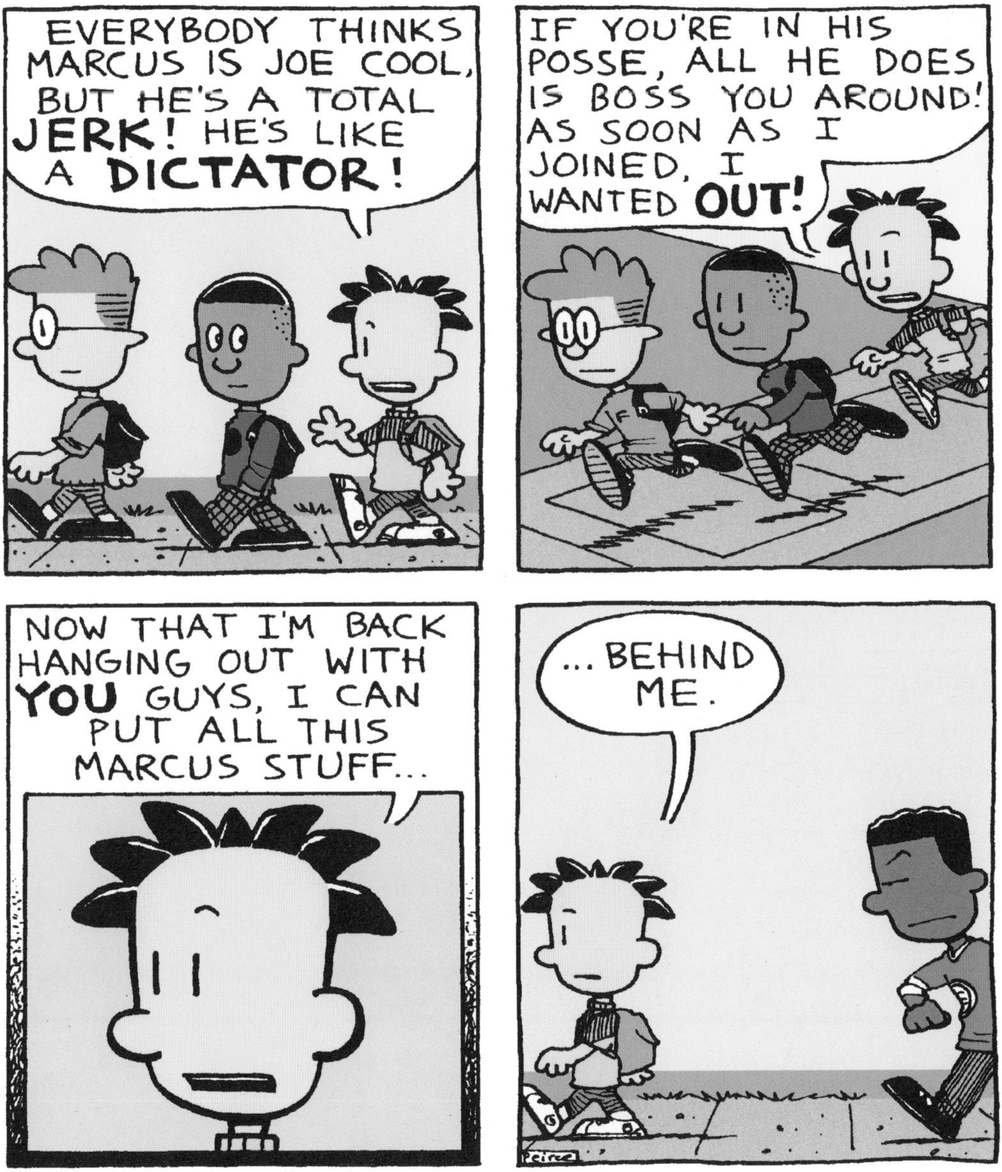
EVERYBODY THINKS MARCUS IS JOE COOL, BUT HE'S A TOTAL **JERK!** HE'S LIKE A **DICTATOR!**
IF YOU'RE IN HIS POSSE, ALL HE DOES IS BOSS YOU AROUND! AS SOON AS I JOINED, I WANTED **OUT!**
NOW THAT I'M BACK HANGING OUT WITH **YOU** GUYS, I CAN PUT ALL THIS MARCUS STUFF...
...BEHIND ME.
Peirce

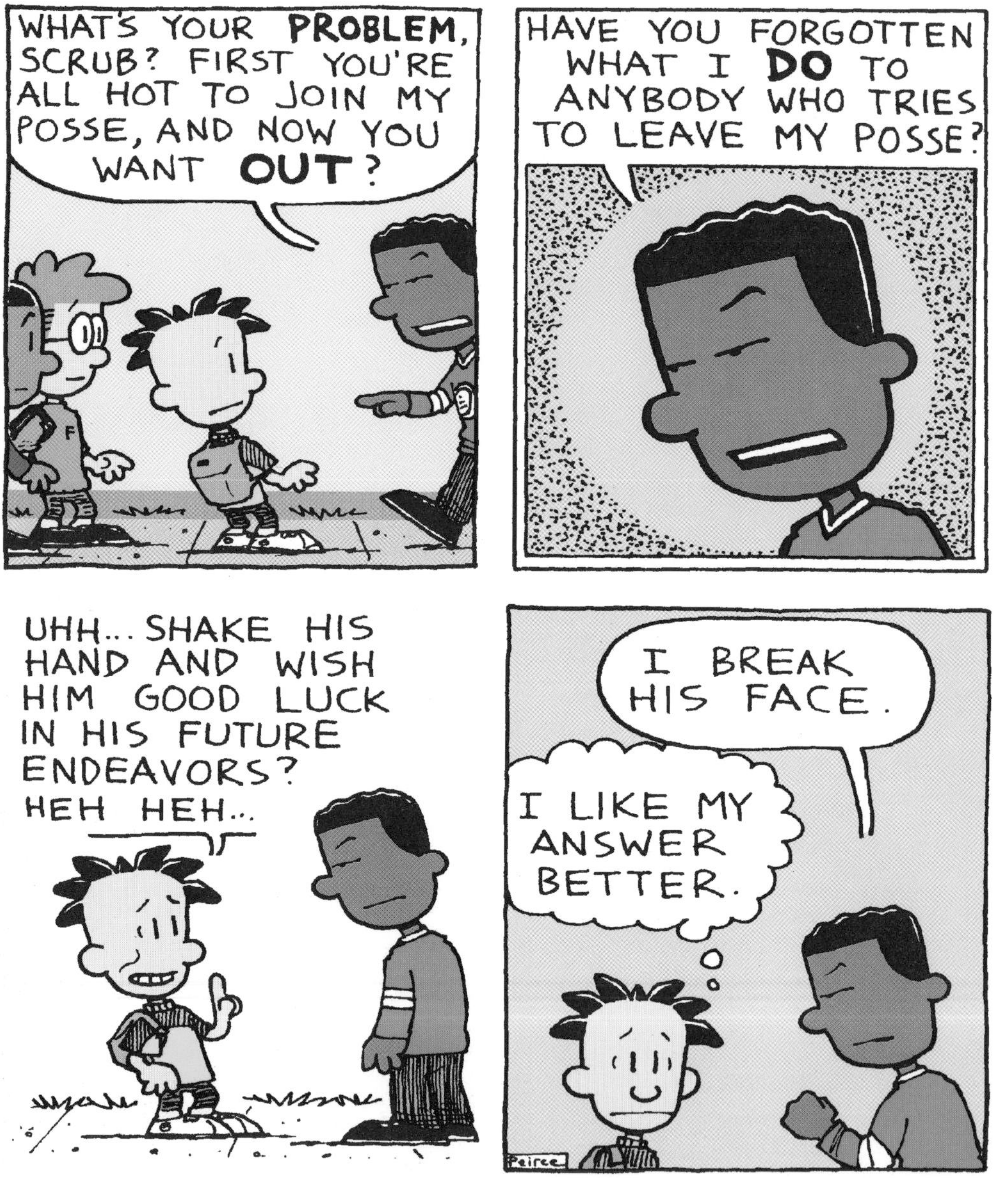
WHAT'S YOUR **PROBLEM**, SCRUB? FIRST YOU'RE ALL HOT TO JOIN MY POSSE, AND NOW YOU WANT **OUT**?
HAVE YOU FORGOTTEN WHAT I **DO** TO ANYBODY WHO TRIES TO LEAVE MY POSSE?
UHH... SHAKE HIS HAND AND WISH HIM GOOD LUCK IN HIS FUTURE ENDEAVORS? HEH HEH...
I BREAK HIS FACE.
I LIKE MY ANSWER BETTER.
Peirce

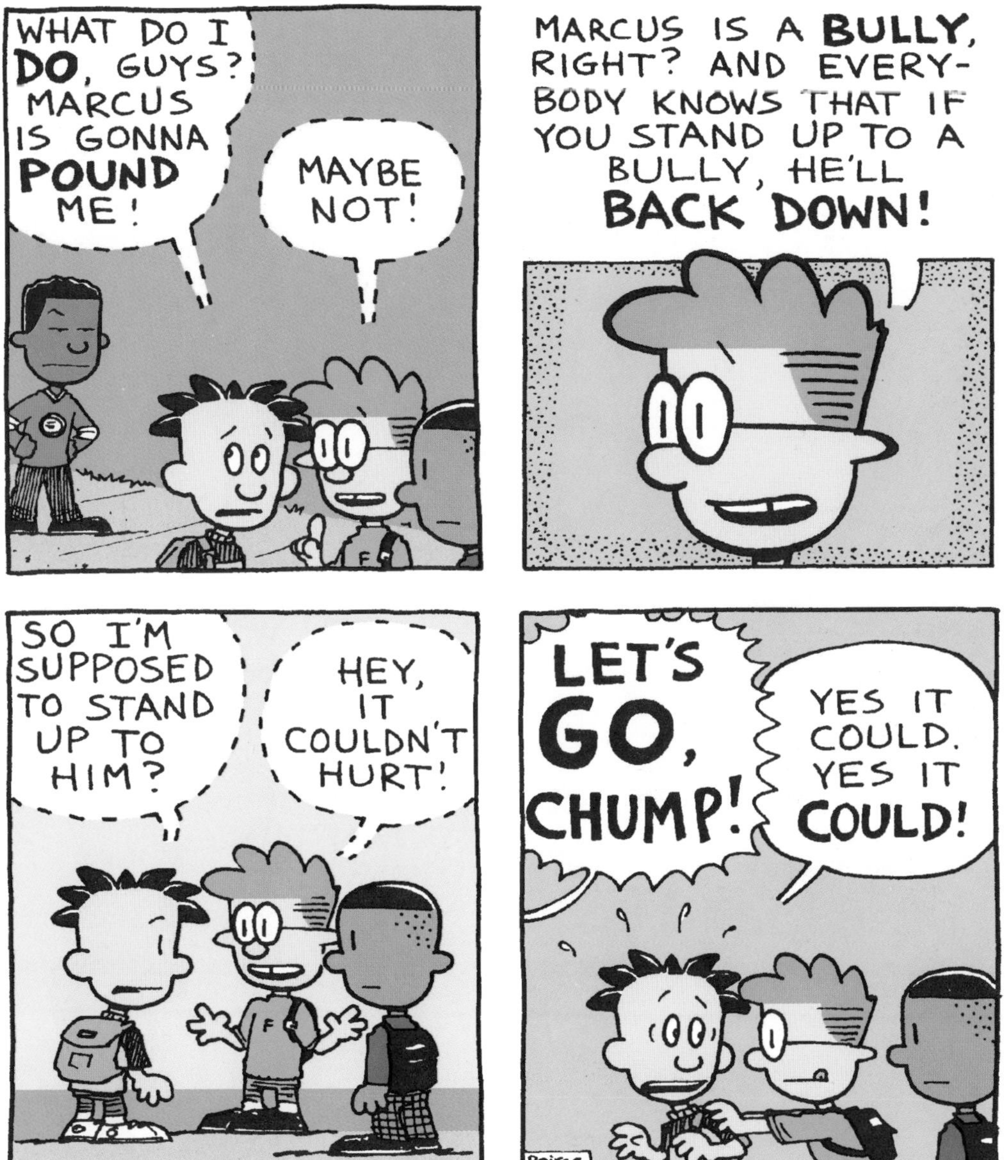
WHAT DO I DO, GUYS? MARCUS IS GONNA POUND ME!
MAYBE NOT!
MARCUS IS A BULLY, RIGHT? AND EVERY-BODY KNOWS THAT IF YOU STAND UP TO A BULLY, HE'LL BACK DOWN!
SO I'M SUPPOSED TO STAND UP TO HIM?
HEY, IT COULDN'T HURT!
LET'S GO, CHUMP!
YES IT COULD. YES IT COULD!
Peirce

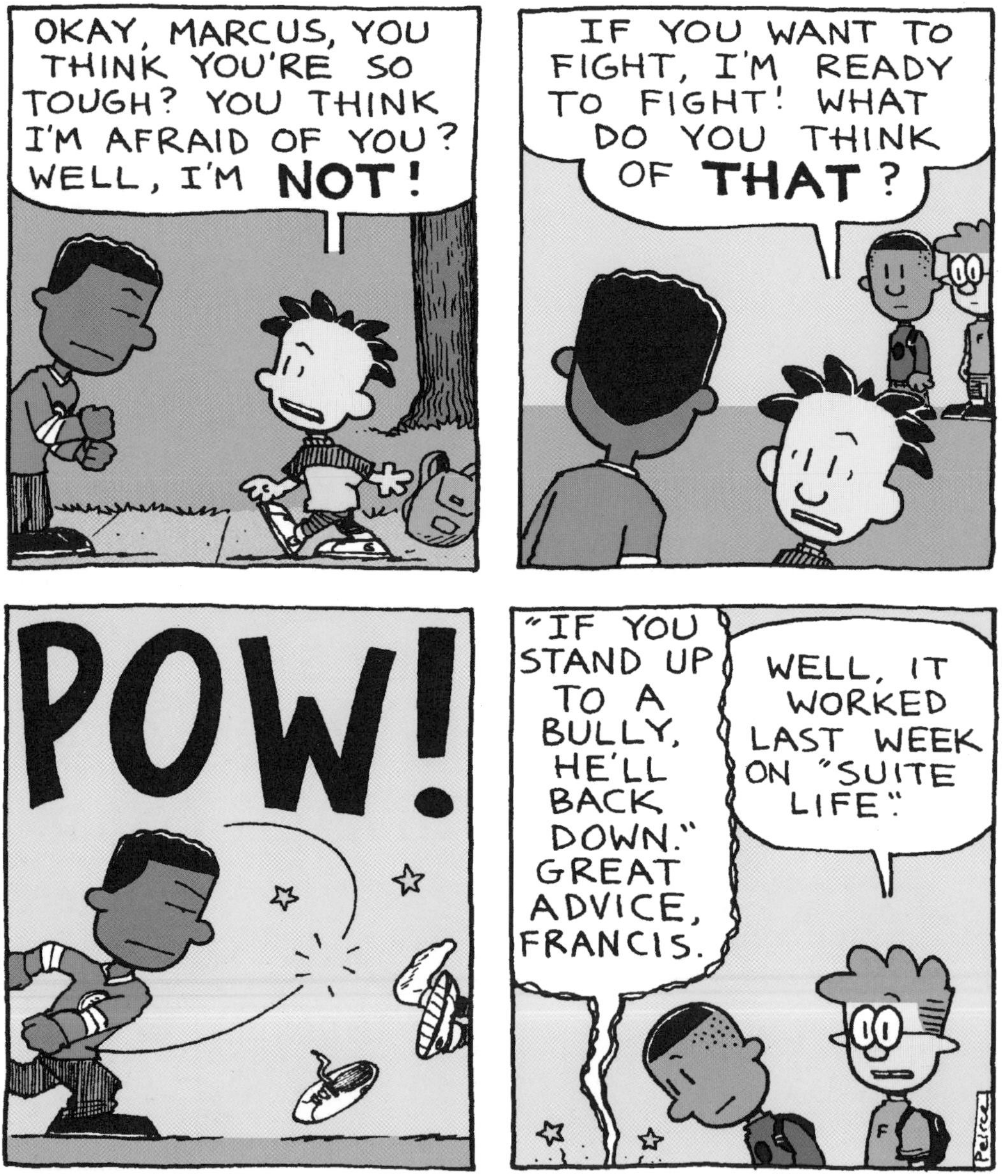
OKAY, MARCUS, YOU THINK YOU'RE SO TOUGH? YOU THINK I'M AFRAID OF YOU? WELL, I'M NOT!
IF YOU WANT TO FIGHT, I'M READY TO FIGHT! WHAT DO YOU THINK OF THAT?
POW!
"IF YOU STAND UP TO A BULLY, HE'LL BACK DOWN." GREAT ADVICE, FRANCIS.
WELL, IT WORKED LAST WEEK ON "SUITE LIFE."
Peirce

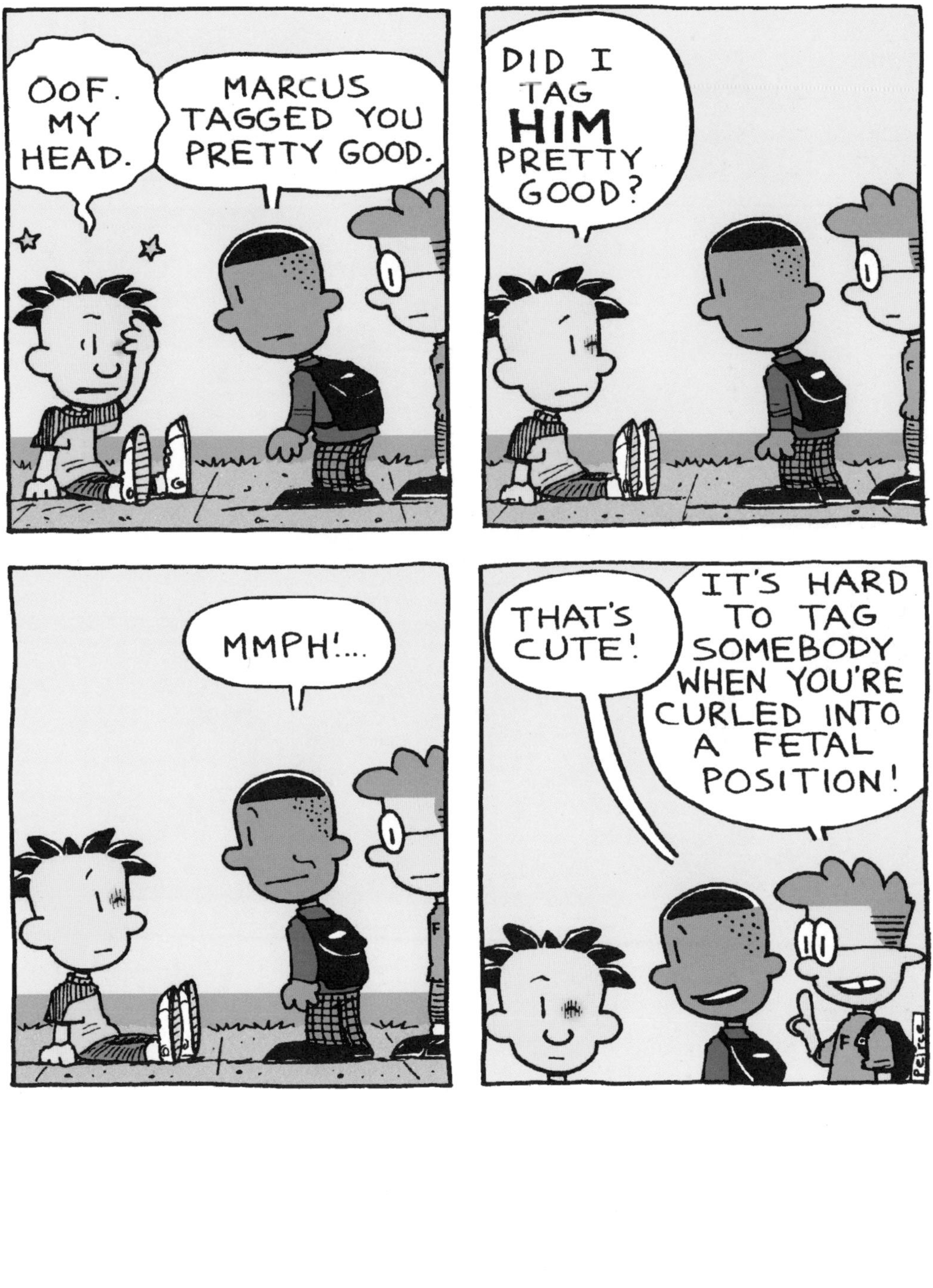
OOF. MY HEAD.
MARCUS TAGGED YOU PRETTY GOOD.
DID I TAG **HIM** PRETTY GOOD?
MMPH!...
THAT'S CUTE!
IT'S HARD TO TAG SOMEBODY WHEN YOU'RE CURLED INTO A FETAL POSITION!
PEIRCE

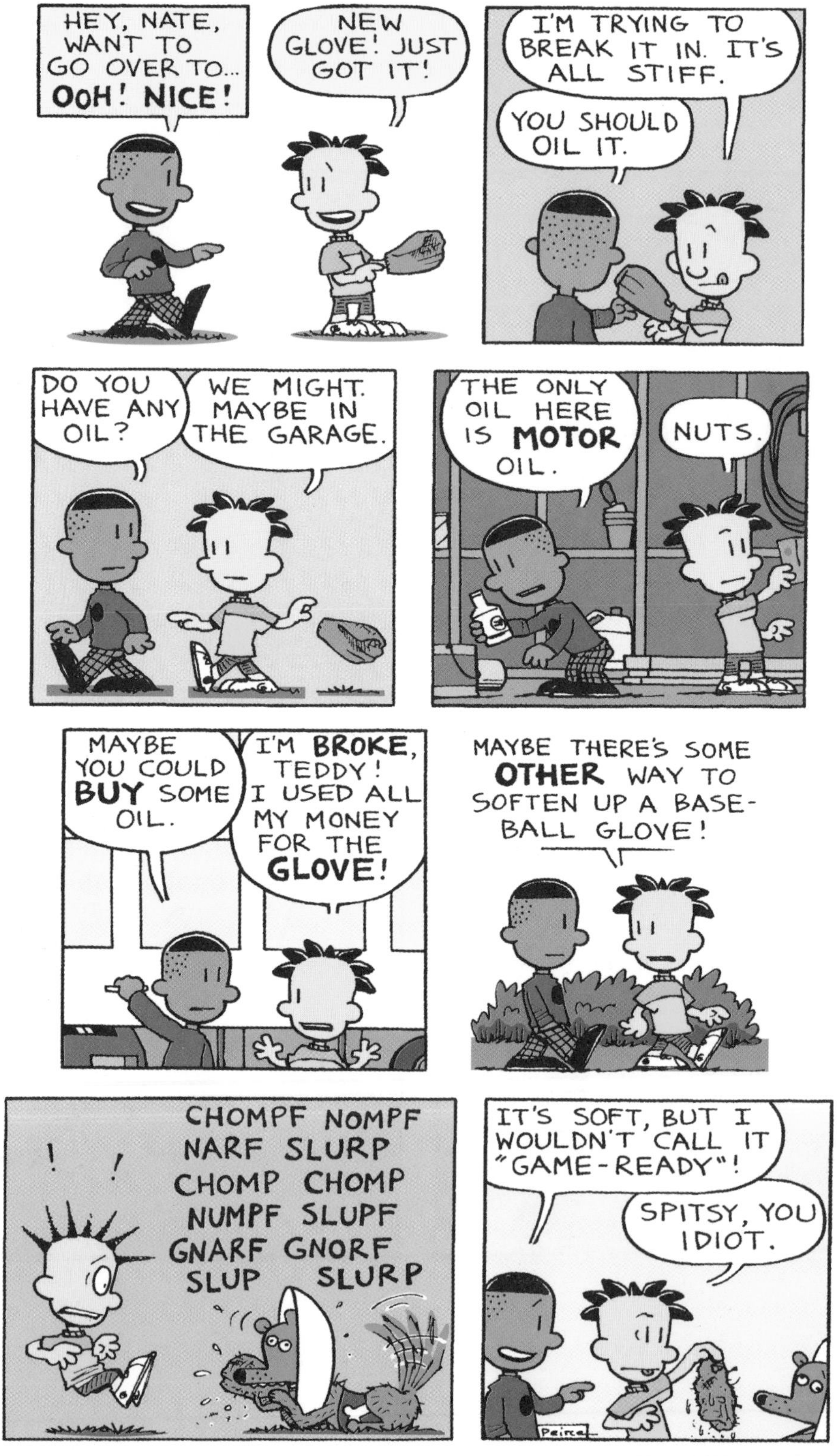

HEY, NATE, WANT TO GO OVER TO... OOH! NICE!
NEW GLOVE! JUST GOT IT!
I'M TRYING TO BREAK IT IN. IT'S ALL STIFF.
YOU SHOULD OIL IT.
DO YOU HAVE ANY OIL?
WE MIGHT. MAYBE IN THE GARAGE.
THE ONLY OIL HERE IS MOTOR OIL.
NUTS.
MAYBE YOU COULD BUY SOME OIL.
I'M BROKE, TEDDY! I USED ALL MY MONEY FOR THE GLOVE!
MAYBE THERE'S SOME OTHER WAY TO SOFTEN UP A BASE-BALL GLOVE!
! !
CHOMPF NOMPF
NARF SLURP
CHOMP CHOMP
NUMPF SLUPF
GNARF GNORF
SLUP SLURP
IT'S SOFT, BUT I WOULDN'T CALL IT "GAME-READY"!
SPITSY, YOU IDIOT.
Peirce

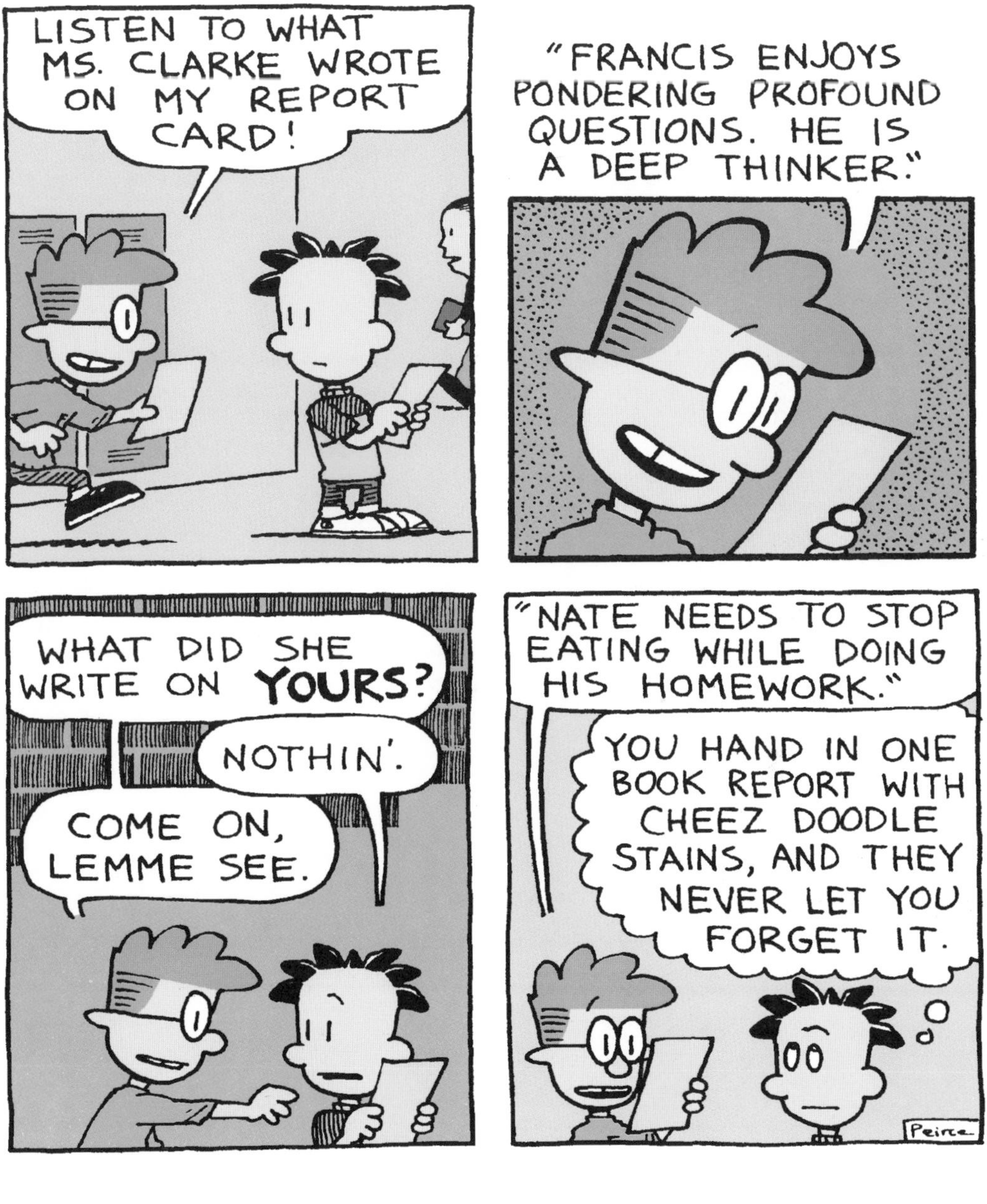
LISTEN TO WHAT MS. CLARKE WROTE ON MY REPORT CARD!
"FRANCIS ENJOYS PONDERING PROFOUND QUESTIONS. HE IS A DEEP THINKER."
WHAT DID SHE WRITE ON **YOURS?**
NOTHIN'.
COME ON, LEMME SEE.
"NATE NEEDS TO STOP EATING WHILE DOING HIS HOMEWORK."
YOU HAND IN ONE BOOK REPORT WITH CHEEZ DOODLE STAINS, AND THEY NEVER LET YOU FORGET IT.
Peirce

HOW COME MS. CLARKE CALLED **YOU** A DEEP THINKER, BUT SHE DIDN'T CALL **ME** ONE?
I GUESS SHE DOESN'T CONSIDER YOU A DEEP THINKER.
BUT I **AM**! I THINK ABOUT DEEP STUFF ALL THE **TIME**!
LIKE WHAT?
LIKE... UHH... LET'S SEE...
FALSE PRIDE?
YES! THAT! WHAT YOU SAID!
Peirce

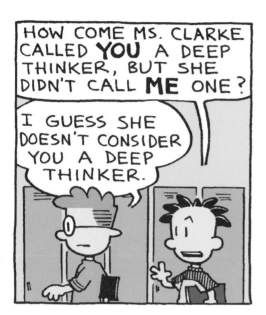

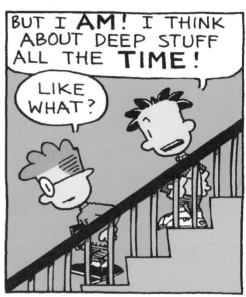

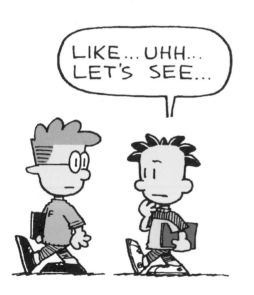

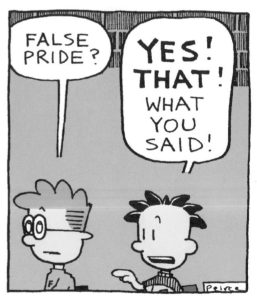

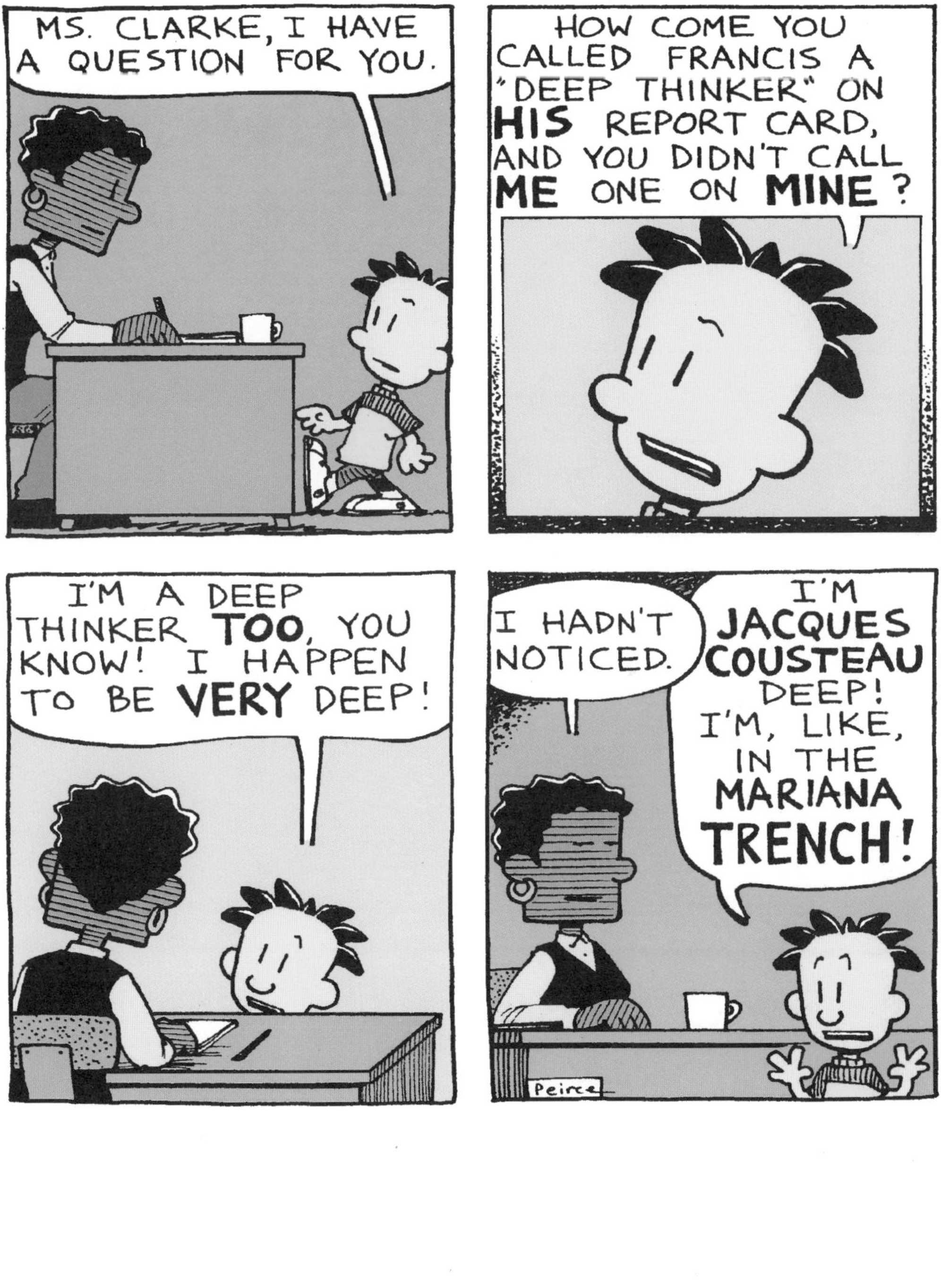
MS. CLARKE, I HAVE A QUESTION FOR YOU.
HOW COME YOU CALLED FRANCIS A "DEEP THINKER" ON HIS REPORT CARD, AND YOU DIDN'T CALL ME ONE ON MINE?
I'M A DEEP THINKER TOO, YOU KNOW! I HAPPEN TO BE VERY DEEP!
I'M JACQUES COUSTEAU DEEP! I'M, LIKE, IN THE MARIANA TRENCH!
I HADN'T NOTICED.
Peirce

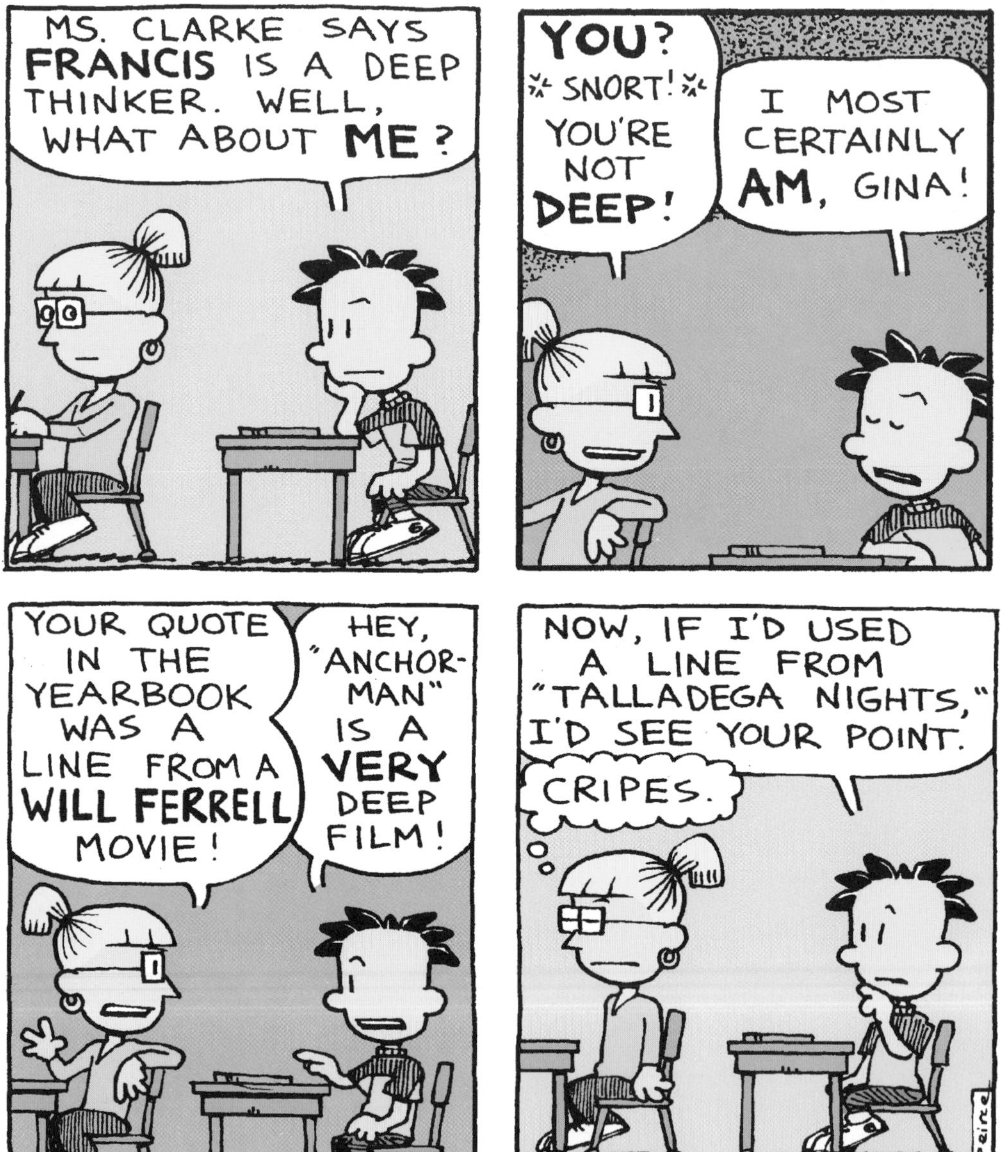
MS. CLARKE SAYS FRANCIS IS A DEEP THINKER. WELL, WHAT ABOUT ME?
YOU? *SNORT!* YOU'RE NOT DEEP!
I MOST CERTAINLY AM, GINA!
YOUR QUOTE IN THE YEARBOOK WAS A LINE FROM A WILL FERRELL MOVIE!
HEY, "ANCHORMAN" IS A VERY DEEP FILM!
NOW, IF I'D USED A LINE FROM "TALLADEGA NIGHTS," I'D SEE YOUR POINT.
CRIPES.
Peirce

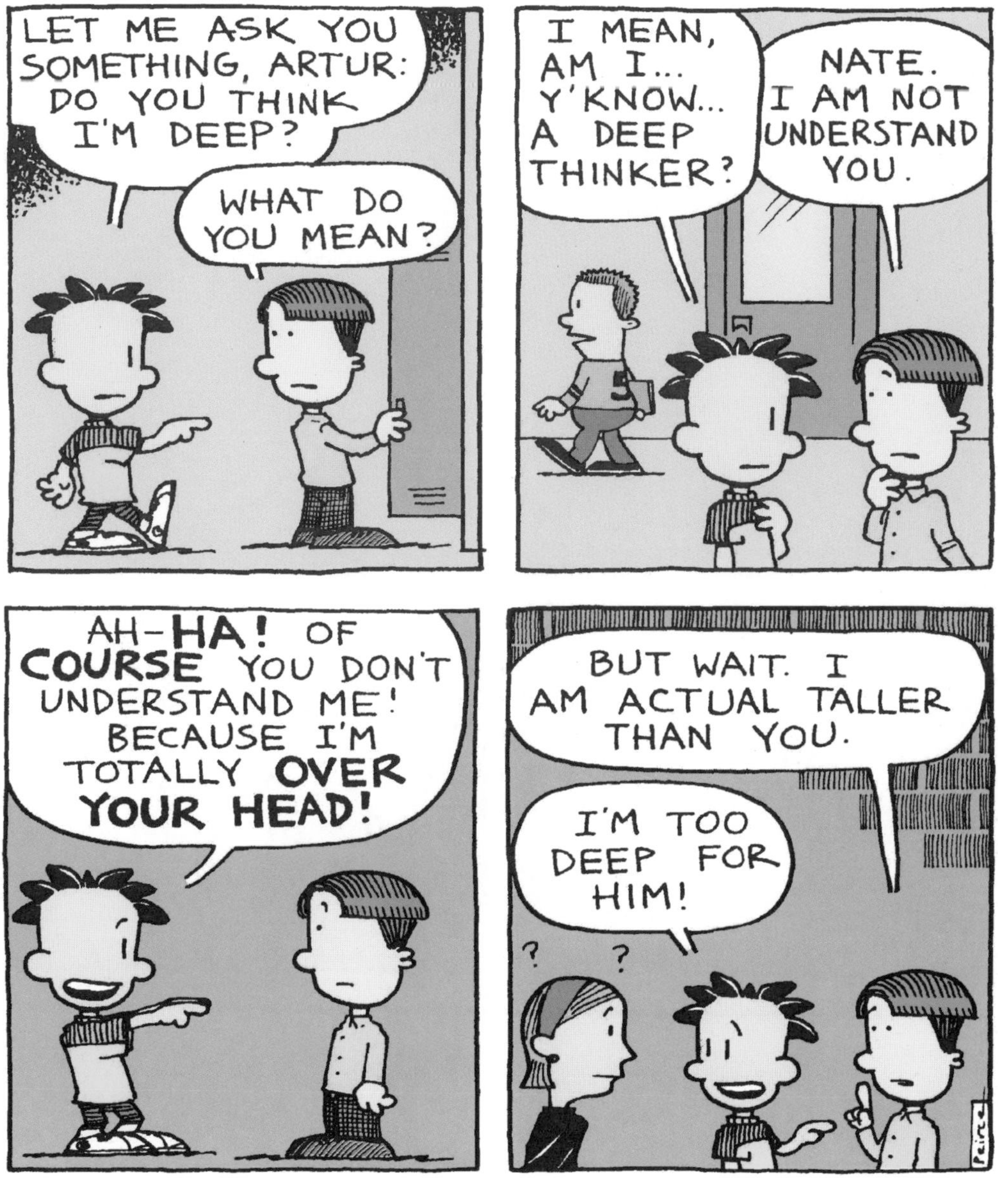
LET ME ASK YOU SOMETHING, ARTUR: DO YOU THINK I'M DEEP?
WHAT DO YOU MEAN?
I MEAN, AM I... Y'KNOW... A DEEP THINKER?
NATE. I AM NOT UNDERSTAND YOU.
AH-**HA!** OF **COURSE** YOU DON'T UNDERSTAND ME! BECAUSE I'M TOTALLY **OVER YOUR HEAD!**
BUT WAIT. I AM ACTUAL TALLER THAN YOU.
I'M TOO DEEP FOR HIM!
? ?
Peirce

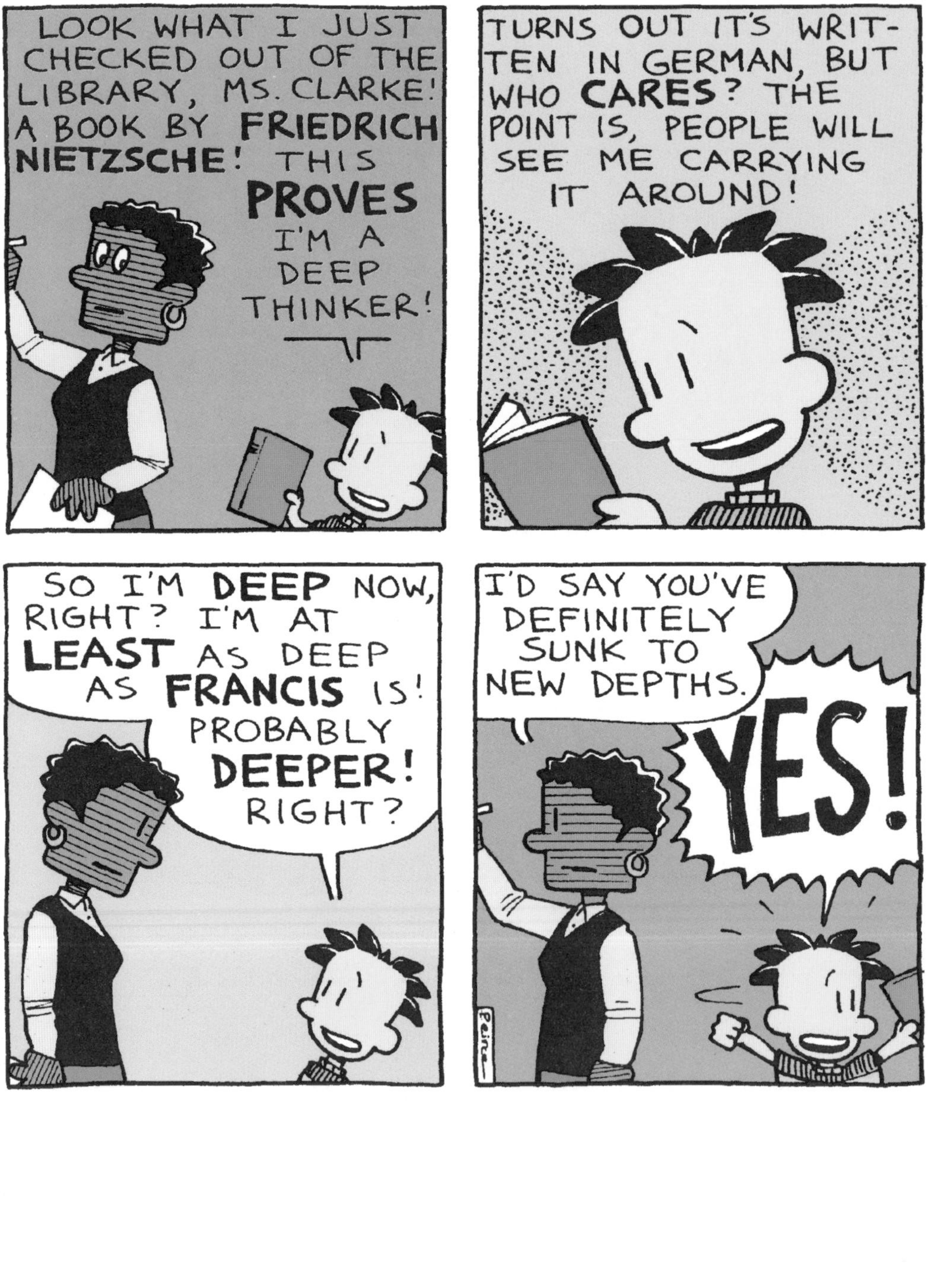
LOOK WHAT I JUST CHECKED OUT OF THE LIBRARY, MS. CLARKE! A BOOK BY FRIEDRICH NIETZSCHE! THIS PROVES I'M A DEEP THINKER!
TURNS OUT IT'S WRITTEN IN GERMAN, BUT WHO CARES? THE POINT IS, PEOPLE WILL SEE ME CARRYING IT AROUND!
SO I'M DEEP NOW, RIGHT? I'M AT LEAST AS DEEP AS FRANCIS IS! PROBABLY DEEPER! RIGHT?
I'D SAY YOU'VE DEFINITELY SUNK TO NEW DEPTHS.
YES!
Peirce

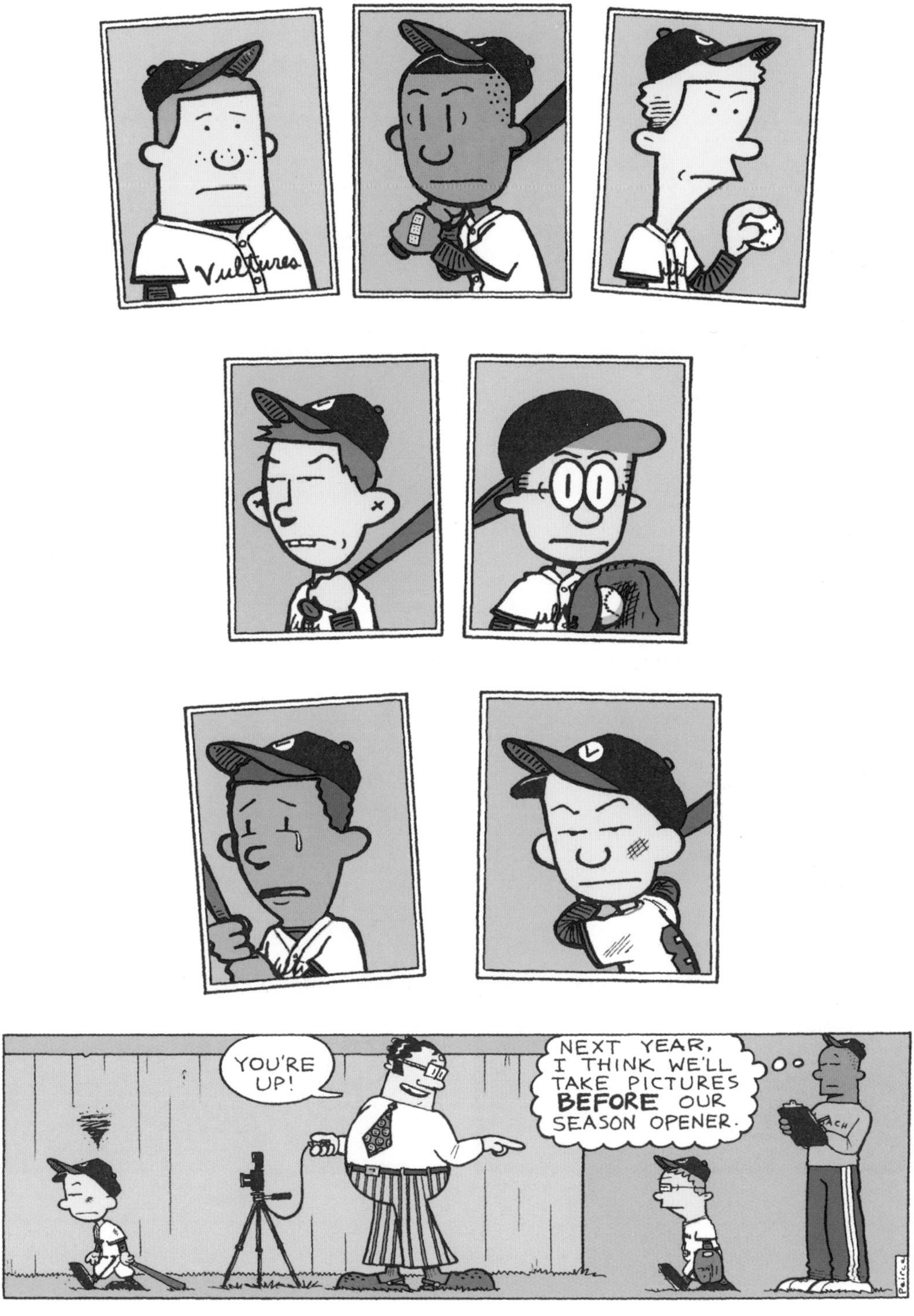
Vultures
YOU'RE UP!
NEXT YEAR, I THINK WE'LL TAKE PICTURES **BEFORE** OUR SEASON OPENER.

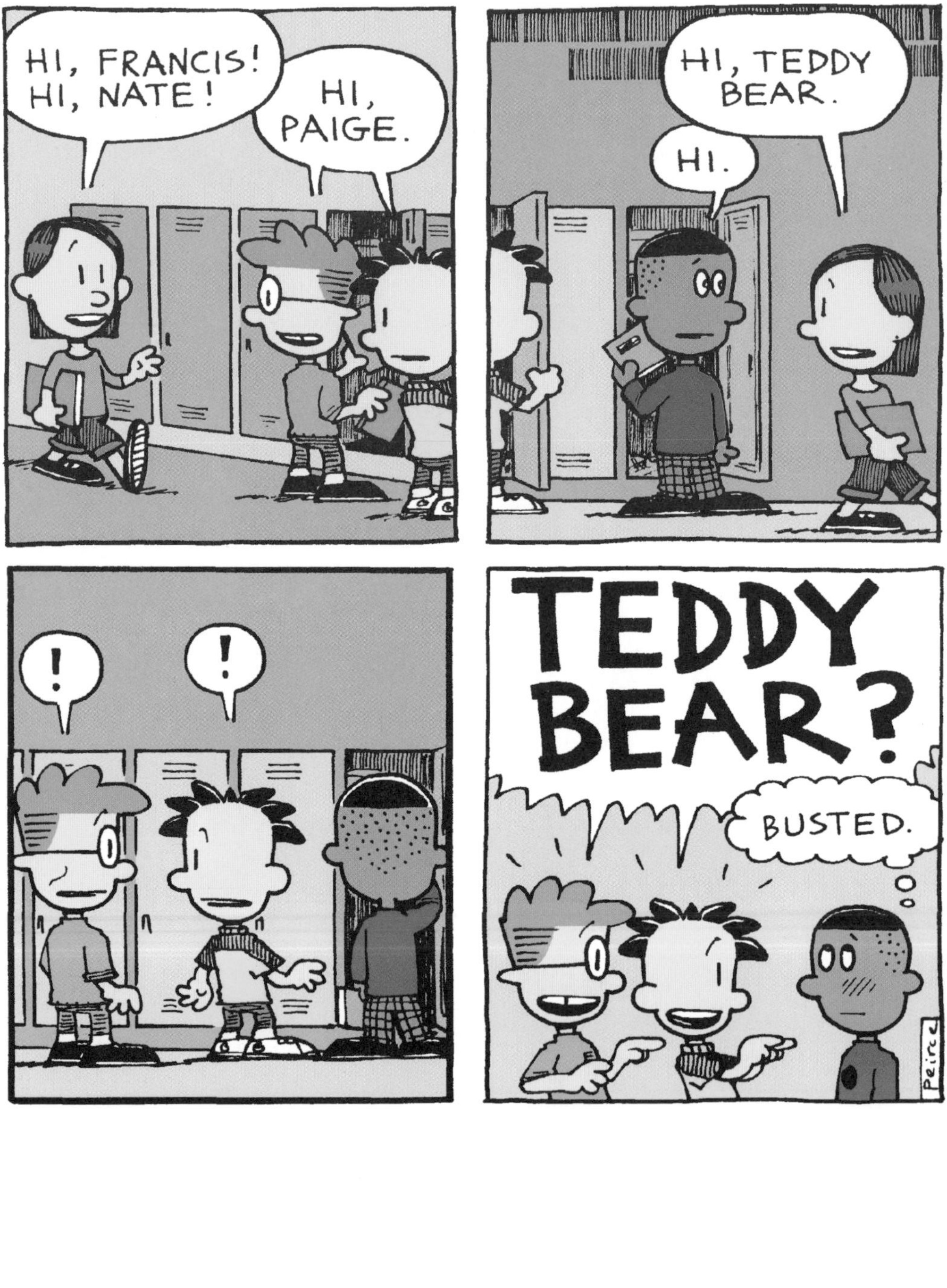
HI, FRANCIS! HI, NATE!
HI, PAIGE.
HI, TEDDY BEAR.
HI.
!
!
TEDDY BEAR?
BUSTED.
Peirce

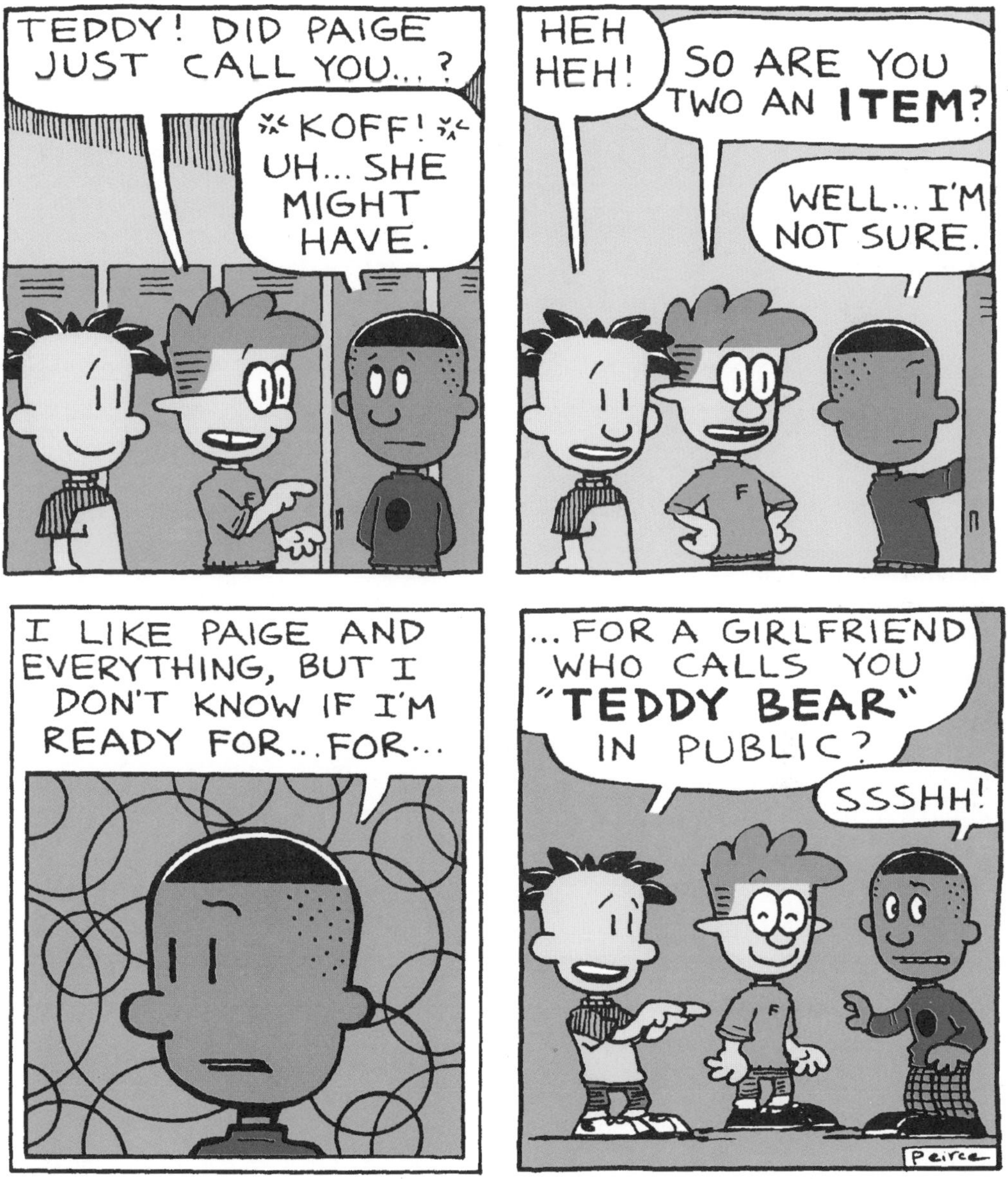
TEDDY! DID PAIGE JUST CALL YOU...?
KOFF! UH... SHE MIGHT HAVE.
HEH HEH!
SO ARE YOU TWO AN **ITEM**?
WELL... I'M NOT SURE.
I LIKE PAIGE AND EVERYTHING, BUT I DON'T KNOW IF I'M READY FOR... FOR...
...FOR A GIRLFRIEND WHO CALLS YOU "**TEDDY BEAR**" IN PUBLIC?
SSSHH!
Peirce

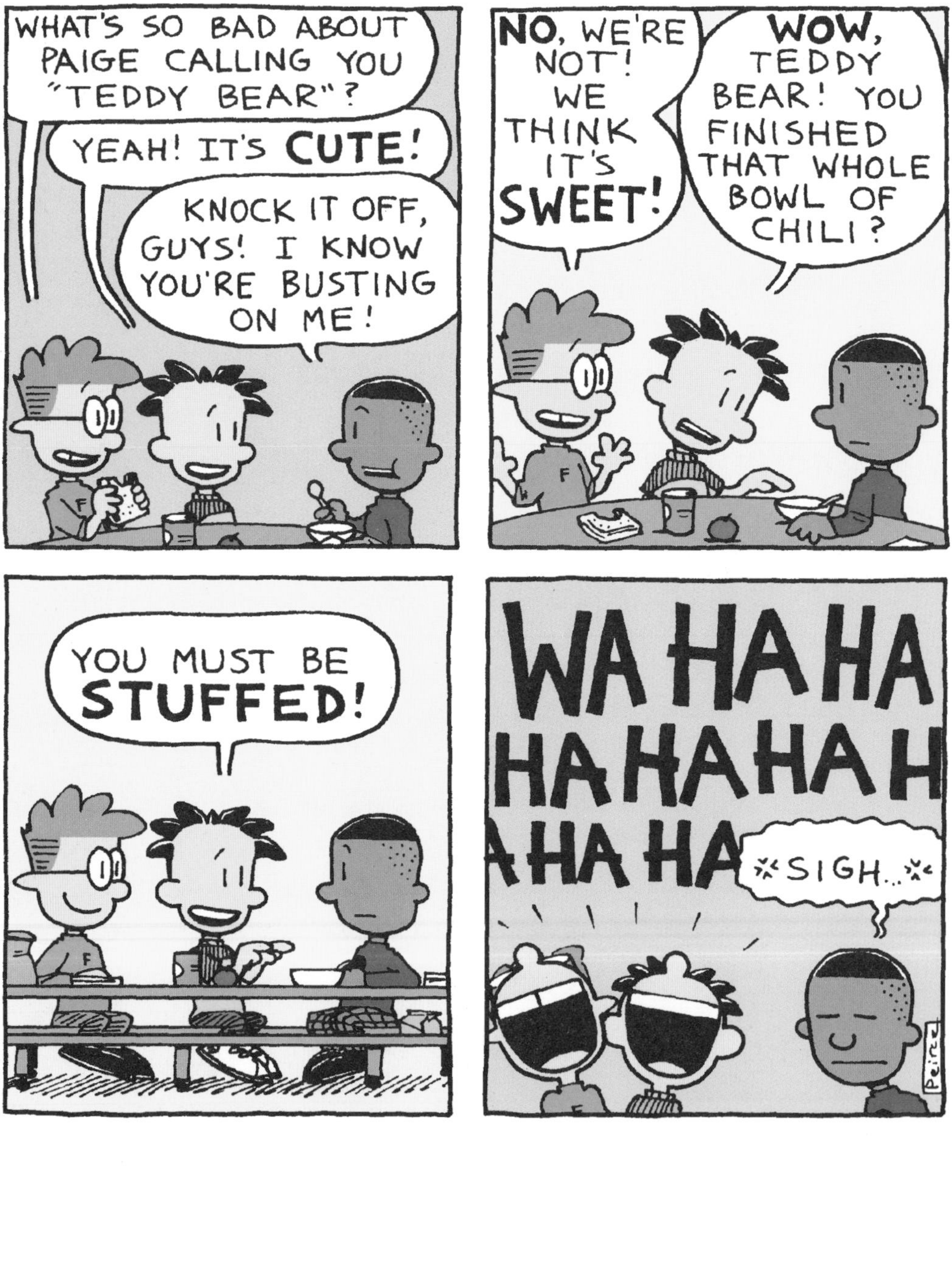

WHAT'S SO BAD ABOUT PAIGE CALLING YOU "TEDDY BEAR"?
YEAH! IT'S **CUTE!**
KNOCK IT OFF, GUYS! I KNOW YOU'RE BUSTING ON ME!
NO, WE'RE NOT! WE THINK IT'S **SWEET!**
WOW, TEDDY BEAR! YOU FINISHED THAT WHOLE BOWL OF CHILI?
YOU MUST BE **STUFFED!**
WA HA HA HA HA HA HA H A HA HA
SIGH...
Peirce

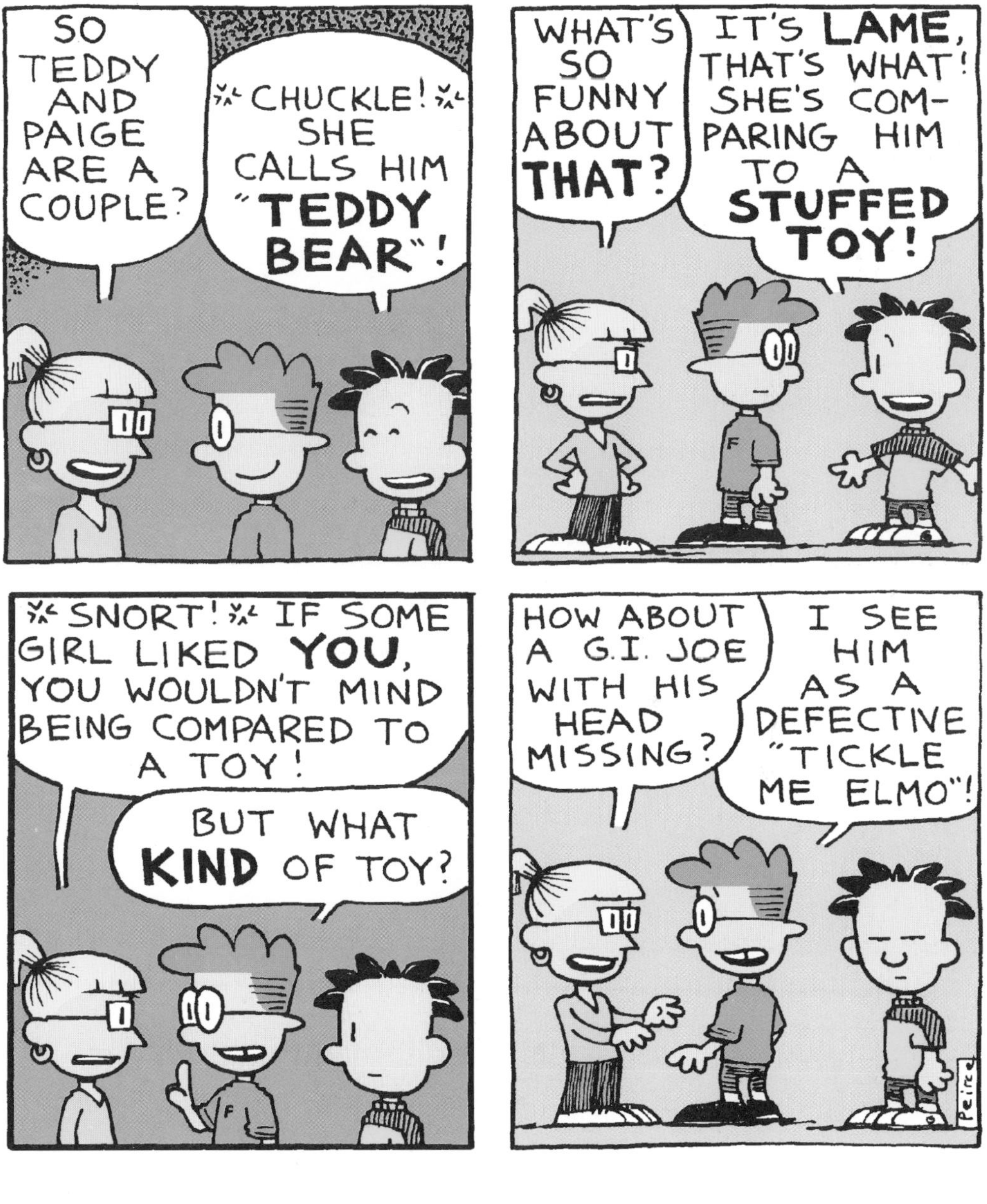
SO TEDDY AND PAIGE ARE A COUPLE?
CHUCKLE! SHE CALLS HIM "TEDDY BEAR"!
WHAT'S SO FUNNY ABOUT THAT?
IT'S LAME, THAT'S WHAT! SHE'S COMPARING HIM TO A STUFFED TOY!
SNORT! IF SOME GIRL LIKED YOU, YOU WOULDN'T MIND BEING COMPARED TO A TOY!
BUT WHAT KIND OF TOY?
HOW ABOUT A G.I. JOE WITH HIS HEAD MISSING?
I SEE HIM AS A DEFECTIVE "TICKLE ME ELMO"!
Peirce

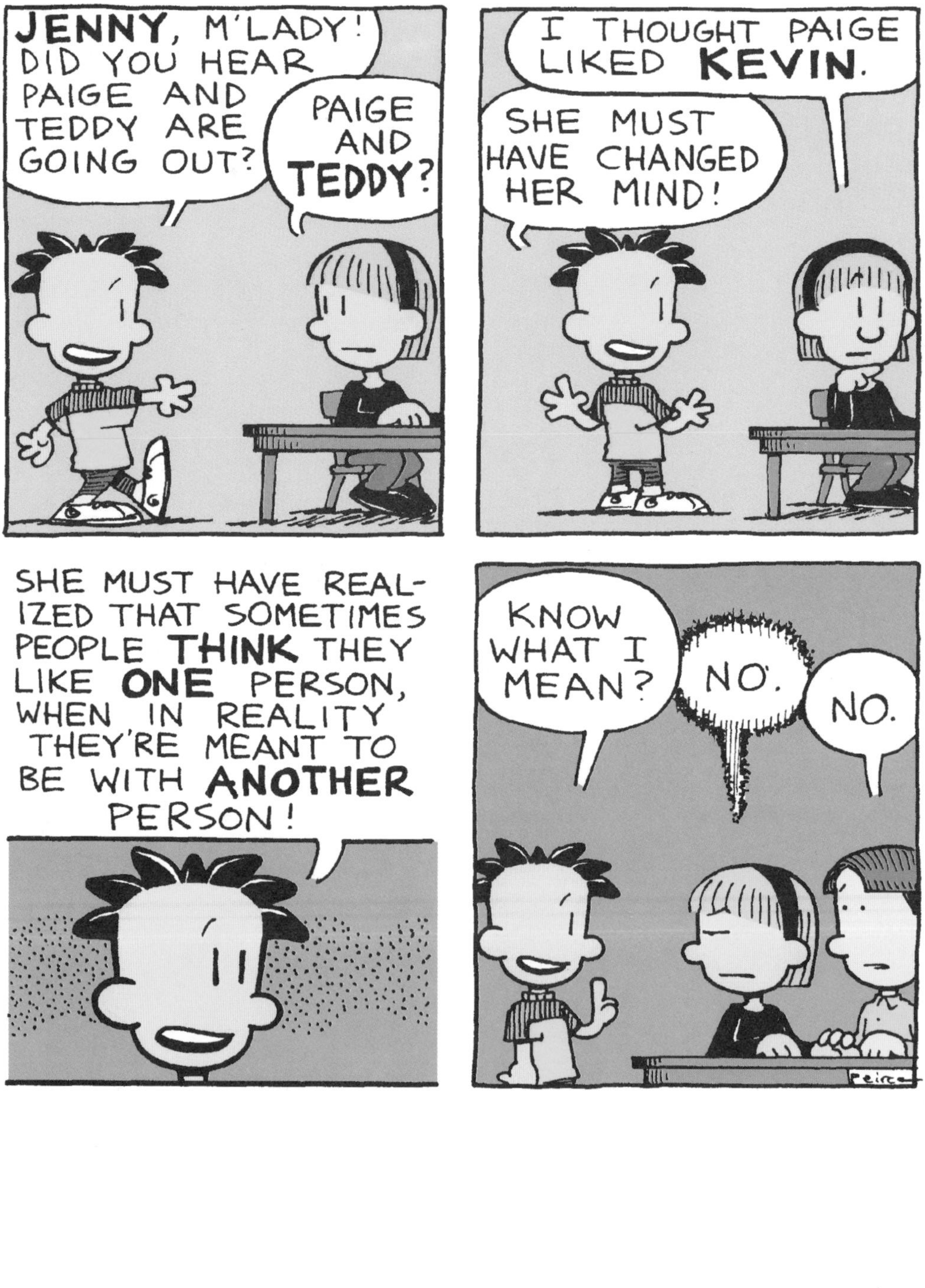
JENNY, M'LADY! DID YOU HEAR PAIGE AND TEDDY ARE GOING OUT?
PAIGE AND TEDDY?
I THOUGHT PAIGE LIKED KEVIN.
SHE MUST HAVE CHANGED HER MIND!
SHE MUST HAVE REALIZED THAT SOMETIMES PEOPLE THINK THEY LIKE ONE PERSON, WHEN IN REALITY THEY'RE MEANT TO BE WITH ANOTHER PERSON!
KNOW WHAT I MEAN?
NO.
NO.
Peirce

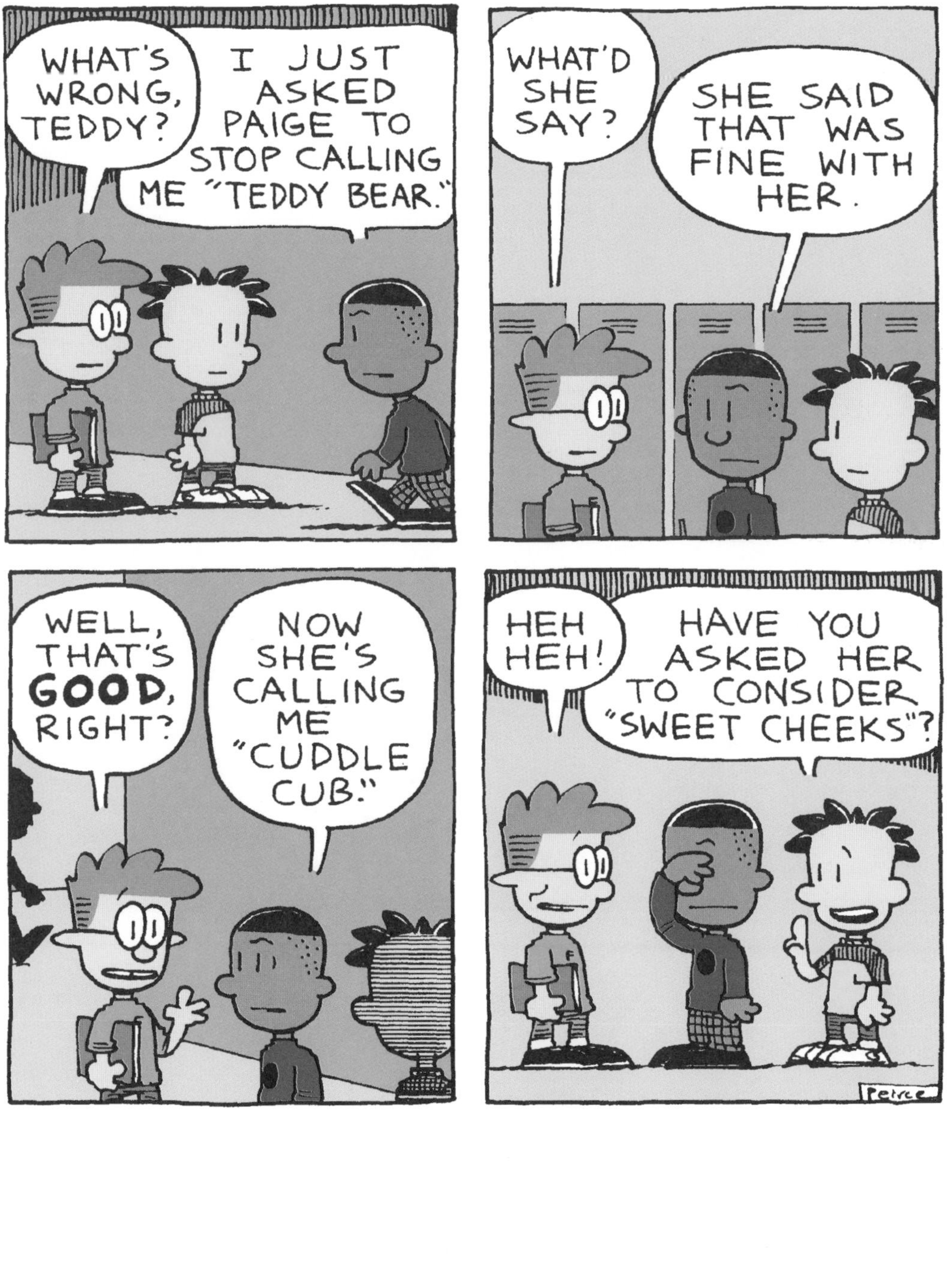
WHAT'S WRONG, TEDDY?
I JUST ASKED PAIGE TO STOP CALLING ME "TEDDY BEAR."
WHAT'D SHE SAY?
SHE SAID THAT WAS FINE WITH HER.
WELL, THAT'S GOOD, RIGHT?
NOW SHE'S CALLING ME "CUDDLE CUB."
HEH HEH!
HAVE YOU ASKED HER TO CONSIDER "SWEET CHEEKS"?
Peirce

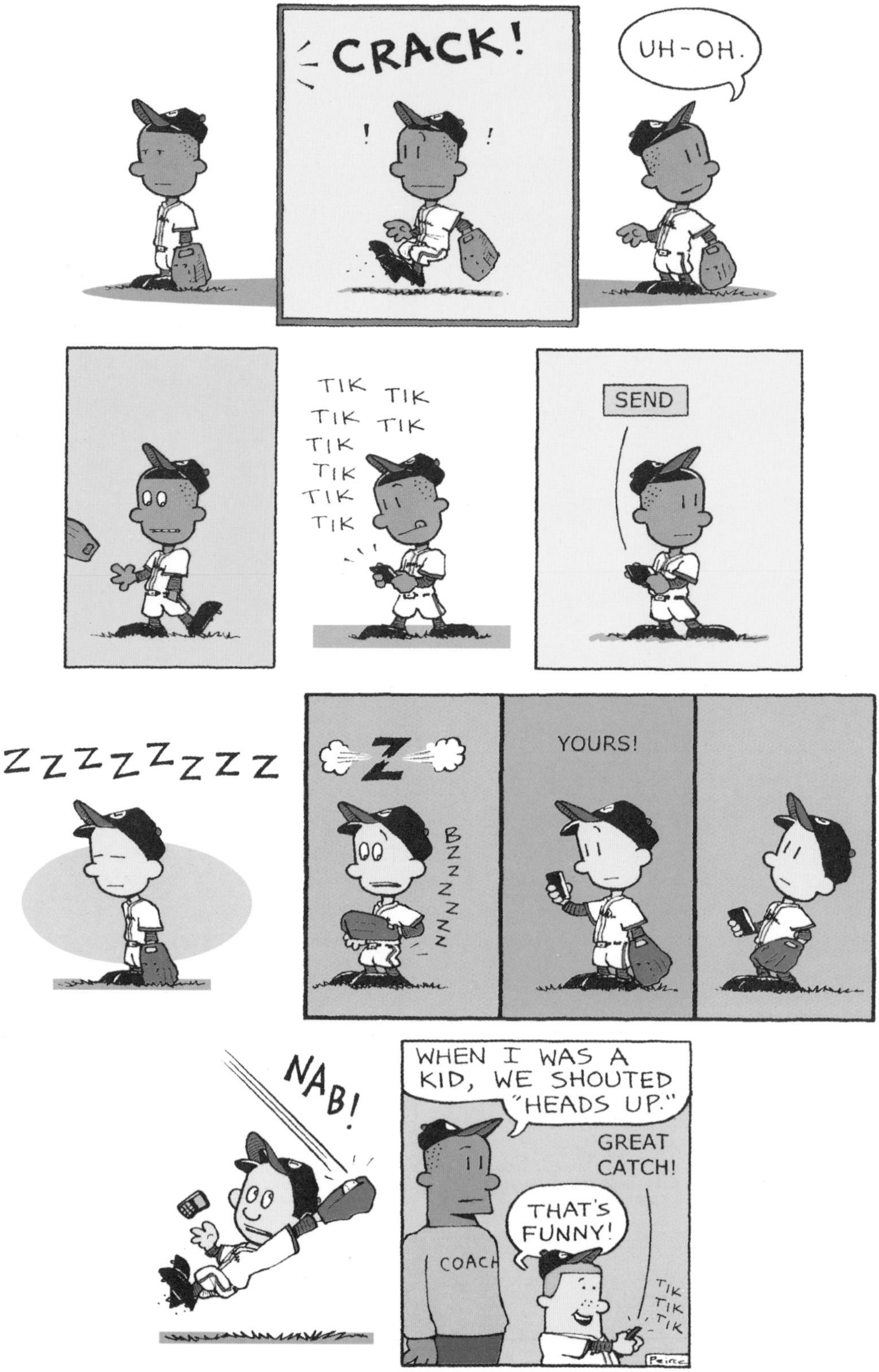
CRACK!
!
!
UH-OH.
TIK TIK
TIK TIK
TIK
TIK
TIK
TIK
SEND
ZZZZZZZZZ
Z
BZZZZZZ
YOURS!
NAB!
WHEN I WAS A KID, WE SHOUTED "HEADS UP."
GREAT CATCH!
THAT'S FUNNY!
COACH
TIK
TIK
TIK
Peirce

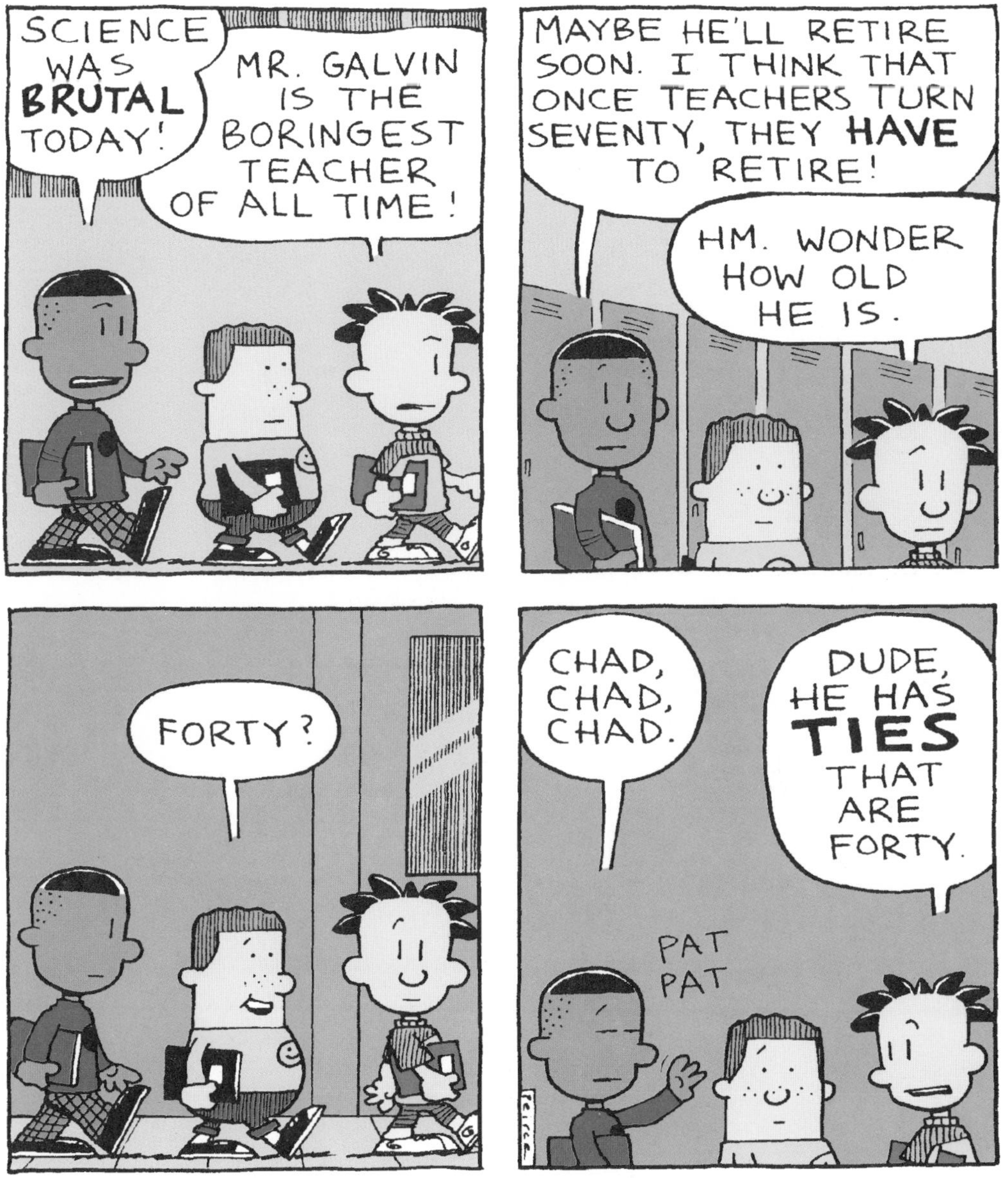
SCIENCE WAS **BRUTAL** TODAY!
MR. GALVIN IS THE BORINGEST TEACHER OF ALL TIME!
MAYBE HE'LL RETIRE SOON. I THINK THAT ONCE TEACHERS TURN SEVENTY, THEY **HAVE** TO RETIRE!
HM. WONDER HOW OLD HE IS.
FORTY?
CHAD, CHAD, CHAD.
DUDE, HE HAS **TIES** THAT ARE FORTY.
PAT PAT

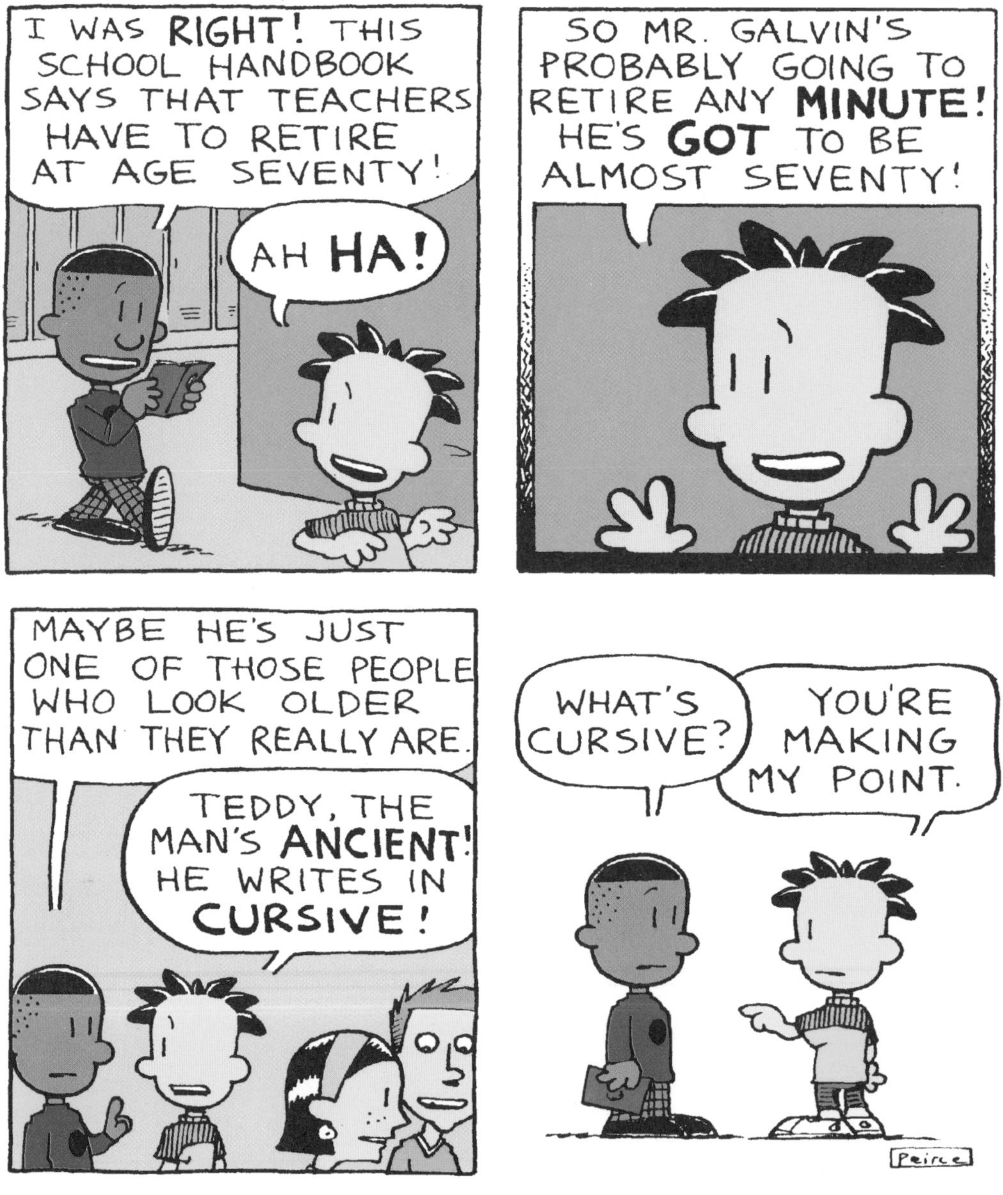
I WAS RIGHT! THIS SCHOOL HANDBOOK SAYS THAT TEACHERS HAVE TO RETIRE AT AGE SEVENTY!
AH HA!
SO MR. GALVIN'S PROBABLY GOING TO RETIRE ANY MINUTE! HE'S GOT TO BE ALMOST SEVENTY!
MAYBE HE'S JUST ONE OF THOSE PEOPLE WHO LOOK OLDER THAN THEY REALLY ARE.
TEDDY, THE MAN'S ANCIENT! HE WRITES IN CURSIVE!
WHAT'S CURSIVE?
YOU'RE MAKING MY POINT.
Peirce

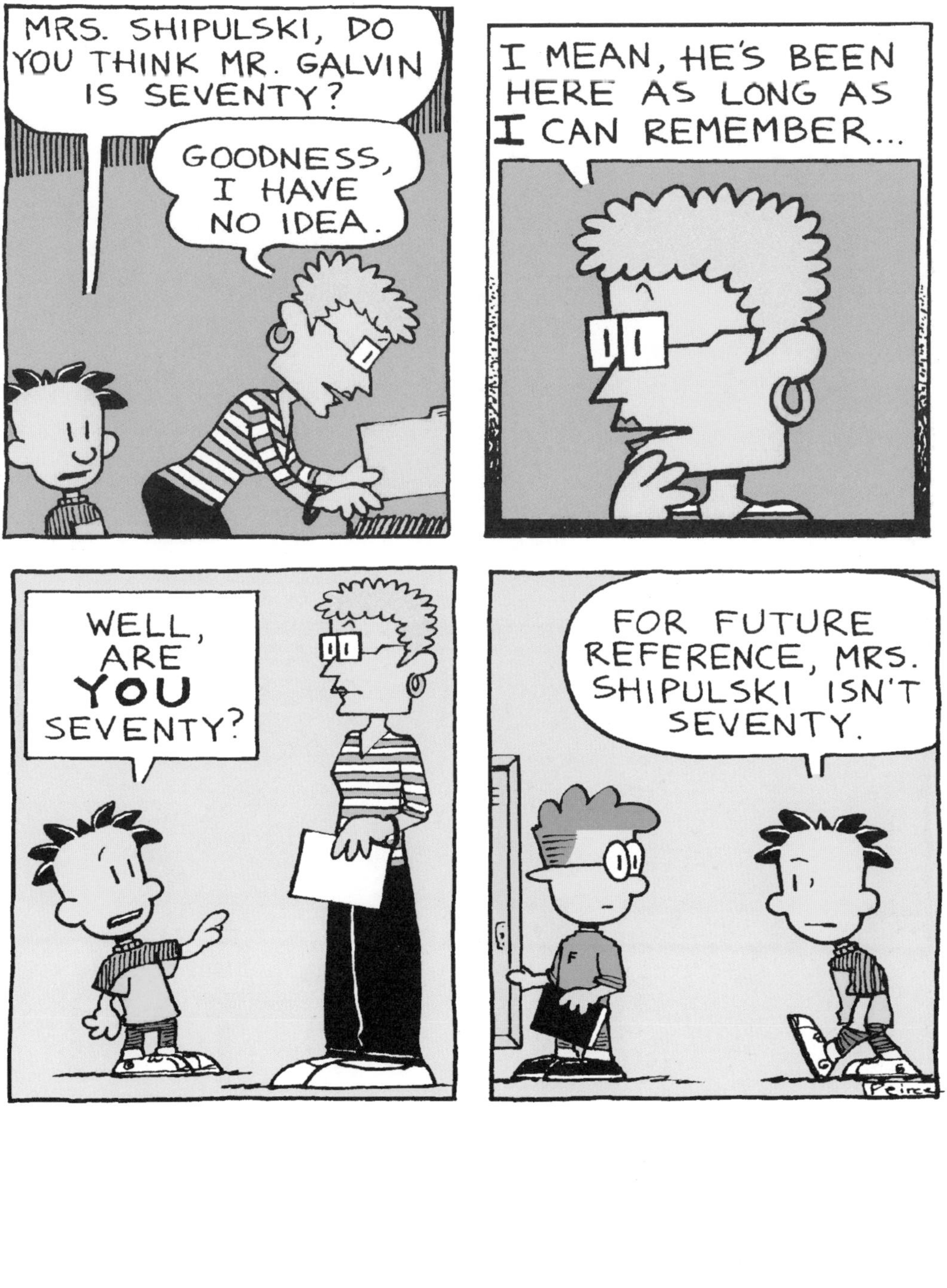
MRS. SHIPULSKI, DO YOU THINK MR. GALVIN IS SEVENTY?
GOODNESS, I HAVE NO IDEA.
I MEAN, HE'S BEEN HERE AS LONG AS I CAN REMEMBER...
WELL, ARE YOU SEVENTY?
FOR FUTURE REFERENCE, MRS. SHIPULSKI ISN'T SEVENTY.
Peirce

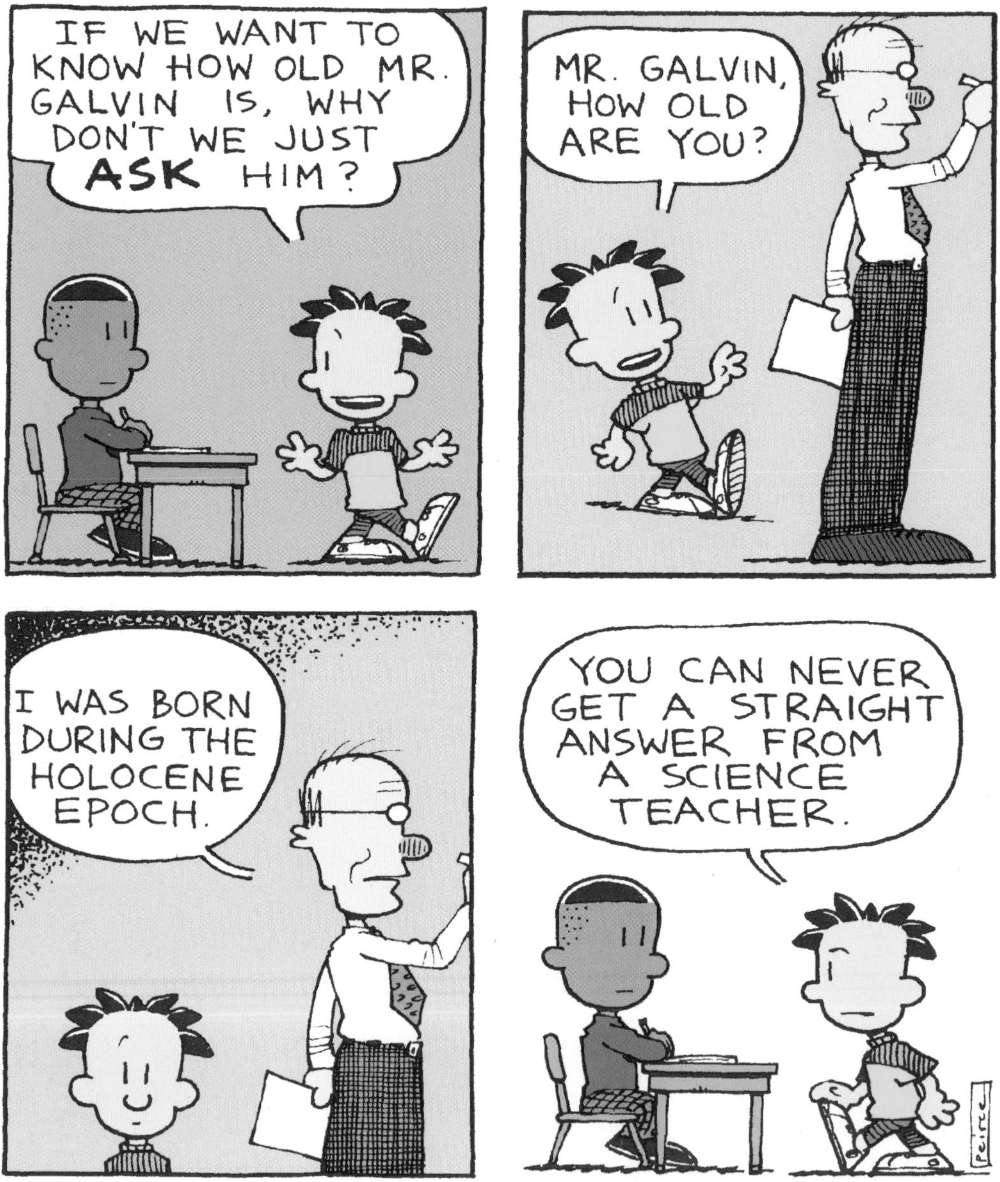
IF WE WANT TO KNOW HOW OLD MR. GALVIN IS, WHY DON'T WE JUST **ASK** HIM?
MR. GALVIN, HOW OLD ARE YOU?
I WAS BORN DURING THE HOLOCENE EPOCH.
YOU CAN NEVER GET A STRAIGHT ANSWER FROM A SCIENCE TEACHER.
Peirce

PRINCIPAL NICHOLS! MR. GALVIN HAS TO RETIRE SOON, RIGHT?
WHY WOULD HE HAVE TO RETIRE?
IT SAYS IN THE SCHOOL HANDBOOK THAT TEACHERS HAVE TO RETIRE AT AGE SEVENTY.
YOU MUST HAVE BEEN LOOKING AT AN OUTDATED HANDBOOK, NATE.
THE SCHOOL DID AWAY WITH THAT POLICY A FEW YEARS AGO.
OH.
Peirce
SO I GUESS YOU WON'T BE REPLACING HIM WITH A HOT SWEDISH STUDENT TEACHER WHO MOON-LIGHTS AS A BIKINI MODEL.
PROBABLY NOT THIS WEEK.

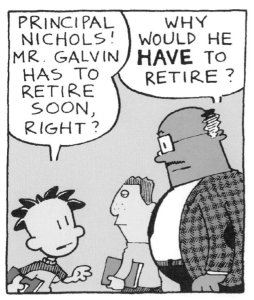

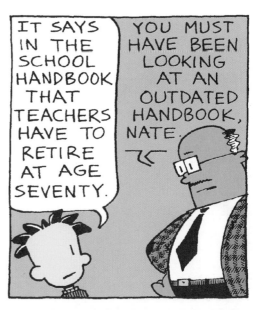

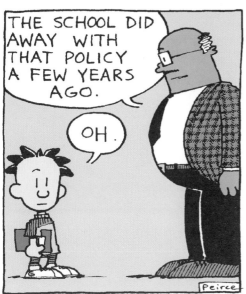

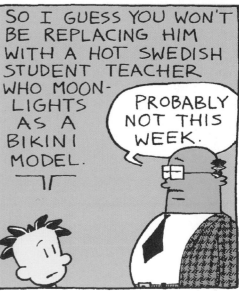

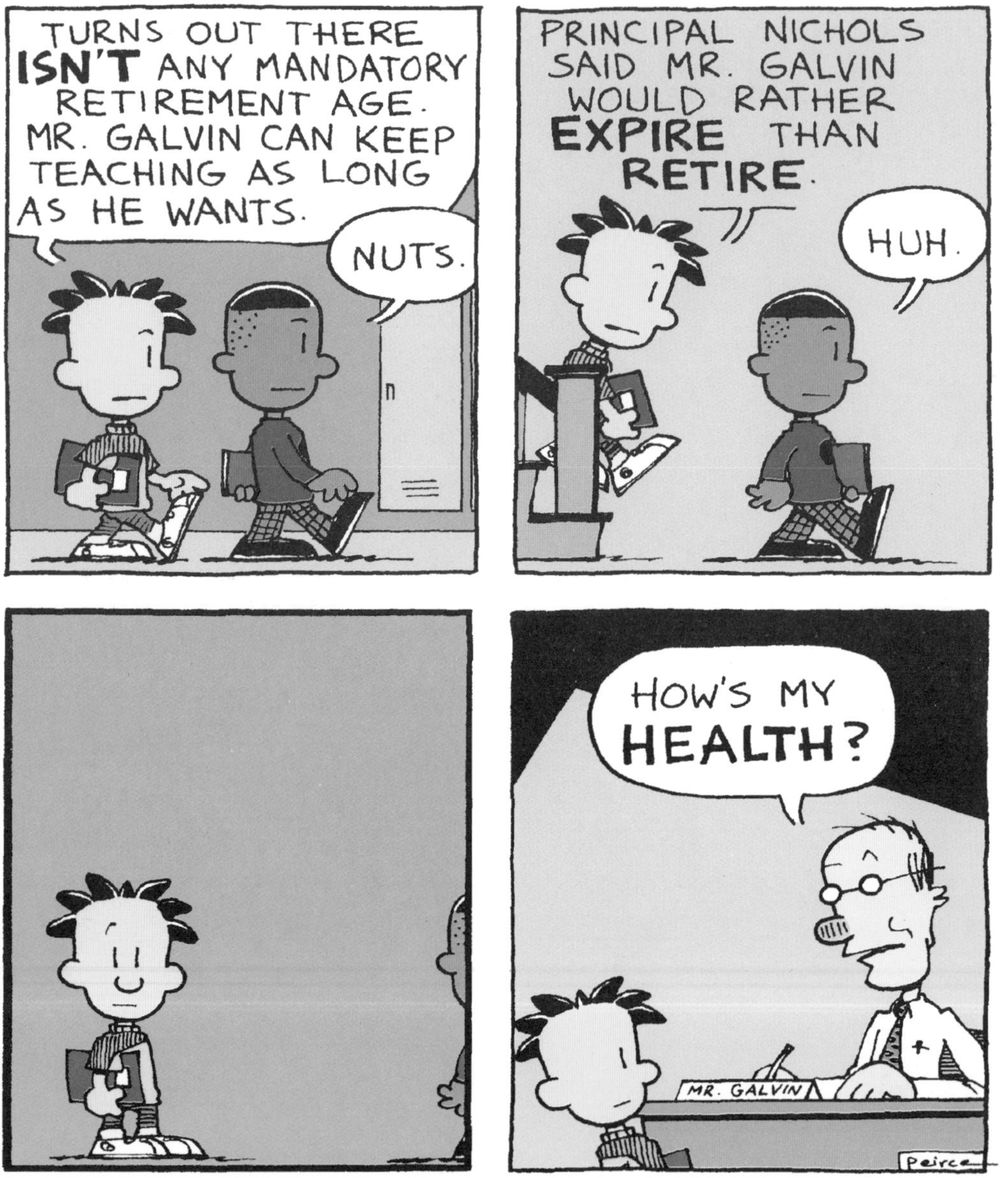
TURNS OUT THERE **ISN'T** ANY MANDATORY RETIREMENT AGE. MR. GALVIN CAN KEEP TEACHING AS LONG AS HE WANTS.
NUTS.
PRINCIPAL NICHOLS SAID MR. GALVIN WOULD RATHER **EXPIRE** THAN **RETIRE**.
HUH.
HOW'S MY **HEALTH**?
MR. GALVIN
Peirce

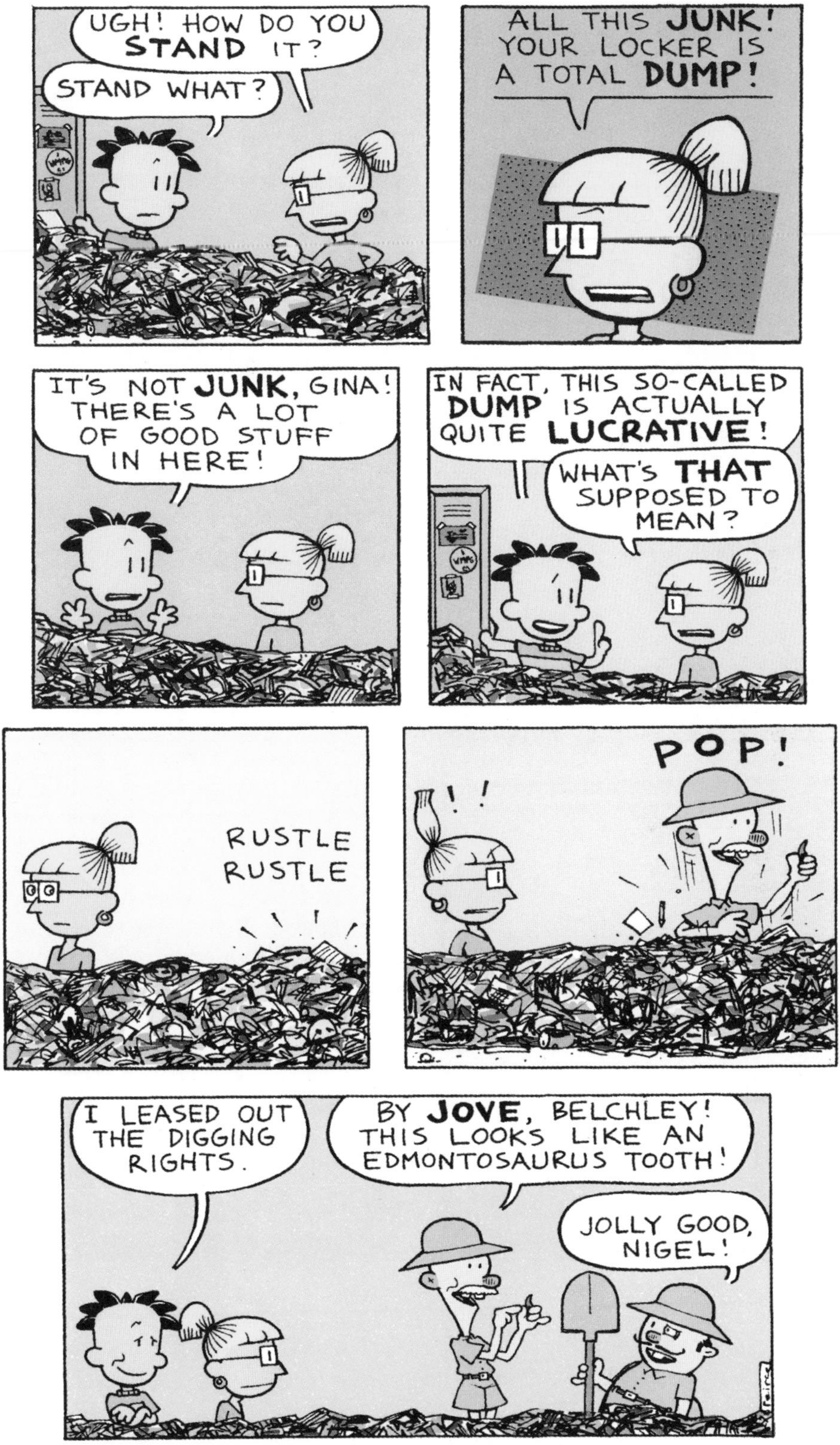
UGH! HOW DO YOU STAND IT?
STAND WHAT?
ALL THIS JUNK! YOUR LOCKER IS A TOTAL DUMP!
IT'S NOT JUNK, GINA! THERE'S A LOT OF GOOD STUFF IN HERE!
IN FACT, THIS SO-CALLED DUMP IS ACTUALLY QUITE LUCRATIVE!
WHAT'S THAT SUPPOSED TO MEAN?
RUSTLE RUSTLE
POP!
! !
I LEASED OUT THE DIGGING RIGHTS.
BY JOVE, BELCHLEY! THIS LOOKS LIKE AN EDMONTOSAURUS TOOTH!
JOLLY GOOD, NIGEL!

IT SAYS HERE THAT YOU CAN TELL A LOT ABOUT PEOPLE BASED ON THEIR FAVORITE **BODY** OF **WATER**!
I'M A LAKE!
I'M A MOUNTAIN STREAM!
I'M A TIDE POOL!
TSUNAMI.
DEFINITELY.
WAIT, **WHAT**?

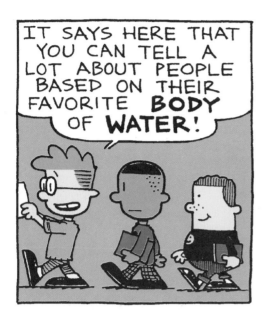

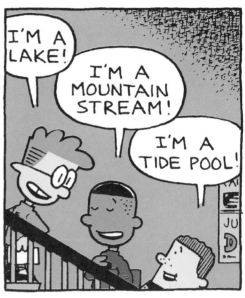

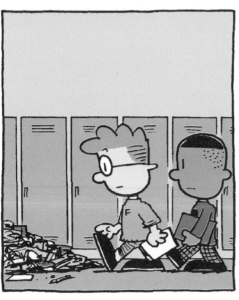

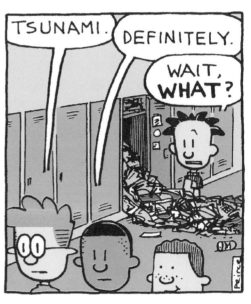

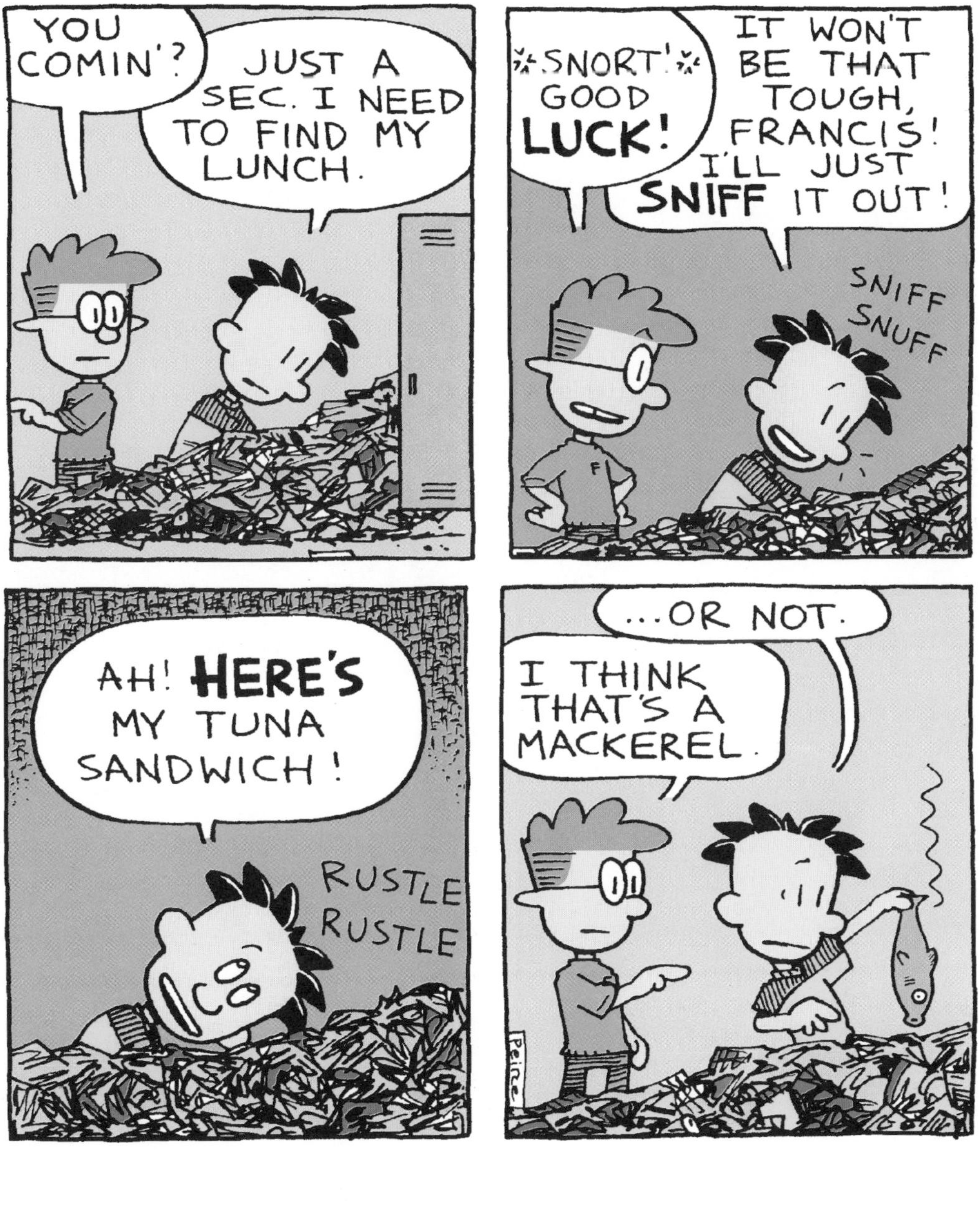
YOU COMIN'?
JUST A SEC. I NEED TO FIND MY LUNCH.
SNORT! GOOD **LUCK!**
IT WON'T BE THAT TOUGH, FRANCIS! I'LL JUST **SNIFF** IT OUT!
SNIFF SNUFF
AH! **HERE'S** MY TUNA SANDWICH!
RUSTLE RUSTLE
I THINK THAT'S A MACKEREL.
...OR NOT.
Peirce

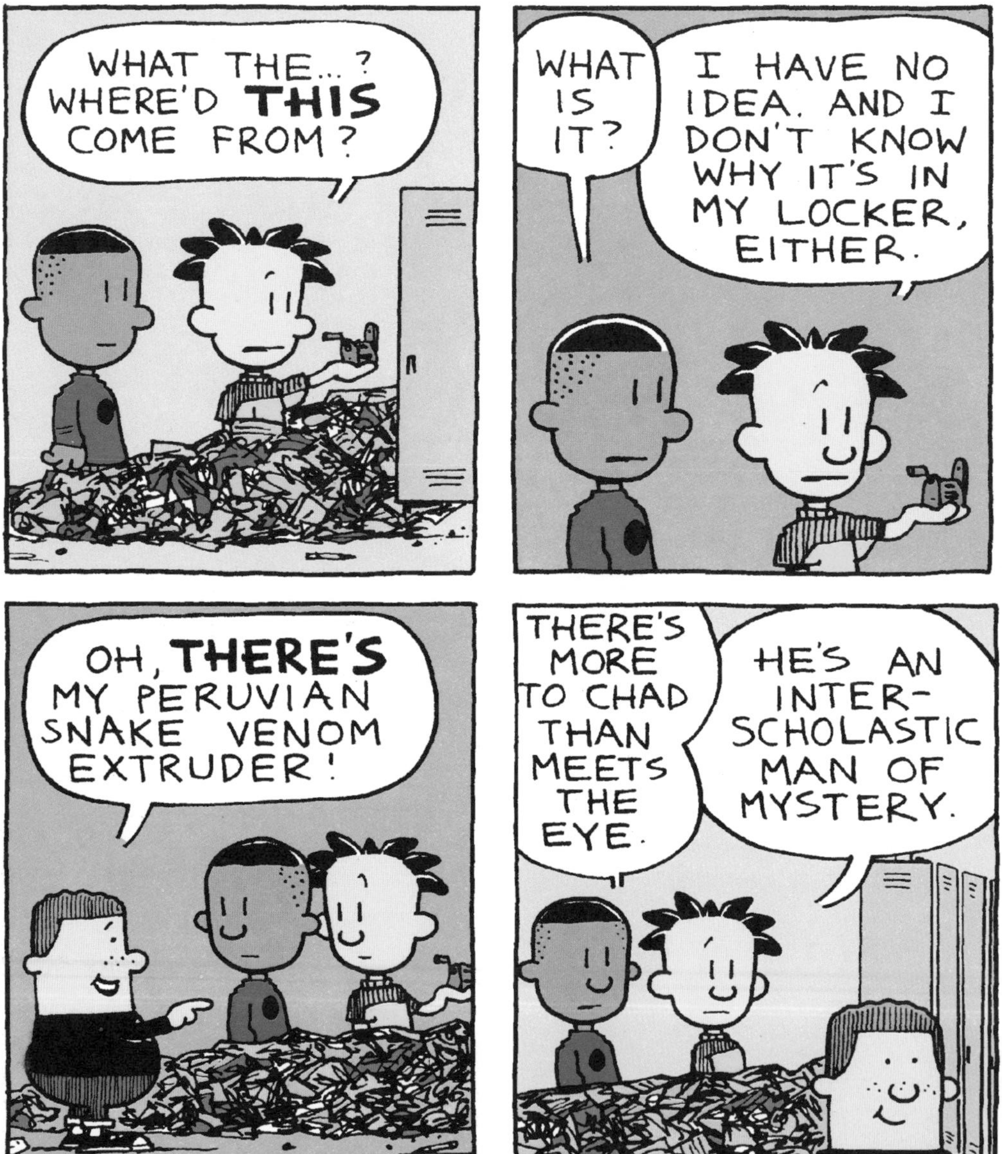
WHAT THE...? WHERE'D **THIS** COME FROM?
WHAT IS IT?
I HAVE NO IDEA. AND I DON'T KNOW WHY IT'S IN MY LOCKER, EITHER.
OH, **THERE'S** MY PERUVIAN SNAKE VENOM EXTRUDER!
peirce
THERE'S MORE TO CHAD THAN MEETS THE EYE.
HE'S AN INTER-SCHOLASTIC MAN OF MYSTERY.

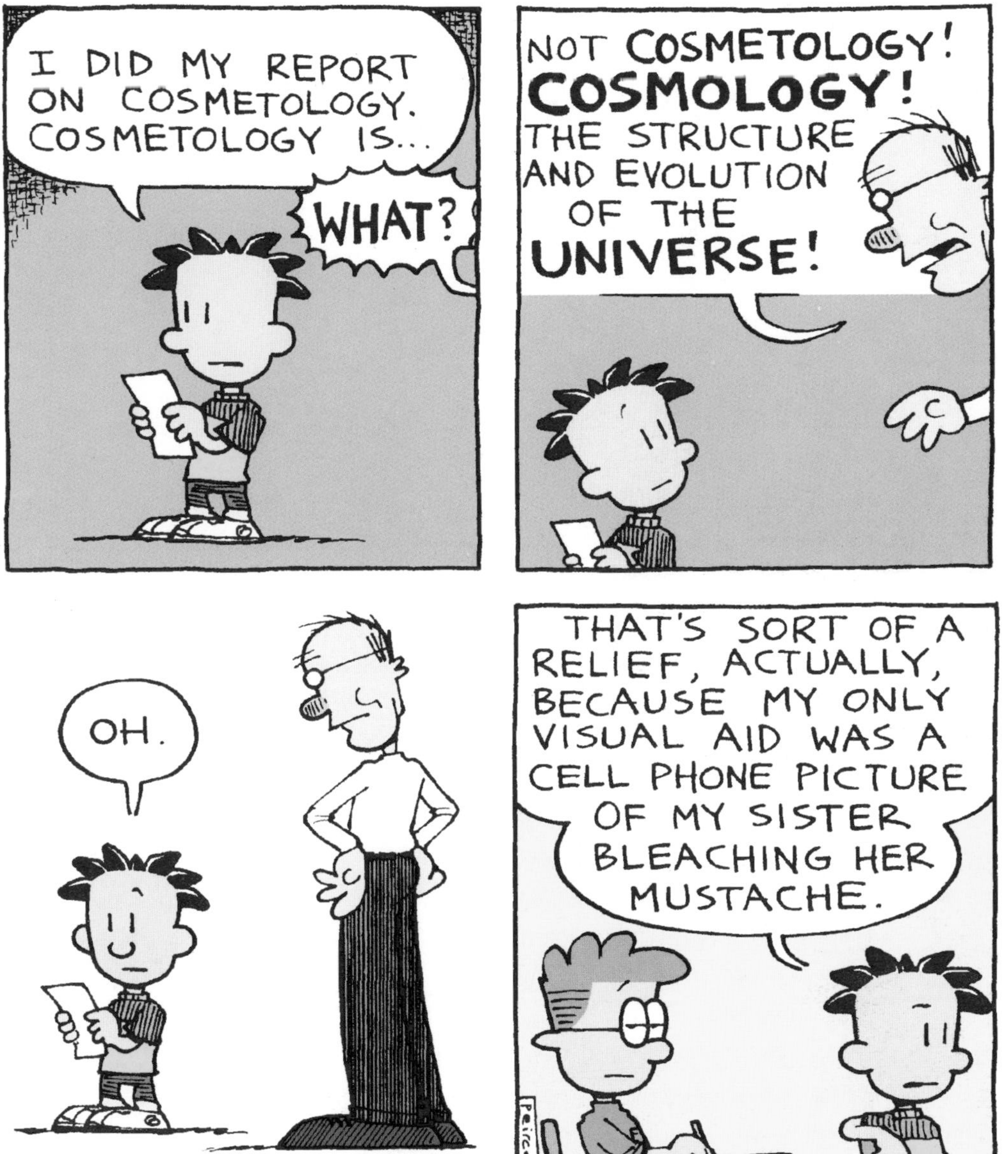
I DID MY REPORT ON COSMETOLOGY. COSMETOLOGY IS...
WHAT?
NOT COSMETOLOGY! COSMOLOGY! THE STRUCTURE AND EVOLUTION OF THE UNIVERSE!
OH.
THAT'S SORT OF A RELIEF, ACTUALLY, BECAUSE MY ONLY VISUAL AID WAS A CELL PHONE PICTURE OF MY SISTER BLEACHING HER MUSTACHE.
Peirce

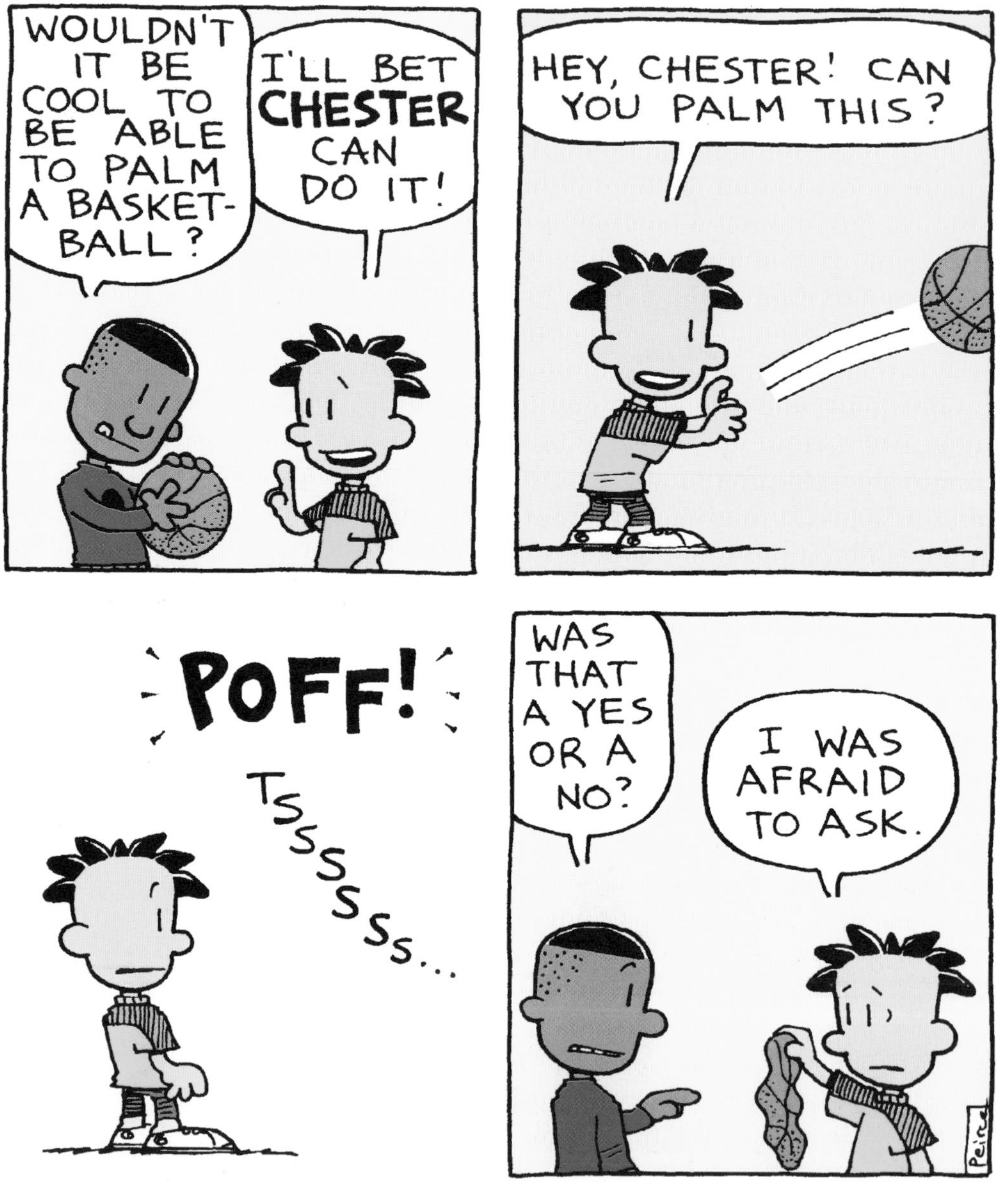
WOULDN'T IT BE COOL TO BE ABLE TO PALM A BASKET-BALL?
I'LL BET CHESTER CAN DO IT!
HEY, CHESTER! CAN YOU PALM THIS?
POFF!
TSSSSSS...
WAS THAT A YES OR A NO?
I WAS AFRAID TO ASK.
Peirce

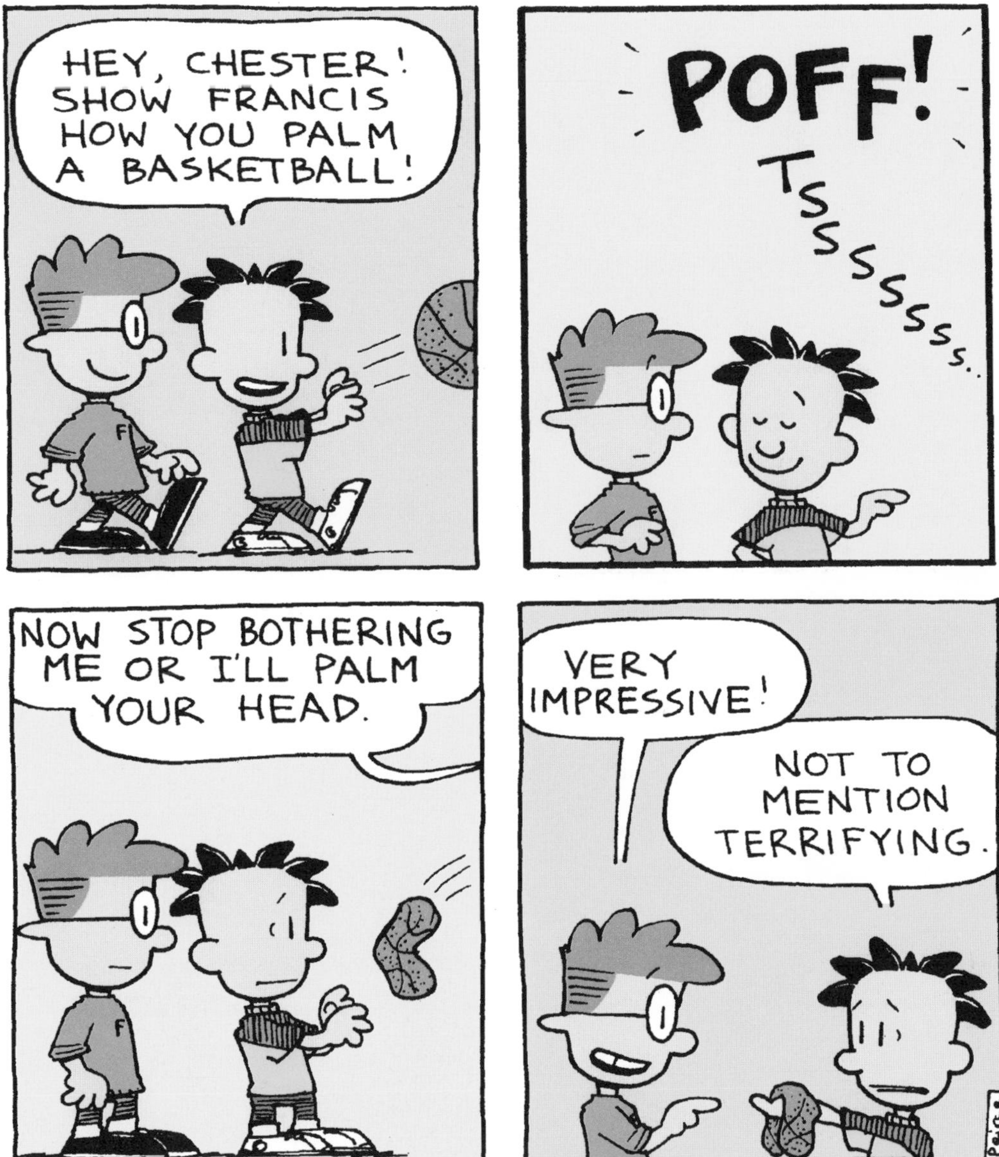
HEY, CHESTER! SHOW FRANCIS HOW YOU PALM A BASKETBALL!
POFF!
TSSSSSSSS...
NOW STOP BOTHERING ME OR I'LL PALM YOUR HEAD.
VERY IMPRESSIVE!
NOT TO MENTION TERRIFYING.
Peirce

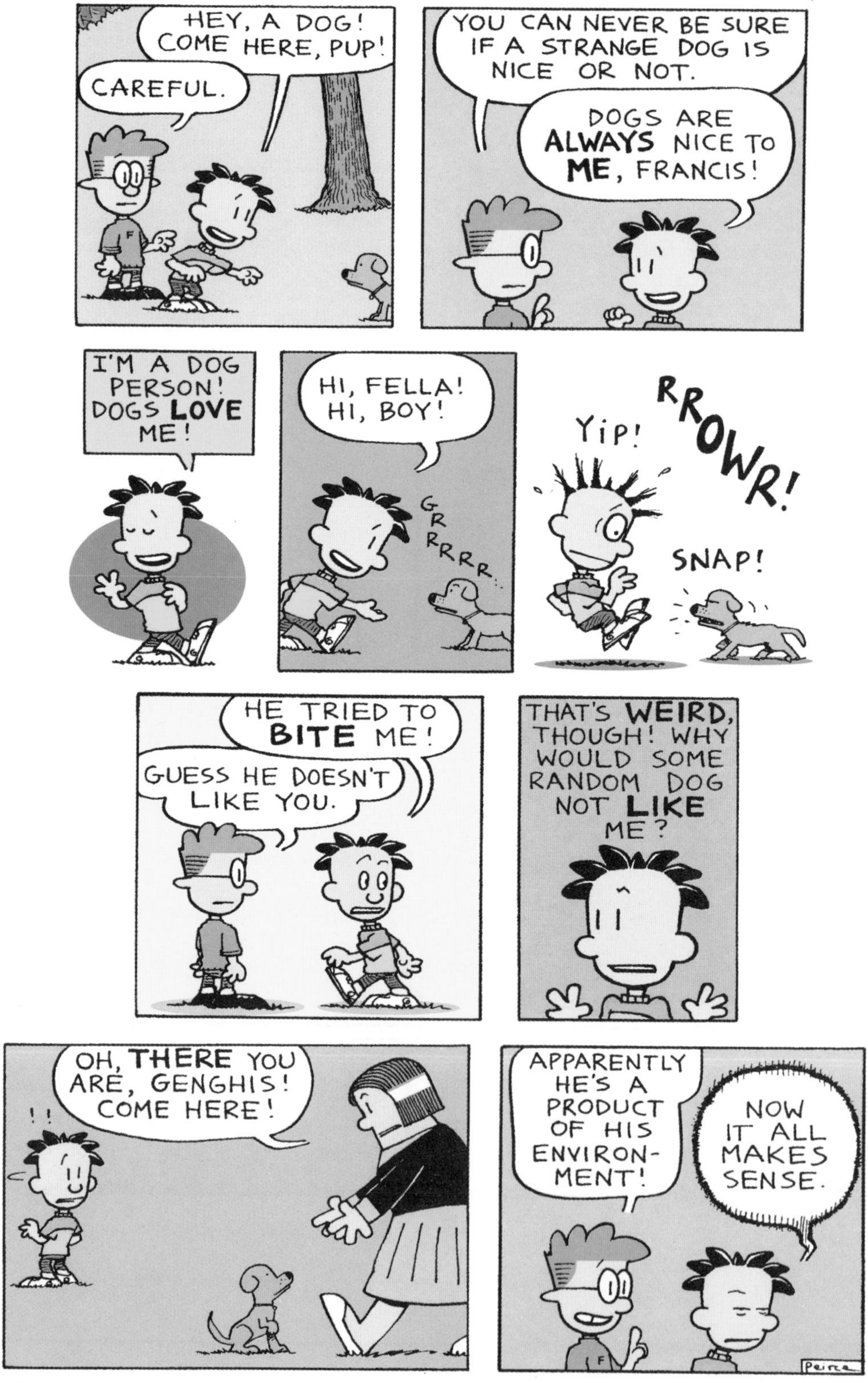

HEY, A DOG! COME HERE, PUP!
CAREFUL.
YOU CAN NEVER BE SURE IF A STRANGE DOG IS NICE OR NOT.
DOGS ARE **ALWAYS** NICE TO **ME**, FRANCIS!
I'M A DOG PERSON! DOGS **LOVE** ME!
HI, FELLA! HI, BOY!
GRRRRRR..
YIP!
RROWR!
SNAP!
HE TRIED TO **BITE** ME!
GUESS HE DOESN'T LIKE YOU.
THAT'S **WEIRD**, THOUGH! WHY WOULD SOME RANDOM DOG NOT **LIKE** ME?
OH, **THERE** YOU ARE, GENGHIS! COME HERE!
! !
APPARENTLY HE'S A PRODUCT OF HIS ENVIRON-MENT!
NOW IT ALL MAKES SENSE.
Peirce

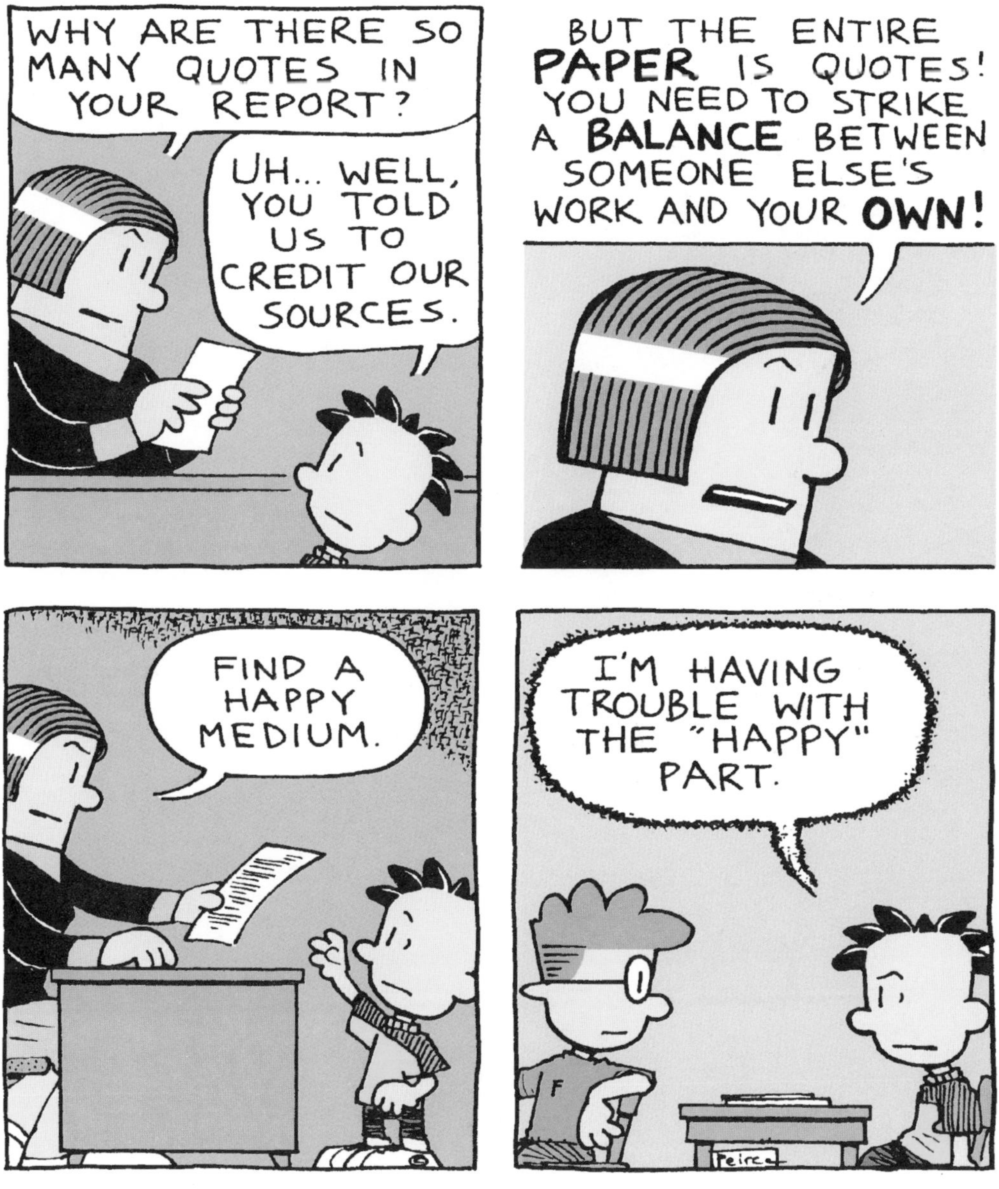
WHY ARE THERE SO MANY QUOTES IN YOUR REPORT?
UH... WELL, YOU TOLD US TO CREDIT OUR SOURCES.
BUT THE ENTIRE PAPER IS QUOTES! YOU NEED TO STRIKE A BALANCE BETWEEN SOMEONE ELSE'S WORK AND YOUR OWN!
FIND A HAPPY MEDIUM.
I'M HAVING TROUBLE WITH THE "HAPPY" PART.
Peirce

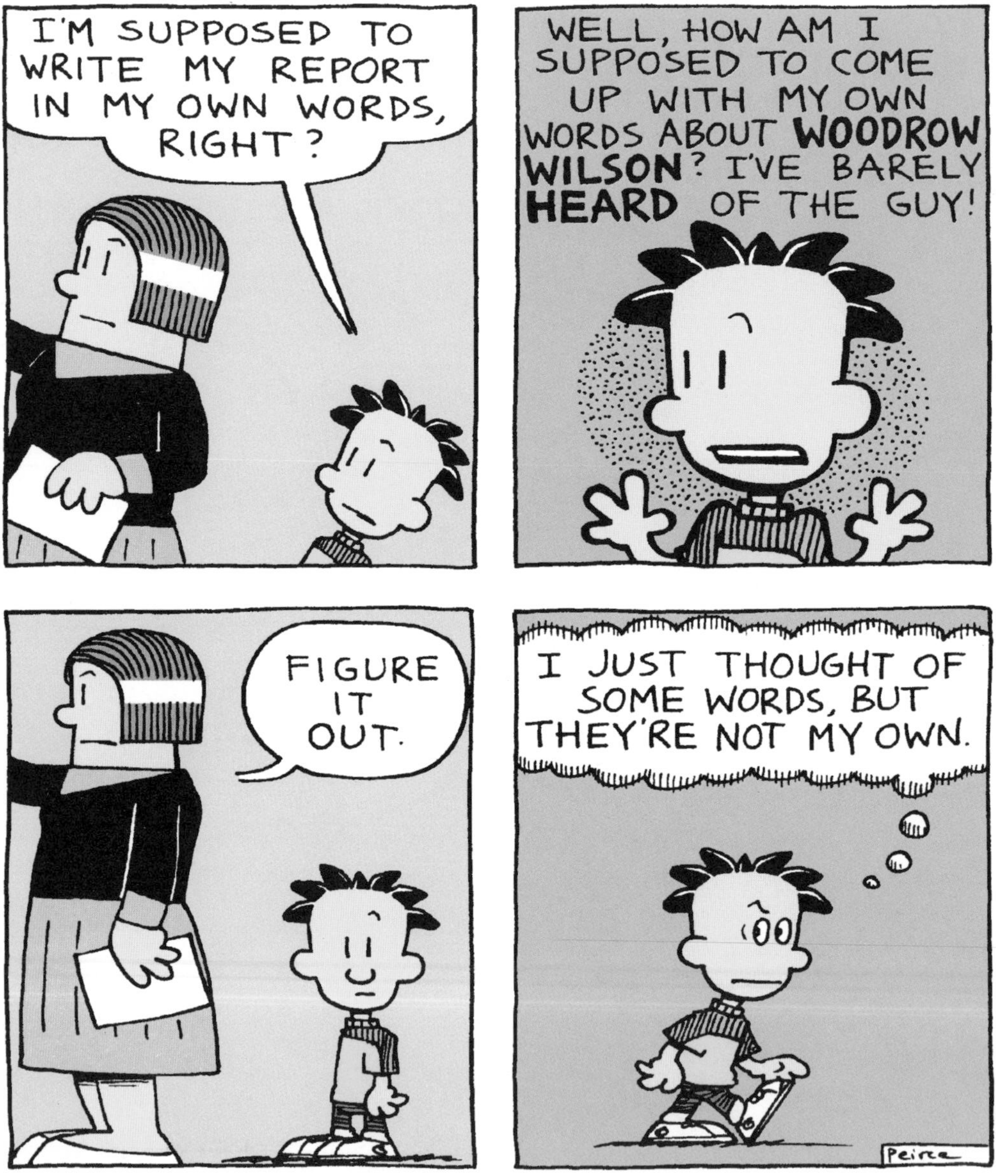
I'M SUPPOSED TO WRITE MY REPORT IN MY OWN WORDS, RIGHT?
WELL, HOW AM I SUPPOSED TO COME UP WITH MY OWN WORDS ABOUT **WOODROW WILSON**? I'VE BARELY **HEARD** OF THE GUY!
FIGURE IT OUT.
I JUST THOUGHT OF SOME WORDS, BUT THEY'RE NOT MY OWN.
Peirce

MRS. GODFREY'S MAKING ME REWRITE MY WOODROW WILSON PAPER!

SHE TOLD ME TO FIND A BALANCE BETWEEN FACT AND OPINION... WHATEVER **THAT** MEANS.

IT PROBABLY MEANS JUST WHAT IT SOUNDS LIKE.

SO EVERY TIME I WRITE SOMETHING FACTUAL, I WRITE AN OPINION IN THE VERY SAME SENTENCE?

RIGHT.

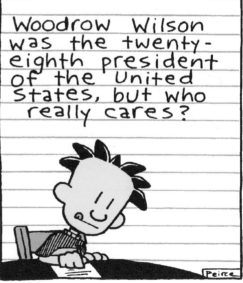

Woodrow Wilson was the twenty-eighth president of the United States, but who really cares?

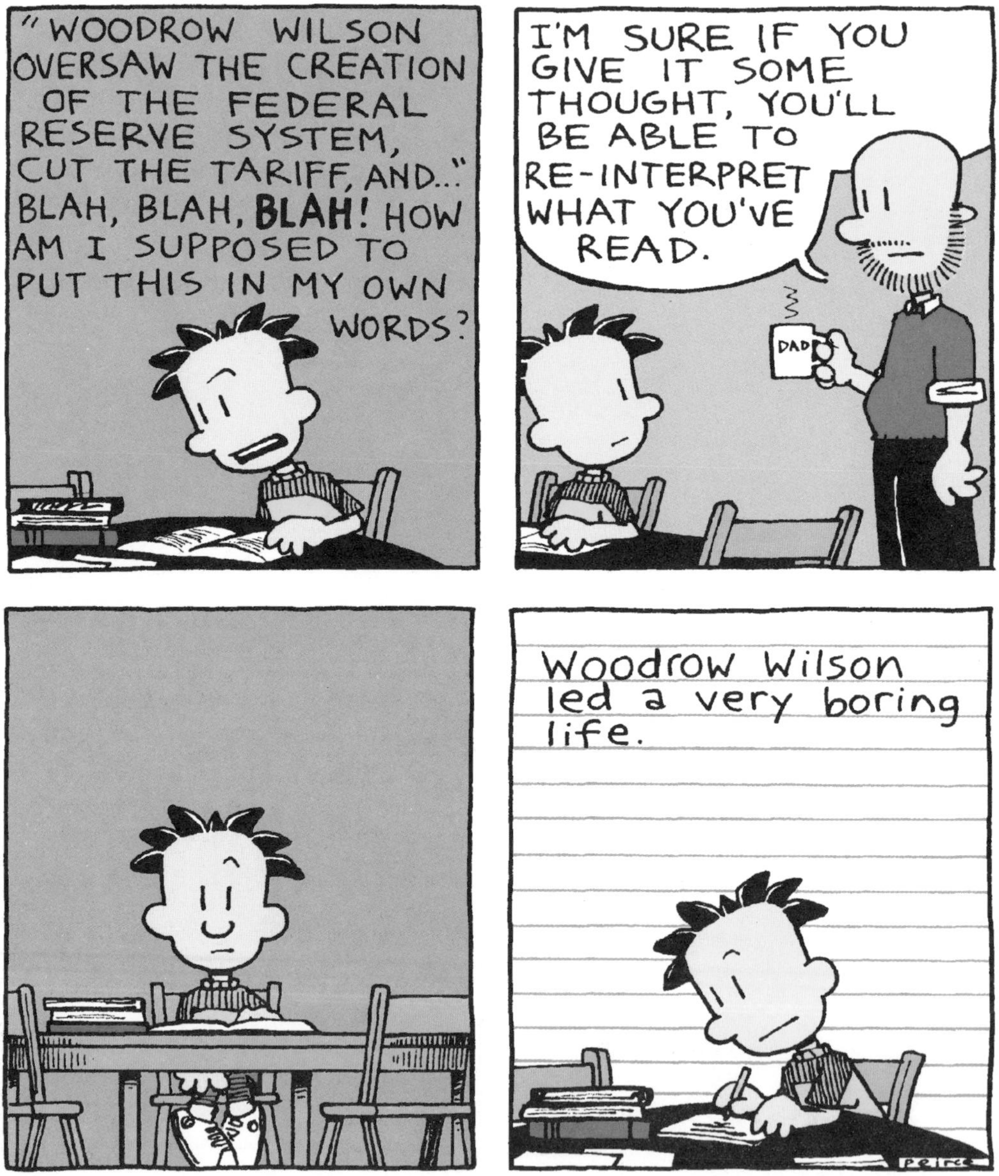
"WOODROW WILSON OVERSAW THE CREATION OF THE FEDERAL RESERVE SYSTEM, CUT THE TARIFF, AND..." BLAH, BLAH, BLAH! HOW AM I SUPPOSED TO PUT THIS IN MY OWN WORDS?
I'M SURE IF YOU GIVE IT SOME THOUGHT, YOU'LL BE ABLE TO RE-INTERPRET WHAT YOU'VE READ.
DAD
Woodrow Wilson led a very boring life.